THE LURE OF THE LION

A Novel

J.P. Fonté

Library of Congress Number:		2003095550
ISBN :	Hardcover	1-4134-2479-1
	Softcover	1-4134-2478-3

This book was printed in the United States of America.

To order additional copies of this book, contact:
Xlibris Corporation
1-888-795-4274
www.Xlibris.com
Orders@Xlibris.com

20012

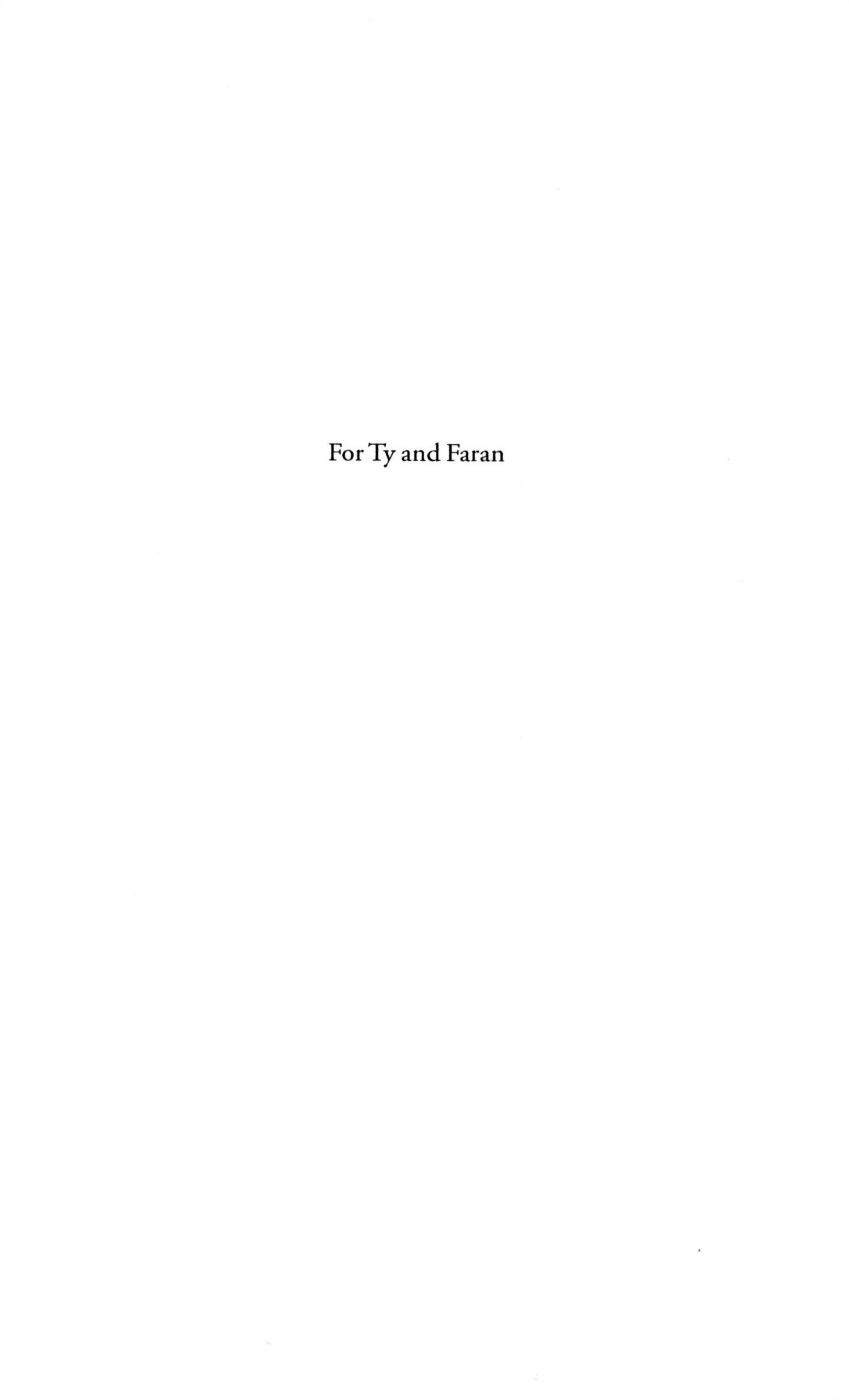

For Ty and Faran

Chapter 1

October 1971. Fort Portal, Uganda. The foothills of the Ruwenzori Mountains—The Mountains of the Moon

The leopard crouched low in the dense tropical forest, the weight of her full teats nearly resting on the ground. It was her first hunt since the birth of her first litter of cubs. Prey had been elusive throughout the night; but as she now studied the young bushbuck, anticipation of the kill mixed with fear, for she had ventured too far into the realm of man. With muscles taut and tail held low, she inched forward each time the bushbuck lowered its head to graze. Desperate to return to her brood, she sprang. The flight of the frightened animal drew her from the shelter of the trees into a field of cultivated tea plants. Within seconds she brought it down. When its thrashing movements ceased, she grasped it behind the ears and dragged it from the field. She did so quickly—for the scent and sound of man were rising with the breaking dawn.

"Damn!" Elon O'Shay exclaimed, his sky-blue eyes flashing an angry shade of gray as he glanced at his watch. "Here, Harun, this should be the last of it!"

The ten-year-old Bugandan boy was nearly bowled over by the piece of luggage being tossed to him. Short and skinny for his age, Harun's smile gleamed brightly against his shiny black face as he added the bag to the precariously balanced mountain of luggage filling the back of the Land Rover.

With trim tapered fingers, Elon combed the dark hair from his sweat-lined brow. Wheeling his tall muscular frame around, he stormed into the house. Harun followed closely, his smile growing with anticipation. *She's going to get yelled at!* the boy thought with pleasure. He nearly ran into him when Elon halted at the door to her room.

"We should have been the hell out of here an hour ago!" Elon told his sister while angrily tapping his watch.

Shauna O'Shay sat at her dressing table attempting to secure her thick red hair onto the top of her head. His words startled her into releasing the mane, which flowed softly over her shoulders and halfway down her shapely back.

"Now look what you made me do!" she whined. "Mila, make him go away!"

Harun's mother, Mila, came from the bathroom where she'd gathered the last of Shauna's toiletries. She packed them into a small bag on the bed before turning toward Elon with a menacing scowl.

"Out!" Mila ordered with one hand planted on her prodigious hip and the stubby forefinger of the other aimed toward the door.

Elon knew better than to argue. Although Shauna was only seventeen, eleven years younger than he, she'd almost always had the upper hand. When she was allied with Mila, Elon didn't stand a chance. He narrowed his eyes with anger before storming away.

Harun hung around the doorway, still smiling, until his mother shot him a stern glance. Mila watched as he followed after Elon. Satisfied they no longer posed a threat, she turned her attention back to Shauna. Seeing that Shauna was on the verge of tears over her hair, Mila gently took the brush from her hand and soon had her locks contained in a neat twist.

As Shauna studied Mila's face, reflected in the mirror, her frustration melted into sadness. "I'll miss you so much," she told her softly. "You've been like a mama to me."

Mila bit her lower lip to keep from crying. She'd cried enough in the past weeks, knowing this child she loved so much, who was indeed like a daughter to her, was going so far away. Careful not to displace her hair, Mila gently cradled Shauna's head against her ample breast. It was Mila's breast that had replaced that of the child's mother, who'd nearly died following Shauna's birth. Mila had been suckling her oldest son, Mutiba, not yet a year old at the time. She had more than enough milk, and love, to sustain them both.

"Come, now," Mila mustered her strength as a single tear descended slowly, glistening against her black cheek.

"Promise you'll visit me in Vienna?" Shauna pleaded while gathering her belongings.

"Humph!" Mila responded, disturbed at the thought of traveling so far from Africa. "No, my child, you must promise to come home whenever you can."

"Home?" Shauna mused, studying Mila worriedly. "Where will home be when Elon sells our share of the farm?"

"Home will be wherever I am," Mila tried to assure her while directing Shauna out the door. She wanted to add that home would always be in Uganda, but her intuition told her otherwise—and Mila's intuition was nearly psychic.

Outside, impatiently tapping his fingers on the steering wheel of the Rover, Elon was about to explode. Starting the engine, he narrowed his eyes and ground the teeth in his chiseled jaw as Shauna and Mila exited the house. Harun twitched with excitement as he sat on top of the luggage stacked in the back of the vehicle.

After adding the last of her belongings to the mountain of baggage, Shauna embraced Mila's short, rotund frame. Taking Shauna's face between her hands, Mila gently kissed her cheeks. Tears from Shauna's emerald-green eyes mingled with those of Mila's.

"Tell Mutiba 'goodbye' again for me," Shauna said as she gave Mila a melancholy smile while climbing into the front passenger's side of the Rover.

Before Mila could respond, Elon flung the vehicle into gear and was headed down the dirt driveway, lined with a blaze of multi-colored roses and bougainvillea interspersed among scarlet-flowering acacia trees.

"Wait!" Shauna screamed at Elon.

Slamming on the brakes, he glared at her with concern.

"I forgot Aran," she told him sheepishly.

With his cheek clenched between his teeth, Elon threw the Rover into reverse and rapidly backed up. Mila was waiting on the veranda, holding the encased violin. She brought it to Shauna, who placed it gently on her lap. Shauna blew Mila a kiss as once again they were off.

Continuing down the long driveway, they passed the predominately Asian workers toiling in the sea of tea fields, which glistened with the morning dew. As Shauna returned their waves of goodbye, she was achingly aware of how much she would miss the only home she'd ever known—which was called Rose Inish.

Turning onto the main thoroughfare, Shauna cupped her hand over her hair when Elon picked up speed. His stern expression kept her from asking him to close his window. In the back, Harun balanced atop the luggage, singing happily into the breeze.

Before Elon, Shauna, and Harun completed the long drive from Rose Inish to Entebbe Airport, Lee Parnell and his wife Rika deplaned from the Uganda Airways flight arriving from Nairobi.

"I'll be right back," Rika said in her soft Dutch accent as she and Lee entered the terminal. Covering her mouth with her hand, she rushed to the ladies' room and barely made it to a stall before losing the lunch she'd fought so hard to keep down.

Lee Parnell headed to the baggage claim area. Brushing away aggressive offers from taxi drivers and safari operators after collecting his bags, he looked around irritably.

When Elon brought the Rover to an abrupt stop in front of the terminal, Harun fell from his perch on top of the luggage. He soon popped up again, smiling brightly. Shauna sadly studied her dust-covered face and tangled mess of a hairdo in the rearview mirror.

"Start unloading!" Elon ordered before quickly making his way inside the building. Heading toward the gate, he passed in front of the ladies' room just as Rika was exiting. He instinctively grabbed hold of her as their bodies collided.

"I'm sorry," he told her. "Are you all right?"

Rika nodded through her nausea and dizziness. Elon continued his hold on her, as she appeared slightly off-balance.

"Just great! Leave my wife alone for two minutes and find her in the arms of another man!" Lee laughed in a thick Texas drawl dripping with studied Southern charm.

Rika managed a weak smile. "Excuse me," she said while extracting herself from Elon's grasp before heading back into the ladies' room.

Elon looked after her with concern.

"Is your name O'Shay?" Lee asked.

Elon turned to look at the man. Lee Parnell was a few inches shorter and considerably stockier than Elon, with sandy-brown hair and dark, brooding eyes. Looking beyond the man's smile, Elon didn't like the expression he saw in his eyes.

"Yes. Elon O'Shay. Dr. Parnell?" Elon asked as he offered his hand.

Lee nodded as he shook Elon's hand. "Was about to think you'd forgotten us."

"Sorry about the delay," Elon said as Rika exited the washroom.

"The little lady with the weak stomach is my wife," Lee explained. "But I see you two have already met."

"Elon O'Shay," Elon introduced himself to her. He noticed that Rika Parnell was younger than her husband, in her early-twenties to his mid-thirties. She was quite petite, with pale-blonde hair and ashen-looking skin. Elon couldn't help but compare her looks to the bronzed and robust beauty of his half-Maori love, Kiri, waiting for him in New Zealand.

"I'm Rika," she smiled softly while offering her hand to Elon.

Elon was concerned at how cool and fragile her hand felt. Unlike Kiri's rich brown eyes, Rika's were a pale shade of green. *Her eyes have the look of a trapped animal and make a lie of her smile,* Elon thought before Shauna and Harun joined them, followed by porters loaded down with Shauna's luggage.

"Doctor, Mrs. Parnell, this is my sister, Shauna, and our young friend, Harun," Elon introduced them.

Still attempting to tame her hair, Shauna nodded in greeting.

Lee's face lit up at the sight of the redheaded beauty. "This country can't be too bad to have produced a fine young filly like you," he told Shauna before the departure announcement for her flight to Nairobi was heard over the intercom.

"Hurry, or you'll miss your flight," Elon told Shauna as he protectively steered her away from Lee.

"How long will you be in Nairobi?" Lee asked Shauna as he and Rika followed them toward the gate.

"Just long enough to catch a plane to Vienna," Elon answered for her in a big-brotherly tone.

"Vienna?" Lee asked with interest.

"To study music," Shauna told him.

"That explains the fiddle," Lee commented as he directed his attention to the encased instrument she was carrying.

Shauna's name was called from the front of the terminal. The group turned to see a tall, lanky black teenager hurriedly making his way toward them.

"Mutiba!" Shauna exclaimed, pleasantly surprised.

Mutiba's long legs carried him to Shauna in a swift, fluid motion. From behind his back he produced a wind-blown bouquet of flowers, which he shyly presented to her.

"Dr. Parnell, Rika, this is Mutiba, Harun's brother," Elon introduced them.

When Mutiba offered his hand to the doctor there was a noticeable hesitation on Lee's part before shaking it. The final announcement for Shauna's flight was heard over the intercom and the group hurried toward the gate, where airline employees whisked the baggage off to the waiting aircraft while Elon tipped the porters.

"Well, it's been short but sweet," Lee told Shauna in parting.

"We wish you luck in Vienna," Rika offered kindly.

"Thank you," Shauna smiled before turning toward Harun. "You be good," she told him while playfully rubbing the top of the boy's head.

Harun smiled sadly. Growing up like brother and sister, they'd had their share of fun and rivalry. But, until this moment of parting, Harun hadn't realized how much he would miss her.

Folding Shauna lovingly in his arms, Elon kissed her gently on the forehead. With tears rising in her eyes, she kissed him on the cheek. When Shauna faced Mutiba, they exchanged a look of urgency before falling briefly into each other's embrace. She kissed him quickly on the mouth before running toward the plane.

"Good luck in New Zealand!" Shauna called back to Elon before disappearing inside the aircraft.

"New Zealand?" Lee asked Elon. "What's in New Zealand?"

"A job," Elon replied. "And my fiancée," he added, turning toward Mutiba.

Mutiba looked surprised. Having grown up together, they had discussed girls and sex . . . and even marriage—with Elon being firmly against the institution. For, although Mutiba and Harun's parents' marriage had been a good one, Elon and Shauna's parents' had not.

"Kiri?" Mutiba asked needlessly.

Smiling, Elon nodded.

"Love," Lee shook his head. "Makes fools of us men. Take me, for example, letting myself get dragged halfway around the world to satisfy one of my wife's whims."

"My grandparents lived in Uganda," Rika explained to Elon and Mutiba. "I grew up in Holland, but would visit them here as often as I could," she said, before adding so quietly that only Elon overheard: "They were the happiest times of my life."

Elon regarded her with compassion.

"Of course buying something in South Africa would make more sense," Lee said.

Rika noticed Mutiba exchange a look of concern with Elon. "Lee will be doing an internship there with Dr. Barnard, the heart surgeon," she explained, not wanting them to think that she and Lee were supportive of South Africa's practice of apartheid—although Rika was speaking mostly for herself.

"That's the doctor who takes the hearts from people who have died and puts them into others," Elon explained for Mutiba and Harun's benefit.

Mutiba nodded his awareness of the procedure, but Harun responded with a wide-eyed look of sickened disbelief.

"If your work is in South Africa, why are you looking for a place to buy in Uganda?" Mutiba asked the Parnells as the group headed away from the gate.

"Like I said, the little lady's got her heart set on this country. I'll practically be married to my work, so she might as well be happy," Lee responded. He made no mention of a more selfish objective; one that would be difficult to accomplish with the U.S.-imposed trade sanctions aimed against South Africa because of apartheid.

Elon sensed a half-truth in Lee's response, but he didn't probe. His objective was to sell his and Shauna's share of Rose Inish, and Elon didn't want whatever plans the rich Texan had for it to concern him.

"I had better return to work," Mutiba said after they'd loaded the Parnells' few bags into the Land Rover.

"How's it going?" Elon asked him. "Mutiba's servicing the Cessna," he told the Parnells.

"The plane's part of the deal, right?" Lee asked.

"Yes, it goes with the farm," Elon responded.

"I'm waiting for some parts to get here from Nairobi," Mutiba told Elon.

"We'll be staying the night at the nearby Lakeview Hotel and leave for Fort Portal in the morning," Elon informed the Parnells. "It's about a five-hour drive."

"Give Mama my love," Mutiba told Harun, as he playfully rubbed the boy's head in the way that Shauna had. "Tell her I'll be flying home soon."

"Don't tell me you're a pilot as well as a mechanic?" Lee asked skeptically.

"He's an excellent pilot," Elon stated in Mutiba's defense.

Mutiba held the door open for Rika. "Welcome to Uganda," he told her. "I hope you find here what you are looking for."

"Thank you," she smiled, although she didn't know what she was looking for; or, more precisely, she didn't want to acknowledge it.

Ignoring Mutiba, Lee got in the vehicle and closed the door. Mutiba and Elon exchanged a look of mutual contempt for the American doctor.

"I'll meet you at the hangar after I get them settled in," Elon told Mutiba.

Sitting in the back seat next to Rika, Harun waved goodbye to his big brother as Elon steered the Rover away from the curb. Returning Harun's smile, Mutiba waved back. But Mutiba's smile soon faded as he recalled Shauna's departure.

Arriving at the Lakeview Hotel, located a few miles from the airport on the shore of Lake Victoria, Elon and the others were greeted by the manager, Rashid Jameel, an exuberant man who was originally from India.

"Welcome! Welcome!" Rashid exclaimed as he directed a bellboy to tend to the luggage. "If there is anything I can do to help make your stay here more—"

"Actually, you can point me to the bar," Lee cut him off.

"Of course," Rashid responded, his smile losing much of its luster.

"I'll be up in a while," Lee told Rika as he gave her a cursory kiss.

Elon noticed the disappointment reflected in Rika's eyes when she watched her husband leave with Rashid. Rika avoided Elon's gaze as she accompanied him and the bellboy to the room.

"Is it all right?" Elon asked when he and Rika were left alone in the room.

Standing at the window looking out at the lake, she turned and gave him a questioning look.

"The room," he explained. "Is it all right?"

"Oh, yes. Quite."

"I imagine you're accustomed to much grander—"

"No, really, it's quite nice," she smiled reassuringly.

Elon's heart ached at the pain the smile couldn't conceal in her eyes. "Can I bring you anything to eat?" he offered.

The mention of food intensified Rika's feelings of constant nausea. "No, thank you. I'd like to just rest."

"Feel free to sleep in late in the morning. We won't be leaving until after lunch," Elon said, while studying her intently.

"Yes?" she inquired, his gaze making her feel uncomfortable.

"I'm sorry. It's just that I have the feeling we've met before."

"No, I don't think so. I'm sure I would have remembered if we had."

"Yes, well, if there's anything I can do . . ."

"Thank you," she responded sweetly. "I'll be fine."

Will you?! Elon wanted to demand of her. "Again, let me know if there's anything you need," was all he said before turning to go.

Rika remained smiling until Elon closed the door behind him. Turning back to the window, her smile slowly dissolved as she covered her slightly protruding belly with her hands. *What a difference time makes,* she thought sadly, recalling how she'd felt the last time she was in Uganda.

Leaning her head against the windowpane, Rika remembered her grandparents' loving embrace and kisses as they greeted her on her previous arrival at Entebbe Airport. Rika was twelve years old at the time, and she didn't notice the teenaged boy who was gazing longingly at the happy reunion. It wasn't until the boy's father harshly demanded his help that Rika's attention was drawn to him. By that time the boy had turned away. He soon slipped from Rika's mind, along with the name by which his father had addressed him: "Elon."

Even if Elon had remembered the girl from when he and his father waited at the airport for the arrival of their safari clients, it's likely he wouldn't have connected her to the now grown woman—as there was a major distinction between the two. For, at that time, the smile in young Rika's eyes had corresponded with the smile on her lips.

Chapter 2

Shauna gazed out the plane's window as it descended toward Vienna. Seeing the lights of the city sparkling in the clear October night, tears of emotion welled in her eyes. Whether they were from exhaustion, excitement, or apprehension, she wasn't sure. All she knew was that she was about to realize a life-long dream. For, longer than she had thought about becoming a professional musician, Shauna dreamed of living in Vienna.

Having never traveled beyond East Africa, Shauna acquired her love of Vienna from the stories her mother and Great-Uncle Eli had told—stories of their beloved native city before the rise of Hitler. Eli had been a farmer and a musician, as well as a Zionist. One of the few items he'd brought from Austria to Uganda was a violin, which now lay in its case on the seat beside Shauna. When she was a child, Shauna nicknamed the instrument Aran, from the Irish Islands where her and Elon's father had been born. In name and spirit, the instrument embodied the union of their parents' differing cultures. As she now laid her hand upon it, Shauna smiled through her tears while the plane touched down.

Making her way with the other deplaning passengers, Shauna scanned the waiting crowd for sight of Herr Muller.

"Fräulein O'Shay! Fräulein O'Shay!" Herr Muller called out to her.

"Herr Muller!" she waved in response.

Short, red-faced, and looking rather disheveled and non-threatening, it was easy to see why Elon and Mila had consented to Herr Muller's offer for Shauna to come to Vienna and pursue her musical interests. As the manager of an Austrian orchestra that toured Africa the previous year, he had met with aspiring young musicians. After enduring numerous auditions, Herr Muller had been most impressed with Shauna. He'd led her and her family to believe he could help her get into a school of music in Vienna.

"I am glad you have arrived safely," he told Shauna in heavily accented English. "Come, we will get your belongings. Do you have a coat?" he asked when noticing she was shivering. "It is not as warm here as it is in Africa!"

"Yes," she replied. "Packed in one of my bags."

When Shauna retrieved the lightweight coat from one of her numerous bags that they barely managed to cram into Herr Muller's Mercedes sedan, he realized it wasn't sufficient. He gallantly wrapped his own coat around her shapely shoulders.

As they drove through the streets of Vienna, Shauna marveled at its grandeur. Although the outside of the Mullers' building didn't overly impress her when they arrived, Shauna's opinion changed drastically when she entered the marble-floored, high-ceilinged apartment with sparkling chandeliers and antique furnishings.

Just as Shauna wasn't prepared for the display of opulence in the Muller home, Frau Muller was even less prepared for the beautiful redhead who now stood before her. She scrutinized Shauna's slender body and sculpted, lightly freckled face. The fact that the lovely creature was wrapped in her husband's overcoat gave added insult to Frau Muller's delicate ego.

Seeing the fire in his wife's eyes, Herr Muller hastily took the coat from Shauna and tried to smooth the way between the two women. But it would be an impossible task, for Shauna would prove to be every bit as headstrong as fat and dowdy Frau Muller.

"So, you are Fräulein O'Shay," Frau Muller snorted in better English than her husband's. "I will show you to your room. Manfred, see to the child's belongings!"

"Yes, my dear," Herr Muller responded meekly before leaving to retrieve the rest of Shauna's luggage.

With Aran in hand, Shauna followed Frau Muller toward the back of the residence to a small alcove nestled behind the kitchen. The room's decor was worlds away from the magnificence of the rest of the apartment. Its furnishings consisted of a single bed that hugged the wall beneath a small window, and an ancient armoire with questionable usefulness. The tiny space was lit by a bare light bulb hanging from the ceiling.

"Frau Schultz, our cook, will wake you in the morning," Frau Muller informed Shauna. "Do not come out until she does," she directed. "You will take your meals in the kitchen. It is understood that you will tend to our sons, Gert and Helmut."

Shauna looked surprised. "It hadn't been mentioned. It was my impression that Herr Muller would be helping me get into a music school and then—"

"You do not expect that we would have you stay here for nothing, do you?" Frau Muller huffed indignantly. "Music schools are not easy to get into. Especially for children of questionable financial means!"

Shauna bristled at being referred to as a child. It was one thing for Mila to do so, but quite another coming from this pig of a woman! Shauna felt like telling Frau Muller what to do with herself and the miniscule space she had designated as her room. But considering Herr Muller's kindness, and the fact that it was the middle of the night and she had nowhere else to go, Shauna held her tongue.

"Perhaps you could show me to the bathroom?" she managed with forced politeness.

Frau Muller led Shauna to the small room at the opposite side of the kitchen. "Do not use any other bath but this one. Understood?" she demanded sternly.

"Yes," Shauna calmly replied through clenched teeth.

Frau Muller snorted in response before leaving. Shauna closed the door and turned on the water at the sink. It ran icy cold and she shivered when splashing it on her face. Studying her reflection in the mirror, a pang of loneliness swept over Shauna as she remembered Mila's kind face reflected in her mirror at Rose Inish.

Forcing the feelings of homesickness from her mind, Shauna shut off the running water. Beyond the closed door she could hear Frau Muller's angry voice as she attacked her husband in a barrage of German.

In the morning, Shauna woke to the smell of chocolate. She opened her eyes and focused on a chunk of it being held in front of her nose. Attached to it was a small, pudgy hand. Shauna followed the hand as it slowly drew away, depositing the chocolate morsel into the mouth of a six-year-old male version of Frau Muller. Shauna's stomach tightened into a knot when she remembered where she was.

"Gert!" a woman's voice boomed.

As the boy ran from the room, Shauna's gaze came to rest on the figure of an imposing woman dressed in a pale-gray uniform with a white apron and cap.

"So, you are the new nanny!" the woman proclaimed sternly in heavily accented English.

The knot in Shauna's stomach tightened. Then an unexpected and wonderful thing happened—the woman smiled!

"I am Ursula. Ursula Schultz," she introduced herself kindly.

Shauna slowly exhaled with relief. "I'm Shauna O'Shay."

"Ya, I know. Come, you must hurry, my child. You need to help get the boys dressed and to school," Ursula told her before leaving.

Shauna didn't take offense at Ursula calling her "child." It was actually somewhat comforting, as Ursula's kindness reminded Shauna of Mila's.

Before allowing any feelings of homesickness to invade her thoughts, Shauna quickly got out of bed. On the way to the bathroom she noticed that her belongings had been stacked against the kitchen wall. With chocolate-smudged fingers, Gert and his eight-year-old brother, Helmut, were attempting to open one of the bags.

"Stop that!" Shauna ordered just as Frau Muller entered the room.

Feigning hurt, the boys ran whimpering to their mother.

"Do not yell at the babies!" Frau Muller barked at Shauna as her sons peered out from behind her ponderous hips. The boys gave Shauna a devious smirk.

Shauna stood tall as her Irish blood took hold. "I will happily not yell at your precious little *babies* if you support the fact that I expect them to act properly!" she proclaimed with a steady gaze.

Shocked at the teenager's audacity, Frau Muller sucked in her breath as her face turned red. Never before had anyone in Shauna's position spoken to her in such a manner! And in her own home! Her eyes darted from Shauna to Ursula, who was stifling a laugh. Frau Muller turned and stormed out of the room, leaving her "babies" completely baffled by the apparent shift of power within their universe.

Ursula gave Shauna an amused wink before turning her attention back to her cooking.

Shauna stared down at the boys, who appeared riveted to the floor. "Now, then, I am Miss O'Shay. You may call me 'Miss Shauna.' You must be Masters Helmut and Gert. Do you speak English?" she asked.

The boys exchanged a glance. Emboldened, Helmut rudely mimicked Shauna's question. "'Do you speak English?'" he sassed.

"I take that to mean 'yes.' In the future I will expect a more polite and direct answer," Shauna responded sternly. "You're how old? Four and five?" she teased.

Both boys puffed up indignantly, looking even more like miniature versions of their mother.

"I am eight!" Helmut proclaimed. "And Gert is six! How old are *you*?" he demanded of Shauna.

"Seventeen—old enough to be treated with the respect owed to an adult. Do you understand?"

Their boldness seemed to waver. Before they could regain it, Shauna reasserted herself. "Do you understand?!" she demanded sternly.

They exchanged a look of uneasiness before nervously swallowing and nodding.

"Good. Now, at six and eight you are old enough to dress yourselves. I expect you to do so and be back here in ten minutes."

They stood staring at Shauna with their mouths open.

"Now!" she ordered with a stamp of her foot.

Nearly knocking each other over, they fled from the room.

"Good work!" Ursula told Shauna appreciatively after the boys had left. "But I suggest you hurry as well."

Removing a clean dress from one of her suitcases, Shauna took it to the bathroom to change. "You'll be all right," she assured herself as she studied her reflection in the mirror, now lit by the morning sun. "You'll be all right," she repeated before splashing cold water on her face.

Chapter 3

Rika woke at the Lakeview Hotel to the sounds of birds chirping and Lee's snoring. She smiled slightly when remembering she was back in Uganda. But her smile waned when Lee reached out for her, sliding her nightgown above her hips. Dispensing with any foreplay or tenderness, he thrust himself inside her. When he was satisfied, he rolled off her and quickly fell back to sleep. Rika turned her head away as the tears stung her eyes. Overcome by nausea, she made her way to the bathroom.

Elon was seated at a table on the tree-shaded patio of the hotel, reading a newspaper, when Rika and Lee joined him.

Avoiding Elon's gaze as he stood and held out a chair for her, Rika directed her attention to where Harun and a group of children were playing a game of rugby on the manicured lawn leading to the edge of the lake.

"What's there to eat?" Lee asked as he picked up the menu. "I'm hungry enough to eat a horse! Or elephant, I should say. Do they serve elephant for breakfast in Africa?"

Although Rika smiled at her husband's question, Elon could still see the pain reflected in her eyes. "It's too late for breakfast. The fish is good," he suggested.

"Fish it is," Lee responded when the waiter came to take their order. "For two. And coffee," he directed without consulting Rika. "You?" he asked Elon.

"I've already eaten," Elon replied as he studied Rika. "Would you prefer something other than fish?" he asked her gently.

She gave him a slightly surprised look. Shaking her head, she directed her attention back to Harun and the other children.

"So, O'Shay," Lee began after the waiter left. "Tell me some more about that plantation of yours. What is it you call it?"

"Rose Inish. Inish is Gaelic for island. My great-grandfather named it," Elon responded in a cool tone that barely masked his contempt toward the American doctor.

"What possessed your kin to settle in Uganda?" Lee asked.

"The railroad," Elon told him.

"'The Lunatic Express,'" Rika stated quietly.

Nodding, Elon's tone and features softened as Rika's eyes met his. "At sixteen, my great-grandfather went to sea," he told her. "When his ship docked at Mombasa, the British were building the railroad through Kenya to Uganda. So he got involved with 'The Lunatic Express,' liked what he found at the end of the line, and stayed."

"And your family's been here ever since?" Rika asked, still locked in his gaze.

"No. My great-grandfather returned to Ireland, married his childhood sweetheart and brought her here. My grandfather was born here. He went to Ireland to find a wife, but my grandmother refused to come to Africa. My father, Quinn, grew up there."

"Where in Ireland?" Rika asked.

"Kilronan. On the Aran Islands."

"How'd they make a living?" Lee inquired.

"Ferrying people from Galway to the islands," Elon responded, the edge returning to his voice as he directed his attention to Lee. "There's a tourist attraction there—the ruins of one of the oldest fortresses in Europe. It sits on a cliff that drops three hundred feet to the sea," he elaborated, not mentioning it was where his grandmother had plunged to her death in a final fit of despair.

"Is that where you were born?" Rika asked.

"No. My father left Ireland and joined his grandparents here," he told her, his voice reverting to its softer tone.

"And your mother?" she inquired.

"My mother, Hanna, came to Uganda when she was eighteen. Her father's older brother, Eli, was one of the Zionist pioneers who—"

"Don't tell me you're an Irish Jew!" Lee snickered.

"Where was your mother from?" Rika hurriedly asked Elon, deflecting Lee's comment.

"Austria," Elon told her, ignoring Lee. "She and her Uncle Eli were the only ones in their family to escape the Holocaust."

Rika's gaze turned sympathetic.

"Enough about my family," Elon smiled softly. "What about yours?"

"You don't wanna know," Lee piped in. "My dear wife's descended from a long line of hard-nosed preachers!"

Elon shot Lee an icy glance before turning back to Rika. His heart went out to her when Elon saw the wounded look reflected in her eyes. "What brought your grandparents to Uganda?" he asked her gently.

"They came here from South Africa during the Boer War," she replied in a flat voice. "My grandfather was a doctor and my grandmother a nurse. They ran a small clinic near Jinja, where my mother was born. She met my father in Holland, where they stayed after they were married. And, yes," she added, glancing vacantly at Lee, "he is, as were his father and grandfather, a minister."

The waiter brought the Parnells their food. Although Lee dug in ravishingly, Rika only picked at hers.

"You mentioned in your letter that you and your sister are only co-owners of that plantation of yours. Who else is in on it?" Lee asked Elon between mouthfuls.

"Mutiba and Harun's mother, Mila," Elon responded coolly.

"That won't be a problem, will it?" Lee asked.

"Not if she likes you," Elon answered in a tone suggesting Mila's opinion of Lee would probably be no more favorable than his own. "We'll stop for tea at Mubende, the half-way point between here and Fort Portal," Elon told Rika, changing the subject. "Are you sure you feel up to the drive?" he asked when noticing she appeared ill. "There's no hurry. We could stay an extra day if—"

"She'll be fine," Lee interjected as Rika forced herself to eat.

Elon continued to study Rika with concern. "I'll be in the lobby whenever you're ready," he said while rising to leave. "Harun, come get cleaned up!" he called to the boy.

Rika watched with a melancholy expression as Harun bid goodbye to his young friends and ran to join Elon.

Nearing the end of the drive to Rose Inish, Rika woke from a nap just as the mist momentarily lifted from the distant mountains, bathed in variegated hues of orange and purple from the setting sun.

At the wheel of the Rover, Elon studied Rika's reflection in the rearview mirror. "The Ruwenzori Mountains," he told her.

"'The Mountains of the Moon,'" she smiled as her features relaxed.

Seeing the smile reflected in her eyes, Elon had the feeling that Rika was awakening from a deep, troubled sleep. Experiencing a sense of relief, he smiled in response as he turned off the main road onto the driveway leading to Rose Inish.

Gazing out at the rich red earth and rolling fields of tea, glimpsed beyond the blaze of roses and blooming acacia trees, Rika's heart swelled with a sense of homecoming.

"It's all so beautiful," she stated reverently when they came to a stop in front of the white stucco, red-trimmed house with matching barn and guest cottages.

Even Lee seemed impressed. "It's a helluva lot better than I'd expected!" he exclaimed regarding the single-story home with welcoming veranda that stretched across the front. The structure was built in a fan shape hugging the circular driveway.

Mila and her sixteen-year-old Asian helper, Nisha, were on the veranda shucking corn. Nisha's face brightened at the sight of Elon. But her delight in seeing him dimmed when she noticed the way he was smiling at the pale-looking woman he was helping out of the Rover. Seized with jealousy, Nisha regarded Rika with obvious contempt. Nisha's expression softened when she focused on Lee.

"Dr. Parnell, Rika, this is Mila Kitande . . . and Nisha," Elon introduced them as they met on the veranda.

"Hello," Rika smiled while offering her hand to Mila.

Even before Mila grasped the frail young woman's hand, she felt an alarming sense of protection toward her—and the child that Mila instinctively knew Rika was carrying.

"Pleased to make your acquaintance," Lee told Mila with a charming smile.

Dismissing his smile, Mila immediately guessed from what, or whom, Rika needed protection. "Welcome to Rose Inish," she told Lee coolly before turning back to Rika. "Come, my child, you must rest before supper. Nisha, take the maize into the kitchen and finish it there," she directed the girl.

Pouting, Nisha did as she was told. Elon and Harun unloaded the luggage from the Rover as Mila led Rika and Lee inside. Before stepping into the foyer, Rika admired the beautifully carved front door, made out of solid mahogany.

"That's the parlor," Mila pointed out the room to the left of the entryway.

Rika glanced into the spacious, hardwood-paneled room with Victorian-era furnishings. At the front of the room a large stone fireplace held a gently burning fire. There were floor to ceiling windows at the back, with a glass door leading onto a veranda offering a view of a manicured lawn that merged with a sloping tea field. Beyond the field, the densely forested foothills rose to meet the mountains.

"This is the dining room and kitchen," Mila pointed out the rooms on the other side of the entryway. "There are six bedrooms with baths, three on each side of the house, and four guest cottages outside, also with baths. You'll be staying in one of the cottages."

"Oh, Mila," Rika smiled, "it's so lovely!"

"You can see it all later," Mila told her. "First you must rest."

Gently clutching Rika's arm, Mila led her and the others out to the back veranda. They descended a few steps to a rose-lined path leading to one of two cottages on the south side of the house. Two other identical cottages were located on the north side.

"My grandparents had roses," Rika stated wistfully as she gazed at the flowers.

They passed under a bougainvillea-entwined trellis that was attached to a short picket fence enclosing a beautifully landscaped little yard. Entering the cottage, Rika admired the simple yet elegantly decorated interior. She inhaled the scent of the cut roses placed in a vase on the bedside table before closing her eyes, letting the soft breeze from the slowly revolving ceiling fan gently caress her face.

"Elon, why don't you and Harun show Dr. Parnell around the farm before it gets too dark?" Mila suggested firmly as they set the luggage down.

"Good idea," Lee agreed as he, Elon, and Harun were practically shooed out of the cottage by Mila.

"Come," Mila turned her attention back to Rika, "you and your baby must rest."

Rika looked alarmed. "How did you—? Do I show that much?"

"No, my child," Mila told her. "You are small and are carrying him lightly." *Much too lightly,* Mila thought with concern.

"Do you also think it's a boy?" Rika smiled as she covered her belly with her hands. "You won't tell anyone, will you?" she pleaded, her smile waning. "You see, I haven't told my husband yet."

Mila gave her a questioning look.

"It's just that . . . well, he has so much to take care of right now," Rika explained hurriedly. "I plan to tell him while we're here—after he's had a few days to relax and has finalized the purchase of the farm . . . or plantation, as he calls it," she elaborated. "I'm almost six months along," she admitted with downcast eyes. "I know I can't hide it much longer."

Mila's concern intensified, knowing as far along as Rika was into her pregnancy, her belly should be considerably more rounded.

"It's our secret," Mila assured her. "You needn't join us for supper. I'll have Nisha bring you something to eat," she offered while pulling back the covers on the bed.

"I'm afraid I haven't been too successful in keeping food down."

"We'll see what we can do about that. Try not to worry. I'm sure you and your son will grow strong," Mila said with a smile that belied her uncertainty.

"Thank you, Mila," Rika whispered as she slipped off her shoes before sinking into the bed. "I've been so in need of a friend," she admitted softly, resting her head on the pillow while closing her eyes against the rising tears.

You have found more than just a friend, Mila wanted to tell her as she gently tucked the covers around Rika's slight frame. Having recently bid a tearful goodbye to a child who was like a daughter to her, Mila felt as though she had now gained another. She remained at Rika's side, softly humming a lullaby, until the young woman drifted off to sleep. Before leaving, Mila spread the mosquito-net canopy around the bed.

An hour later, Nisha entered the cottage with a tray of food. She set it on the bedside table before glaring disdainfully at the sleeping woman. When she left, Nisha slammed the door loudly behind her. Rika woke with a start. Through the mosquito netting she noticed the tray of food. Pushing the netting aside, she sat up and began to eat.

"When he was a teenager, growing up in Vienna, Great-Uncle Eli became a Zionist," Elon told Lee and Rika following supper on their second evening at Rose Inish.

A fire blazed in the fireplace as they sat in the parlor while Nisha served coffee and Mila showed Rika a photo album that chronicled the history of Rose Inish.

"Uganda had been offered by the British as a substitute to Palestine for a Jewish state, and Eli was one of the first Zionists to come here," Elon continued. "Although the offer was later rejected by the Zionist Congress of 1903, he decided to stay. He tried to convince his younger brother, my grandfather, to move here with his family from Austria. But only my mother came for what was supposed to be a short visit, in the spring of 1938."

"Thank you, Nisha," Rika told the girl sweetly as she was handed a cup of coffee.

Ignoring Rika, Nisha offered Elon a cup along with a seductive smile. Her smile turned to a look of resentment when she saw his attention was focused on Rika. Handing a cup to Lee, Nisha was pleasantly surprised to see he was studying her in a way that she had always hoped for, but never managed to elicit, from Elon. Her smile returned.

Mila was the only one to notice the suggestive exchange between Nisha and Lee. "That will be all, Nisha. You may be excused," she told her firmly.

Nisha pursed her lips into a pout and cast her eyes down demurely before leaving.

Lee's gaze followed Nisha's firm young hips as she sashayed from the room. "So, tell us how you got involved with this here Irish Jew," he then directed his smile at Mila while motioning toward Elon.

"My grandfather and Elon's great-grandfather met during the building of the railroad," Mila told him. "This land had belonged to my ancestors. They started growing tea on it when Uganda became a British protectorate."

"Isn't it sad for you to have Elon and Shauna sell their share of it?" Rika asked.

"Their dreams lie elsewhere," Mila said. "My sons and I will still have our share of the land, but they don't have the same passion for it that their father did," she added sadly while glancing out the large windows to where the moon had broken through the clouds, gently illuminating the manicured lawn.

"What happened to your husband?" Lee asked.

"He was killed in the same accident that took Elon's father," Mila answered simply.

Elon directed his gaze to his steaming cup of coffee. He was grateful for the way in which Mila had worded her response, as it was Elon's father who was responsible for the auto accident that took his and Mila's husband's lives.

"How did your mother and father meet?" Rika asked softly of Elon.

"Great-Uncle Eli was overseer here at Rose Inish," he began.

"It is because of Eli that Rose Inish became so successful," Mila interjected.

"So your folks met here, fell in love, and lived happily ever after," Lee speculated.

Elon and Mila shared a look of sarcasm in response to Lee's comment.

"Was growing tea the only way your families made a living?" Lee asked.

"No," Elon replied. "My father also ran a small safari operation."

"For hunting?" Lee asked with increased interest.

Elon nodded reluctantly after glancing at Rika, who seemed disturbed by her husband's question.

"Too bad the ole boy's no longer around, as I'd be interested in his services," Lee said. "Perhaps you could fill in for him?"

"I don't share the same interests as my father did," Elon told him with an edge to his voice.

"I'm glad," Rika responded quietly.

"My wife, the bleedin' heart animal lover!" Lee snorted with mock contempt.

"I don't consider the killing of animals to be sporting," Elon stated adamantly.

"Elon has always been one to rescue, not hurt animals," Mila said. "Ever since he was a baby, he's had a way with them. Except for the time when a mother gorilla—"

"We don't need to bore our guests with childhood stories," Elon cut her off.

"Do tell us about the gorilla!" Rika beseeched Mila.

"I found a baby gorilla in the forest behind the house," Elon spoke up, hoping to save face by relating the story himself. "I assumed it was orphaned, brought it home, and then let it go. End of story."

"Not quite," Mila corrected, shaking her head at the memory. "Somehow it had just gotten separated from its mother, who came looking for it and practically destroyed everything in her path to get to it!"

"Bet you got your butt whipped for that one!" Lee laughed in Elon's direction.

"Tomorrow I thought we could tour the Toro Game Reserve," Elon changed the subject, not wanting to dwell on the whippings he'd received from his easily provoked father. "Perhaps spend the night there at the Semliki Lodge."

"Sounds good," Lee said. "So, what kind of wildlife is there in this part of the country?"

As he studied the wealthy doctor with misgivings, Elon had to remind himself of his objective to sell his and Shauna's share of Rose Inish and return to New Zealand—and Kiri—as soon as possible.

"In the nearby forest and surrounding area, there are chimpanzees, monkeys, various types of antelope, a few buffalo, and elephants. No more gorillas . . . poachers," he explained sadly.

"No predators?" Lee asked with disappointment.

"An occasional leopard. In fact, there's been one sighted recently," Elon said. "We'll see lion and other predators at the Toro Reserve."

"I've been admiring the drawings," Rika said as she gestured toward the framed sketches of animals hanging on the walls. "Are they originals?"

"Mutiba did them," Elon told her, recalling his father's animal trophy heads that were previously mounted on the walls. Removing them was one of the first things Elon did when he returned to Rose Inish after his father's death.

"He is extremely talented," Rika told Mila.

Mila smiled at the compliment to her eldest son's artistic ability.

"What can you tell me about President Idi Amin?" Lee asked Elon while removing a cigar from his shirt pocket. Before he could light it, Mila snatched it from his mouth and stuffed it back in his pocket. Lee chuckled in resignation.

"Politically, the country seems to be on a much better course now that Amin is at the helm," Elon told him.

Lee let out a loud belch. "Excuse me! It's that great cooking of yours!" he teasingly accused Mila. "It'd sure be great if you could stick around and cook for us here. Maybe even come to Texas and show them how it's done?"

"Humph!" Mila responded with feigned disapproval.

"Oh, Mila," Rika pleaded, "I do wish you'd consider staying!"

Mila raised her eyebrows in a way that suggested she might. "Leave those," she told Rika when she started collecting the coffee cups.

"Are you sure? I'm not used to being waited on," Rika said.

"You should get some rest," Mila suggested kindly.

"I am a little tired," Rika admitted. "I look forward to tomorrow," she told Elon as he stood to bid her goodnight.

"I'll be there shortly, my dear," Lee told her.

"Goodnight," Rika smiled at Elon and Mila as she left.

"Goodnight," Elon called quietly after her.

"Think I'll slip out back and have a smoke," Lee winked at Mila as he again pulled the cigar from his pocket.

"Don't go far," Elon warned. "The leopard," he reminded Lee reluctantly.

"I could put an end to it," Lee offered brightly.

"That won't be necessary," Elon responded coolly.

"'Night then," Lee stated, saluting him and Mila with his cigar before leaving.

As Elon watched Lee settle onto the divan on the back veranda, he sensed Mila's stare penetrating through his shirt. "What?" Elon turned to look her in the eye.

Mila's expression was enough of an answer.

"I know you don't like him any more than I do," he told her quietly. "But they're the only perspective buyers we've got. If you do stay on, I'm sure you can keep him in line."

"Humph," Mila responded in a tone suggesting she was seriously considering the offer. "Someone has to tend to that sweet child he married," she rationalized as she gathered up the cups.

Elon furrowed his brow as he looked toward where Rika had disappeared into the guest cottage. He then turned his attention back to her husband, who was polluting the crisp night air with the stench of his cigar.

Lee still reeked of cigar smoke when he and Rika left with Elon early the next morning. Elon drove from Rose Inish to the Toro Game Reserve with his window slightly rolled down, although he offered to close it should Rika become chilled from the cool morning air. But she said she was fine, and reacted enthusiastically to the sights along the way.

Entering the reserve, Elon stopped for a pride of lions that were marching defiantly toward them in the center of the road. As the pride parted around the Rover, a cub passed within inches from where Rika sat. Suppressing the urge to open the door and pet it, she smiled at its swaggering little walk as it tried to keep up with the others.

"More than anything else," Elon contemplated as he watched the pride regroup behind the vehicle, "it's the lion that draws people to Africa."

"The bait that sucks them in, huh?" Lee responded. "They're like a lure—the lure of the lion," he smiled at his inventiveness.

"'The lure of the lion,'" Elon repeated quietly, nodding in agreement as they continued on.

They passed a sign stating: ELEPHANTS HAVE THE RIGHT OF WAY.

"No shit!" Lee responded to the sign's directive.

Rika laughed. No longer plagued by morning sickness, she felt vibrantly alive—even happy! She resolved to tell Lee of her condition before the day was through.

"Look! Crowned Cranes!" she exclaimed, pointing toward a pair of tall, elegant gray birds with black, white, and red markings.

"The national bird of Uganda," Elon offered, smiling at her enthusiasm.

Continuing on, they admired the reserve's varied landscape of open rolling plains to steep forested escarpments. They encountered herds of Uganda kob, Jackson's hartebeest, buffalo, and the small Congo forest variety of elephant. They were entertained by the antics of a warthog family—the babies following their mother's mechanical trot with tails held straight in the air like skinny little flags.

Arriving at Lake Albert, they left the Rover and walked along a path leading through the tropical foliage to the water's edge.

"Hippo," Elon pointed to the semi-submerged beasts that scrutinized them from the lake.

They watched as, following a dive, the hippos surfaced like whales, spraying water from their nostrils. The animals often opened their jaws with impressive yawns, or emitted a rollicking bark/laugh. Some clashed tooth-to-tooth with formidable aggression.

"How's the fishing?" Lee inquired as he gazed out at the lake.

"Ever hear of Nile perch?" Elon asked.

"We've got perch at home," Lee said.

"That grow up to six feet and weigh almost two hundred pounds?"

Lee emitted an appreciative whistle. "Where can we look into it?"

"At the lodge," Elon said as they headed back to the Rover.

The Semliki Safari Lodge was located in the center of the reserve next to the Wassa River. Following a supper that dimmed in comparison to Mila's cooking, Rika excused herself.

"I think I'll turn in early," she said, giving Lee an inviting smile.

"Go right ahead, my dear," he responded. "Think I'll have a drink and a smoke."

Elon saw the disappointment reflected in Rika's eyes as her smile melted. He stood when she rose to leave.

"Thank you for a very enjoyable day," she told him.

"It was my pleasure," he replied.

There was a fleeting, almost desperate exchange as their eyes met. Glancing down guiltily, Rika hurried away. Elon watched her go with a look of compassion . . . and longing.

"Coming?" Lee asked him as he headed for the bar.

Reluctantly, Elon followed.

"Whiskey," Lee demanded of the bartender. "You?" he inquired of Elon.

"Just tonic."

"What? An Irishman who doesn't drink? Bet your daddy's rolling in his grave over that one!"

"It was drink that put him there," Elon stated under his breath.

After paying for the drinks, Lee turned his attention to a group of Brits who were engaged in an animated conversation relating their day's events.

"Got him right behind the ears," one of them boasted. "The bugger never knew what grabbed him!"

"They say the buffalo is the most treacherous," another said. "Will circle around and hunt the hunter!"

"Nothing is as ferocious as the ratel, or honey badger," yet another stated. "I've heard tell of its climbing up a victim's leg and biting off the genitals, causing it to bleed to death!"

Every man within hearing distance squirmed uncomfortably—except Elon, who smiled as he sipped his tonic. He was amused at the men's ignorance, not the story about the ratel, which was true. Elon felt like informing the group that the animal responsible for the most human fatalities in Africa was the hippo. But, from the sound of their conversation, Elon doubted the information concerning an animal which many hunters considered to be just an oversized pig would be appreciated.

"Took six shots to bring down that elephant this morning," the first Brit stated. "Bloody piece of work," he added with a grin.

Elon's smile faded.

Lee approached the group. "Mind if I join you gentlemen?" he asked.

"Please," one responded as he motioned for Lee to take a seat. "American, hey?"

"Right outta Texas," Lee replied. "Houston, more precisely. Couldn't help but overhear your conversation. Sounds like you men have had some excitement!"

From the bar, Elon slowly nursed his tonic as he listened to the men trade stories of a pastime he could never understand. He'd seen the symptoms more times than he cared to count—the disease that drove men, and sometimes women, to track and destroy another creature for the sole pleasure of what? To see it die an often slow and agonizing death? Or to simply have "dominion" over it? *That's it,* Elon speculated: *It's about exercising the most heinous act of power that a human being can exert over another living thing—the power to kill!*

The fact that African wildlife was the most dangerous, and therefore the most appealing to the killers, didn't escape Elon. But there was something else. In Africa, more than anywhere in the world, animals have the most freedom. *It's that freedom which hunters resent so much that they'd travel thousands of miles and spend thousands of dollars to take from another creature,* Elon surmised. *Because in their narrow, regimented worlds, they hate the fact that there are creatures that roam the earth at will—that have no need and often no fear of man . . . a creature that demands to be feared! And commands it through the barrel of a gun, or the use of a whip! Like Quinn O'Shay!*

Elon forced the memory of his abusive father from his mind as he angrily gulped down the last of his tonic. He also had to suppress his feelings of growing attraction to Rika. Ordering a refill, Elon let his thoughts wander back to New Zealand . . . to Kiri's waiting arms and ample breasts.

"If you gentlemen will excuse me," Lee eventually told his newfound friends after downing numerous drinks. "I've got a little woman keeping my bed warm," he smiled suggestively as he left with a slight stagger.

Elon shot Lee a look of resentment as he went to join Rika.

Entering their room, Lee collapsed on the bed and immediately fell asleep, snoring loudly. Rika studied him sadly before turning away.

Chapter 4

When Elon and the Parnells returned to Rose Inish from their tour of the Toro Game Reserve the following afternoon, the Cessna was parked on the grassy airstrip next to the barn. Mutiba and Harun came from the house to greet them.

"Mutiba has joined the air force!" Harun blurted excitedly.

"Recruited, actually," Mutiba corrected. He noticed Elon's look of concern. "As a mechanic," Mutiba reassured him.

"Good things can come outta the military," Lee commented as the group made its way toward the house. "Met my little wife on a medical tour in 'Nam," he explained while putting his arm around Rika. "She was with the Red Cross. Best little scrub nurse of the bunch. 'Course she made me marry her before I could see any action!"

Rika's eyes shot down in embarrassment as the color rose in her cheeks. Elon and Mutiba exchanged a look of shared disgust toward Lee's insensitive remark.

"Tea is ready," Mila told them as they entered the house. Glancing at Rika, she could see that something was wrong. Taking her away from Lee's grasp, Mila led Rika to where Nisha was serving tea on the back veranda.

Harun followed after Lee and the women, but Elon and Mutiba hung back.

"When are you due back in Entebbe?" Elon asked.

"Day after tomorrow," Mutiba responded distantly.

"How are things going?"

Mutiba shook his head sadly. "People are disappearing. Mostly friends of Obote's," he explained in reference to the former president, who was ousted by Idi Amin's regime.

Elon looked concerned. "Are the Israelis still around?" he asked.

Mutiba nodded. "They're still working with the air force."

"Good. Come, we mustn't keep our guests waiting," Elon told him.

Mutiba arched his eyebrows in a sarcastic response. When they joined the others, he noticed the suggestive smiles that Lee shared with Nisha. Mutiba wondered why Rika didn't seem to be aware of what was going on. But her attention was directed toward the mountains, which were becoming obscured by ominous clouds.

"If you'd like, and the weather permits, we could fly to Murchison Falls tomorrow," Elon suggested to the Parnells as Mutiba and Harun began a one-on-one game of rugby on the lawn.

"Murchison Falls?" Lee responded. "Isn't that one of the places you wanted to see, my dear?" he asked Rika. "Tell you what," he continued before she could respond, "why don't you two go? I have some business I'd like to take care of in Fort Portal."

Rika shot him a look of concern.

"Perhaps we should all go into town?" Elon offered, noticing Rika's discomfort.

"No," Lee insisted. "My business wouldn't be of interest to either of you."

"Rika?" Elon inquired as to her opinion.

The gentle tone of Elon's voice, and the caring look in his eyes, made Rika feel like crying.

"Of course she'll go," Lee answered for her.

"We'll leave at dawn, if that's all right with you," Elon told her.

Rika nodded her consent while directing her gaze to her now lukewarm tea.

"Good flying weather," Elon said when Rika joined him at the plane the following morning.

Rika surveyed the farm, which sparkled in the early sunlight following the night's storm. *It's so beautiful!* she thought as she closed her eyes and deeply inhaled the rose-scented air.

Mila joined them with a picnic-basket in hand. "I've packed enough for breakfast and lunch," she stated.

Elon took the basket from her and loaded it inside the aircraft.

"Are you sure you feel up to flying?" Mila asked Rika with concern.

"Yes," Rika assured her.

Mila turned to Elon with a stern expression. "No acrobatics!" she warned, wagging her finger at him.

"Don't worry, I'll be good," he promised.

"Humph! See that you are!" Mila directed.

Elon helped Rika into the plane and then kissed Mila on the cheek before boarding the craft himself. Adjusting the radio headphones at his mouth and over his ears, he motioned for Rika to do the same.

"Contact," Elon announced before turning on the ignition. "Can you hear me?" he asked Rika over the buzz of the propeller.

Smiling, she gave him a thumbs-up. He taxied the craft down the grassy airstrip and turned it around, halting momentarily before applying full throttle. Rika felt her heart race as the plane gathered speed and lifted into the air. She waved down at Mila as they circled Rose Inish before climbing parallel to the mountains.

Rika closed her eyes and leaned her head back. "' . . . And he never got home to early tea,'" she recited softly, forgetting Elon could hear her through the headphones.

"What's that?" he asked.

Opening her eyes, Rika appeared surprised and embarrassed that he'd heard. Her first reaction was to say it was nothing. But it wasn't Lee who asked the question. *Maybe Elon won't think I'm silly,* she reasoned.

"'The bumblebee, the bumblebee, he flew away from the tulip tree. He made a mistake and flew into the lake, and he never got home to early tea,'" she recited with a smile. "It's just a poem that was mentioned in my favorite movie, *Two For the Road,* with Audrey Hepburn and Albert Finney," she explained with slight embarrassment.

"Why's that?"

"Why is what?"

"Why is it your favorite movie?"

"I don't know," Rika replied slowly, having never analyzed the question. "Perhaps because of what it says about relationships . . . marriage mostly. Maybe it's because of the closeness and playfulness—the love between the two characters . . . in spite of all they went through," her voiced trailed off sadly as she looked away, directing her attention to the passing landscape below.

Elon guessed the reason for Rika's sadness was because the romance depicted in her favorite movie hadn't played out for her in real life. And then he did something that caused her to turn to him with a look of amazement and delight—he started whistling the theme music from the film, which coincidentally was one of Elon's favorites as well.

I was right to trust him, Rika thought with a smile before again directing her attention out the window. As they flew over Lake Albert, she studied the small fishing boats that dotted the water below.

The further they flew, the more relaxed Rika became. While sharing the breakfast Mila had prepared, Rika nodded appreciatively when Elon pointed out a waterfall nestled in a tropical inlet framed by the steep Bunyoro cliffs.

"The Victoria Nile," he announced when they reached the mouth of the river.

As Elon nosed the plane down to where it practically skimmed over the water, hippos scampered for shore while monstrous Nile crocodiles, basking on the banks, bounded into the water.

Steering the craft respectfully around a small herd of elephants making its way through the shallows toward a little island, Elon then banked to the west where a lodge was situated on the crest of a bluff overlooking the river.

"The Paraa Lodge," he told Rika before heading toward a nearby airstrip, where he brought the plane in for a bumpy landing on the uneven dirt. By the time they taxied to a stop, a jeep was making its way toward them.

"So good to see you!" the driver of the vehicle told Elon while pumping his hand.

"I'd like you to meet Mrs. Parnell. This is Sahid Jhani," Elon introduced Rika to the man of East Indian descent. "Sahid runs the boat launch here," he explained.

"Welcome to Murchison Falls National Park!" Sahid said while pumping Rika's hand enthusiastically.

Rika smiled at his exuberance.

"You are just in time!" Sahid told them. "Would you care to get something to eat at the lodge before we start?"

"That won't be necessary," Elon responded as he removed the picnic-basket from the plane. "Mila has already taken care of it."

"Ah, Mila! And how is the lovely woman?" Sahid asked with a sparkle in his eye. "And her sons? And Shauna? I was very sorry to hear of your father's and Mila's husband's passing. Such a terrible accident!" he shook his head sympathetically.

"Yes," Elon remotely agreed.

"Come," Sahid told them. "I have a boat waiting to take us to the falls."

Leading them toward his jeep, Sahid drove to the launch area where a group of tourists were disembarking from a canopied tour boat. He helped Rika board a smaller vessel, and then directed the helmsman to push off when he and Elon were settled in.

As the craft faced into the current for the leisurely cruise upriver, Sahid gleefully pointed out the wildlife along the way. Rika smiled at the antics of a group of monkeys frolicking in the tree branches that stretched out over the water. The helmsman carefully maneuvered the boat around hippos that eyed them suspiciously while snorting their displeasure with sprays of water. Huge crocodiles lay motionless on the banks of the river with their mouths open wide to help circulate the air throughout their bodies.

When the boat got too close to an exceptionally large croc, it suddenly snapped its mouth shut and sprang into the water with a powerful burst of speed. Startled, Rika nearly jumped onto Elon's lap. Protectively folding his arms around her, he closed his eyes and took in the sweet scent of her hair. Rika trembled in his grasp. When Elon loosened his grip, she slowly moved away.

Arriving in Fort Portal with Mutiba at the wheel of the Rover, Lee looked around derisively. "They call this a town?" he sneered.

"Where would you like to go?" Mutiba asked.

"The District Commissioner's Headquarters."

Mutiba gave Lee a questioning look, but did as he was directed.

"You needn't come along," Lee told him when they arrived at the DC's building. "It shouldn't take long."

Mutiba watched Lee disappear inside before he headed toward the post office.

"I'd like to speak with the District Commissioner," Lee informed the man sitting at a desk in the reception area.

The man regarded him with suspicion. "Wait here," he said before leaving.

Looking around the room, Lee's gaze came to rest on some photographs pinned to the wall. They were mostly pictures of white hunters proudly displaying their trophies. Lee smiled appreciatively.

"How may I help you?" the DC asked from behind him.

Lee straightened up at the sight of the imposing black Ugandan official. "I'm Dr. Parnell, cardiologist from the States. I'm buying the O'Shay place," he explained with a charming smile. "Is there somewhere we can talk?"

"Joseph Tabaro, District Commissioner," the man introduced himself. "Right this way," he motioned.

Before leading Lee to his office, Mr. Tabaro and the receptionist shared a look of distrust aimed at the American physician.

"How can I help you?" Mr. Tabaro repeated, motioning for Lee to take a seat in his office.

"I'll get right to the point. I was told you were the person to see about getting a permit for obtaining animals."

"Are you inquiring about a hunting license?"

"No. We want them alive."

"'We'?"

"Some buddies and I are getting together a little enterprise—an African wildlife park in Texas. Only it won't be any bleedin' heart animal refuge, if you get my drift."

"You mean you want to transport live animals to America to be used for hunting purposes?" Mr. Tabaro asked flatly.

Lee nodded. "We could stock the place with animals from zoos and such, but that'd be like shooting a cow. Real African animals would fit the bill just fine."

"Why don't your friends simply come here to hunt?"

"In our profession we're rather short on time, but long on capital. We can make it well worth your time if you'd help us out."

Mr. Tabaro smiled vaguely.

"I'd appreciate it if you kept our little discussion under your hat," Lee told him while rising to leave. "I hope to sew up the deal on the O'Shay place by the end of the week, and then head off to South Africa. I'll be in touch before I leave," he added, turning to go without so much as a thanks or goodbye.

The smile eased from Mr. Tabaro's face as Lee disappeared around the corner. Entering the office, the receptionist exchanged a look of concern with his superior.

Having picked up the mail, Mutiba was waiting outside in the Rover.

"Home, James," Lee joked with a satisfied grin.

Before driving away, Mutiba noticed the receptionist standing in the doorway of the building, shaking his head disapprovingly.

As their boat approached Murchison Falls, Elon and the others could hear the roar before turning a bend and coming into view of the cascading water, framed by a shimmering rainbow. Rika's breath caught in her throat at the beauty of it all.

"Feel up to a hike?" Elon asked her above the noise of the falls.

Nodding her consent, Rika avoided looking him in the eye. The feel of his embrace when the crocodile startled her had been both reassuring and frightening—and she resolved to keep her distance from him, physically as well as emotionally. So, when the helmsman brought the boat to shore, Rika refused Elon's hand and instead accepted Sahid's help in getting out. She followed after Elon while Sahid and the boatman remained with the craft.

Halfway up a narrow winding trail, Elon stopped at a clearing that afforded a panoramic view. He motioned for Rika to have a seat on a small boulder while he divided the lunch between them. They ate in silence, gazing out at the river as it snaked away from the falls.

Closing her eyes, Rika forced the thought of Elon's embrace from her mind and instead concentrated on the life growing within her. Thinking of Lee, Rika reminded herself of his charm and other good qualities—qualities that had endeared him to her when they first met in Viet Nam.

When Lee returned to Rose Inish from Fort Portal, he entered the guest cottage as Nisha was making the bed.

"That won't be necessary," Lee told her suggestively while slowly approaching.

Nisha stood her ground as Lee scanned her body with his gaze. She made the first move by slowly unbuttoning his shirt. While she loosened his pants, he slipped the straps of the dress from off her shoulders. As the garment floated softly to the ground, Nisha stood in front of him wearing only bikini undies—her firm young breasts proudly exposed to his scrutiny.

Fondling her nipples, Lee smiled as they hardened to his touch. She lowered his slacks and stood back while admiring his erection. He kicked off his boots before stepping out of his pants. Backing her onto the bed, he laid her face down while roughly sliding the panties from off her slender, honey-colored bottom. She dug her fingers into the mattress with pleasure as he fell on top of her.

At the crest of Murchison Falls, Elon studied Rika as she gazed at the water beating with such force against the narrow rock divide that it whipped up froths of foam. The rainbow was so close it seemed as though she could reach out and touch it. Overcome by the majesty of the moment, Rika closed her eyes against the rising tears. When she opened them, she made the mistake of looking into Elon's gaze. What she saw melted her resolve.

After gently wiping the tears from Rika's cheeks, Elon tilted her chin up as his lips moved slowly toward hers. Their kiss was soft and gentle. Rika visibly relaxed, surrendering to the moment. But not for long—as the child kicked within her. Her eyes sprang open, and in them Elon saw fear and confusion. He watched sadly as Rika quickly made her way to the trailhead leading back to the waiting boat.

Not a word was spoken between them on their return to Rose Inish, as Rika pretended to be asleep throughout the flight. When they landed, she hurried toward the cottage.

Sitting alone on the front veranda while shelling peas, Mila looked worried as Rika rushed by her without speaking. Remaining at the aircraft, Elon met Mila's questioning gaze before looking away. Mila shook her head sadly.

Entering the cottage, Rika froze at the sight of Lee lying naked and asleep on top of Nisha. A malicious smile spread slowly across the girl's lips as she peered through a soft curtain of dark hair into Rika's startled eyes. Rika mechanically backed out of the cottage and quietly closed the door.

On weakened legs, Rika went to the side of the building and vomited into the grass. Making her way to the back veranda, she curled up in a fetal position on the sliding divan. Mila soon joined her. Gently placing Rika's head on her lap when sitting beside her, Mila tenderly stroked her hair while softly singing a lullaby. The rocking of the divan, along with Mila's soothing song and gentle touch, soon lulled Rika to sleep.

Mila glanced up when Nisha exited the cottage. Without a break in her song, Mila narrowed her eyes with anger as the girl slunk out of view.

Mila remained with Rika until dusk mingled with storm clouds, darkening the land. When Elon took over so she could tend to supper, Mila gently placed a pillow under Rika's head and covered her with a blanket. Sitting in a chair near the divan, Elon kept watch as Rika continued to sleep.

As night encroached upon the farm, the leopard crept closer to the house. Her growing cubs were making increasing demands on her supply of milk, and she felt compelled to take chances that she wouldn't have ordinarily taken.

Keeping vigil over Rika on the back veranda, Elon caught a glimpse of the leopard. Rika woke when a monkey screeched in alarm. Focusing on Elon, she followed his gaze to where the lawn met the tea field just as the clouds parted, exposing the leopard in a shaft of moonlight. Rika sat up with a frightened gasp.

"Don't worry," Elon quietly reassured her. "She knows we see her."

The clouds again obscured the moonlight. When they parted, the leopard had disappeared. Rika regarded Elon with more concern than she'd shown toward the cat.

"How do you know it's a 'she'?" Rika asked.

Elon detected a note of anger in her voice. "Only a wounded animal or a nursing mother would venture so close to the house," he responded in a gentle tone. "She didn't appear wounded. Besides, I could see her full teats," he smiled.

Feeling herself being drawn into his gaze, Rika forced herself to look away. "Yes," she contemplated softly, "her motherly instincts would overpower any concern for her own safety."

Elon studied her with compassion. "Why are you with him?" he asked.

"What do you mean?" she feigned ignorance.

"Your husband. He doesn't deserve you."

"Don't," she warned. "You don't understand—"

"You're right—I don't understand why you married someone like him. What was it? The money? Prestige? What?"

"When we first met," she began in a quiet voice, "he was the most charming man I'd ever known. It wasn't until . . ." her voice trailed off sadly.

"Why do you stay with him?"

"Because I'm pregnant," she admitted softly.

Her admission took Elon by surprise. And it made him angry. "And he still treats you the way he does?" he demanded.

"He doesn't know."

"How can he not know?"

"Why? Can you tell?" she glared at him.

"No. But I'm not your husband."

She looked away. "There's more to it than that," she said. "Lee has a son, named Cole. He's seven years old, and I'm the only mother he has. I love him as if he were my own. He'll be staying here with me while Lee is in South Africa."

"What happened to his real mother?"

"She died," Rika replied, omitting the fact that the woman had killed herself. It had happened before Rika came into Lee's life. "Tell me about New Zealand," she asked, changing the subject.

"What do you want to know?"

"What is it you do there?"

"Field research in wildlife conservation for an organization based out of Christchurch."

"Tell me about your fiancée."

"Kiri's an oceanographer."

"'Kiri,'" Rika repeated softly. "Is she as lovely as her name?"

Feeling a sense of guilt, Elon looked away. "Yes," he admitted. "She's half-Maori—tall, with raven hair. Quite lovely."

"When will you marry?"

"To be honest, she doesn't know yet that we're engaged. Not that we haven't talked about it," he added hastily. Elon didn't divulge that his and Kiri's conversations regarding the subject had been more argument than discussion.

"Why haven't you asked her?"

"Because marriage wasn't something I was particularly keen on."

"What changed your mind?"

"Perhaps absence does make the heart grow fonder. Perhaps it was putting my father in the ground. Who knows, maybe more than one demon was laid to rest that day," he quietly mused.

Silence settled between them as they studied the moonlit landscape.

"There were times I felt like I hated my mother for staying with him," Elon eventually confided in a flat tone. "I have no doubt his abuse and infidelity helped put her in her grave. When she became ill, she didn't have the will to live," he added sadly, remembering his mother's passing. "You could do so much better," he accused Rika.

"You have no right!" she shot back. "You have no one to answer to! Your parents are both dead! Your sister is thousands of miles away! And you say you're engaged to a woman who doesn't even know it? You obviously know nothing about commitment!"

"You're right," he admitted in a gentle tone. "What I *do* know is that I care about you, and it upsets me to see you hurt."

His gentleness threw Rika off-balance. She was prepared for a fight, and had no defense against his kindness. "I must go to my husband," she stated weakly.

Elon stood and blocked her way. He wanted desperately to take her in his arms and once more feel her soft lips on his. He wanted to keep her safe . . . to protect her from herself as well as the world!

Rika stood rigid in front of him, refusing to meet his gaze. She knew if she did it could compromise all that she'd been taught she must be. Reluctantly, Elon stepped aside and she ran into the night. He watched as she disappeared into the cottage.

That night Kiri slipped into Elon's dreams. Her bronzed, naked body glided softly across the fog-shrouded New Zealand beach. Her teasing gestures drew Elon into a game of chase among the breaking waves. Her silken, ebony hair flowed across her playful face as she ran into the tropical forest bordering the sand. Elon followed her into the dense foliage, where she faded from sight. The leopard appeared in Kiri's place. It also lured Elon into a game of chase before fading away. Kiri reappeared, but again vanished before reappearing elsewhere. When Elon tired of the game, she made her way seductively toward him. He closed his eyes as their lips slowly met. When he opened them, Elon was neither surprised nor disappointed to find that it was Rika whom he had kissed. Her pale-green eyes smiled up at him as she gently stroked the head of the leopard, purring contentedly at her side.

Elon woke with a start as the shriek of an owl pierced the predawn hour. His breathing was labored and sweat soaked his body as he replayed the dream in his mind. He felt it wasn't surprising that he had dreamt of Kiri, as he greatly missed their sexual trysts. But when he recalled the look in Rika's eyes when she had taken Kiri's place in his dream, Elon realized it was only sex that kept him and Kiri together—whereas in Rika he'd found a kindred soul. *But she's married to another man—a man who doesn't deserve her!* Elon reminded himself with renewed anger.

The owl shrieked once more, sending a shiver through Elon's body. Refusing to dwell on the sense of foreboding he felt from the bird's call, he rose to face the new day.

Entering the dining room, Elon acknowledged Mila with a gloomy nod as he helped himself to a cup of tea while she set the table for breakfast.

"There's a letter for you," she told him. "From New Zealand."

She watched as he sat down and opened the letter. As he began to read, the look on Elon's face confirmed what Mila had suspected—that Kiri had found someone else.

Mutiba entered the room and greeted his mother with a kiss on the forehead. "What's wrong?" he asked, seeing her worried look. He followed her gaze to Elon.

"It's Kiri," Elon responded, feeling their eyes on him as he returned the letter to its envelope. "It seems she's in love."

"I should hope so," Mutiba smiled.

"With someone else," Elon said, directing his attention out the window to where the morning sun bathed the farm with growing light.

Mila disappeared into the kitchen as the smile slid from Mutiba's lips.

Mutiba regretted adding to Elon's bad news, but he knew he had to tell him what he'd learned. "Yesterday, after I brought the doctor back here, I returned to Fort Portal to see what he was up to. It seems he had a talk with Tabaro."

"What about?" Elon asked with concern.

"Using Rose Inish as a base for capturing animals to be shipped back to America, where they would be kept in a reserve to be hunted by him and his rich Texas friends."

Elon's eyes narrowed with anger. Mila returned with plates of food.

Mutiba sat down to be served. "Where's Nisha?" he asked before digging in.

"Humph!" Mila responded, not wanting to explain why she'd let the girl go.

Studying Mila's expression, Elon realized that Nisha had something to do with Rika's falling asleep on the divan the previous evening. What it was wasn't difficult to guess.

Mila met Elon's gaze with a knowing look as she set his breakfast in front of him.

"'Morning," Lee greeted them cheerfully while entering the room. "Can't remember when I've slept so well!" he added with a luxurious yawn.

Elon regarded him with an icy stare. Mutiba looked warily from Elon to Lee and back.

"Will Rika be joining us?" Mila asked coolly of Lee. "Or should I take something to her?"

"Thank you, Mila, but that won't be necessary," Rika responded with forced cheerfulness as she entered the room.

Elon stood and politely pulled out a chair for her. Nodding her thanks, Rika avoided eye contact as she sat down. Taking his seat, Elon again glared at Lee. Mila went to the kitchen, soon returning with Rika and Lee's breakfast.

"I'll be leaving for Entebbe within the hour," Mutiba said, breaking the heavy silence that had settled in the room.

"Do you need me to fly you back?" Elon asked in an angry tone.

Mutiba knew Elon's anger was directed at Lee, not him. "A friend will be picking me up," he responded. His eyes again darted between Elon and the doctor, who was attacking his meal with glee.

"Another culinary delight!" Lee complimented Mila between bites. "Sure hope you'll be staying on when the place changes hands."

"The 'place' won't be changing hands," Elon countered with stony conviction. "At least not into yours."

All eyes, including Rika's, regarded him with surprise.

"What are you saying?" Lee asked in a venomous tone.

"I'm saying that I will not permit you or anyone else to use Rose Inish as a base for acquiring wildlife to be shipped to the States and slaughtered in the name of sport," Elon responded in a controlled voice that belied the anger seething in his eyes.

Shocked, Rika looked from Elon to Lee. Mila gently placed her hand on Rika's shoulder in an attempt to reassure her. Mutiba stifled a smile as he resumed eating.

"I can take legal action against you!" Lee threatened Elon.

"Go right ahead. But I will not sell you Rose Inish," Elon responded, coolly meeting Lee's angry stare.

"Very well!" Lee shouted, throwing his napkin on the table as he rose to leave. "Come on, Rika, we've got packing to do!"

"You don't have to leave," Elon told Rika gently.

"So *that's* how it is?" Lee sneered at her. "I should have known! You whore!" he hissed.

Elon sprang from his chair with such force that it fell to the floor. Before he could punch Lee in the face, Mila grabbed hold of Elon's arm.

"You can get a ride back to Entebbe with Mutiba!" Elon told Lee through clenched teeth. "He leaves in an hour!"

"Forty minutes," Mutiba corrected, smiling broadly while checking his watch.

Lee looked angrily from Elon to Mutiba and then to Rika, who sat in stunned silence. "If you're not with me in five minutes, you're outta my life and outta my pocketbook forever!" he snarled at her. "*Understood?!*"

What little color Rika had acquired from her brief stay at Rose Inish was now completely drained from her face. Attempting to stand, she found she was unable to move. She blinked uncomprehendingly as Lee stormed from the room.

"You'll be all right," Elon told her softly while gently covering her hand with his.

The feel of his touch, and the kindness in his voice, gave Rika a semblance of strength. She slowly slid her hand out from under his. "I must go to him," she stated weakly. She stood but, in her compromised condition, managed only a few steps before fainting.

Elon caught her before she hit the floor. Lifting her limp body into his arms, he gave Mila a worried look.

"Bring her to Shauna's room," Mila told him while leading the way.

Carrying the unconscious Rika, Elon followed after Mila. They passed Harun at the entrance to the dining room. Rubbing the sleep from his eyes, the boy looked with bewilderment from Elon to Mutiba, who shook his head for him not to say anything. From outside, they heard the honk of a horn as Mutiba's friend arrived.

"He's early," Mutiba said as he glanced out the window.

Harun's look of confusion turned to sadness as he followed Mutiba outside.

In Shauna's room, Mila pulled back the covers before Elon laid Rika on the bed.

"She's going to have a baby," he stated softly.

"Yes," Mila responded as she gently tucked the covers around Rika.

"You knew?" Elon asked with a hint of disappointment.

Mila nodded while glancing out the window to where Mutiba and Harun greeted Mutiba's friend, who had arrived in a jeep.

"I'll stay with her," Elon offered. "You go say goodbye to Mutiba."

Mila left to join her sons. From the window, Elon saw Mutiba load his duffel bag into the jeep. Seeing him, Mutiba waved goodbye. Elon waved back. He then watched as Lee stormed from the house and angrily tossed his bags into the vehicle.

Mutiba kissed Mila goodbye, and then gave Harun a playful nudge before enclosing him in a bear hug.

At the window, Elon held his breath with anticipation. He expected Lee to storm back in the house to reclaim his wife. *That's what I'd do if I were her husband!* Elon reasoned. But Lee didn't even look back as the vehicle pulled away.

When Rika moaned softly from the bed, Elon turned away from the window and settled into an overstuffed armchair. He studied her with concern as she tossed in a fitful state of unconsciousness. Elon knew better than to feel secure in Rika's remaining at Rose Inish, for she'd done so unwittingly. And he knew that he cared for her too much to ever hold her against her will.

Chapter 5

Shauna shivered in the crisp December air as she waited to walk Helmut and Gert home on their last day of school before the Christmas break. Although she had seen snow from a distance on the peaks of the Ruwenzori Mountains, Shauna had actually been in it only once before—when she and her family climbed Mount Kilimanjaro, in Tanzania. *How different everything in Austria is compared to Africa,* she thought as she stamped her boots in an attempt to keep warm while gazing at the banks of snow cleared from the walkway. *Yet how much more exciting!* she smiled.

In spite of the cold Shauna loved Vienna, especially now when the city was filled with the trappings of her first Christmas in Austria. She loved how the lights sparkled in the clear nights and played upon the moonlit snow. She loved all the sights and smells. And the food! The artistry and flavor of the food were unbelievable!

Ursula's cooking was the best Shauna had ever tasted. It wasn't surprising that everyone in the Muller family had a problem with their weight; a problem that Shauna didn't succumb to, as she was able to push back her plate when full. It was only one of the many things Frau Muller hated about her.

Shauna smiled somewhat smugly as she tightly wrapped the fur-lined coat Herr Muller had given her around her lithe frame. The coat, more than anything else Herr Muller had done for Shauna, was a sore spot with Frau Muller. Shauna had heard the argument that ensued over it; although, as with all the Muller's "discussions," it had been more of a one-sided event wherein Frau Muller had exercised her formidable vocal chords.

Another reason Frau Muller despised Shauna was because the young woman couldn't be cowed. But Frau Muller needed someone to help with the boys—only not someone as attractive as Shauna O'Shay, whom her sons had bonded with all too easily.

Helmut and Gert's devotion to Shauna was evident in the way they now ran from the school and happily grabbed hold of her gloved hands. Like the other children, they were dressed in little uniforms and overcoats that made them look like miniature soldiers.

"Good afternoon, Miss Shauna," Helmut addressed her in proper English.

"Good afternoon, Masters Helmut and Gert," she responded with warmth.

Gert smiled shyly. As he walked proudly at Shauna's side, it was obvious the tall redheaded beauty had captured his little six-year-old heart.

"Did your day go well?" Shauna asked.

"Oh, yes!" Helmut stated enthusiastically.

"What about you, Gert?" she asked gently.

Gert sadly shook his chubby-cheeked head. School was not his favorite activity. Then his face brightened. "But we have four weeks off for the holiday!" he exclaimed.

"Yes!" Helmut concurred. "And we will be going to our home in the mountains where I will teach you how to ski!" he told Shauna emphatically.

Shauna smiled. The boys had been appalled to learn that she had never even attempted the sport. It was the only form of physical activity they truly enjoyed—an enthusiasm for which their father had instilled in them at an early age.

"We'll see!" Shauna laughed at Helmut's suggestion.

"Don't worry, we won't let you fall," Gert offered lovingly.

"How sweet of you," she responded, bending down to give the youngster a gentle kiss on the cheek.

Gert's smile widened and the color rose in his cheeks as he tightened his hold on Shauna's hand while they continued to walk home in the snow. When they arrived, Ursula greeted them with warm almond-paste cookies and hot chocolate brimming with whipped cream. The boys dug in ravishingly.

"Now, now!" Shauna admonished them gently. "What have I told you about acting like gentlemen?"

They sat down guiltily and began eating with controlled politeness.

Ursula smiled at the effect Shauna had over them. "Here," she stated kindly while directing Shauna to a chair. "You eat as well."

"I'll have just one. I don't want to spoil my appetite for supper," Shauna said with an accusatory glance at the boys.

"Will you play Aran for us?" Gert begged with a whipped cream mustache.

Shauna gently wiped his mouth with a napkin before going to her room and returning with the instrument. As she treated Ursula and the boys to a medley of Christmas tunes, Herr Muller arrived home from work and joined them.

"Bravo!" he clapped when Shauna had finished. He helped himself to a handful of cookies, stuffing them eagerly into his mouth.

"Father, you must eat like a gentleman!" Helmut parroted Shauna's directive.

Herr Muller smiled distraughtly. "I am afraid I have some bad news," he stated with much difficulty, not meeting Shauna's gaze. "Frau Muller has secured someone else to be the boys' nanny."

As Helmut and Gert sat in stunned disbelief, Ursula and Shauna didn't appear surprised. They both knew it was only a matter of time until Frau Muller succeeded in convincing her husband that Shauna must leave.

"No!" Gert wailed. "We don't want Shauna to go!"

"I am sorry, Gert," his father responded sadly. "Shauna, I know you do not want to leave Vienna yet," he turned to her reassuringly. "I have made arrangements for you to stay with one of our orchestra members, Vivian Wilcox—if that is all right with you. She lives in a lovely place in the old section of town. And of course I will help you financially until you are able to find work. I regret I was not able to get you into a school, but I . . ." his voice trailed off sadly.

"Don't worry, Herr Muller," Shauna assured him. "You've been very kind to me and I appreciate all that you've done. How soon will I be leaving?"

"Now, I am afraid," he said with his head bowed.

Shauna and Ursula exchanged a look of dismay.

"No!" Helmut objected as tears stung his eyes. "Shauna was going to come to the mountains with us!"

"And we were going to teach her how to ski!" Gert said while crying openly.

Shauna gathered them in an embrace. "It will be all right," she assured them lovingly. "We will still be able to see each other," she added with an imploring glance at Herr Muller.

"Of course," he lied.

"Come, I will help you pack," Ursula told Shauna sadly while gently prying the boys away from her.

"Please bring only what you immediately need. I will send the rest later. It is best that we are gone before Frau Muller returns," Herr Muller instructed.

Shauna nodded before following Ursula to her room.

"I am so sorry," Ursula said.

"I'll miss you and the boys terribly," Shauna said while returning the violin to its case. "But you must admit we knew it wouldn't last . . . not with the way Frau Muller feels about me,"

"Ya," Ursula agreed as she helped Shauna gather up a few of her belongings.

Most of Shauna's suitcases had never been unpacked, but had been stashed under the bed or piled in a corner of the room. After stuffing a few clothes and toiletries into a small bag, Shauna removed a framed photograph from the windowsill. It pictured herself, Elon, Mila, Mutiba, and Harun at Rose Inish. Shauna smiled sadly as she gently caressed the image of Mutiba's face before placing the photo in her purse. Carrying Aran, she left the room without looking back. Ursula followed with the small bag.

Shauna hugged Gert, Helmut, and Ursula goodbye. Herr Muller took the bag from Ursula as he and Shauna left.

"We will see Miss Shauna often," Ursula told the crying boys as she kept them from following after Shauna. But the sadness in her face belied the hopefulness in her voice.

Outside, as Shauna and Herr Muller were about to pull away in his Mercedes, Frau Muller arrived in a taxi. A benign-looking red-faced woman, who surpassed Frau Muller in both age and girth, accompanied her. Shauna's heart ached for the boys. She knew it wouldn't be long until they reverted back to their sullen, belligerent ways.

"Fräulein Wilcox is quite talented on the cello," Herr Muller said as he drove Shauna toward the city's historic district. He wished he could add that Vivian Wilcox was someone whom Shauna would like, but that probably wouldn't be the case. Vivian was a spoiled and demanding auburn-haired beauty, whom Herr Muller knew was civil to him only because he paid for her favors. *Her expertise in playing the cello is not the only thing at which she excels!* he thought with a leering smile.

Arriving in front of a massive wooden gate with ornate hand-wrought ironwork, Herr Muller honked the horn. A man of about sixty opened the gate and then closed it behind them as they drove onto the cobble-stoned courtyard. Even with the snow, Shauna could tell that the courtyard was beautifully landscaped.

"Johann, this is Fräulein O'Shay," Herr Muller introduced Shauna to the man.

"Welcome," Johann solemnly stated as he tipped his hat in greeting.

Taking Shauna's bag from Herr Muller, Johann directed them inside. Shauna followed with Aran in hand. A rather pudgy, dark-haired girl of fifteen regarded them shyly as she met them at the door.

"This is Johann's niece, Tanya," Herr Muller introduced the girl. "Tanya, this is Shauna O'Shay."

With downcast eyes, Tanya curtsied politely before taking Shauna's bag from Johann.

"Is Fräulein Wilcox home?" Herr Muller asked.

When Tanya only nodded and indicated they should follow, Shauna wondered if the girl could speak. But her thoughts soon turned to her surroundings; for although the Mullers' home had been impressive to Shauna, it was nothing compared to what she now encountered. She had never seen such an ornate and lavishly furnished residence. The fourteen-foot ceilings were adorned with sculpted plaster reliefs and crystal chandeliers that practically blinded the eye. The walls were painted a pale shade of blue, and were accented with gold-leaf trim that complimented the rich, black walnut framework of the doors and windows.

As she followed Tanya and Herr Muller, Shauna was bombarded by an eclectic display of artwork and expensive furnishings. There were Greek and Roman statues, mostly of nude men, scattered between Louis Quatorze and modern Danish furniture. Shauna felt somewhat disoriented by the incongruity of it all, and was so distracted that she barely noticed the soft music being played on a cello. Entering a large sitting room dominated by a highly polished grand piano, Shauna's attention was drawn to the woman who straddled the instrument.

With her eyes closed and her skirt pulled up around her shapely legs, twenty-two-year-old Vivian Wilcox drew the bow across the cello so sensuously that Herr Muller's face became flushed. When she finished, Vivian opened her violet eyes and gave him an alluring smile.

Herr Muller cleared his throat. "Fräulein Wilcox, I would like you to meet Fräulein O'Shay," he announced with a considerably higher pitch to his voice.

"Herr Muller told me you are from Africa," Vivian addressed Shauna in a cultivated British accent and manner that masked her lower working-class roots.

"Yes. Uganda," Shauna smiled.

"'The Pearl of Africa,'" Vivian commented rather derisively. "According to Winston Churchill, that is."

"Actually it was Sir Henry Morton Stanley of the Dr. Livingston fame who first called it that," Shauna offered.

"Yes, well, it's just a shame that it's a third-world country," Vivian sniped. "Or is Uganda a fourth-world country?"

Shauna's smile faded.

"Vivian is from England," Herr Muller informed Shauna.

"Tanya, why don't you show Miss O'Shay to her room?" Vivian suggested to the girl who remained standing shyly to one side.

"Again, I am sorry I was not able to help more," Herr Muller told Shauna sadly.

"I understand. I do hope to see Ursula and the boys again, though."

"Perhaps I can bring them here sometime?" he suggested brightly.

"Wouldn't that be lovely?" Vivian responded with open sarcasm.

"Goodbye, Herr Muller. And thank you again for all that you've done," Shauna told him before following after Tanya.

"You didn't tell me she was so fetching," Vivian accused Herr Muller when Shauna and Tanya were out of sight.

"Not as fetching as you, my dear," he responded while turning her toward him. Although almost a head taller than Herr Muller, Vivian gave no resistance as his mouth closed around hers and he groped at her skirt. Sliding his hand up her panties, he thrust his finger inside her. Vivian gyrated a few times before pulling his hand away.

"Not now, you nasty little thing!" she scolded him playfully, her accent slightly reverting to its original coarseness.

"When?" he pouted.

"I'll let you know. Until then you run along, you naughty little boy! Or Mama will have to pull down your pants and give you a sound spanking!"

A smile rose with the color in his cheeks as the image aroused Herr Muller even further. "Promise?" he whined.

With her arm laced through his, Vivian walked him to the front door. Before leaving, he pulled some money from his wallet.

"This is for Miss O'Shay's keep," he offered. "And a little extra for yourself."

Vivian took the money and gave him an open-mouthed, full-tongued kiss before shoving him out the door. She tucked the money inside her bra.

Shauna hid her disappointment upon entering the small and comparatively drab room Tanya led her to; although she was grateful that it was considerably larger than the one she had occupied at the Mullers' residence.

"Miss Wilcox' home is quite beautiful," she commented to Tanya.

"Oh, it is not her home," the girl responded in a soft, melodiously-accented voice. "It belongs to Herr Kessler. Fräulein Wilcox is just the sister of a friend of his. Do you know Herr—"

"That will be all, Tanya," Vivian told the girl sternly, entering the room while overhearing her remark. Vivian's accent and bearing had returned to their acquired refinement.

Tanya's eyes shot down with a look of guilt as she quickly left. Shauna watched her go with a mixture of compassion and curiosity before busying herself with unpacking the few items she had brought. Removing the photo from her purse, Shauna placed it on the nightstand. Vivian studied it from a distance before moving in for a closer look.

"Is that your family?" she sneered sarcastically in reference to the image of Mila and her sons. Then her eyes widened as she picked up the photograph, focusing on Elon. "Who is *that?*" she asked while practically drooling.

It wasn't the first time Shauna had seen a woman show such an obvious interest in her brother. But the thought of someone as snippy as Vivian being so enthralled with him was rather unsettling to Shauna.

"That's just my brother," she responded dismissively, taking the photo from Vivian and placing it back on the nightstand.

Vivian continued to study Elon's image. The two things she admired most in men were their looks and their pocketbooks. Other than Franz Kessler, Vivian had met few men who had both. But she knew that Franz was already taken. And, knowing of Shauna's situation, Vivian correctly surmised that her brother was not a man of financial means. *His looks are means enough!* she thought with delight.

"Is he a model? Or an actor?" she asked Shauna.

"Hardly. He's a wildlife conservationist."

"What's his name?" Vivian asked, hiding her distaste for his occupation.

"Elon."

"'Elon O'Shay,'" Vivian quietly savored the name. "Will he be visiting you here?" she asked hopefully.

"It's doubtful. Does Herr Kessler live here?" Shauna changed the subject.

Detecting a slight barb in Shauna's question, a sly plan took shape in Vivian's devious mind. "Sometimes—when he's not at his castle near Hallstatt, or his flat in Paris, or off gallivanting around the world. He's deliciously rich . . . and handsome!" she clasped her hand over her heart for emphasis. "Yes, I'm anxious for the two of you to meet! Oh, and my brother Harry stays here occasionally," she added matter-of-factly.

"Harry's a doll," Vivian elaborated. "He's involved with a gorgeous woman who *is* a model. He works for an investment company—one of Franz' companies, actually. That's how we all met. Franz inherited a string of banks and such from his parents, who were killed in a plane crash a few years ago," Vivian explained, omitting the rumor of his family having greatly increased their wealth when the Nazis confiscated the assets of Viennese Jews.

"So, how's your cooking?" Vivian asked, suddenly changing the subject.

Shauna looked somewhat surprised, although she hadn't expected to stay without helping in some way. "Not too good," she admitted. "But I'm willing to give it a try."

"Good. Tanya could use some help in the kitchen."

"She seems rather young. And quiet."

"She's fifteen. She hasn't been here very long. Her aunt and uncle have worked for the Kesslers for years, long before Franz was even born. Her aunt recently died, which is rather a shame as she was a fantastic cook," Vivian said, showing more remorse for her stomach than the woman's passing. "We've been trying to find someone to take her place."

"I may know of someone," Shauna offered as Ursula came to mind. "But she works for the Mullers. I doubt she would—"

"The Mullers?" Vivian cut in, amused at the thought of stealing their cook. "Tell me, what do you think of that cow of a woman our dear little Herr Muller is married to?"

Shauna rolled her eyes with disdain.

"I'll bet she just loved having you around!" Vivian laughed. "Herr Muller tells me you're quite good on the violin," she said, glancing at the encased instrument lying on the bed.

"I had hoped to get into a music school here," Shauna stated sadly.

"They're rather difficult to get into. And expensive," Vivian responded, suppressing the urge to suggest a way in which Shauna could profit financially from her fresh, innocent beauty. "Perhaps you would be so kind as to play something for me?"

"Now?"

With Vivian nodding her encouragement, Shauna took Aran from its case and positioned it on her shoulder. As the notes drifted throughout the rooms, they drew Tanya from her work in the kitchen. She stood in the open doorway to Shauna's room, mesmerized by the music.

Entering his home, Franz was similarly drawn to Shauna's room. Unnoticed by the three young women, he stood behind Tanya and watched as Shauna played on. When she finished, he reacted the most enthusiastically.

"Splendid!" he clapped.

Regarding Franz with surprise, Shauna found herself transfixed by the sight of the most gorgeous man she had ever seen. In his late-twenties, his blonde hair was impeccably styled and his clear blue eyes seemed to penetrate her soul. Shauna's breath caught in her throat and her knees gave out as she sank onto the bed.

"Franz!" Vivian exclaimed happily as she threw her arms around his neck and kissed his cheeks. "Come and meet our new houseguest, Shauna O'Shay."

"My pleasure," Franz told Shauna as he took hold of her hand, which still grasped the bow, and kissed it gently. "Allow me to introduce myself. I am Franz Kessler," he stated in slightly accented English.

Shauna lost herself in his gaze as he smiled the most endearing smile she'd ever seen.

"These just arrived by taxi," Johann announced in heavily accented English as he entered the room loaded down with some of Shauna's suitcases. "There are more outside. Where would you like them, Fräulein?"

"Not in here, Johann. Take them to my mother's room," Franz kindly directed. "You'll be more comfortable there," he explained to Shauna.

Tanya smiled as she helped her uncle with Shauna's luggage. "This way," she indicated for Shauna to follow them to the other room.

Still somewhat dazed, Shauna rose from the bed with Aran in hand. Franz watched as she followed after Johann and Tanya.

Seeing that Franz was distracted, Vivian retrieved Shauna's photograph from the nightstand and hid it behind her back. "We weren't expecting you so soon," she told Franz, slipping her arm through his as they followed the others. "How was Paris?"

"My business there didn't require as much time as expected," he replied. "Tell me about Miss O'Shay," he whispered.

"Lovely, isn't she?" Vivian whispered back. "I knew you'd like her. And it appears the feeling is quite mutual!" she enthused suggestively.

"Now, isn't this better?" Franz asked Shauna when entering his late mother's bedroom, which had an adjoining sitting room. Decorated in shades of pale-peach and cream, the sunlit rooms reflected the taste of an extremely elegant woman who had been quite comfortable with her femininity.

Shauna could only nod in response to Franz' question, as her voice was again lost in his gaze. Neither of them noticed as Vivian laid Shauna's photograph facedown on the nightstand.

Johann stoked up a fire in the room's marble fireplace before leaving with Tanya to collect the rest of Shauna's suitcases.

"Well, my dear, why don't you freshen up and come join us in the parlor?" Vivian suggested to Shauna.

"Feel free to make yourself at home," Franz told Shauna kindly before Vivian steered him out of the room.

Released from the hold Franz had on her, and with Aran still clutched in her hand, Shauna collapsed onto the beautifully crafted bed. She stared in disbelief as she surveyed her surroundings. Never in her wildest dreams had she imagined making herself at home in such a splendid environment! Nor had she ever hoped to encounter anyone as breathtakingly handsome as Franz Kessler!

"This is all of it," Johann told Shauna when he and Tanya brought the last of her belongings.

"Thank you, Johann, Tanya. You've been so kind," Shauna smiled.

"If there is anything we can do for you, please do not hesitate to ask," Johann told her.

Noticing the sadness reflected in his eyes, Shauna remembered what Vivian had said about Johann's recent loss of his wife. Shauna surmised that they must have loved each other very much. "Thank you again," she told him sweetly.

"If I may say so, it is nice to have you here," he stated shyly.

Tanya nodded in agreement before leaving with her uncle.

Remembering Vivian's invitation to join her and Franz in the parlor, Shauna placed Aran back in its case and then rummaged through her bags for something appropriate to wear. "Everything's so childish!" she whined, until settling on her most sophisticated dress—if it could be called that.

She quickly changed and ran a brush through her hair, studying her reflection in the huge mirror attached to an antique dressing table. Scrunching her nose with displeasure over her freckled face, she pinched her cheeks to bring out the color, took a deep breath, and then went to join the others. All thoughts of Rose Inish, and of Mutiba in particular, were far from Shauna's mind as she ignored the photograph lying facedown on the nightstand.

"May I get you something to drink?" Franz asked Shauna when she found her way to the parlor as he was handing Vivian a glass of white wine.

"The same," Shauna responded, trying to sound sophisticated while motioning to Vivian's glass, although she really didn't care for alcohol.

"Vivian has informed me that you would like to attend music school," Franz stated while pouring the wine. "Although I, for one, can find no fault in your musical ability."

"That's because you are practically tone-deaf, my dear," Vivian teased him.

"Be that as it may," he responded good-naturedly while handing Shauna the wine, capturing her once again in his gaze. "If you are intent on taking lessons, I am sure I can arrange for a private instructor."

"No, I couldn't possibly—" Shauna started to object.

"And perhaps a few items for her wardrobe?" Vivian suggested to Franz, eyeing Shauna's dress derisively.

"It would be my pleasure," Franz smiled. "On the condition that I may come along," he added hopefully.

"Oh, goody!" Vivian exclaimed. "A shopping spree!"

Shauna looked alarmed. "No, I couldn't . . . I wouldn't want you to spend—"

"Nonsense, dear," Vivian chided her. "As I told you, money is of no concern to Franz. Simply tell him 'thank you' and leave it at that."

"Thank you," Shauna complied, blinking back tears of amazement and gratitude.

"Good. Now then, what plans have you made for the holiday?" Franz asked.

Shauna shook her head sadly as she recalled the aborted ski trip with Helmut and Gert.

"Excellent!" Franz responded brightly. "I insist that you join us in Hallstatt!"

"Yes!" Vivian enthused before Shauna could object. "Wait until you see the castle! And the town! They're absolutely picture-perfect gorgeous!"

Pulling her gaze away from Franz' smile, Shauna buried her eyes in the wineglass. Not wanting to appear immature, she suppressed the urge to wrinkle her nose as she sipped the bittersweet liquid.

Before leaving for Franz' castle in Hallstatt, he and Vivian were good on their word to take Shauna shopping. Although at first they had to practically drag her from boutique to boutique, she eventually surrendered to their enthusiasm in seeing that she was provided with more clothes than she could have ever hoped for.

"I don't know what I'll do with all the clothes I brought with me," Shauna shook her head as they stepped in for tea and pastries at a darling little café. "Or how I can ever repay you," she told Franz worriedly.

"Consider it a Christmas present," he smiled.

"That and a trip to a storybook castle!" Vivian exclaimed.

On the train ride from Vienna to Hallstatt later that week, Shauna pressed her nose to the window so as not to miss any of the passing sights. She stared with awe as they entered the snow-covered wonderland of the picturesque Salz Mountain Range. Franz showed obvious delight at her enthusiasm, and took pleasure in making sure she didn't miss any points of interest along the way. Tanya often smiled at Shauna's appreciation while Vivian, unimpressed by the scenery, either napped or read fashion magazines throughout the trip.

"I have a surprise waiting for you when we arrive," Franz told Shauna as they neared the rail-stop for Hallstatt.

"What is it?" she asked excitedly.

"It wouldn't be a surprise if I told you, now would it?" he admonished her gently.

Shauna feigned a pout before directing her attention back to the passing landscape.

It wasn't long until they reached their destination, where a smiling Johann met them at the station. He had arrived a few days ahead of the others to prepare the castle for their arrival.

"Welcome!" he greeted them enthusiastically with a tip of his woodsman's hat. Dressed in traditional Austrian attire, he looked as though he had just stepped out of a postcard. "Let me have those!" he offered as he took Shauna and Vivian's bags. In addition to his unusually exuberant behavior, Shauna noticed his eyes twinkled in a way that she hadn't seen before.

"This way," Johann directed, leading them to where a team of white Lipizzans stood harnessed to a large antique sleigh.

Shauna smiled with delight as Franz and Johann helped her, Vivian, and Tanya into the sleigh, bundling them up with blankets made of fur. When Johann eased the horses into a prancing trot, the bells on their harnesses rang melodiously throughout the forest as they traveled under a canopy of evergreens laden with fresh powdered snow.

Turning a bend in the road, Shauna's breath caught in her throat when Franz' castle came into view. It indeed looked like something out of a storybook. It reminded Shauna of an elaborate Russian cottage seen in the movie *Doctor Zhivago,* only on a much grander scale.

"It dates from the middle of the last century, and was originally designed and built for the Russian Ambassador to Austria," Franz told Shauna, confirming her assessment of the castle's architectural style.

Gazing across the ice-lined lake that bordered the castle, Shauna could see the little town of Hallstatt, nestled at the foot of Dachstein Mountain. The town and mountain, along with patches of brilliant-blue sky showing between puffs of white clouds, were reflected in the mirrored surface of the lake.

"It's all so spectacular," Shauna stated reverently.

Franz smiled at her reaction, and in anticipation of the surprise he had in store—which became known as soon as Johann brought the horses to a halt in front of the castle.

"Shauna!" a familiar voice called out to her.

"Ursula!" Shauna exclaimed as the dear woman came running toward her.

Like Johann, Ursula was also dressed in traditional attire. She and Shauna embraced excitedly.

"She came highly recommended," Franz responded to Shauna's tearful, questioning look.

"I can't believe you're here! How are Helmut and Gert?" Shauna asked Ursula.

"I am afraid Frau Muller's *babies* are back to their old habits. Still, it was hard for me to leave them. If Herr Kessler had not made me an offer I could not refuse . . ." Ursula smiled in Franz' direction.

"Ursula, I'd like you to meet Fräulein Wilcox and Johann's niece, Tanya," Franz introduced them.

"Shauna says you're an excellent cook," Vivian addressed Ursula. "Perhaps you could give her and Tanya some lessons?"

"Perhaps you as well?" Ursula offered, quickly assessing Vivian's true nature. "Come, there is fresh-baked strudel waiting!" she announced before Vivian could respond.

Shauna's smile broadened as Ursula took her by the hand and led her up the stone steps through the massive leaded-glass doors opening into the castle. Once inside, Shauna stopped in amazement. The castle's interior gave her the sensation of having stepped back in time. As Vivian, Tanya, and Franz passed by her and Ursula on their way to the kitchen, Johann stood to one side with Shauna and Vivian's suitcases in hand.

"Thank you, Johann," Shauna told him softly.

"No, Fräulein," he smiled, "it is *I* who should thank *you.*"

Noticing the way he was looking at Ursula, and how her dear friend was blushing, Shauna guessed the reason for the twinkle in Johann's eyes. She was delighted by the thought of her robust Ursula paired with the tall, lanky gentleman. *A rather handsome gentleman for his age,* Shauna realized as he made his way up the grand staircase to deposit the bags in her and Vivian's designated rooms, located on the upper floor.

"Ursula?" Shauna asked suggestively of the interchange between her and Johann.

Ursula tried to ignore her, but her smile and the color in her cheeks gave her away.

"Who would like to join me in getting a tree?" Franz asked as Ursula led Shauna into the kitchen, where Tanya was serving the apple strudel and hot chocolate.

"Now?" Vivian whined.

"Why not?" Franz responded cheerfully while checking his watch. "There are still a few hours of daylight left. Let's take a vote. All in favor raise their hand."

Every hand but Vivian's shot into the air. "Fine," she reluctantly yielded. "But first let me finish this delicious strudel!"

As Shauna sat down to the hot chocolate and warm strudel, she savored the smell of apples and spice that permeated the air. She admired the massive kitchen with its open fireplace and antique utensils hanging among large copper pots. The room's ambience gave Shauna a surreal feeling—as if she were in a place where time had stood peacefully still. The feeling intensified when she finished the snack and followed Tanya up the staircase to the room that had been prepared for her.

"I feel like I'm dreaming," Shauna said on entering a bedchamber fit for a princess. Tanya smiled before leaving her alone in the room.

Shauna ran her hand over one of the intricately carved posts of the canopied bed, which practically required a ladder to climb onto. She caressed the thick down-filled comforter before going to the window to take in the view. She watched as the ferry from Hallstatt cut through the mirrored-surface of the lake with passengers bound for the train ride back to Vienna. Remembering the Christmas tree, Shauna retrieved a pair of slacks and a sweater from her bag and hurried to change.

By the time Shauna joined the others outside, Johann had hitched a gentle giant of a draft horse to a long flat-bedded sleigh. He held the reigns proudly as Ursula sat contentedly at his side.

"Here, let me help you up," Franz offered as he lifted Shauna onto the bed of the sleigh.

The feel of his gloved hands around her waist sent chills of excitement through Shauna's body. She found it difficult to look him in the eye—fearful of having her feelings known. Together with Tanya, she huddled in a sea of soft fur blankets.

When Vivian joined them, she appeared somewhat put out. But she didn't want to be left behind. Franz helped her onto the sleigh before jumping up beside her. As Johann urged the horse forward, Franz led the group in a medley of carols. *Vivian was right,* Shauna thought with a smile as she sang along—*Franz is rather tone-deaf!*

Johann steered the gentle horse along a windy wooded trail to a clearing where he was able to turn the sleigh around. Shauna jumped off and paired up with Tanya as the group dispersed into the forest, searching for the perfect tree. Their cries periodically pierced the cold, quiet air with shouts of "Here's one!" or "What about this one!" Eventually Vivian exclaimed "This is it!" and they all agreed.

Franz and Johann took hold of opposite ends of a two-handled saw they'd brought along. The tree quivered as it was being cut. With the powered snow drifting from its limbs, it slowly fell through the branches of its neighbors before coming to rest on the ground. Everyone helped drag it to the waiting sleigh, where they secured it as best they could—although a third of its length extended beyond the bed.

Ursula offered to give her up her seat beside Johann, but no one accepted. Following the sleigh on foot, Vivian had Franz, Tanya, and Shauna lock elbows and join her in singing:

"We're off to see the Wizard! The Wonderful Wizard of Oz!
We hear he is a wonderful whiz if ever a whizzz there waaas!"

Their voices echoed through the forest as they skipped over the snow in badly-synchronized step.

With difficulty, the group managed to drag the tree into the castle's grand sitting room. While Johann and Franz nailed a wooden base to the bottom of the trunk, the women brought the decorations down from storage. When they eventually stood the tree upright, it almost brushed against the eighteen-foot ceiling. They stood back and admired it with a collective "Ahh!"

"Is that the best you could find?" a man asked cynically from behind them.

"Harry! Lisl!" Vivian exclaimed with surprise as she turned to greet her brother and his tall, radiantly beautiful, blonde girlfriend.

They exchanged kisses before Vivian led them toward Shauna. "Harry, Lisl, I'd like you to meet Shauna O'Shay," she introduced them.

"Harry, as in Vivian's slightly-older brother," he explained to Shauna with a charming smile. Quite handsome in a rather refined way, his accent and friendly manner were considerably more genuine than his sister's.

"Hello, my darling Tanya," he acknowledged the girl with a brotherly kiss on her forehead, causing her to smile and glance down shyly.

"You should have told us you were arriving early!" Franz scolded Harry as the two men embraced.

"What? And spoil the surprise?" Harry countered.

Franz kissed Lisl on both cheeks. "I am so glad you and Harry are here!" he told her.

"How did you arrive from the station?" Johann asked Harry with concern.

"Johann, my man!" Harry greeted him warmly. "We took a romantic stroll in the moonlight. And who is this lovely young woman at your side?" he inquired regarding Ursula, who blushed at the attention.

"Ursula Schultz," Johann proudly introduced her. "Our new cook."

"Pleased to make your acquaintance," Harry said, gallantly kissing her hand.

Ursula fanned her heated cheeks. "Speaking of cooking, I had better see to supper," she managed weakly while regrettably retrieving her hand from Harry's.

"Charming," Harry smiled as he watched her leave.

"Would you like me to help with your bags?" Johann offered.

"No need," Harry responded, putting his arm around Johann's shoulder. "They'll keep at the station until morning. No, I see we have more pressing business to attend to here!" he commented while scrutinizing the tree. "Such as what to do with this god-awful tree!"

"'God-awful tree'?" Vivian feigned offence.

And so began a round of good-natured kidding as Vivian and Franz joined sides against Harry and Lisl in a heated debate over how to best decorate the tree. Tanya excused herself with a smile and went to help Ursula in the kitchen. Shauna offered to go with her, but the others wouldn't hear of it. As Johann busied himself feeding the fire in the massive stone fireplace, Shauna tried to remain neutral in the battle over the tree.

"What do you think, Shauna?" they often asked, attempting to draw her into the debate. When realizing she couldn't be coerced, they dubbed her "Little Switzerland."

They voted for Shauna to put the finishing touch on the tree. As Johann and Franz held the ladder steady, she climbed to the top and placed what she assumed was a rhinestone-studded star. It didn't occur to Shauna that it was actually made out of real diamonds.

When Franz helped Shauna from the ladder, she trembled at their closeness as she stood beside him when Harry turned off the overhead lights. The flames from the fireplace cast an eerie glow around the room until Johann plugged in the tree lights and it sparked brilliantly to life. Everyone clapped and cheered at the masterpiece.

Basking in the warmth of the fire, and the rapport with her new friends, Shauna breathed a sigh a relief when realizing she was going to have a fabulous Christmas after all. Whatever feelings of homesickness she had for Africa, and the people she left behind, were now eclipsed by the joy of the moment . . . and her growing attraction to Franz.

Shauna had no idea how difficult it would be for Franz to

reciprocate her feelings, for she didn't see the way he and Harry often looked at one another. And, even if she had, Shauna's innocence would have prevented her from suspecting that the two men were lovers.

Chapter 6

Christmas music blared from the PA system at Houston International Airport where little Cole Lightfoot waited at the terminal with as much patience as possible for a seven-year-old. One of his hands was lost in the grip of his father's black chauffeur, Isaac. In his other hand Cole held a small bouquet of slightly wilted roses, secured with a red bow that he had obviously tied by himself.

Cole strained to see the familiar faces of the man who was his father in fact, if not in name—and the woman who may not have given birth to him, but who loved him with a mother's heart. It was mostly she whom Cole searched for in the sea of deplaning passengers.

"Welcome home, sir," Isaac greeted Lee Parnell as he made his way toward them.

"Isaac, Cole," Lee responded distantly while handing Isaac his bag.

Cole gave his father a tentative smile before craning his neck for sight of Rika.

"Come along," Lee told the boy brusquely, taking Cole's hand from Isaac's.

"Won't Miss Rika be joining us?" Isaac asked with concern.

"No! Miss Rika will not be joining us!" Lee shot back.

Cole continued to glance over his shoulder as he was being led away. He refused to accept the fact that Rika would not appear and take him in her arms, smiling in the way she had of making him feel all was well with the world. When Cole realized she was nowhere to be seen, he fought bravely to keep the tears from escaping his dark brown eyes, framed by soft brown curls. As his father practically dragged him along, the roses slipped from Cole's grasp and were soon trampled by the crowd.

"I want her cut off from everything!" Cole heard Lee yell at his lawyer over the phone the next day. The boy stood undetected on the other side of the door leading to the den in the Parnell mansion, which was located in an exclusive Houston neighborhood.

"Are you saying you want to divorce Rika?" Walter Hansen, Lee's lawyer, asked from the other end of the line.

"No," Lee responded ominously. "No divorce. If that's what she wants, she'll have to beg for it! In the meantime I want you to make things miserable for her! And that son-of-a-bitch Elon O'Shay!"

It wasn't the first time Cole had heard that name. He knew Elon O'Shay had something to do with Rika not returning from Africa . . . and Cole hated him for it.

"What about Cole?" Walt asked with concern.

"What about him?" Lee asked.

"Will he be going with you when you return to South Africa?"

"No. I've made arrangements for him to stay at the ranch with the Bennetts. I want you to draw up papers for guardianship. Plus I'll give them five-hundred-a-month for their trouble."

"Perhaps I should draw up papers giving the boy your name while I'm at it?" Walt suggested.

"Hold off on that."

"Look, Lee, his mother's dead and Rika's no longer around," Walt tried to reason with him. "You're only hurting—"

"You're my lawyer, Walt! Not my damn shrink! Just do as I say!" Lee barked before slamming down the receiver.

Cole went to his room where Isaac's wife, Vera, who worked as Lee's maid, was packing the boy's belongings for the trip to the ranch. Like her husband, Vera was in her mid-twenties. Seven months pregnant with their first child, she watched sadly as Cole scooped his collection of plastic African animals into a backpack.

"Goodbye, sweetie," she told Cole with a hug when Isaac came to collect the bags.

"'Bye, Vera," Cole responded, trying hard not to cry as she kissed him gently on the cheek. "Will you let me know when the baby comes?" he asked hopefully.

"Of course," she told him. She and Isaac shared a look of sympathy for the boy before Cole followed Isaac from the room.

"You mind the Bennetts now, you hear?" Lee demanded sternly of Cole as he walked with him and Isaac to the limousine.

Cole nodded before climbing into the back seat of the vehicle. He sat tall and brave as Isaac steered the limo away from the mansion. When they were out of his father's sight, Cole scampered over to the front seat and stretched out with his little head resting on Isaac's lap. Isaac laid his hand reassuringly on the boy's shoulder as Cole slept throughout most of the four-hour drive to the ranch, located north of San Antonio.

When they arrived at the ranch, Simon and Juanita Bennett greeted them warmly. In their mid-fifties, they were an engaging couple with graying hair and endearing smiles. Their Border collie, Lucky, lavished slobbering kisses on Cole.

"Hello, Lucky!" the boy responded happily.

"That's enough, girl! I imagine he's already had a bath," Simon told the dog. "Hey, Isaac," he extended his hand.

"Mister Simon, Miss Juanita," Isaac returned their smiles as he shook Simon's hand.

"Good to see you, Isaac," Juanita said before turning back to Cole. "Look how you've grown!" she exclaimed, scooping the boy into a loving embrace.

"Now, 'Nita, don't go smothering the boy!" Simon admonished her gently.

"Nonsense," she countered. "He enjoys being smothered!"

Cole couldn't help but smile. Although it was sometimes embarrassing, he was grateful for the love the Bennetts showered on him. Cole knew they never had children of their own; and that he was the closest thing they'd ever have to a grandchild.

"Come on in the house," Juanita directed him kindly. "You, too, Isaac. I've got some sugar cookies that are just begging to get frosted!"

"Thanks, ma'am," Isaac replied as he and Simon removed Cole's few bags from the limousine. "But I'd best be getting back. Have a good holiday!"

"Same to you and Vera. Give her our love. And let us know as soon as that baby of yours arrives," Juanita smiled while steering Cole toward the modest, but well maintained, single-story home. The boy waved goodbye to Isaac before disappearing inside with Juanita and Lucky.

Simon remained outside with Isaac. "These are papers for legal guardianship," Isaac told him while handing over a large envelope. "Also a record of his shots and all for getting him into school. The doctor's address in South Africa is in there, too. He said to tell you a check will be sent to you and Miss Juanita each month from his lawyer, Mister Walter Hansen, for your 'trouble'—as the doctor puts it."

"We both know that boy won't be any trouble," Simon responded with more than a hint of anger directed at Cole's father.

Isaac nodded. "Oh, and there's some money in there from the doctor and Mister Hansen, to get something for Cole for Christmas. Plus a little from Vera and me."

"That's mighty nice of you and Vera. And Mister Hansen," Simon told him. "Is it true that the doctor and Miss Rika have separated?"

"It appears so," Isaac replied sadly.

"That's a shame. For Cole's sake."

"Yes, for the boy's sake," Isaac agreed. "He's just fortunate to have you and Miss Juanita. What he needs most, you two have plenty to go around."

"That's kind of you to say."

"Can I help with the boy's bags?" Isaac offered.

"I can manage. You run along. And don't you and Vera be strangers around here, you hear?"

Isaac smiled at the invitation. He and Simon shook hands in parting before Isaac got in the limousine and drove off. Simon carried Cole's bags inside the house, where the boy was seated on a stool in the kitchen with his face and hands smeared with frosting while licking a large spoon.

"I need to feed the animals," Simon stated after placing the bags on the floor. He and Juanita shared a conspiring glance.

"Can I come?" Cole asked excitedly.

"Only if you wipe that icing off your face," Simon told him. "You want them to like you for who you are, not for what you're wearing."

"Why don't we all go?" Juanita suggested as she helped Cole get cleaned up. When she was finished, Cole rushed outside with Lucky barking happily at his side.

"Lucky, go get the sheep!" Simon directed.

They watched as Lucky darted into the pasture, quickly rounding up the small herd into a corral adjacent to the barn.

"Good girl!" Cole rubbed her head when she came panting to him for approval. The boy then helped Simon and Juanita pour grain into a trough for the sheep before scattering feed on the ground for the chickens, ducks, and geese.

"What about the horses and cows?" Cole asked.

"They're still up on the high pasture," Simon told him as he and Juanita turned back toward the house.

Cole and Lucky started to follow, until a faint whinny was heard from the barn.

"What was that?" Cole asked.

The Bennetts played ignorant. "I didn't hear anything. Did you, 'Nita?" Simon asked innocently.

Another whinny, this time louder, was heard. "It's coming from the barn," Cole told them with concern.

"Perhaps we'd better go see," Juanita suggested in a curious tone.

Cole and Lucky raced to the barn with Simon and Juanita not far behind. Adjusting his sight to the dimly lit interior, the boy made his way toward the sound of the whinnying. His eyes grew wide when he peered into one of the stalls. There, with the sunlight filtering in from a small window onto her shiny chestnut coat and flowing mane and tail, stood the most beautiful horse Cole had ever seen. The mare had one white stocking and a small white star between her large, gentle eyes.

As Cole stood transfixed at the sight of the mare, Simon removed a note pinned to the gate of the stall. "What's this?" he asked, showing the note to Cole.

"'MERRY CHRISTMAS, COLE,'" the boy read slowly from the large-lettered note. He blinked uncomprehendingly at Simon, who took the note and began reading it himself:

"'MERRY CHRISTMAS, COLE. HER NAME IS STAR AND SHE'S ALL YOURS. SORRY I COULDN'T WAIT 'TIL CHRISTMAS TO GIVE HER TO YOU, BUT YOU KNOW HOW BUSY I AM. LOVE, SANTA CLAUS.' Santa Claus?" Simon feigned surprise as Cole slowly digested the content of the note.

"All mine?" the boy muttered in disbelief.

"All yours," Simon smiled.

"It looks as though Star is an Arabian," Juanita told Cole, still playing innocent. "Arabians are the oldest pure breed of horses in the world. In the desert the Bedouin would let them sleep with them in their tents, they were that valuable. And they only rode the mares into battle. They called them 'The Daughters of the Wind.'"

Still unable to believe that Star was actually his, Cole stared with his mouth open.

"Merry Christmas," Juanita smiled.

"Merry Christmas," Simon added.

Cole looked from Juanita to Simon, and then to Star.

"Would you like to meet her?" Simon asked.

When Cole nodded enthusiastically, Simon led him inside the stall. Juanita waited outside, with Lucky sitting patiently at her side. They watched as Star lowered her head toward the boy, who reached out and stroked her soft, velvety nose. Cole felt as though his little heart would burst from happiness. And, for the first time since his father had returned from Africa without Rika, Cole momentarily forgot the pain of missing her.

Half-a-world-away from where Cole spent Christmas with the Bennetts, Elon and Harun paced impatiently on the back veranda of Rose Inish. The sun was about to set beyond the mountains and now dormant tea fields. They had waited since dawn to hear the sound that finally came to their ears—the soft cry of a newborn infant. Elon and Harun stopped in their tracks and exchanged smiles. But it wasn't until Mila joined them that Elon was able to breathe a sigh of relief.

"They are both doing well, although the baby is rather small from having been born early," Mila told them. She looked and sounded exhausted.

"What is it?" Harun asked excitedly.

"A boy," Mila smiled.

"Can we see him?" he asked hopefully.

"First help me with supper."

"I've already taken care of it," Elon told her.

Mila nodded her appreciation. "Give them time to rest, then you can take Rika something to eat," she said before leaving.

Elon felt torn between keeping his distance and wanting to run to Rika. It'd been two months since Lee had left her at Rose Inish. During that time they hadn't heard anything from him. Rika had written a letter to Lee's young son, Cole. When Elon mailed it, he surmised that it was an attempt on Rika's part to assure the child that she still loved him. The letter had been returned from Texas, unopened.

Rika had not yet fully recovered from the shock of Lee having left her when she went into labor almost a month prematurely. Prior to that, she had mentioned only once that she felt she should go to her husband. But Mila had pointed out that traveling could risk the welfare of her unborn baby—and Rika knew she was right.

Although Elon's feelings toward Rika had grown by the day, he had no illusions regarding their relationship. He realized it was for her child's sake that Rika had remained at Rose Inish. *For her and Lee's child,* he reminded himself often. Elon was determined not to let himself become attached to the infant. But, when he quietly brought a tray of food into Shauna's room where Rika had given birth, the sight of the sleeping mother and child captured Elon's heart.

Rika woke just as he was leaving. "Wait," she told him weakly. "Would you like to hold him?" she asked when Elon turned back.

Elon's first reaction was to say "no." But he didn't want to hurt Rika's feelings. As she gently handed him the tiny bundle, Elon's resolve not to become attached to the newborn completely evaporated. He smiled faintly as the infant stretched and yawned before settling in his arms.

What a wonderful man, Rika thought as she studied Elon. She marveled at the feelings reflected in his face—*feelings of love for a child that isn't even his own!*

"His name is Christiaan," she told him. "After my grandfather."

"Hello, Christiaan," Elon stated softly.

Watching the bond developing between Elon and her child, Rika felt a pang of guilt. "I should let Lee know he has another son," she stated weakly.

Her words pierced Elon's heart and his smile dissolved. He gently returned Christiaan to Rika's arms before turning to go. Rika shut her eyes against the stinging tears as her mind spun with pain and confusion.

Hesitating at the door, Elon turned back. "He never deserved you! And he certainly doesn't deserve that beautiful little boy!" he stated with quiet anger.

"If he were yours, wouldn't you want to know?" she asked softly.

"If it were me, I would never have left you!"

As their eyes locked, Elon could see her confusion. "If you let me . . ." he stated haltingly, " . . . I know I can be a good father to him."

"What are you saying?" she asked hesitantly.

"I'm saying . . . I am begging you . . . marry me."

Studying his expression, Rika saw that he was sincere. "If it were only that simple," she stated tearfully.

A soft knock was heard at the door. "May we come in?" Mila asked from the other side.

"Of course," Rika said as she wiped away the tears.

On tiptoes, Harun followed Mila into the room.

"Harun, this is Christiaan," Rika introduced them.

Harun gazed down at the sleeping infant with an expression of pure awe.

"Would you like to hold him?" Rika asked.

Harun looked hopefully to Mila, who nodded her approval. When Rika transferred the infant into his arms, Harun's grin stretched from ear to ear.

Studying the look of love reflected on Mila and her son's faces, as well as Elon's, Rika realized Elon was right . . . that the best thing she could do for Christiaan would be to not take him away from Rose Inish. Meeting Elon's gaze, Rika slowly nodded her consent to his proposal as the tears again rose in her eyes.

A look of relief spread across Elon's face. But, as Rika had implied, their getting married would not be a simple matter. When she wrote to Lee requesting a divorce, Rika received no reply. She didn't inform him of Christiaan's birth, as she knew it would complicate her request. Nor did Rika allow herself to become intimate with Elon, who respected her wish to stay in Shauna's room until she was free from Lee.

When four months had passed and they still hadn't heard from Lee, Rika and Elon talked about taking the matter into their own hands.

"We could meet with a divorce lawyer in Kampala," Elon suggested one evening as they sat on the back veranda watching Harun play ball with some of the workers' children.

The uncertainty in Elon's voice expressed his and Rika's awareness of how difficult it would be for her to divorce Lee while in Africa. They both knew the entire continent was a man's world;

and that divorce rarely favored the woman, who would be expected to relinquish her children to the father.

"I was thinking I should take care of it in Holland," Rika said.

"We could both go," Elon offered.

"No," she responded adamantly. "I need to go alone."

Detecting the fear in her voice, Elon remembered Lee's comment about Rika's father being a "hard-nosed preacher." He felt the man would be far from amenable to the idea of his only child getting a divorce. Elon also knew that if he went to Holland, it could aggravate the situation. As hard as it would be to let Rika go on her own, Elon realized he had to—even though it could mean his losing her forever. For, although there was no doubt that he loved her, Elon had difficulty telling her so. And, though Rika had consented to his proposal of marriage, she had remained faithful to her vows to Lee.

"Before you leave for Holland, perhaps you and Christiaan would take a little holiday with me," Elon mentioned hopefully.

Rika gave him a questioning look.

"Some dear friends of my family's, Devin and Yvette MacKail, have a home on Lamu," he told her.

"Lamu? On the ocean?" she brightened.

Christiaan's faint cry was heard from Shauna's room as he woke from his nap. Mila's singing soon quieted him as she changed his diaper before bringing him outside to be nursed. Out of respect, Elon stood and moved away. He kept his gaze locked on Harun and the other children as they played ball on the lawn.

Latched onto his mother's breast, Christiaan reached for her face with his little hand. Rika playfully pretended to nibble on his fingers, causing him to smile and break the suction on her nipple. He took hold of it with renewed vigor.

"Ouch!" Rika laughed. "You're a little hyena!" she lovingly accused.

Mila smiled at the baby's tenacity. "Supper is almost ready," she informed Rika and Elon before leaving.

"When can we leave?" Rika asked Elon when Christiaan had finished nursing.

He turned and gave her a questioning look.

"For Lamu," she reminded him.

"Soon," he responded, breathing a sigh of relief.

"Soon," Rika agreed as a sense of foreboding swept over her. She was not looking forward to going to Holland and confronting her father.

On their flight to Lamu, Elon first landed the Cessna at Entebbe Airport, where Mutiba met them. Wearing the dark-blue overalls of an air force mechanic, he greeted them warmly. Taking Christiaan in his arms, it was obvious the baby recognized and adored Mutiba, from his visits to Rose Inish.

"How are things now that the Israelis are gone?" Elon asked Mutiba quietly when Rika went to change Christiaan in the ladies' room.

"The British are here now," Mutiba answered, trying to sound optimistic.

"Good," Elon responded. But his expression showed his continued concern over what was happening in the country under Idi Amin's leadership. People were reported missing, or showed up dead, on a daily basis. There were also rumors of systematic executions of former President Obote's supporters—many of whom were said to have been tortured to death.

Also disturbing was the fact that Idi Amin had formed an open alliance with Libya, whose leader, Colonel Muammar al-Quaddafi, welcomed an Islamic stronghold in East African. As a result of that alliance the Israeli military advisors, who had been instrumental in training the Ugandan Air Force as well as designing and building both the old and new civilian airport facilities, had recently been expelled from the country.

When Rika rejoined them, she hugged Mutiba goodbye before re-boarding the Cessna with Elon and Christiaan to continue the flight to Lamu. Mutiba watched as the plane lifted into the air, then looked around worriedly before returning to his duties.

Landing at the airstrip on Manda Island in northeast Kenya, Elon and Rika were met by a young man who led them toward a little pier where he waved down a dhow. With its sail stored, the boat motored toward them. Behind it two dhows under full sail crisscrossed in the narrow channel. On the opposite bank, gleaming like pearls in the bright sunlight, were the buildings of Lamu—the oldest continually occupied town in Kenya.

After the two crewmen helped their passengers board the ancient-looking craft, the helmsman deftly motored it around those under full sail. They smiled at Rika's obvious appreciation of the unique vessels with tall, slanted triangular sails that glided effortlessly across the water.

"They call the town of Lamu the 'Katmandu of Africa,'" Elon told Rika as their dhow veered toward a stretch of sand that fronted a homestead nestled in a grove of palm trees.

The MacKails' three large dogs barked excitedly at the arrival of the craft as it neared the shore. Since the home lacked a dock, and it wasn't possible to beach the vessel, one of the boatmen carried Rika through the gentle surf to the glistening sand. Elon held Christiaan above his head as he slipped into the tepid water and made his way to shore, followed by the other boatman hoisting Elon and Rika's bags above his head.

Hearing the dogs barking, Devin and Yvette came from the house to greet their guests. Although in their mid-seventies, the MacKails were a strikingly handsome couple. Tall, trim, and almost totally bald, Devin towered above his petite wife, whose silver hair still held traces of natural golden-blonde.

"Now, now!" Devin admonished the barking dogs.

"Welcome!" Yvette exclaimed as Elon kissed her on both cheeks. "Who have we here?" she asked delightedly of little Christiaan, gurgling happily in Elon's arms.

"Yvette, Devin, I'd like you to meet Christiaan and his mother, Rika," Elon introduced them.

"A pleasure to meet you!" Devin smiled while gallantly kissing Rika's hand. "And you, too!" he tickled Christiaan, who giggled in response.

"Welcome, my dear," Yvette greeted Rika with a warm hug. "Come, you must get dry," she told Elon while taking Christiaan from him.

The baby reached his little hand toward Yvette's face and she smothered it with kisses. Rika smiled at the rapport the MacKails had with him.

Devin helped Elon with the bags as they and Rika followed Yvette up a flight of stairs to a guesthouse separated from the main residence. Rika stopped to admire the view of the channel from the open-fronted porch, framed by palm fronds.

"Tea is ready whenever you are," Yvette told her guests as she transferred Christiaan to Rika's arms.

"Perhaps we could all go for a swim after you've settled in," Devin said with a slightly lecherous look that suggested an interest in seeing Rika in a bathing suit.

"Now, dear, we're not going to monopolize their time," Yvette scolded him gently. She turned back to their guests. "If you two would like to spend some time alone, don't hesitate to leave the little one with us," she offered

"Thank you so much for your hospitality," Rika smiled.

"Not at all! Consider us family!" Devin said before planting a gentle kiss on Christiaan's forehead.

"Come along, old man," Yvette steered him away. "Make yourselves at home," she directed Elon and Rika before leaving with her husband.

"Perhaps I should have warned you about him," Elon told Rika after the MacKails had left.

She gave him a questioning look.

"Devin MacKail is one of the last of the true 'Great White Hunters,'" he explained. "But four-legged creatures weren't his only prey. At least not until Yvette came into his life."

"I think they're adorable," Rika said. "How long have you known them?"

"Devin and my father were in the safari business together since before I was born. Then Devin got involved with filmmaking. He met Yvette on one of the shoots."

"Do they have any children?"

"Yvette has a daughter from a previous marriage, who lives with her husband on an estate Devin owns in Scotland. Devin and his first wife had a son who was an RAF pilot. He was killed when his plane was shot down over Normandy during World War Two."

"How sad," Rika sympathized. She appeared uncomfortable as she glanced at the large bed with a mosquito-net canopy.

"I'll sleep in the next room," Elon offered, sensing her unease. "You and Christiaan take the bed," he said. Taking his bag to the adjacent room, he closed the door before changing out of his wet clothes.

Rika lay on the bed, offering her breast to Christiaan. "You look so much like your father," she whispered solemnly while gently stroking the baby's cheek as he nursed. *What if I'm making a terrible mistake by divorcing Lee?* she agonized. Overcome by uncertainty and exhaustion, she drifted off to sleep.

Elon knocked softly. Opening the door to the bedroom, he saw that Rika and Christiaan were sleeping. He studied them longingly before quietly leaving the guesthouse from the adjacent room.

"Rika will be joining us later," Elon told the MacKails when he joined them for tea on the patio. He playfully acknowledged the dogs before they settled at his feet.

"She has such a sweetness about her," Yvette said, handing him a cup of tea.

Elon nodded while watching the dhows sail serenely in the channel. "The baby's not mine," he stated needlessly. "She's married to someone else," he added quietly.

"But you love her, don't you?" Devin smiled knowingly.

"Whether he's in love with her or not is none of our business!" Yvette chided him. "The last thing they need is a couple of old biddies nosing around!"

"'Old biddies'?" Devin feigned offense at being included in her reference to little old ladies.

"You two stay out of trouble while I see to supper," Yvette instructed the men sternly before turning to go.

"Yes, dear," Devin answered contritely. "How are Shauna and Mila and her boys?" he asked Elon after Yvette had left.

"Shauna seems to be doing well in Austria. Mila's been thrilled to have a baby to look after. Harun is as chipper as always. And Mutiba's keeping busy in the air force."

"What's the buzz on Amin?"

Elon shook his head worriedly.

"You know why he kicked the Israelis out of the country, don't you?" Devin asked.

Elon gave him a questioning look.

"It seems your president got angry when they wouldn't give him what he wanted in order to bomb Tanzania," Devin said.

Elon studied him with concern and skepticism.

"The Brits and Israelis have come to realize they helped spawn a monster," Devin continued in a quiet voice. "I've heard that when the lights go out in Kampala, it's because the generators at Owen Falls Dam are clogged with the mutilated bodies of Amin's victims . . . That prisoners are given sledgehammers to kill fellow prisoners, and then are killed in the same way by others . . . That people have been forced to eat their own flesh and genitals . . . And that Amin keeps the heads of his worst enemies in a refrigerator."

Elon listened with revulsion. "Mutiba says the Brits are there now," he stated, as if to suggest the situation could improve.

"Not for long."

"Why do you say that?"

"Because Amin is sleeping with the Libyans. Quaddafi has succeeded in manipulating him into becoming a crusader for Islam. What's troubling is the prospect of Amin going to bed with the more extremist Arab factions, who are backed by the Soviets. If so, Amin is in a position to provide them with the one thing their more moderate Arab cousins won't."

"What's that?"

"An air force."

Elon studied his old friend with misgivings, until a smile slowly spread across his face. "If I didn't know better, I'd say you were a spy," he teasingly accused Devin.

Devin's solemn expression confirmed what Elon had thought was only a joke. For, in addition to his having been a Great White

Hunter, Devin was also an Interpol agent who worked closely with the Mossad—the Israeli secret service.

"There's something I need you to promise," Devin stated ominously as Elon's smile evaporated. "That when I tell you to get the hell out of Uganda, you'll get the hell out of Uganda!" he demanded quietly.

Visibly disturbed by Devin's directive, Elon slowly nodded.

Devin relaxed slightly. "And I suggest, as soon as you get back, that you sign complete ownership of Rose Inish over to Mila and her sons. At least until the political situation improves."

"I'm not sure where I'd go," Elon stated worriedly.

"I know your father left you and Shauna financially strapped. Quinn was my friend, but he was also a major son-of-a-bitch. I've always looked on you as a son—okay, perhaps more like a grandson," Devin smiled. "Yvette and I would like to help in any way we can. We were hoping you'd consider taking over the camp in the Mara. If things get too dicey there, you can always go to our place in Scotland. Oh, and one more thing," he added before Elon could respond, "don't let Rika get away."

Thinking about all that Devin had told him, Elon's mind spun with confusion . . . *the Mara . . . Scotland . . . Rika!*

The dogs rose from their place at Elon's feet and silently ran to greet Rika as she approached with Christiaan asleep in her arms. Her hair damp from showering, she had changed into a long, sleeveless sheath. She looked radiant, but Elon noticed the fear and uncertainty reflected in her eyes.

"Well, my dear," Devin stood to greet her. "So glad you two could join us."

Rika returned Devin's smile before looking with concern at Elon, who had directed his attention toward the channel. She could see by Elon's expression that he was also troubled.

"Good, you're just in time for supper," Yvette told Rika as she came from the house. "Here, let me take the little one," she offered.

Rika transferred the sleeping Christiaan into Yvette's outstretched arms.

"I've borrowed a bassinet from the neighbors," Yvette said as together they headed inside the house. "We'll have Elon carry it to your room after we've eaten."

As if weighted down, Elon stood up slowly. He had arrived in Lamu already emotionally drained, fearing Rika might not return from her upcoming trip to Holland. Devin's words had added to Elon's concerns. The one bright spot was the prospect of making a home at the MacKails' camp near Kenya's Maasai Mara Reserve. *But only if Rose Inish is no longer an option—and as long as Rika and Christiaan are by my side!* Elon realized. The thought of losing them was more than he could bear.

Devin put his arm around Elon's shoulder as he steered him toward the house. "No need to worry the women with what we were talking about," he suggested quietly.

As they entered the dining room, which opened onto the patio, Devin pulled out Rika's chair for her when she and Yvette returned from the bedroom where they had laid Christiaan in the bassinet. Rika regarded Elon worriedly, as he remained aloof while the MacKails' two helpers served them their food. Rika's spirits lifted, however, when Devin and Yvette engaged her in their animated conversation.

"I know it's been a long day, dear," Yvette told Rika when they finished eating.

"Yes," Rika admitted. "But it's been a lovely day. And I'm very much looking forward to seeing more of the island tomorrow," she added brightly in Elon's direction.

He responded with a faint smile.

"I'm afraid you'll have to see it on foot or by donkey," Devin said. "The only person allowed a motorized vehicle here is the District Commissioner."

"How charming!" Rika responded. "Donkeys?"

"Yes," Yvette said in a slightly sour tone. "Just watch where you step."

Rika smiled at the advice as Elon went to gather up Christiaan and the bassinet.

"Again, we'd love to watch him for you," Yvette stated after giving the sleeping baby a gentle kiss on the forehead. "Goodnight, dear," she gave Rika a hug.

"Goodnight. And thank you," Rika smiled as Devin kissed her on both cheeks.

"Get some rest," Devin told Elon while patting him on the shoulder.

Elon kissed Yvette goodnight. Carrying Christiaan in the bassinet, he followed after Rika.

"That boy's a fool if he lets her get away," Devin told Yvette as they watched Elon and Rika disappear toward the guesthouse.

"I told you, it's none of our business. Besides, it's not up to him," Yvette said.

"Then *she's* a fool if she lets *him* go!" Devin restructured his statement.

"The only one who's a fool around here is you, old man," she teased. "Come on, it's time for bed."

They exchanged a gentle kiss as he patted her on the bottom.

"You behave!" she ordered with mock sternness.

Devin growled like a ravenous lion. Yvette ran to the bedroom, giggling like a schoolgirl as he hurried after her.

Through most of the night, Elon lay awake in the front room of the guesthouse, stretched out on the sofa. Staring at the closed door leading to the bedroom where Rika and Christiaan slept, he thought about all that Devin had said . . . especially about Rika. Elon dreaded the thought of her and Christiaan going to Holland without him. *I should tell her not to go—that it doesn't matter to me if she's married to another man,* he tried to convince himself. But it did matter. And he knew how much it mattered to her.

Rika was also experiencing a restless night. By the light of the moon filtering through the slats of the window blinds, she studied Christiaan's shallow, rhythmic breathing as he lay sleeping beside her. There was so much about him that reminded her of Lee. Rika thought back on how it was when she and Lee first met in Viet

Nam . . . how he seemed like such a gentleman . . . how all the nurses adored him . . . how she'd been thrilled to have him show an interest in her—especially when all those other women were throwing themselves at him!

Listening to the sounds of the night blending with the surf lapping gently on the shore, Rika was transported back to Viet Nam—where she had arrived scared and uncertain of her recently acquired nursing skills. In 'Nam she'd been exposed to many horrors, as well as blessings. Lee, at that time, had been among the latter.

Perhaps I haven't given my marriage enough time, Rika reasoned, as she lay awake in the guesthouse. She felt she was being selfish in depriving her child of his real father . . . and, in doing so, risking alienation from her own father.

And then thoughts of Elon slipped into Rika's mind . . . how gentle and kind . . . how good he was with Christiaan. *Elon!* Just the sound of his name brought a sense of peace to Rika's heart—a peace that was being shattered by the workings of her mind! *Why couldn't we have met before I met Lee?* Rika agonized. *But it's because of Lee that we did meet!* The irony of it all was just too confusing for her. *Is God playing a cruel joke? Or has He taken pity on me by bringing me to the one man who can truly love me?*

But Elon had never told Rika that he loved her. His emotional distance at supper was quite disturbing to her. *Has he given up?* she wondered. *Has it become too difficult for him to be involved with a woman who has so many strings attached?* The thought of Elon turning against her was unbearable. Overwhelmed by feelings of loss and confusion, Rika eventually drifted off to sleep.

Rika woke at dawn to the rhythmic prayer of a Moslem muezzin echoing from a nearby minaret. Christiaan was content in having found her nipple on his own. As he nursed, Rika stroked the silken hair on his little head.

Following a light breakfast, Rika took Yvette up on her offer to watch Christiaan so she and Elon could explore the island. Stepping out of the MacKails' front door, Rika felt as though she'd been transported to another world in an ancient time.

A living museum of Arabic customs and architecture, Lamu was quite intoxicating to Rika who, in turn, was admired by the men of the island. Dressed in traditional white robes and kofia caps, many of them eyed her salaciously. But they maintained their distance in deference to Elon, who stayed close at her side.

The women of Lamu wore the black wrap-around buibui that, contrary to conservative Islamic custom, often framed their shapely bodies and fell short of their ankles. And their beautifully sculpted faces were exposed, rather than being hidden behind the repressive veil.

While Elon led the way through the narrow winding streets, Rika noticed with amusement that there seemed to be donkeys everywhere—and that Yvette was right, you had to be careful where you stepped! Elon smiled when Rika stopped to pet a friendly mare and its young foal.

Sampling some of the culinary treats the island had to offer, Rika savored the aroma of spices that permeated the air and mingled with Arabic music blaring from transistor radios. *What an eclectic blend of sights, sounds, and smells!* she marveled. *How exciting—yet surprisingly relaxing! How contradictory!* she smiled as she felt a tremendous weight lift from her soul.

Wanting desperately to hold her in his arms, Elon studied Rika with longing. The look in his eyes gave her the strength to follow her heart. And so, when they found themselves standing pensively on the sands of Sela Beach, watching the dhows glide beyond the waves in the Indian Ocean, Rika took a deep breath and gave voice to what her heart had decided.

"I want you to know . . . how much I love you," she told him softly.

Elon gave her a questioning look, not sure that he'd heard correctly. But her smile told him he had. He slowly moved closer, searching her eyes with his own. Only their lips touched in a slow, soft kiss. When they pulled away, they smiled through their tears. Taking her by the hand, he led her back to the guesthouse.

The dogs greeted them quietly as they approached the main house from the shore. Still holding hands, they looked in on the MacKails. Yvette had fallen asleep on the settee with an open book on her lap. Devin sat in an overstuffed armchair with his eyes closed and Christiaan sprawled across his chest, fast asleep.

Elon and Rika smiled at the tranquil scene before leaving. Devin opened one eye and watched as they made their way hand-in-hand toward the guesthouse. He grinned smugly before joining Christiaan in slumber.

Entering the guesthouse, Rika glanced through a small collection of eight-track tapes. Choosing one that suited her, she slipped it into the player. She kept her back to Elon as the soft guitar intro to *The First Time Ever I Saw Your Face* began to play. As he gently turned her to face him, Rika smiled shyly. Enclosing her in his arms, he led her in a slow dance as Roberta Flack's soulful voice filled the room:

> "The first time ever I saw your face,
> I thought the sun rose in your eyes . . ."

Rika gazed up at Elon with tears in her eyes. Resting her head on his shoulder, she surrendered to their dance:

> "And the moon and the stars were the gifts you gave,
> To the dark and the endless skies, my love.
> To the dark and the endless skies . . ."

The tenderness of Elon's touch caused Rika to tremble in his grasp. Cradling her in his arms, he asked nothing of her as she began to sob uncontrollably:

> "And the first time ever I kissed your mouth,
> I felt the earth move in my hand.

Like the trembling heart of a captive bird,
That was there at my command, my love.
That was there at my command . . ."

In the days that followed, the love Elon and Rika had been so hesitant to proclaim could no longer be suppressed. They held hands constantly, as if fearful of losing what they thought had been impossible to find. During the day they played in the gentle surf; and in the evenings they strolled along the moonlit beach:

"And the first time ever I lay with you,
I felt your heart so close to mine . . ."

Their feelings transcended sex, as their first few nights together were simply spent curled up in each other's arms, fully clothed. Until the night Rika faced Elon in the pale-moonlight. Easing the nightgown from her shoulders, she let it float softly to the floor as his eyes roamed lovingly over her body. When he held his hand out to her, she slowly melted into his embrace. They tenderly kissed while caressing each other's nakedness with gentle, electrifying strokes:

"And I knew our joy would fill the earth,
And last 'til the end of time, my love.
And it would last 'til the end of time, my love . . ."

When they became one, it was as much of a spiritual sensation as it was sensual:

"The first time ever I saw your face.
Your face . . .
Your face . . .
Your face . . ."

The last night they spent together on Lamu, as their lovemaking became more intense, Rika knew instinctively when the moment of conception occurred—when they had created a bond between them that only death could sever. Although it was questionable if even in death they could be parted:

> "And I knew our joy would fill the earth,
> And last 'til the end of time, my love.
> And it would last 'til the end of time, my love . . ."

Chapter 7

Even without her powers of perception, Mila could see when Elon and Rika returned from Lamu that the situation had changed between them. Wordlessly, she helped Rika move her and Christiaan's belonging from Shauna's room into Elon's. There was no more talk of Rika going to Holland; at least not for the time being. Although everyone wished Rika to be free of Lee Parnell, for her to do so could jeopardize her custody of Christiaan . . . and the welfare of the new child growing within her. So, for all concerned, it seemed quite natural and right for Rika to settle into being Elon's wife in appearance, if not in fact.

A few months after Elon and Rika's holiday in Lamu, Mutiba arrived at Rose Inish for a visit. Uncharacteristically grim and reticent, he spent the days helping in the tea fields. The only time he let down his guard was when he played with Christiaan. Mutiba was extremely gentle and solicitous with him, and the baby thrived on the attention.

Mila smiled whenever she watched Mutiba interact with Christiaan. But she sensed the pain her eldest son was harboring, and it worried her. Although Mila could see that Mutiba wasn't sleeping well, she knew better than to question him . . . that it would be best to wait until he was ready to talk.

But it was too difficult for Mutiba to speak of the horrors he'd seen. Horrors that flooded his mind whenever he closed his eyes. What he mostly relived was the blood-splattered room in which soldiers suspected of being loyal to former President Obote had been blown apart by grenades.

As a witness to the atrocity, Mutiba could still hear the screams of the condemned men—and recall the horror of having to help remove what was left of their bodies. Shovels were needed to scrape up the bloody remains, which were put into plastic bags and thrown into Lake Victoria.

"How are things at Entebbe?" Elon asked when he and Mutiba were working together in the barn one afternoon during Mutiba's visit to Rose Inish.

Mutiba simply shrugged his shoulders as he sharpened a scythe.

Elon studied him with concern. "Talk to me," he quietly implored.

Stopping what he was doing, Mutiba stared out the barn door toward the mist-shrouded mountains. He took a deep breath before speaking in a quiet, distant tone. But he only voiced what he had heard, not what he had personally seen . . . which was too repugnant for him to put into words.

"I have heard of people being tortured and buried alive . . . That at the barracks in Mbarra and Jinja, officers were on the parade ground being reviewed by Amin when they were slowly crushed to death by tanks . . . It was said that Amin stood by and laughed . . . That he claims God talks to him in dreams . . . That he thinks he's doing God's work."

Elon remembered what Devin had told him about the lights going out in Kampala because of the mutilated body parts clogging the generators at Owen Falls Dam.

"Devin suspects things may get worse," he told Mutiba sadly.

"Yes, we've spoken," Mutiba admitted.

Elon looked surprised, as well as concerned. "Be careful," he warned when realizing Mutiba had been recruited into Devin's clandestine activities. "Devin suggested that I sign over Shauna's and my interest in Rose Inish to you, your mother, and Harun—which I've done."

Mutiba nodded. "Only until things get better," he responded with forced hopefulness. "Until things get better," he repeated quietly as he turned his attention back to the task of sharpening the scythe.

But the situation in Uganda got progressively worse instead of better. And, although Elon tried hard to shield Rika and the others from the terrors eating away at the country, it was impossible for him to do so completely.

Because of its seclusion, Rose Inish was relatively safe. Weeks and then months went by without incident, creating a false sense of security. Until September 5th, when the world came crashing in on them. As Elon sat in the parlor one evening with Rika, Mila, and Harun, listening to the Radio Uganda broadcast of the Olympic games being held in Munich, they were stunned to learn of the massacre of Israeli athletes, who had been taken hostage by Palestinian terrorists.

"Germany is the right place," Idi Amin's voice boomed across the airwaves in response to the incident, "where, when Hitler was prime minister and supreme commander, he burnt over six million Jews. This is because Hitler and all the German people know that the Israelis are not people who are working in the interest of the people of the world and that is why he burned the Jews alive with gas in the—"

Elon shut off the radio, but not before he and the others had come to realize the extent to which their beloved Uganda had fallen into the hands of a madman.

On the heels of the Olympic massacre, Amin ordered the expulsion of all Asians. Over ninety thousand families prepared to leave the country. Among them were Sahid Jhani and his family, who stopped at Rose Inish on their journey to Tanzania from Murchison Falls National Park. While there, they lavished their attention on little Christiaan, who was now at the age where he gleefully tried to demolish everything within crawling distance. They were pleased to learn that Rika was expecting another child.

"Don't worry," Sahid tried to reassure them when he and his family were leaving. "I am certain we will be allowed to return soon."

Although Elon and the others smiled as they waved them goodbye, they were painfully aware that Sahid's words held no promise.

A few days later, Elon drove Nisha and her family into Entebbe to catch a bus to Mombasa. He felt bad that he had nothing more than a hug or handshake to offer them in gratitude for their years of service. Before boarding the bus, Nisha clung desperately to Elon, weeping openly until her father pulled her away.

Elon watched helplessly as, just before the bus drove off, soldiers unloaded the luggage from the belly of the vehicle. They tossed it into army trucks and sped away.

Elon drove to the Lakeview Hotel to see if Rashid Jameel and his family were still there.

"My friend! My friend!" Rashid exclaimed as he and Elon embraced. "I can think of no one else whom I would like to spend our last evening with in Uganda!"

"I'm afraid I can't stay," Elon told him sadly.

"But you must," Rashid responded in a low, authoritative tone. "You should not be on the roads after dark."

Studying his dear friend's face, Elon realized that, like Mutiba, Rashid had personally witnessed his share of horrors.

"Come," Rashid said, looking around cautiously. "I will show you where to park the Rover so it will be safe."

They got in the vehicle and drove to where Rashid indicated.

"What's happened to the country, Rashid?" Elon asked, shaking his head as they remained inside the Rover.

"What has happened is that the devil walks the earth."

"I wish there was something I could do."

"Actually there is, if you wouldn't mind. We could use a ride to the airport tomorrow. Unfortunately, we have been relieved of all our vehicles."

"Of course. And, if I may suggest, don't bring more than you can carry . . . or wear," Elon cautioned, remembering the soldiers stealing the luggage from the bus.

"For once my wife will have to not mind looking a few pounds heavier," Rashid smiled.

"Where will you be going?"

"London, first, to visit family. Then perhaps we will go to Kenya. And you? Will you be staying?"

"Things have been relatively quiet around Fort Portal, although it will be difficult to keep Rose Inish going now that . . ." Elon's voice trailed off sadly as a heavy silence settled between them.

"It is the end of an era," Rashid eventually stated as he stared sadly into space. "But, there are always new beginnings, are there not?" he brightened while turning toward Elon. "Mutiba has told me about your new family!"

"We're going to have another baby," Elon stated proudly.

Rashid nodded knowingly. "On the day you first brought Rika here with that man who claimed to be her husband, I wanted to feed him to the crocodiles!"

Elon laughed. "I need to use your radio to let her know I won't be coming home tonight."

"Of course," Rashid replied as they left the Rover.

Lying awake that night at the Lakeview Hotel, Elon listened to the sound of distant gunshots punctuated by periodic screams. *So much has changed since the last time I was here!* he realized. Elon agonized over the welfare of his displaced friends. And he worried about how he would manage Rose Inish with only Mila, Harun, . . . and Rika. Seeing her face in his mind's eye, peace enfolded Elon and he finally drifted off to sleep.

In the morning when he bid goodbye to Rashid and his family at the airport, Elon noticed the flood of Arabs arriving on incoming flights. A sense of foreboding swept over him and he decided to look for Mutiba.

"Can you get away for a while?" Elon asked when he located Mutiba at the barracks next to the old airport terminal building.

Although Mutiba saw some of his colleagues regarding him with suspicion, he got in the Rover with Elon. Out of habit, Elon drove back toward the Lakeview Hotel. As they passed by, they saw soldiers carelessly throwing Rashid's family's belongings into trucks. Elon narrowed his eyes with anger, while Mutiba sadly shook his head and looked away.

Elon parked the Rover near the edge of the lake. They sat in silence for a few moments before he spoke.

"I just took Rashid and his family to the airport. There were a lot of Arabs—"

"Palestinians," Mutiba stated with disdain. "They're taking over the government jobs that had been held by the Asians."

Elon nodded solemnly as he stared out at the lake. He vaguely noticed the vultures that were waiting on shore.

"When you get back to Rose Inish, do not leave," Mutiba quietly warned him.

Elon studied Mutiba worriedly. Turning his attention back to the lake, he noticed something bobbing in the water. When the object floated onto shore, the vultures quickly set upon it. Elon felt ill when realizing it was a human torso. Outwardly, Mutiba appeared unaffected by the sight.

They drove back to the barracks in silence.

"It's best you don't come here again," Mutiba told Elon before leaving the Rover.

Elon watched sadly as Mutiba disappeared inside the barracks. Desperate to return to Rika, he headed home.

That night in bed, Elon listened to Rika's soft breathing as they lay naked in each other's arms. When he kissed the top of her head, she woke with a smile. As he ran his hand slowly down her back, she arched her body toward his. Starting on her slightly protruding belly, he worked his way up her torso with soft kisses. Gently caressing her breasts, he buried his kisses in the hollow of her throat and then up her chin until their lips met. Moving her fingertips sensuously down his spine, she wrapped her leg around him as they made love in gentle strokes—careful of the life growing within her.

It wasn't long until Elon knew why Mutiba had warned him to stay close to Rose Inish. From their base in Tanzania, an ill-equipped and largely untrained contingency of Ugandans loyal to ousted President Obote launched a heroic but short-lived assault against the Amin regime. There were only a few professional soldiers among the fighters—most were students or teachers. The fortunate ones died quickly in battle. Those that were captured were subjected to hideous torture and publicly executed.

Mutiba personally witnessed a group of suspected rebel sympathizers being made to lie face up in a deep pit with their hands tied behind their backs. Bulldozers then slowly covered them with dirt, burying them alive.

Mutiba was also on hand when five Hercules transport planes arrived at Entebbe Airport with armaments and approximately four hundred Libyan troops—a gift to Idi Amin from Colonel Muammar al-Quaddafi. Hiding his disdain for the Arab soldiers, who often took a perverse and sadistic pleasure in helping Amin maintain his stranglehold on the country, Mutiba quietly took note of their numbers, where they were located, and their weapons. In forwarding this information to Devin in Lamu, Mutiba was careful to use different payphones throughout Kampala.

In his need to appear loyal to Amin, Mutiba nearly became schizophrenic. The horrific acts that he was witness to, and even participated in, were so far removed from whom and what he was that Mutiba often had the feeling they involved someone else.

The only reality Mutiba dared to recognize—the only place where he could find a semblance of peace—was at Rose Inish. He would retreat there as often as possible. While helping to fight the vegetation that was swallowing the fields of tea, Mutiba found some release from the demons that festered inside him. But he would attack the wild growth with such vengeance that Elon and Mila often exchanged looks of dismay.

Sometimes late at night, after lying awake in his bed at Rose Inish while staring at the ceiling in an attempt to ward off the nightmares, Mutiba would slip into Shauna's room. There, curled up on her bed with her pillow close to his heart, he would quietly cry himself to sleep.

Chapter 8

Two evenings before her second Christmas in Austria, Shauna participated in a chamber orchestra that performed at a party hosted by Franz at his home in Vienna. The orchestra also included Vivian, who played the cello so sensuously that many of the male guests were compelled to loosen their collars. Franz and Harry, however, only had eyes for each other. Although Lisl was at Harry's side, she seemed oblivious to his and Franz' stolen glances.

"Excuse me, my dear, I'll be right back," Harry told her as they clapped following one of Shauna's solos.

Lisl smiled sweetly as Harry rose to leave. Making his way toward the kitchen, he caught Franz' eye. With a slight tilt of his head, Harry indicated to Franz that he'd like to speak with him.

Franz followed Harry to a small alcove adjacent to the dining room. Harry glanced around nervously to make sure no one saw them.

"What's the matter?" Franz asked with concern.

Harry regarded his lover sadly. "Lisl is pregnant," he managed weakly.

Surprise, then sadness, spread across Franz' face as he turned away.

"I didn't mean for it to happen," Harry told him.

"But it has," Franz responded flatly.

Silence weighed between them until Harry answered Franz'

unspoken question, confirming his worst fear. "We will be getting married."

"Congratulations," Franz offered vaguely as he turned to face Harry. "When?"

"Soon. I know this is difficult . . . It's quite difficult for me . . . It's only for the sake of the baby . . ."

Franz nodded his understanding.

"I hope you can find it in your heart to stand in as best man?" Harry asked tearfully.

"Of course."

"Perhaps you and Shauna might someday—"

"Perhaps. But for now she's still rather young."

"Yet quite lovely."

"Quite," Franz agreed as his own eyes misted with tears.

"I am so sorry," Harry said, his voice faltering.

Franz smiled sadly while offering Harry his hand. "It's all right," he assured him lovingly.

As they shook hands, the tears flowed freely down Harry's cheeks. "It's you I'll always love," he whispered sincerely.

The handshake evolved into a hug. Looking imploringly into each other's eyes, their lips slowly came together—softly at first, and then with unrestrained passion. Neither of them noticed Tanya as she entered the alcove from the dining room. Stunned by the sight of the two men locked in a kiss, she froze momentarily before backing away. She leaned against the wall and took a deep breath before returning to the kitchen to help Ursula.

"What's wrong?" Ursula asked, noticing the girl's stricken look.

Tanya shook her head as she mechanically went about her business. She knew she would never tell anyone what she had seen. How could she? She could barely comprehend it, let alone put it into words.

Thousands of miles away from Vienna, at the ranch near San Antonio, eight-year-old Cole lay awake in a sleeping bag on a bed of straw outside the stall where Star was due to foal. Lucky was curled up beside him and a large flashlight lay within Cole's reach, but it wasn't needed as the full moon filtered in through the high window above the stall.

Lucky wagged her tail in silent greeting as Simon entered the barn. Looking in on Star, Simon saw that her time was near. He put his finger to his lips for Cole to remain quiet while they watched in awe as the miracle of birth unfolded before them.

Tears of amazement misted Cole's eyes as Star welcomed her newborn with a soft whinny. The foal lay exhausted on the ground as its mama licked it dry. Eventually, after a few comical attempts, it managed to stand on long wobbly legs before collapsing again on the soft straw.

"Is it okay?" Cole asked Simon fearfully.

Simon smiled and nodded. "It's a filly. A girl," he stated softly.

They continued to watch in silence as once again the little one managed to stand, this time finding her way to her mother's teats.

"Would you like to say 'hello'?" Simon asked Cole when the newborn had finished nursing.

Cole blinked with disbelief. Witnessing the birth had been an overwhelming experience for the boy, and he couldn't imagine being able to get close! To perhaps even touch the little one! All Cole could manage was an incredulous nod.

Simon gave Lucky the signal to stay, and she readily obeyed. He then took Cole by the hand and led him into the stall, where Star whinnied a friendly greeting.

"First tell Star what a good job she did," Simon quietly advised as he let go of Cole's hand and stood off to one side. "Don't forget her when you fuss over her baby."

"Good girl," Cole whispered while gently stroking Star's soft nose.

The mare lowered her head and closed her eyes in peaceful exhaustion. Standing on uncertain legs, the foal regarded Cole with a look of curiosity.

"Just stay where you are," Simon told Cole quietly. "Let her come to you."

Cole remained at Star's head as the little one wobbled over to touch noses with its mama before inspecting the boy. When Cole sank to his knees on the straw, the foal nibbled at his hair and smelled around his face. Finding Cole's ear, she enclosed it in her little mouth and sucked on it gently with her gums. Cole giggled as chills ran through his body. Rediscovering the boy's face, the newborn licked the tears of joy from his cheek.

Juanita quietly entered the barn and stood outside the stall, petting Lucky. She and Simon shared a loving smile. Watching the foal interact with the boy, Juanita began to softly hum *The First Noel*. It would be from that carol, and the fact that dawn was about to break on the morning of Christmas Eve, that Star's baby would get her name: Noelle.

As Star was welcoming her newborn into the world, it was already the afternoon of Christmas Eve at Rose Inish.

While preparing supper with Rika, Mila felt an overwhelming sense of foreboding. She glanced worriedly at Rika, now almost eight months pregnant. Mila masked her concern when Rika turned to her with a smile before gazing out the kitchen window to where Elon and Mutiba hacked away at the intruding weeds that were threatening to overrun the barely manicured lawn. Beyond it the tea fields were no longer recognizable, having been swallowed by the wild growth because of a lack of maintenance following the expulsion of the Asian workers.

Rika's smile widened as she watched Harun play with Christiaan on the lawn. Gently rolling a ball, Harun laughed as the toddler retrieved it on uncertain little legs. When the ball rolled past Christiaan to the edge of the tall weeds, Mila looked up from her work with a sense of alarm. She joined Rika at the window.

"What is it?" Rika asked, seeing the worried expression on Mila's face.

Watching Christiaan alternately walk and crawl after the ball, Mila shook her head, not knowing what was causing her to feel so distraught. And then she saw the menace as it raised its body to almost half its length and flared its hooded head, towering over the child. The two women froze in fear as they watched Christiaan smile up innocently at the forest cobra.

"Oh my God!" Rika found her voice, recoiling in horror at the sight of the snake. "No!" she screamed as she forced herself to run on legs that seemed made of rubber. "Noooo!" her voice echoed as she ran across the lawn toward Christiaan.

Looking in the direction Rika was headed, Elon and Mutiba saw the snake. In shock, Harun remained where he was. Mila tried desperately to catch up with Rika. They all watched in helpless horror as Christiaan extended his chubby little hand toward the black wavering serpent with a yellow-striped underbelly. In relatively slow motion for a snake, the cobra struck the child on the wrist. Christiaan seemed surprised that the beautiful creature would harm him.

In swift fluid strides, Mutiba ran toward the snake. It felt the vibrations from the man's approach and turned to face him. In the unique way the forest cobra has of pursuing its prey, it remained poised in striking position as its lower body carried it headlong in Mutiba's direction. Just as it struck at him, Mutiba swung the sharp-edged scythe and severed the snake's head with one sweeping motion. The head flew to one side; but the body flipped about, splattering blood onto Mutiba's bare chest before coming to rest on the ground.

Mutiba slowly lowered the scythe and watched with a dazed expression as Rika swept Christiaan into her arms. Elon was soon at her side. He had drawn his knife from its sheath on his belt and was prepared to amputate the child's arm in an effort to save his life. He watched helplessly as Rika shook her head numbly, knowing it was too late. The bite had gone directly into a vein.

As the cobra's venom surged through Christiaan's little body, he looked pleadingly into his mother's eyes. His own eyes began to glaze over from a lack of oxygen when his swollen windpipe prevented the air from reaching his lungs, which were already shutting down. He made a soft gurgling sound and a trickle of blood eased from the corner of his mouth as his baby teeth bit into his tongue. His cheeks lost their color and his lips turned blue as his little heart gave out. He convulsed violently before lying still in his mother's arms.

Rika sank silently to her knees, rocking Christiaan's limp body against her breast while staring with unseeing eyes toward the mountains. Elon and the others regarded her with looks of anguish.

Gathering Rika up from the ground, Mila slowly guided her toward the house. Clutching her dead child, Rika went meekly. Elon and Mutiba watched with stricken expressions as the women walked away. Harun was the only one who wept.

Mila sat Rika down in the parlor. She and Elon remained by Rika's side throughout the night as she cradled Christiaan's body in her arms. At dawn, Rika allowed Elon to take the child's body from her before Mila led her to her and Elon's room.

With Mila at her side, Rika lay in bed staring blankly at the ceiling as Elon, Mutiba, and Harun buried little Christiaan that Christmas morning in a beautifully carved cedar box that had belonged to Elon's mother. At the gravesite, Elon and Mutiba stood in dazed silence as Harun sat on the ground with his arms folded around his knees, rocking back and forth while sobbing uncontrollably.

That night the leopard came from the forest and inspected the fresh earth, marked by a small white cross. She sniffed around curiously before stretching out on the soft dirt covering Christiaan's grave.

In the days that followed, Elon and Mila took turns keeping vigil over Rika. She had not cried, nor even spoken, since Christiaan's death. On the third day after they'd laid the child in the ground, Rika silently went into labor.

"It's too early," Elon told Mila worriedly. "We may need a doctor."

"There are no more decent doctors," Mila reminded him.

It was true, as the most qualified physicians had left the country in the Asian exodus. The Palestinian doctors that replaced them weren't even a consideration. And so, as a thunderstorm raged around Rose Inish, Rika delivered her child in silence with Mila and Elon at her side.

When Mila placed the tiny infant girl in his hands, an indescribable feeling swept over Elon and he couldn't control the tears that escaped from his heart. Like Rika, he hadn't been able to cry following Christiaan's death. To cry was to acknowledge the horrible tragedy. But there was no denying what Elon now held—the most precious gift, next to Rika, that he knew he'd ever receive.

"She's not crying," Elon whispered fearfully as Mila cleaned the newborn.

"She has come before her time, and her lungs aren't yet fully developed. But don't worry, she'll be all right," Mila assured him.

"How can you be so certain? She's so incredibly tiny."

"Because I had a dream."

"Oh?" Elon questioned with raised eyebrows. "And what did you see in your dream?"

"I saw the child full of light and life."

"You and your dreams," Elon shook his head before bringing the little one to Rika. But Rika turned her head away from the infant.

Yes, Mila silently agreed, *me and my dreams!* She'd had another dream on the night before Christiaan died—an extremely disturbing dream. In it Mila saw four bright figures and three others that were obscured by shadows. Although the figures were human, they were indistinguishable and had no facial features. Mila had no doubt what the dream meant, as she now knew that Christiaan was one of the shadowy figures.

Mila studied Rika with concern. Dream or no dream, Mila knew the newborn's survival was dependent upon the mother's. Seized with anger, Mila slapped Rika hard across the face. Rika blinked slowly as she looked into Mila's raging eyes.

"How dare you!" Mila scolded her. "How dare you shut yourself away when you are needed? If you want to die, then do so later! For now your daughter needs you. I will not stand by and see her harmed by your selfishness!"

Mila took the infant from Elon and introduced her to Rika's breast. Elon stood back, shocked by Mila's behavior. He'd never seen her so angry! He watched as Rika allowed the newborn to suckle, but Elon could see that her mind had retreated back to its place of refuge. When the infant fell asleep at Rika's breast, Mila gently wrapped her in a towel and handed her back to her father.

"You must give her a name," Mila told Elon. "And she must be held constantly."

Elon looked down at the sleeping baby's tiny, angelic face. He knew Mila was right; that the greatest cause of infant mortality in animals was the sense, or state, of isolation.

"We had decided on 'Anika,' after Rika's grandmother," he told Mila quietly.

"'Anika,'" Mila nodded approvingly as she repeated the name. "We must keep her warm. And, when she gives the slightest indication of being hungry, we must bring her to her mother."

Elon gazed with love and concern for his daughter as Mila left to join Mutiba and Harun in the parlor, where they regarded her with frightened, beseeching looks.

"It's a little girl," Mila told them. "She will be fine," she assured them, wishing she could say the same about the newborn's mother.

Looking slightly relieved, Mutiba nodded. In slow, labored strides, he left through the glass door leading from the parlor and headed toward the guest cottage that he'd moved to following his recruitment into the air force. Watching him leave, Mila knew it would be a long time before any of them would recover from Christiaan's death.

Mila turned her attention to Harun, whose tearful, stricken expression hadn't changed since the toddler's death. Taking him by the hand, Mila led him to a rocking chair. Although he was almost twelve years old, Harun was still quite small and skinny for his age. He offered no resistance as his mother folded him onto her lap and rocked him gently.

"I'm so sorry," the boy sobbed. "If we hadn't been playing . . . If I'd watched Christiaan better—"

"It's not your fault," Mila told him gently. "It's no one's fault," she added adamantly. But Mila knew how hollow her words must sound to him; and that the only person who could give him any sense of peace, or forgiveness, was Christiaan's mother. Mila had no doubt Rika would do so—when, or if, she survived the emotional trauma of her first child's death, followed so closely by the birth of her second.

In his and Rika's room, Elon studied her worriedly as he sat in the overstuffed chair with tiny Anika asleep in his arms.

"She looks just like you," Elon whispered to Rika. "So incredibly beautiful."

With her arm shielding her eyes, Rika turned her head away.

"Please, God," Elon quietly prayed for the first time in years, "keep Anika and her mama safe. And please have the angels watch over little Christiaan," he wept softly.

A single tear escaped from beneath Rika's closed eyelids.

In the week following her birth, Anika grew strong—due in most part to her father's and Mila's efforts . . . as well as Harun's. With Elon and Mila's encouragement, the boy soon bonded with the newborn. Mutiba, however, kept his distance from the infant.

In spite of Elon and Mila's efforts, Rika was slipping away.

"Mama!" Rika cried out in her tormented sleep one night not long after Anika was born. "Mama," she repeated, as Elon lay awake next to her, studying her with concern.

The following morning, Elon contacted Shauna in Vienna by radio and asked if she would find Rika's parents to let them know their daughter needed them.

More than happy to be of help, Franz flew with Shauna on his private jet to Amsterdam, where they located Rika's parents in the tiny enclave of Holyport. Rika's father, Owen van Zaun, made it quite clear to Franz and Shauna that they were not welcome in his home. Especially Franz. However, Rika's mother, Xandra, did agree to accompany Shauna to Uganda. Franz arranged for the two women, along with a surprise Xandra had for her daughter, to fly commercially from Amsterdam to Entebbe. Only Rika, had she been coherent, would have known the strength it took for her mother to defy Owen van Zaun and go to Uganda.

Mutiba flew the Cessna from Rose Inish to Entebbe to meet the women. Standing on the tarmac dressed in civilian clothes, he looked around nervously as the Ugandan soldiers and Palestinian guards eyed him suspiciously. When Shauna greeted him warmly upon her arrival, Mutiba maintained an emotional as well as physical distance. She regarded him with disappointment.

"Mutiba, this is Rika's mother, Xandra van Zaun," Shauna introduced him to the diminutive woman.

Mutiba regarded Xandra with uncertainty. He was concerned by the fact that she was smaller and even paler looking than her daughter—if that was possible.

"Welcome to Uganda," Mutiba told her flatly. "I hope you don't mind another flight."

"Not at all," Xandra responded in a soft voice reminiscent of Rika's. "But first I must tend to something," she told Mutiba while surveying the unloading of the baggage from the aircraft.

"Wait 'til you see," Shauna told him.

Two baggage handlers lifted a large animal crate from the hold of the plane. When one of them glanced inside, he quickly recoiled in terror, dropping his side of the container while chattering and gesturing excitedly. The other handler dropped his end of the crate and also backed away fearfully.

"Please be careful," Xandra told the men as she hurried toward them.

Responding to the concerns of the baggage handlers, two soldiers rushed toward the crate with their rifles poised to shoot.

"There, there," Xandra told them quietly. "You will scare the poor thing."

The soldiers regarded the tiny woman with looks suggesting they questioned her sanity. They watched with their weapons still poised as Xandra opened the container while talking softly in Dutch. A beautiful tawny-coated beast emerged from the crate. At first glance it looked like a young lion . . . but it was a dog—a large golden dog with dark markings on its face and dangling ears.

Mutiba and the others stared with amazement as the animal gently licked the little woman's face. When Xandra motioned for it to follow, it stretched luxuriously before trotting obediently at her side.

"He's still just a puppy," Shauna told Mutiba. "Barely half-grown."

Mutiba's jaw dropped at the statement. The "puppy" was practically as big as the little woman who was leading it to a grassy strip beside the tarmac where it relieved itself.

"It's a Leonberger," Shauna explained. "Rika's parents raise them. His name is Rafi—short for Rafiki."

Knowing "Rafiki" was the Swahili word for "friend," Mutiba shook his head. *With a friend like that, a man would have few enemies!* he concluded.

With his plumed tail curled loosely over his back, Rafi trotted happily at Xandra's side as she collected her suitcase before making her way back to Shauna and Mutiba. "We may go now," Xandra informed them.

Mutiba took her and Shauna's bags and, after clearing customs, helped the women into the Cessna. He appeared concerned about the young dog running loose in the plane. But Mutiba needn't have worried, as Rafi was quite the gentleman. Filling the floor space between the front and back seats, he slept throughout most of the flight.

Mutiba flew to Rose Inish in silence. Since he and Shauna had last been together, he had kept her memory alive in his dreams. It was the only thing that gave Mutiba a sense of peace. But now that she was so near, and so real, he found her presence to be almost unbearable.

Shauna regarded Mutiba with concern. They'd been apart only fourteen months, but he seemed like a stranger to her. Experiencing a tremendous sense of loss, she directed her attention to the passing scenery below.

Noticing the way Shauna had looked at Mutiba, and seeing his unresponsiveness, Xandra shook her head sadly. Gazing out the window, she was reassured to find that the landscape had remained much as she'd remembered it from the last time she was in Uganda. Then she thought of the soldiers and Palestinian guards at the airport. *Nazis!* Xandra shuddered, fighting the memory of when Holland had been occupied by the Germans, and she was a member of the Dutch resistance. Closing her eyes, she let the drumming of the plane's propeller lull her to sleep.

When they landed at Rose Inish, Elon was also concerned by the daintiness of Rika's mother. And he was worried that Xandra would hold him responsible for her daughter's misfortunes. But, when he looked into the little woman's eyes, Elon couldn't detect any condemnation. And, from the way Rafi responded to her, Elon knew she had a good heart. He had never seen such a happy yet well-mannered animal, and he felt the young dog's behavior had much to do with its devotion to the diminutive woman.

Elon also appreciated the loving way in which Xandra accepted little Anika—and how she got along so well with Mila. The two women immediately took to each other like long lost friends. Elon soon felt that, even if her mother were to convince Rika to leave him, he'd been right in asking her to come to Uganda. For if anyone could lift the gloom that had settled over Rose Inish as a result of Christiaan's death, perhaps it would be Xandra van Zaun.

"He was such a good-natured little boy," Elon told Xandra sadly at the gravesite.

Rika had been asleep when her mother arrived at Rose Inish, and Xandra didn't want to disturb her. After being introduced to Mila, Harun, and her tiny two-week-old granddaughter, Xandra had asked Elon to take her to Christiaan's grave. Elon had been surprised by the request, but Mila understood the woman's need. She had shown Xandra a photograph of baby Christiaan being held by Elon and Rika. The photo was one taken by Devin when Elon and Rika were in Lamu, and was placed in the album of Rose Inish.

"Mila told me you treated him as if he were your own," Xandra said to Elon while kneeling beside the grave, with Rafi at her side.

Elon nodded sadly as his throat tightened from grief.

"Thank you," Xandra looked up at him with sincerity. "Thank you for bringing such love and happiness into my daughter's life."

Her words took Elon by surprise, as he had steeled himself for a barrage of accusations like those he repeatedly hurled at himself. And her kindness released Elon's pain. With the strength draining from his limbs, he sank to the ground and bowed his head as his body shook with sobs.

Xandra held him tight. "All will be well, my son," she told Elon quietly as Rafi whimpered with concern. "All will be well."

She let Elon cry himself out before they returned to Rika.

"Mama?" Rika asked weakly from the bed.

"Yes," Xandra smiled softly as Rafi eased his nose under Rika's hand.

"Hans?" Rika questioned as she slowly stroked Rafi's head.

"No. His name is Rafiki, which you know is Swahili for 'friend.' We call him Rafi. He's Gretchen's and Hans' son," Xandra told her.

"Mama, is it really you?" Rika whispered, fearing she might be dreaming.

"Yes," Xandra assured her.

"But how . . . why . . ."

"I will tell you later. First you must eat. Mila!" Xandra called.

Elon and Mila, holding a tray of food, were waiting outside the room. When Xandra called for Mila, Elon opened the door for her and was about to shut it when Xandra addressed him.

"Elon, come in," she directed.

He entered the room rather hesitantly. Seeing that he'd been crying, Rika's pain intensified, and she had to look away.

"Now, then," Xandra said, "Elon, see that she eats. Mila, perhaps you would be so kind as to show me to my own room?" she asked while glancing at her suitcase, which had been placed in the corner of Elon and Rika's room.

"We thought you might want to stay in here with—" Elon started to explain.

"It is *your* place in here, not mine," Xandra told him gently.

Elon appeared surprised . . . and grateful. Closing her eyes, Rika bit her lip against the rising tears.

"I have another room waiting," Mila told Xandra as she took hold of her bag.

"When you are done eating," Xandra addressed Rika, "Shauna will bring Anika to you."

"Shauna?" Rika opened her eyes with surprise. "Shauna is here, too?"

"Yes. She and I have come a long way to be with you," Xandra smiled lovingly.

Rika stared blankly at the ceiling as she responded in an emotionless tone. "I don't deserve it. God has punished me for—"

"It was not God's will that a beautiful, innocent child was lost," Xandra cut her off gently. "What has happened simply happened. God did not have a hand in it. He is there to help us deal with the tragedies that befall us—not to cause them."

Rika appeared confused by her mother's words. "That's not what Father would say if he—"

"Your father is not here," Xandra again interrupted in a gentle tone. "I am here, as are Mila and her sons, and Shauna and Elon—the father of your beautiful daughter, whom I have no doubt was conceived in love. So give thanks to God for all the good that He has done, and try not to dwell on what is lost. And now, Mila, if you will kindly show me to my room," she requested.

Stunned, Rika watched as her mother left with Mila. As had happened with Elon, Xandra's kindness released a flood of emotion within her daughter. Unable to hold back the tears, Rika began to sob uncontrollably. When Elon gathered her into his arms, they clung to each other desperately. Rafi remained in the room, looking sad and confused by the people's behavior.

Shauna, with Anika asleep in her arms, met Mila and Xandra in the hallway.

"Give them some time," Mila told Shauna quietly.

Mila led Xandra to Mutiba's old room, while Shauna carried Anika to the back veranda where Mutiba sat on the steps, smoking. Seeing Shauna with the infant, he quickly turned away while extinguishing the cigarette on the ground.

"I thought the habit disgusted you," Shauna said.

Mutiba ignored her comment.

Shauna turned her attention to Anika, asleep in her arms. "Your mama and papa love you very much, little one. As does Great-Auntie Mila and Uncles Mutiba and Harun. As for me, I think I'll reserve my opinion until you've proven yourself. I just know you're going to be terribly spoiled, and that there should be someone around to keep you in line!" she quietly teased.

Mutiba's expression remained hard as he studied the spot where Christiaan had been bitten by the snake. "If I had only gotten there in time," he stated distantly.

Sitting beside him, Shauna regarded him with concern. "You shouldn't blame yourself," she told him gently.

He glared at her with anger. "I should have gotten there in time!"

Feeling sad and helpless, Shauna tried to think of what to say, or do, to help ease his pain. "I need you to hold her," was all she could come up with as she held Anika out to him.

With anger still burning in his eyes, Mutiba looked at Shauna as if she were crazy.

"I need you to take her for a while," Shauna stated with desperation.

Before he could object, Shauna handed him the sleeping infant and then quickly left. But she went only as far as the doorway, where she watched as Mutiba gingerly settled the baby in his grasp. The tiny bundle fit easily into one of his hands.

Mila came and stood beside Shauna, who motioned for her to keep quiet. Together they studied Mutiba. It was the first direct contact he'd had with the infant, and Mila was grateful to Shauna for making it happen.

Anika yawned and stretched her little arms into the air before stuffing her tiny fist into her mouth. Glancing around fearfully for help, Mutiba saw Shauna and Mila regarding him with patronizing looks.

"I think she's hungry," he told them with forced anger.

Mila took Anika from him. "You can change her later, if you'd like," she offered.

"No, thank you," Mutiba responded, pretending to be disgusted—although he'd often changed Christiaan's diapers.

Shauna again sat beside him as Mila left with Anika.

"You tricked me," he accused, turning away from her.

Shauna could tell from the way his jaw had relaxed that his anger wasn't real. She kissed him gently on the cheek. "I've missed you," she told him.

Mutiba regarded her with amazement before the anger shot back into his eyes. Shauna put her finger to his mouth to keep him from speaking, and then slowly replaced it with her lips. Closing his eyes, Mutiba lost himself in their kiss. When their lips parted, his eyes remained shut. He cupped his head in his hands as his shoulders sagged. When Shauna again reached out to him, he drew away and fled into the approaching night.

With their bodies entwined for the first time since Christiaan's death, Elon and Rika slept so soundly that they were unaware of Anika's need to nurse during the night. In the cradle beside her parents' bed, the infant sucked on her fist and whimpered softly. Rafi woke from where he was sleeping on the floor and raised his head. It hadn't taken the young animal long to realize how he could be of the most help in his new home. He nudged Elon awake.

"What is it, boy?" Elon asked groggily as Rafi looked toward the cradle and barked. "Good dog," Elon praised him as he gathered up Anika.

Rafi barked again while wagging his tail at the compliment.

"It seems little Anika has a four-legged nanny," Elon told Rika as he transferred the infant to her arms. He watched lovingly as Rika brought Anika to her breast.

Rafi ran to the door, barking to be let outside. Elon slipped on a pair of trousers and made his way through the darkened house with Rafi at his side. When he opened the door to the back veranda and Rafi took off like a bullet, Elon realized he'd made a mistake. He had forgotten about the leopard.

"Rafi! No!" Elon yelled.

But it was too late, as the dog had already disappeared toward the forest. If the leopard was on the prowl, Elon felt Rafi wouldn't have a chance—in spite of his size. Elon had seen what a leopard could do to a dog, and the knowledge made him desperate.

"Rafi, come back!" he yelled louder.

The lights went on in the house.

Half-dressed and holding a rifle, Mutiba came running barefoot from the cottage, looking genuinely afraid. "What's wrong?" he asked hoarsely.

"Rafi may have gone after the leopard," Elon told him worriedly.

Mutiba visibly relaxed. "Is that all?" he asked.

"What happened?" Shauna asked fearfully as she, Mila, Xandra, and Harun joined them.

Mutiba felt as though his heart would burst from the sight of Shauna standing before him in a lightweight nightgown. He achingly realized that the girl he'd grown up with no longer existed—but had been replaced by a strikingly beautiful woman. Seeing she was studying his rifle with concern, Mutiba lowered it to his side.

Xandra put her fingers to her lips and emitted an ear-shattering whistle. Everyone regarded her with amazement. They were all relieved when Rafi came barking toward them from the woods. He greeted them happily, despite the scolding he was getting in Dutch from Xandra.

"There doesn't seem to be a scratch on him," Elon concluded after looking him over. "Do you realize how lucky you are?" he demanded sternly, taking the dog's head between his hands. "That leopard could have been the end of you!"

Rafi seemed to smile at the attention as he wagged his tail.

"You needn't have worried," Xandra assured Elon. "When my parents and I lived in this country, we had Leonbergers. They were never bothered by leopards."

"Leonberger . . . 'mountain lion,'" Shauna translated into English. "Not too many leopards would tangle with a lion, right?"

"Some lion," Elon responded sarcastically.

"Tomorrow we will establish the boundaries for him," Xandra informed the group. "Until then, goodnight."

Harun rubbed his sleepy eyes as he followed Xandra back inside the house. When Elon and Rafi returned to Rika, and Mila had gone to the kitchen to heat a kettle of water for tea, Shauna and Mutiba found themselves alone on the veranda.

Shauna studied Mutiba's tall, trim frame, clothed in nothing but a pair of khaki shorts. Although he wasn't looking at her, Mutiba could feel her eyes upon him. He sat on the divan with the rifle on his lap.

"Did you intend to use that on the leopard?" she asked, regarding the weapon.

He visibly tensed as she sat beside him.

"Have you done any sketches since I left?" she asked, attempting conversation.

Mutiba shook his head while glaring into space.

"What's happened to you?" Shauna asked quietly. "It's more than Christiaan's death, isn't it?"

He continued to stare blankly into space.

"Talk to me, Mutiba," she implored. "We used to talk all the time."

He forced himself to look at her. "You must not stay in the country long," he warned in an ominous tone.

"Why?"

"Because the Uganda you left a year ago is not the Uganda that now exists!"

"Nothing remains the same," she replied softly. "You're not the same. Nor am I. But our friendship—"

"Tell me about Austria," he cut her off brusquely, changing the subject while looking away.

"Austria is much as I had hoped . . . yet in some ways not."

"You had written about your friends," he stated with a hint of fear.

"Yes, I've made a few friends," she said, studying his chiseled profile. "One in particular," she looked away somewhat guiltily. "His name is Franz. He's been kind enough to pay for my music lessons, which has helped me get a job with a small orchestra."

Shauna sensed Mutiba's fear of having lost her to another man. Realizing how much he obviously still cared for her, she knew that her attraction to Franz was nothing compared to the deep love she felt for Mutiba.

"Franz and I are just friends," she told him. "There will never be anyone as special to me as you are."

Relief, uncertainty, and then anger flashed across Mutiba's face. "You must forget about me!" he ordered.

"Forget about you?" she demanded angrily. "How can you say that? I've cared about you for as long as I can remember! How dare you tell me I should just forget you! What a selfish, rude boar you've become! No matter what's happened to you—you don't have the right to shut me out of your life!"

Shauna practically shook with indignation. "I love you, damn it!" she continued. "I've always loved you! And I know you love me! And, like it or not, neither of us will ever be able to forget about the other!"

Mutiba regarded her with amazement as the tears spilled onto her cheeks. When he gently wiped them away, she brought his hand to her lips and kissed it softly. Placing the rifle on the divan, Mutiba gathered her in his arms as her eyes gazed imploringly into his. Shauna leaned her head on his shoulder as he carried her away.

Mila came from the kitchen with two cups of tea. She watched as Mutiba carried Shauna toward the cottage. When they disappeared inside, Mila set the cups down. She picked up Mutiba's rifle and brought it inside the house.

High in a tree at the edge of the forest, the leopard surveyed Rose Inish. Satisfied that the humans and lion-like dog no longer posed a threat, she made her way down and ran into the woods.

Inside the cottage, Mutiba and Shauna's lovemaking was slow and gentle. And although it was the first time for both of them, it was in no way awkward. They were so attuned to one another that there was no need for words. When at last they fell into exhausted sleep, they continued to cling to each other as if their lives depended on it. At the break of dawn, however, Shauna woke alone to the sound of a honking horn.

"Mutiba?" she asked hopefully.

Realizing he was gone, Shauna grew fearful. She slipped into her nightgown and wrapped the blanket around her before fleeing from the cottage. Running through the house, she stopped on the front veranda.

"Mutiba!" Shauna called as he was flinging his duffel bag into the waiting jeep.

He turned to face her.

"Mutiba!" she uttered with soft urgency.

He made his way toward her, holding the rifle as a barrier between them. "You must promise you'll soon leave Uganda—and not return until I tell you to!" he ordered.

Shauna glanced fearfully from him to the rifle, and then to the driver of the jeep, who regarded them with a smirk on his face.

"Promise!" Mutiba demanded of Shauna in a hushed, angry tone.

Looking deep into his eyes, Shauna swallowed her tears while slowly nodding.

"And you must never forget how much I love you," Mutiba told her softly. "But we can never be!" And with that he turned to go.

Shauna remained on the veranda, shivering in the cool morning air, as Mutiba drove away. When Mila quietly approached, Shauna turned to her with a mournful look. Sobbing, she fell into the dear woman's embrace.

Mila comforted Shauna as best she could, although she was also in need of being comforted. For Mila knew that her son was returning to the depths of hell—and she could only pray he would find his way back home again.

Chapter 9

Over the course of three-and-a-half years from the time he admitted his love for Shauna, Mutiba witnessed or was involved in many disturbing events—such as being forced to attend numerous executions of suspected rebels.

He was in attendance when President Amin greeted Libyan leader Colonel Muammar al-Quaddafi on his visit to Uganda. Mutiba also took part in a military parade that performed when the Russians came to visit; and was present when a squadron of Mig fighters arrived in Entebbe from the Soviet Union. And he watched with concealed regret when the United States closed its embassy and its citizens left the country.

Mutiba listened stoically to the whispered accounts of atrocities: such as the report of Amin ordering his surgeon to cut up the body of one of his wives who had died from a botched abortion. It was said that Amin had the doctor sew the woman's arms onto her pelvis, and her legs onto her shoulders. Then Amin displayed the corpse to their young children, telling them it's what God does to those who disappoint Him.

Mutiba also heard rumors of the tortures and murders carried out by Amin's infamous agencies: such as the "Public Safety Unit," "State Research Bureau," and "Anti-Corruption Unit." Many good people were either disappearing, or leaving the country of their own volition.

Mutiba often wondered if his and Elon's families should leave as well. But they waited for the word to come from Devin MacKail before doing so. In the meantime, Mutiba knew his services were needed if his beloved Uganda were to ever extract itself from the clutches of an increasingly insane dictator. But he hated being a spy.

In the summer of 1976, the time finally arrived when Devin deemed it wise for his friends to leave Uganda. The hijacking of an Air France airbus en-route to Paris from Athens was what prompted his decision.

At approximately 3 a.m. on the morning of Monday, June 28, Mutiba and his fellow airmen were wakened and told to bring their weapons and stand in attention at the edge of the runway leading to the old airport terminal building. Shivering in the pre-dawn mist rising off Lake Victoria, they weren't told that they were waiting for the hijacked plane to land at Entebbe.

Mutiba noticed President Amin standing beside his black Mercedes. The imposing six-foot-four, two hundred and eighty pound president was surrounded by four of his armed and uniformed Palestinian bodyguards. Amin was talking amicably with two other men, one of which was a somewhat handsome Palestinian with a mustache whom Mutiba had seen for the first time a few days earlier. From the way the other Palestinians had deferred to the man, it was apparent to Mutiba that he was held in high esteem.

The other man waiting with Amin wasn't familiar to Mutiba. He had a thicker, longer mustache that drooped at the edges. He moved with a slouching gait and was deferred to by Amin and the others with extreme respect. Mutiba felt there was something exceptionally strange and ominous about the second man. Perhaps it was the moustache and hair, which protruded out from under a hat. Mutiba guessed they weren't real—and that it was extremely important to the man not to be recognized. Instinctively, Mutiba felt the man's presence could be of significant importance. When the man turned toward him, Mutiba studied his features with an artist's scrutiny.

Mutiba watched as a car pulled up next to Amin's Mercedes. Five Palestinians, all unknown to Mutiba, quickly got out. They each carried a submachine gun and were greeted cordially by Amin and the others. Three of the newcomers ran into the deserted terminal building and appeared to give it a cursory inspection. Glancing at the vehicle the five Palestinians had arrived in, Mutiba noticed it had diplomatic plates.

At the sound of an incoming aircraft, Mutiba turned his attention to the sky. The plane's lights pierced the darkness and then disappeared as it landed at the new airport facility a mile away. Mutiba watched as Amin and the more suspicious-looking man bid goodbye to the Palestinians. The two then got into Amin's Mercedes and drove off with Amin's bodyguards. When the airbus taxied to a stop not far from where Mutiba stood, he and his fellow servicemen were ordered to surround it with their weapons drawn.

Bright searchlights flickered to life from the old control tower. Mutiba briefly saw the frightened faces of some of the plane's passengers before the shades were drawn over the windows. Glancing toward the cockpit at the gray-haired captain, Mutiba saw he had a pistol held to his head by an Arab. In his other hand, the Arab held a grenade. Mutiba's gaze wandered over the plane's fuselage and came to rest on the Air France logo.

A man and a woman, each carrying an automatic pistol, got off the plane and were greeted enthusiastically by the Palestinians waiting on the ground. Mutiba studied the couple. They looked European—in their late twenties, maybe early thirties. The woman wore a dark skirt and light-blue blouse. Her face was scared by acne and her hair was dark, but it didn't appear natural. Mutiba suspected she was wearing a wig. She had a harsh, frantic look about her. The man appeared more relaxed. When they spoke between themselves, Mutiba recognized it to be in German.

The man and woman were each given a submachine gun and ammunition from the trunk of the car with diplomatic plates that the Palestinians had arrived in. Two of the Palestinians accompanied the Germans as they re-boarded the airbus. The Palestinians that remained behind appeared quite relaxed as they shouldered their weapons. *Of course they can relax,* Mutiba thought with a sneer, *since we're doing their job for them!* But for what end, Mutiba didn't want to guess.

For hours Mutiba and his fellow servicemen were made to guard the aircraft. When the air temperature rose with the sun, they were permitted to relax on the tall grass lining the runway. Mutiba was quite concerned for the welfare of the people being held hostage on the plane. The aircraft's electrical systems had been turned off, and Mutiba knew the heat inside the cabin would be stifling. Finally, around mid-morning, the hostages were allowed to deplane.

Mutiba and the others were ordered to shoulder their weapons and stand guard as, one-by-one, the hostages made their way down the gangplank. Following the Palestinians, they were herded into the old terminal building. The Palestinians who weren't guarding them placed explosives and detonators around the structure. *They're making a show of it for the benefit of the hostages,* Mutiba thought derisively. Some of the people seemed oblivious to the threat as they smiled and waved what they thought was goodbye to their captors. However, like Mutiba, most of them realized that the ordeal was far from over. Mutiba's heart caught in his throat at the sight of the children included among the hostages.

Positioning himself near the entrance to the building, Mutiba watched as the hostages tried to make themselves comfortable in the large, hot, and dusty room. Most of them had to sit directly on the filthy concrete floor, as there weren't enough chairs. When a young father requested something for his small children to lie down on, the German woman flew into a rage. Fearfully, all the hostages fell silent.

Mutiba was among a handful of servicemen who were told to get more chairs. When they returned, the hostages were being served food. Mutiba overheard one of them mention to the airport manager, who had arrived with the women serving the meal, that it must be hard to look after so many new guests. The manager smiled and admitted he'd been expecting them. His comment confirmed what Mutiba had already concluded—that the landing of the airbus in Uganda, perhaps even the hijacking itself, had been orchestrated with the full knowledge and cooperation of President Amin.

That afternoon, Mutiba watched as Amin's helicopter landed amidst much fanfare. The president descended from the craft with his eight-year-old son, Sharon. Mutiba knew the boy was named after a hotel in Israel where Amin had once stayed. Father and son wore identical uniforms, down to matching medals and ribbons. Amin also sported the Israeli paratrooper wings that had been bestowed upon him during the time when the two countries and their leaders had been close.

"Welcome! Welcome to Uganda!" Amin greeted the hostages repeatedly while smiling and laughing profusely.

Mutiba had heard that the president's reverberating laugh was the last sound many of his victims heard before succumbing to horrible deaths. He watched as Amin strutted around the room, trailed by television and newspaper cameramen. Shaking the hands of many of the hostages, Amin would often stop and pose, smiling for the cameras.

"Some of you know me, some of you don't," Amin told the hostages. "For those who don't, I am his Excellency al-Hajji Field Marshal Doctor Idi Amin Dada, holder of the British Victoria Cross, DSO, MC—and appointed by God to be your savior!"

The hostages appeared uncertain as to how to respond to the jovial president. Most, like Mutiba, knew the term "al-Hajji" referred to Islamic pilgrims who had traveled to Mecca. Amin's use of the title "Doctor" was new to Mutiba. Instinctively, Mutiba felt it might have some significance.

"I will do everything possible to see that your stay in Uganda is a comfortable one," Amin assured the hostages. "It was *I* who arranged with the Palestinians to have you removed from the plane and into these more comfortable surroundings. I—"

Cut off by applause from some of the hostages, Amin smiled and nodded before continuing.

"I also arranged for you to have food, and will see that you are provided with whatever is needed."

He was rewarded with more applause.

"It is my hope that this whole matter can be concluded quickly," he said. "The Palestinians are a fair and just people. They are entitled to a state of their own. Zionist imperialists are depriving the Palestinians of a state," he added, his voice hardening.

Seeing the looks of concern on the faces of the hostages, Amin gave them a reassuring smile.

"I have recently been to Damascus," he explained in a more pleasant tone, "and have visited its Jewish community. And a synagogue! I can assure you that the Syrians are taking very good care of the Jews in their country, and they are supplying all of their needs. As I am doing for you!"

There was only faint applause from the hostages.

"Make yourselves comfortable—but remember, do not try to escape. This is very important!" Amin warned. "I shall arrange for your release as soon as possible. Until then, look at me as your host and Uganda as your home!"

The applause was more heartfelt.

"Excuse me, Mr. President," the tall, slim, gray-haired commander of the aircraft addressed Amin. "I am Captain Michel Bacos, the pilot of the airbus," he introduced himself in a heavy French accent. "These passengers and crewmembers are my responsibility. I have been told nothing as to why we are being held here. We are a French airline and have nothing to do with the Palestinians."

"Captain! It is good to meet you! Always good to meet a fellow pilot!" Amin smiled while shaking the captain's hand, although he appeared somewhat uncomfortable that the media was documenting the encounter. "I hope you and the others enjoy your stay here in Uganda," Amin responded simply before quickly leaving.

Mutiba watched as Amin and his young son returned to their helicopter and were whisked away. A Palestinian doctor and a Ugandan nurse then conducted cursory medical exams of the hostages for the benefit of the cameras.

Trying not to appear conspicuous, Mutiba received permission to leave the premises. He went to his barracks and changed into civilian clothes. Borrowing a jeep, he drove to the nearby town of Entebbe to use one of the few remaining British-made, red-painted phone booths that afforded privacy.

"Cheers," Mutiba stated into the phone. He gave the number he was calling from and then hung up. It was the procedure Mutiba had been instructed to follow. He knew the location of the number he'd dialed wasn't that of Devin's home in Lamu, but it was apparently nearby.

Holding down the receiver, Mutiba pretended to talk into the mouthpiece for the benefit of the people waiting to use the phone. In approximately ten minutes, the phone rang.

"Cheers," Mutiba answered quickly.

"I hear you have some unexpected company," Devin began on the other end of the line.

"Yes, about two hundred and fifty guests, hosted by Father and his new friends."

"Father" was the thinly masked code name for Amin. It corresponded with the word "Dada" in the president's self-appointed title.

"How many 'new friends'?" Devin asked.

"It looks like eight Arabs and two Europeans who speak German, one is a woman. And there's a man who doesn't look like an Arab. Whoever he is, he doesn't want to be recognized. Father and his friends obviously think quite highly of him."

There was a slight pause on Devin's end of the line. "Is that man staying with Father's guests?" he asked.

"No. I've only seen him once, with Father just before the guests arrived."

"How are Father and his new friends getting on?"

"Extremely well."

"Are the guests comfortable?"

"Yes, considering."

"Where are they?"

"In the lounge at the old terminal building. Cheers."

Mutiba quickly hung up. The information was more specific than he'd intended, but he couldn't think of any other way to state it.

Some of the people waiting for the phone were pounding on the booth, yelling for him to hurry. When Mutiba left, he was unaware that a fellow airman was waiting in line. The airman regarded him with suspicion as Mutiba got in the jeep and drove away.

Early the next morning, June 29, Elon sat in the parlor at Rose Inish listening to the Radio Uganda report on the hostage situation:

"We now bring you the special announcement you have been waiting for regarding the Air France airbus and passengers which were rerouted to Entebbe out of Athens by members of the Popular Front for the Liberation of Palestine—" the announcer began excitedly as three-and-a-half-year-old Ani, as Anika preferred to be called, joined Elon. Ani's constant companion, Rafi, was at her side. Now full grown, the gentle giant of a beast towered above the golden-haired, green-eyed child.

"Papa," Ani uttered, rubbing the sleep from her little eyes.

Elon lifted her onto his lap and folded his arms around her. Rafi settled at Elon's feet as the broadcast continued:

" . . . have taken control of the aircraft to denounce France for selling Mirage jets and a nuclear reactor to the fascist Israelis," the announcer stated. "And it was done to avenge the murder of innocent Palestinians throughout the world by the bloodthirsty imperialist state of Israel. The French are enemies of the Arab people, and are working hand-in-hand with the fascist Israelis. The port of Djibouti in Somalia-land is still being held by the French to preserve Israel's sole route to the Far East and Africa.

"The murderous Zionists are enemies of the Arab people and should be expelled from the land of Palestine," the broadcaster continued. "President Amin supports the cause of the suppressed Palestinians against Zionism and fascist imperialists. He is negotiating with the revolutionaries for the release of the Air France airbus and its passengers, but the Israelis are not cooperating. The revolutionaries are calling for the release of fifty-three of their—"

Rika entered the room and quickly turned off the radio. She glanced at their daughter before giving Elon a disapproving look.

"Papa," Ani lifted her little head from his chest, "what is 'Zion—'?"

"Ani, go to Mila, she has your bath ready," Rika interrupted sternly.

"I don't want a bath!" the child whined. "I want to stay with Papa!"

Elon kissed his daughter on the top of her head before lifting her from his lap. "Do as Mama says," he told her gently.

Puckering her little mouth into a pout, Ani left with Rafi. Elon and Rika shared a look of concern over the fate of the Air France hostages.

Their second day in Uganda progressed rather quietly for the hostages, although some of them had heard the morning's broadcast over a small transmitter radio. Unlike Elon, they listened to the entire news segment; which went on to state the terrorists' threat to blow-up the aircraft and begin killing the hostages if their demands weren't met by noon Thursday—three days away.

In spite of the terrorists' threats, the hostages remained calm. During the day the women and children were allowed on the grassy area in front of the building, where the youngsters played games. The peacefulness of the scene was periodically disrupted when two Ugandan Mig jets made a few passes overhead.

At seven in the evening, the fragile semblance of peace was shattered when the hostages with Israeli passports were systematically separated from the others and moved into a small adjoining room.

Mutiba was on duty at the time, helping to guard the hostages. He watched with a blank expression as the terrorists confiscated the few belongings the Israelis had with them. Some of the women were crying. The word "Selekzia" was uttered by a few of the older Jews. Mutiba's heart ached as Israeli families with small children made their way through a makeshift hole in the wall leading to the separate room. Unable to tolerate the scene any longer, he wandered out of the building.

Returning to the barracks, Mutiba lay on his cot, staring at the ceiling. The night was young and he couldn't sleep. He felt compelled to talk to Devin and decided to risk driving into Kampala, about twenty miles away. Before doing so, Mutiba changed into his air force uniform and tucked a pistol inside his shirt. Looking around cautiously, he borrowed a jeep. He failed to notice the airman who had seen him at the phone booth. As Mutiba drove away, the man followed at a distance.

Mutiba drove carefully through the streets of the decaying capital, which had been plunged into financial ruin when the Asians left. He was wary of the night. Even in his uniform, Mutiba knew he wasn't safe. But he was willing to take the risk because he knew it would be harder to trace a call coming out of Kampala. The information he needed to convey to Devin was crucial. Prior to the separation of the Jews from the other hostages, Mutiba had held out hope that the terrorists weren't serious in their threat to harm the captives. He now knew otherwise.

As he placed the call, Mutiba didn't see the airman come to a stop nearby.

"They are all still being held in the old terminal building," Mutiba told Devin openly after informing him of the separation of the Jews. "There are nine terrorists with them—the German man and woman and seven Palestinians, all armed with Kalachnikovs, although the hijackers only had automatic pistols and grenades when the plane landed. I haven't seen the more suspicious-looking man again, but the Palestinian who was with him comes and goes in an official vehicle with some of Amin's bodyguards. He seems to be the one in command, not the Germans. About eighty to a hundred of our soldiers and airmen are in the area."

"What about anti-aircraft defenses?" Devin asked as he met the gaze of the blonde Israeli intelligence agent who sat beside him, taking notes while listening on another extension.

"There are ten Migs parked at night in front of the new airport. I'm not sure how many missiles and howitzers. There's maybe thirty Migs and fifty combat aircraft based around Entebbe. There are numerous tanks—one parked next to two helicopters near the old terminal. I don't know how many armored vehicles."

"Is Amin still at his residence in Entebbe?" Devin asked after reading the Mossad agent's silent mouthing of the word "Father."

"As far as I know. He seems to be enjoying his part in all of this. He visits the hostages often, with his bodyguards, who are mostly Palestinians but also include about six large women from his tribe. They are all heavily armed."

"Good work," Devin complimented Mutiba as the Mossad agent nodded.

"I'll call if anything changes. Cheers," Mutiba said before hanging up.

Leaving the phone booth, he looked around cautiously. The airman ducked down behind the wheel of his vehicle when Mutiba looked his way. Mutiba hadn't noticed him, but in the nearby bushes he thought he saw someone crouching in the shadows. Removing the pistol from inside his shirt, Mutiba held it at his side as he made his way toward the jeep.

When the person lunged at him with a knife, Mutiba fired a single shot. The would-be-attacker was blown backwards onto the ground. On close inspection, Mutiba regrettably realized he'd shot a teenaged boy. The boy's frightened eyes regarded Mutiba pleadingly as the life eased from his body. Mutiba saw that the bullet had pierced the boy's heart.

Mutiba's remorse was compounded by the fact that the boy reminded him of Harun. After gently closing the boy's glazed eyes, Mutiba got in the jeep and sped away. He didn't see the airman follow at a distance. Racing his vehicle through the deserted streets, Mutiba bit his lip with anger and regret. On the outskirts of the city, he pulled the jeep over. Getting out, Mutiba vomited into the tall grass. The airman sneered at the sight as he drove past Mutiba on his way back to the barracks.

"Yvette isn't feeling well, and we're leaving for Nairobi to see a doctor," Devin told Elon over the radio at Rose Inish two mornings later. "You and all the family should meet us there," he stated adamantly.

"I hope it's nothing serious," Elon played along, realizing it was his friend's way of telling him it was time to leave Uganda.

"We won't know until we get there," Devin said.

After signing off, Elon went to inform the others that they needed to leave soon.

"No!" Mila refused as Elon and Rika tried to convince her to go with them.

"We're not about to leave you here alone!" Elon told her sternly.

"She won't be alone!" Harun piped up defensively. Almost fifteen, the boy had grown about a foot in the three-and-a-half years since Ani's birth. But he was still as skinny as a rail.

"But, Harun," Rika told him gently, "it isn't safe here anymore."

"What isn't safe?" Ani asked in her sweet little voice, rubbing her eyes with her blankie as she joined them from her nap. As usual, Rafi was practically glued to her side.

Rika picked up her daughter and gave her a tender kiss. "We'll be going away for a little while," she informed the child. "All of us," she looked hopefully in Mila's direction, but the woman shook her head firmly.

"Rafi, too!" Ani insisted.

"Rafi will be staying here with Mila and Harun," Elon stated regrettably, recognizing defeat in insisting that Mila and Harun come with them. As much as he hated separating Ani from her pet, Elon felt somewhat better knowing Rafi could help keep an eye on things while they were gone.

"I won't go without Rafi!" Ani whined as Rika carried her from the room. The big dog barked with concern as he followed after them.

Mutiba's voice was heard over the radio and Elon went to answer it. "I'm glad it's you," Elon told him after signing on.

"How are things?" Mutiba asked. Radioing from the barracks, he needed to be careful in what he said.

"Fine," Elon lied. "Although a friend is ill and wants to see us in Nairobi. We were hoping your mother and brother would come along, but they insist on staying."

Mutiba appeared worried. "When will you be leaving?"

"Later this afternoon," Elon replied, checking his watch. He calculated how long it would take to prepare the plane and get packed.

"Radio before you leave. Perhaps I can meet you at the airport."

"Will do," Elon responded before signing off.

Mutiba's worried look intensified. He felt like driving to Rose Inish to convince his mother to leave. But, like Elon, he knew it would be impossible if she'd made up her mind otherwise. Besides, the situation with the hostages was still quite precarious—although the terrorists had freed forty-seven of the captives, who were now on their way to France. None of those released, however, were Israelis.

Knowing it was important that he stay close to the hostages, Mutiba felt an overwhelming sense of despair. He wanted desperately for things to be better—for his country to emerge from this terrible nightmare. He wished there was something more he could do. As he thought of the children that were still being held captive, a dangerous plan took shape in Mutiba's mind.

Grabbing his sketchpad and a pencil from the bureau drawer next to his cot, Mutiba left the barracks. Taking the jeep, he drove to a secluded shady spot next to the lake. He turned off the ignition and began to draw.

At noon, Mutiba was again on guard duty when President Amin and his son paid the hostages another visit. As previously, father and son wore matching uniforms and were trailed by cameramen.

"I am pleased to tell you that I have succeeded in getting the Palestinians to extend the deadline for negotiations until eleven a.m. this Sunday, July fourth," Amin informed the remaining non-Israeli hostages, who were in the main lounge area of the old terminal building.

"The negotiations have failed until now because of the stubbornness of the Israeli government," Amin continued. "Their position is very dangerous for the Israeli hostages. Their government must agree to the terms of the Palestinians. I have been in contact with the Israeli government through the offices of my good friend,

Colonel Baruch Bar-Lev. Oh, yes, I almost forgot to tell you! I have also arranged for the release of all non-Israeli hostages!"

It took a moment for his words to register with the people. When they did, there was enthusiastic applause.

"Yes! Yes!" Amin smiled as he and his son made their way through the group, shaking hands. "Have a good journey! Now I must talk with the Israeli hostages. Remember how well I have treated you—and that I am your friend!"

Mutiba watched as Amin approached the area where the Israeli hostages remained separated from the others. "Shalom! Shalom!" Amin told them as he ducked through the makeshift hole leading to the other room.

Unable to hear what Amin was saying to the Israelis, Mutiba directed his attention to Captain Bacos, commander of the hijacked airbus. He was talking to his crewmembers in French, who nodded in agreement. Mutiba watched as Captain Bacos then approached the male German terrorist, who had proved to be less volatile than his female compatriot.

"Excuse me," Captain Bacos stated in an authoritative tone. "But my crew and I will not be leaving. Our responsibility lies with the passengers and, as long as you continue to hold even a single one, we shall remain."

Mutiba admired the pilot's courage—and apparently the German did also, as he simply shook his head before walking away. The bravery and determination of Captain Bacos and his crew bolstered Mutiba's resolve. Leaving the scene, Mutiba drove the short distance to the new airport, where he bought a box of candy at the gift shop. He then drove to the lake and stopped where he had parked earlier that morning. Opening the box, Mutiba emptied the candy onto the ground. Taking the folded sketches out from inside his shirt, he placed them in the box and then retied it with the ribbon.

At Rose Inish, Elon and Harun rolled the Cessna out of the barn where it had been hidden, and onto the grassy airstrip. Ani and Rafi approached from the house.

"Can me and Rafi get in?" the child asked innocently.

Wiping the grease from his hands, Elon bent down to her level. "Ani, I told you, Rafi has to stay here and take care of Mila and Harun."

"Then I'm not going!" she huffed indignantly as she reached up to hug Rafi.

"I don't have time to discuss—"

"If Rafi isn't going, I'm not going!" she stamped her little foot.

"Listen, young lady, you'd better mind or you're going to get spanked!" Elon warned, his patience growing thin. "Now go tell your mama that she and Mila can start bringing the bags."

Her father's threat held no bite, as neither he nor her mother had ever laid a hand on the child. Ani *did* know what a spanking was, however, as she'd gotten one once from Mila. She had needed only one. But the prospect of getting another wasn't as disturbing to Ani as was the thought of being separated from her beloved pet. So, when Elon and Harun turned their attention back to the aircraft, she and Rafi made their way stealthily into the barn.

Ani led Rafi to their secret hiding place, enclosed by stacks of dried tealeaves. Making their way through the winding maze leading to the cave-like space, the big dog had to crawl on his belly to keep up. Once there, he had barely enough room to stretch. Ani had him lie down beside her, and within minutes they were asleep.

"Have you seen Ani?" Rika asked Elon when she brought some of the bags to the plane.

"I sent her in to you," he replied, unconcerned.

"Harun, would you please help with the bags?" Rika asked sweetly. "I'm afraid your mama and I got a little over zealous with our packing."

As Harun sprinted toward the house, Rika tuned to Elon with a melancholy gaze.

"We won't be gone long," he tried to reassure her as they shared a gentle kiss.

She nodded and smiled faintly before leaving. Elon continued to work on the Cessna until he heard Rika and Mila calling for Ani. When Rika's calls turned frantic, Elon raced toward the house.

"You haven't seen her?" he asked worriedly.

Her eyes filled with fear, Rika shook her head as she bit back the tears.

"Harun, go look in the barn!" Elon sprang into action.

The boy took off like a shot as Elon went to the parlor and unlocked the gun cabinet. Removing a rifle, he loaded it with shells. Rika and Mila studied him worriedly.

"You're sure she's not in the house or any of the cottages?" Elon asked.

Both women nodded. Elon clicked the chamber shut on the rifle and then stuffed his pocket with ammunition.

"Don't worry, I'm sure she's all right," he stated, trying to sound reassuring. "Besides, Rafi's with her," he added before heading out back toward the forest.

"Ani!" Harun called as he entered the barn. "Rafi!"

In their hiding place, Rafi lifted his head at the sound of his name being called. But Ani remained asleep. Ignoring Harun's calls, the big dog rested his chin back on his paws and closed his eyes.

Returning to the house, Harun shook his head sadly in response to Rika's fearful, questioning gaze. "Where's Elon?" he asked his mother as Rika collapsed onto a chair.

Mila motioned toward the back of the house while attempting to comfort Rika. Harun ran to join Elon. When he caught up with him in the forest, Elon was studying the leopard's prints in the soft dirt.

Elon saw from Harun's expression that Ani wasn't in the barn. "There's no sign of them here," Elon said as he looked around the clearing, softly mottled with shafts of light filtering through the trees.

"Rafi wouldn't let her come out here," Harun stated adamantly.

"Let's search out front," Elon suggested as they turned back.

Elon knew from the fresh tracks that the leopard was nearby. Only yards away, she had regarded them with eyes that pierced through the glade. Her lip was curled into a snarl and her tail twitched with anger over the human invasion of her sanctuary.

Walking the driveway toward the main road, Elon used the tracking skills that had been drilled into him by his father. He was soon able to conclude that Ani and Rafi hadn't gone that way. Harun followed him back to the cottages, where they conducted a thorough search. When they returned to the house, Rika was frantic.

"Do you think someone has taken her?" she asked fearfully.

"No one would take her with Rafi around!" Harun objected.

Appreciating the faith the boy had in the prowess of the big dog, Elon had to agree. "He's right, we would have heard something. What do you think, Mila?"

"I think she's hiding somewhere," Mila replied in a calm voice.

"Hiding?" Rika questioned. "Why would she be hiding?"

"Because I told her again that we couldn't bring Rafi with us," Elon responded as the explanation slowly dawned on him. "Maybe they slipped into the plane," he stated hopefully, before leaving with Harun.

When their search of the aircraft proved futile, Elon and Harun went into the barn.

"Anika! Rafi!" Elon called. "Answer me, young lady!" he added sternly after being met with silence.

Now awake, Ani huddled with Rafi. As she placed her little hands over his muzzle to keep him quiet, the poor dog looked sadly conflicted.

"So help me, Ani!" Elon continued. "If I find you've been—"

"Devin just radioed," Mila told Elon as she joined him and Harun in the barn. "He said Yvette's taken a turn for the worse and that it's important you meet them soon in Nairobi," she explained. "I told him what's happened."

"Elon!" Rika called from the house. They rushed to her. "Mutiba's on the radio," she told Elon, her eyes frantically searching his.

Elon shook his head sadly before making his way to the radio.

"Did you find her?" Mutiba asked worriedly when Elon answered.

"Not yet. But when I do, you can bet she'll never do anything like this again!"

"When you do find her, you'll go to Nairobi?" Mutiba's voice sounded urgent.

"Yes. Call back in the morning."

After signing off, Elon looked to Rika. "Don't worry," he tried to reassure her.

"Come, we should all eat," Mila said, directing Rika toward the dining room. They mostly just picked at their meal in silence. Before retiring, Mila left a plate of food on the kitchen table for Ani and set out Rafi's meal in his bowl on the floor.

Lying awake in bed, with the door to their room open, Elon held Rika tight as she listened fearfully to the sounds of the night.

Ani remained with Rafi as long as possible in the dark and scary barn. When her stomach started growling and an owl hooted she hurried out from hiding.

With Rika dozing fitfully in his arms, Elon thought he heard the front door creak open, followed by the sound of Rafi's paws on the hardwood floors. Then he heard Ani's voice as she tried to whisper for Rafi to remain quiet. Elon waited until they'd had time to eat before gently slipping his arm out from under Rika and leaving the room.

Ani and Rafi had just finished eating and were about to return to the barn when Elon switched on the kitchen light.

"Where the hell have you been?" he demanded.

Fear gripped the child's stomach. "In the barn," she admitted tearfully.

"*Where?!*"

She swallowed hard as the tears spilled onto her cheeks. "In the barn."

"*In the barn? Didn't you hear us call for you?!*" Elon asked, seething with anger.

Ani bowed her head and nodded tentatively as Rafi looked from her to Elon. The big dog had never heard the girl's father talk to her in such a harsh tone, and he seemed quite disturbed by it.

Fuming, Elon stood in the doorway with his hands on his hips. When Rika rushed by, he grabbed hold of her arm before she could go to Ani.

"Leave us," he told Rika flatly, not taking his eyes from the child.

Ani started to leave.

"Not you!" Elon told her sternly.

Ani gave her mother a pleading look before Rika turned to go. Mila and Harun met her at the doorway.

"Is Ani here?" Harun asked hopefully.

"Yes," Mila answered for Rika in a stern voice. "Go back to your rooms," she ordered both Harun and Rika.

As they left, Mila remained at the doorway with her arms folded across her ample breast, looking down at Ani. She knew Elon had no choice but to discipline the child. But Mila also knew how difficult it would be for him to do so—as his greatest fear in life was of becoming like his father.

If Elon couldn't punish his daughter, then Mila was prepared to do so—although it was far from how Mila wanted Ani to remember her when she and her parents left Rose Inish. During the time they'd be apart, Mila didn't want the child to think of her only as a disciplinarian.

Elon pulled a chair away from the kitchen table and sat down. "Come here," he told Ani. "Now!" he ordered when she didn't move.

With tears streaming down her face, Ani did as she was told. Rafi cocked his head with uncertainty as he watched Ani's father pick her up and lay her across his knees. Just as Elon was about to bring his hand down on the child's bottom, Rafi sprang toward him with a deep, menacing growl.

Elon's hand froze in mid-air as he regarded the ferocious-looking beast. He knew Rafi didn't want to harm him, but would do so to protect his beloved charge.

Resting his chin on Ani's little butt, Rafi looked up at Elon with a mournful expression. Elon shook his head while exhaling a slight laugh. He knew he was beat. He set Ani on her feet and tried to appear serious as he tilted her chin to look him in the eye.

"If you ever do anything like that again—! So help me, child, you won't be able to sit down for a month! Do you understand?" he demanded of her.

Her face contorted in sobs, Ani nodded.

"Go with Mila!" he told her sternly.

Ani ran to Mila, who was also shaking her head in defeat. She carried the child to Rika. Rafi started to follow, but he turned back toward Elon.

"Come here," Elon told him softly.

With his head lowered and tail tucked between his legs, Rafi obeyed.

"I know you love her," Elon told him gently as he stroked the dog's head. "And I'm grateful for that. I wish we could take you with us, but I can't now, more so than before. She's got to learn how to mind—someday her life could depend on it. But I promise you this, my dear brave friend . . ."

Rafi wagged his tail and appeared to be smiling as Elon continued.

"I will be back for you. As soon as I get Ani and her mother settled in Kenya, I'll be back for you and Mila and Harun . . . and Mutiba."

Rafi planted a wet, sloppy kiss on the man's face.

"Enough!" Elon laughed. "Go on now!"

Barking excitedly, Rafi ran from the room. When he met up with Ani, the child's mother was smothering her with kisses.

"Come along," Mila told Ani as she led her out of her parents' bedroom. Rafi followed them to Ani's room.

Joining Rika, Elon tried to appear serious. But his shoulders sagged with defeat when she gave him a loving smile and caressed his face before their lips came together in a gentle kiss.

Chapter 10

"Take this with you," Mila told Rika, handing her the photo album of Rose Inish as Rika waited to board the Cessna with Ani for the flight to Nairobi. Tucked inside the album was the letter Rika had written to Cole almost five years earlier, which had been returned from Texas unopened.

"Perhaps it would be safer here," Rika said as she regarded the album with a look of nostalgia. "Surely we won't have to stay away long."

Mila exchanged a knowing glance with Elon, suggesting they felt otherwise. He and Harun were loading the last of the items into the aircraft.

"I wish you'd change your mind," Elon told Mila. "It's not too late for you and Harun to come with us."

"And Rafi?" Ani asked hopefully as she leaned her little head against the big dog's body.

Elon bent down to her level. "No," he told the child firmly. "Rafi needs to watch over Mila and Harun," he explained in a softer tone. "Now tell them all goodbye."

"'Bye, Mimi," Ani said, using her nickname for Mila as they hugged and kissed. "'Bye, 'Arun."

"'Bye, little one," Harun told her, rubbing the top of her head in the way that Shauna and Mutiba had rubbed his when he was younger.

"'Bye, Rafi," Ani buried her face in the dog's tawny coat. "No," she cried softly when Elon pulled her away from her pet.

Rafi barked with concern. Elon nodded for Harun to slip the rope he was holding around Rafi's neck.

"Ani, stop crying," Rika told her gently. "You're making Rafi feel really bad. Now tell him what a good boy he is and ask him to stay." She knew Ani's command was the only thing that would keep the big dog from attempting to go with them.

Ani tried hard to swallow her tears. "I love you, Rafi," she told him from her father's arms. "But you have to stay here."

Rafi wagged his tail slowly. His face had a quizzical expression as he watched Elon place Ani inside the aircraft.

"Goodbye, Harun, Mila," Rika hugged and kissed them lovingly. "Hopefully we'll see you very soon."

Mila bit back her tears as she watched Rika board the plane.

"I'll radio you when we get to Nairobi," Elon told Mila while embracing her. "If need be, I'll be back for you soon. All of you," he said, glancing at Rafi.

"Looks like you're the man around here now," Elon turned toward Harun with a smile. They shook hands like two adults, until Elon opened his arms and Harun fell into his embrace.

Elon then took Rafi's head between his hands. A simple "Thank you" was all Elon could manage before turning away and boarding the plane. Mila and Harun stepped back as Elon turned on the ignition.

At first Rafi obeyed Harun's command to sit and stay but, as the aircraft began to taxi, he started barking furiously. Breaking away from Harun, Rafi almost caught up with the craft. He snapped at its tires as it lifted into the air.

Banking the plane over Rose Inish, Elon watched as Rafi desperately followed its path from the ground.

By the time Rafi made his way around the house, the Cessna had flown out of sight. Stopping at the edge of the forest, he howled pathetically.

On guard duty at the old airport terminal in Entebbe, Mutiba listened as President Amin addressed the Israeli hostages. They had been allowed to rejoin the Air France crew in the main lounge area. All the other hostages had been released. Accompanied by one of his wives and their young son, Gamal, Amin paraded before the Israelis and flight crew wearing a wide-brimmed hat.

"If your government continues to refuse to negotiate with the Palestinians, it will be very grave for you," Amin warned the Israelis. "The building has been surrounded by explosives and will be blown up if your government does not cooperate. I am leaving now for Mauritius to attend a conference of the Organization of African Unity, of which I am chairman. I will return either this evening or tomorrow. While I am gone, I suggest that you write a letter to your government. Tell them it would be wise to accept the terms of the Palestinians. If they do not, there may be nothing more I can do to help you!"

Detecting anger and disappointment in Amin's voice, Mutiba sensed the president had come to realize that he had considerably less control over the fate of the hostages than he'd previously thought.

"I will go now to Mauritius to plead for your cause," Amin told the group in parting. "When you write the letter to your government, be sure to tell them how much I have done for you. Shalom!" he concluded with a forced smile.

After Amin and his wife and their son had left, Mutiba overheard the hostages' debate on whether or not to write the letter. A few of the Israeli family men and Air France crewmembers were in favor of doing so; but most of the others, including Captain Bacos, were not. Mutiba listened as a somewhat heated argument grew out of the debate.

One of the hostages, a young man whom Mutiba had heard being jokingly referred to as "the barman," made his way among the group cheerfully offering tea or coffee. An older man, whose name Mutiba had heard was "Pasko," accompanied the barman. Mutiba presumed the pair were father and son, not knowing they'd been complete strangers prior to being taken hostage. Noticing the tattooed-number the older man bore on his forearm, Mutiba realized he'd been in a Nazi concentration camp. Mutiba was amazed that, despite that experience, Pasko was as jovial as the barman.

Glancing at his watch, Mutiba left his post and made his way toward the jeep to drive to the new airport terminal to meet Elon and his family. He froze at the sight of the airman who, unknown to Mutiba, had been following him. The man had removed the candy box from under the front seat of the vehicle and was about to open it.

"That's a gift for some friends," Mutiba told the man with forced calmness as he approached and took the box from him.

"I didn't think you'd miss any," the airman responded somewhat sheepishly.

"I'm going to meet them now," Mutiba said. "If you'd like, I'll pick up a box for you at the terminal," he offered.

"No, but I'll drive there with you," the airman said as he got into the vehicle.

Not wanting to appear suspicious, Mutiba didn't object to the man's accompanying him. When they arrived at the new terminal they went their separate ways, although Mutiba was aware that the man was watching him from a distance.

Landing at Entebbe, Elon and Rika shared a look of concern over the numerous Ugandan soldiers and Palestinian guards. When they entered the terminal to clear customs, the Palestinian workers regarded them with open contempt.

While Rika and Ani headed for the ladies' room, Elon looked around for Mutiba. He noticed him standing in a far corner of the terminal with his rifle in one hand and a small box in the other. Their eyes met briefly before Mutiba looked away. Elon knew they needed to meet privately. Pretending to read a magazine at the gift shop, he watched from of the corner of his eye as Mutiba entered the men's room. Elon waited a few moments before following nonchalantly.

With the rifle slung across his shoulder, Mutiba was washing his hands when Elon entered the room. They ignored each other until satisfied they were alone.

"Tell Devin the Israeli hostages are back in the main lounge of the old airport terminal," Mutiba whispered hurriedly. "The Air France crew is with them. Amin will return from Mauritius sometime before Sunday's deadline. I have no doubt the hijackers will follow through with their threats. Give this to Devin," he handed Elon the candy box before turning to leave.

"Wait," Elon stopped him.

Mutiba turned to face him. Although his expression was hard, Elon could detect the sadness in his eyes. Elon removed an envelope from his pocket and handed it to him.

"It's my father's ring," Elon explained quietly. "And some American currency. I gave Mila some money as well. I'll be back for you. For all of you," he assured him.

Mutiba studied the envelope before pocketing it. "Tell Rika and Ani I'm sorry I couldn't say goodbye."

Elon extended his hand as they looked into each other's eyes. Skipping the handshake, they quickly embraced. Elon watched sadly as his lifelong friend left.

Suspecting that the airman was still watching him, Mutiba didn't look around as he hurriedly made his way through the terminal.

"Did you find Mutiba?" Rika asked Elon when she and Ani joined him.

"Come along," was all he said as he led them back toward the Cessna.

"What's that?" Ani asked when she noticed the small box he was carrying.

Elon looked at the box as if he'd forgotten he had it. "Just some candy," he replied absently.

"Can I have some?" Ani asked sweetly.

"Wait until we get back in the air," Elon said as he picked her up and held her tight. He wanted to protect her from the stares of resentment they were getting from the Ugandan soldiers and Palestinian guards. Elon felt like running toward the plane, but he knew better than to move too quickly.

Rika gave him a worried look as she walked quietly at his side.

The airman followed Mutiba at a distance. Noticing he no longer had the box of candy, the airman looked around to see whom Mutiba might have given it to. When he spotted Elon and his family as they were leaving the terminal, he hurried after them.

While getting Rika and Ani settled in the back of the Cessna, Elon glanced up at the terminal and instinctively zeroed in on the airman, studying him through the large windows. Before closing the door to the aircraft, Elon absently handed the candy box to Ani. Settling into the pilot's seat, Elon took a deep breath and steadied his shaking hands before preparing for take-off. Looking to see if he was still being watched, he noticed the airman was no longer there.

It wasn't until they were airborne and heading across Lake Victoria for the flight to Nairobi that Elon slowly exhaled a sigh of relief.

"There's no candy!" Ani whined after opening the box and unfolding one of Mutiba's sketches.

Glancing at Ani, Rika sat up in alarm. Taking the box from the child, she unfolded the rest of the drawings. Worriedly, Rika handed them to Elon.

Sweat beaded on Elon's brow as he leafed through the meticulous sketches of the terrorists and hand-drawn map of where the hostages were being held. On the map there were written details of the manpower and armaments surrounding the area. Elon felt ill when thinking about what could have happened to them if Amin's forces had discovered the material. But then Elon realized what a tremendously brave thing Mutiba had done.

"Hand me my camera," he told Rika while giving the sketches back to her.

After handing Elon his camera, Rika folded the sketches back in the box and tucked it into one of their bags.

Elon banked the Cessna over the lake and headed back toward the airport. Circling at an angle, he snapped numerous shots of the old and new airport facilities and surrounding area before resuming the course toward Nairobi.

When Elon handed the camera back to Rika, she nodded gravely. Fully aware of the risk he had taken, she was proud of him for doing so.

"I'm so glad you made it!" Devin greeted them warmly when they arrived at Williams Airport, a small private facility near Nairobi. "And this lovely little lady must be Anika!"

"I'm Ani," she countered, letting it be known that she preferred her nickname.

"This is Uncle Devin," Rika informed Ani after exchanging hugs with him. "Yvette isn't really ill, is she?" she asked Devin worriedly.

"Don't worry, she's fine," he responded while helping Elon carry their overnight bags to his car. "I hope you don't mind, but I've secured a room for you at the Nile Star," he told them as they drove toward town.

Elon and Rika exchanged a look of concern. The Nile Star Hotel was way beyond their financial means.

"Don't worry, its taken care of," Devin assured them, seeing the look on their faces.

"I gave Mila and Mutiba almost the last of my currency," Elon explained. He noticed Devin was studying the rearview mirror. Glancing over his shoulder, Elon saw that they were being followed.

Arriving at the historic Nile Star Hotel, Devin didn't get out. He handed Elon a key to the room. "You're already checked in," he told him.

"I do hope we can see Yvette soon," Rika said.

"To be honest, my dear," Devin stated, "I saw her off to Scotland yesterday."

Rika looked only vaguely surprised. "Give her our love," she said, kissing Devin on the cheek before getting out with Ani.

"I'd like a word with you after you've gotten them settled in," Devin told Elon. "I'll wait here. Oh, and bring your camera."

A bellhop rushed to help Elon and Rika with their bags. After glancing at the key, Elon told him the number of their room—but the boy seemed to already know. Elon noticed the vehicle that had followed them from the airport was now parked across the street. The two men inside appeared to be purposely ignoring him. The one sitting in the passenger seat was the blonde Israeli intelligence agent who was with Devin in Lamu when Mutiba had called.

On entering their bungalow suite with her parents, Ani inspected the culinary treats waiting for them. Her eyes grew large at the sight of all the fruit and sweets.

Elon offered the bellhop a tip, but it was refused.

"All has been taken care of," the boy smiled before leaving.

"'All has been taken care of' quite nicely," Rika stated worriedly as she glanced around. "This must be costing Devin a fortune!"

"I don't think it's coming out of his pocket," Elon responded distantly.

She gave him a questioning look.

"I'm not sure what's going on," he told her, half-truthfully. "I'll know more after I've talked with Devin. While I'm gone, I think it's best that you don't leave the room."

They shared a look of concern before Rika turned her attention to Ani. Remembering what Devin had said about bringing his camera, Elon took the time to snap a photo of Rika and Ani as they smiled next to the mound of fruit.

"Don't forget this," Rika said, taking the candy box from one of their bags and handing it to Elon.

Realizing Rika had guessed that Devin would know what to do with the sketches, Elon gave her a worried look as he took the box from her. He gazed into her eyes as she silently mouthed the words "I love you." Their lips came together in a tender kiss until Ani's giggles broke them apart.

"You be good," Elon told the child, giving her a hug before he left.

Outside the bungalow, Elon noticed a man and a woman seated near a large aviary. The couple quickly glanced away. Two men in business suits strolled purposely by him and three black Kenyans, dressed as gardeners, worked on landscaping that didn't need improving. It wasn't difficult for Elon to guess who all the people actually were.

"Mossad?" he asked Devin, glancing at the vehicle that once again followed them as they pulled away from the curb. "And at the hotel?"

Devin smiled. "Your father taught you well."

"I'd like to think you had as much to do with it."

"I'd like to think the same," Devin nodded gratefully.

"Where are we headed?"

"The park. We can talk better there."

They drove the few miles to Nairobi National Park, followed by the two Mossad agents. When they stopped on a rise overlooking a plain doted with herds of various game, Elon handed Devin the candy box.

"You should take some photos," Devin suggested as he studied Mutiba's sketches.

Aiming his camera out the window, Elon pretended to focus it on the two Israeli agents, sitting inside their vehicle parked in a nearby grove of trees. Both men quickly ducked out of sight.

"I'd forgotten what an excellent artist Mutiba is," Devin stated appreciatively.

"They're going in after them, aren't they?" Elon asked from behind the camera.

"They're not certain yet," Devin responded sadly as he returned the drawings to the box. "Perhaps this information will help them make up their minds."

"So, how long have you been a part of all this?" Elon asked, studying his friend with misgivings.

There was a thoughtful pause on Devin's part before answering. "I started working for Interpol when I was about your age. And with the Israelis since 1948."

Elon nodded gravely. "Two questions: Why haven't they gone in by now? And what the hell makes them think they can pull it off if they do?"

"It's the most difficult hostage situation the Israelis have ever had to face," Devin said. "It's complicated by the distance involved and the fact that it concerns a country whose leader is openly abetting the terrorists. In answer to your second question . . . no doubt they'd say because God is on their side."

"As would Amin and the Palestinians," Elon responded quietly.

Starting his vehicle, Devin drove to where the Israelis were parked. Getting out of their auto, the blonde agent got into the back seat of Devin's.

"Shalom," the agent and Devin greeted each other. The Israeli was about the same age as Elon, with handsome Germanic-looking features.

"Giora, this is Elon O'Shay," Devin introduced the two men, who shook hands.

Devin spoke briefly to Giora in Hebrew while handing him Mutiba's sketches.

Giora studied the drawings with a mixture of disbelief and appreciation. "Your friend Mutiba is extremely talented . . . and brave," he told Elon in slightly accented English. "We are tremendously indebted to him."

"He told me the remaining hostages are with the Air France crew in the main lounge of the old terminal building," Elon relayed Mutiba's message. "And that Amin is due back from Mauritius before Sunday's deadline. He feels the hijackers *will* follow through with their threats."

Giora nodded gravely. "Shalom, chavim," he told them in parting.

"Wait," Elon said as he wound and removed the film from his camera. "There are some shots in there that might interest you," he explained while handing the roll of film to Giora.

Giora nodded his thanks. Pocketing the film, he left to join the other agent.

Elon studied the other man's profile, whose eyes were obscured by sunglasses. The man had dark, brooding features. Elon sensed he was someone a person wouldn't want to have as an enemy.

As the Israelis drove away, Devin removed a thick envelope from under the seat and handed it to Elon.

"What's this?" Elon asked.

"Open it."

Removing three airline tickets, Elon turned to Devin with a questioning look.

"They're to Amsterdam," Devin told him. "Plus three British passports and ten-thousand dollars in American currency. And the deed to my camp in the Mara."

"I can't—"

"I'm flying to Scotland this evening," Devin cut him off. "It's doubtful Yvette and I will ever be back in Africa. Your flight leaves tomorrow afternoon at three. The tickets have an open return, but I suggest you monitor the situation here before you decide when, or if, to come back. Until then, the camp is staffed and can manage on its own."

"I can't accept all this!" Elon told him resentfully as he tried to hand the envelope back.

"It isn't charity!" Devin responded sternly, refusing to take the envelope. "As far as Yvette and I are concerned, you're my only heir. The camp is our gift to you and Mila and your families. You're free to dispose of it, or use it in any way you see fit. As for the money and tickets, they're gifts from our friends."

"But you don't understand, I need to go back to Rose Inish and—"

"You've got to get out of Africa. Tomorrow."

"I can't leave without knowing that Mila and her sons are safe!"

"Damn it, Elon!" Devin exploded. "You're going to be on that plane tomorrow if I have to see to it personally!"

Reminded of his father, Elon glared resentfully at Devin.

"If you don't go, you place Rika and Ani in tremendous danger," Devin said, tempering his anger. "If you're out of the country before the shit hits the fan in Uganda, it will be easier for you to return to Kenya when the dust settles. Rose Inish is lost," he added sadly. "Leave it to the Israelis to get Mila and her sons out."

Elon turned his attention to the animals grazing peacefully on the plain below. Devin's words confirmed what Elon had feared regarding Rose Inish. He also knew there was a good chance Mila and her sons, and Rafi, were doomed as well.

"Promise me you'll be on that flight tomorrow," Devin demanded gently.

"I promise," Elon lied, not looking him in the eye.

Satisfied, Devin headed back to the Nile Star. "If Holland doesn't work out," he told Elon when they arrived, "Yvette and I would love to have you and the family join us in Scotland."

Elon managed a weak smile as he and Devin shook hands, and then hugged, before parting. Watching his dear friend drive off, Elon's smile dissolved.

That night Elon held Rika tight as she slept intermittently. Ani slept peacefully at their side, although a bed had been prepared for her on the sofa. As Elon watched over the sleeping mother and child, he wished the night would never end. But, all too soon, he found himself at Embakasi International Airport hugging them goodbye.

"You've got money," he reminded Rika quietly as he buried his face in her sweet-smelling hair. "You don't need to stay with your parents if it's too uncomfortable."

She kissed him softly on the mouth. "We'll be all right," she assured him while gently stroking his cheek. "You just worry about Mila and the boys. And join us as—"

She was interrupted by the final boarding call for the flight to Amsterdam.

Elon gathered Ani into his arms. "You mind your mama," he told her lovingly.

Taking his face between her little hands, Ani peppered it with sweet kisses. Elon and Rika shared a lingering kiss before she and Ani headed toward the plane. Turning back, they smiled and waved one last time. Elon felt as though his heart would burst as he watched them disappear inside the aircraft.

Elon waited at the terminal until the plane was just a dot in the sky. Hailing a taxi, he directed the driver to take him to Williams Airport. Elon was determined to go back for Mila, Harun, and Rafi—and Mutiba, if at all possible.

The taxi hadn't gone far before it was cut off by the Mossad agents' vehicle. Giora got out and opened Elon's door. "Come with us," he directed Elon.

Elon hesitated before taking his bag and reluctantly doing as the man requested. Giora paid the taxi driver and then joined Elon in the other vehicle.

"We suspected you wouldn't leave," Giora told Elon.

"Giora, is it? And . . ." Elon inquired as he studied the reflection of the driver in the rearview mirror. It was the same agent who'd been with Giora at the park. As before, dark sunglasses obscured the man's eyes and his jaw seemed to be set in stone.

"Zev," Giora told Elon the man's name.

Zev ignored the introduction as he turned the vehicle around.

"I don't suppose you could drop me off at Williams Airport?" Elon asked as they headed back toward the international airport.

"I'm afraid that wouldn't be wise," Giora said.

"Look, you admitted that you were indebted to my friend Mutiba!" Elon responded angrily. "Why not let me try to rescue his mother and brother?"

"We have informed Mutiba to meet us at Rose Inish by dawn tomorrow," Giora told him.

Elon seemed to relax, but not for long. "You'd better have room for a rather large dog," he told Giora sullenly.

"Rafi," Giora nodded with a slight smile.

"So, what did I have for breakfast?" Elon asked sarcastically. Although annoyed, Elon wasn't surprised that the Israelis knew so much about him and his family.

Giora turned to face him. "You have a choice. Either you're on the next plane to Amsterdam . . . or you stay a while and help us."

"Will you take me with you when you go for Mutiba and his family?" Elon asked.

"It isn't for me to say," Giora replied.

"I'm staying," Elon stated adamantly.

"If it's learned that you're involved with us, you may never be able to return to Uganda—or perhaps anywhere in Africa. And you and your family's safety cannot be guaranteed anywhere in the world," Giora warned.

The look on Elon's face showed he didn't take Giora's warning lightly. "Our safety was compromised the day Idi Amin came to power," he replied solemnly.

Giora nodded.

Looking into Giora's sky-blue eyes, Elon sensed that in addition to their closeness in age and the color of their eyes, they were alike in temperament as well.

"So, tell me, is playing James Bond your only occupation?" he asked.

Giora shook his head. "I teach school on a kibbutz."

"Married?"

Giora nodded. "Two young sons. From the looks of your family, you're quite fortunate as well," he added, taking a thin packet of photographs from his pocket and handing it to Elon.

Thumbing through the few developed photos from the film he'd given to Giora the previous day, Elon wasn't surprised that all the ones of Entebbe Airport weren't among them. As he studied the photo of Rika and Ani that he'd taken at the Nile Star, Elon was consumed with the pain of missing them. He gazed sadly out the window.

"'Elon' is a good name," Giora said in an attempt to divert Elon from his melancholy thoughts. "It means 'the strength of an oak tree.' There was a Hebrew judge named Elon."

"What does 'Giora' mean?" Elon asked vacantly.

"Giora was a Hebrew leader who fought bravely against the Romans."

"And 'Zev'?" Elon glanced at the driver, who continued to ignore him.

"'Zev' means 'wolf,'" Giora replied with a slight grin.

"No doubt appropriate," Elon speculated as they arrived at a secured area adjacent to the international airport. "This isn't the terminal," he stated needlessly.

Recognizing the two Israeli agents, the armed Kenyan soldiers waved them inside the gate. They drove to a large hangar holding two El Al Boeing 707s. As the massive hangar doors opened and then closed behind them, Elon focused on the workers. Some of them wore the starched white overalls of East African Airways mechanics, while others were dressed in civilian clothes. There were a few young women among them. Elon quickly, and correctly, surmised that everyone inside the hangar was an Israeli.

"Wait here," Giora told him as he got out of the car and bounded up the stairs, disappearing inside one of the 707s.

Glancing into the rearview mirror, Elon saw that Zev had removed his sunglasses and was studying him with a cold expression. The look in the Mossad agent's dark eyes gave Elon the impression that, unlike Giora, Zev was a natural-born killer.

Giora soon reappeared, motioning for Elon to join him. Following Giora inside the 707, Elon stepped into the Israeli command center from which the rescue of the Air France hostages would be orchestrated. Approximately half of the aircraft's seats had been replaced by equipment needed to track and coordinate the mission. Israeli Air Force personnel, dressed in business suits, manned the stations.

Elon appeared mesmerized by the scene. He slowly shook his head with wonder and appreciation for what the Israelis were preparing to do.

"You'll have to excuse me for not introducing anyone to you," Giora apologized to Elon. "Security reasons," he explained.

Elon noticed that copies of Mutiba's sketches were posted on a nearby bulletin board—along with some of the photographs Elon had taken of Entebbe Airport, which had been enlarged.

"They are exceptional," Giora told Elon in reference to the drawings. "It took a tremendous amount of courage for your friend Mutiba to draw them. As well as for you to take these," he added, regarding the photographs. "We have flown the originals to Israel. They could help save the lives of more than a hundred innocent people—including eleven children."

"What can you tell me about the hijackers?" Elon asked. "Unless doing so means you'll have to kill me," he added half-jokingly.

"We suspect this is Gabriele Kroche-Tiedemann," Giora said as he pointed to the sketch of the acne-scarred woman. "German, mid-twenties. Involved in the kidnapping of oil ministers from the OPEC meeting in Vienna last December. She was the girlfriend of a German terrorist, Bernard Hausman, who had been recruited by the PFLP to carry two bomb-rigged suitcases into Ben-Gurion Airport last month. He and a female Israeli security officer were killed when Hausman was asked to open them. Apparently he hadn't been told by the PFLP that the suitcases were set to go off when opened."

Giora pointed to the likeness of the less-volatile terrorist. "Wilfried Bose," he identified the man. "Also German, and a member of the Baader-Meinhof urban guerrillas. He is a known companion and technical advisor to the most wanted terrorist in the world—The Jackal."

Having heard of the elusive terrorist, Elon gave Giora a look of concern.

"What we've learned from the released hostages and other sources," Giora told him, "is that Bose and Tiedemann, along with these two Palestinians," he pointed to the sketches of the two men, "boarded flight 139 in Athens. All four had arrived in Greece on a Singapore Airlines flight from Bahrain. Conveniently, and rather suspiciously, there was a strike of ground personnel at the Athens airport when the terrorists checked in for the Air France flight. Because of the strike, the security was lax and they were able to bring onboard automatic pistols and grenades, hidden in large cans of dates.

"After being hijacked, the airbus landed briefly at Benghazi," Giora continued. "But it's obvious that Entebbe had been determined as the final destination. Prior to the plane's arrival, President Amin had sent his personal jet to Somalia to bring the leader of the terrorists to Uganda. His name is Doctor Wadi Hadad," Giora pointed to Mutiba's drawing of the man. "Perhaps it's because of him that Amin has added the term 'Doctor' to his self-appointed title," Giora shook his head at Amin's pretentiousness.

"Hadad apparently took control of the operation when the airbus landed at Entebbe. He is considered the mastermind of the PFLP, and has a hand in practically all their terrorist operations. He's a known ladies' man, and has been described by our psychological profilers as 'behaving like a 19th-century Russian anarchist who derives an almost mystical satisfaction in living by his own rules.'

"These six Palestinians were with Hadad when flight 139 landed at Entebbe," Giora pointed at their likenesses.

"Although it's difficult to determine with the wig and fake mustache, we suspect that this is Ilich Ramirez Sanchez," Giora explained regarding the sketch of the man whom Mutiba had seen with President Amin before the hijacked plane arrived at Entebbe. It was the man Mutiba had considered to be the most important, as well as the most suspicious-looking.

"Also known as Carlos Ramirez," Giora elaborated, "he had been personally involved in the killing of two Paris police officers, the kidnapping of delegates to the Vienna conference of OPEC, and numerous other acts of terrorism. As I mentioned earlier, he's the world's best-known and most-wanted terrorist—The Jackal."

Overwhelmed, Elon shook his head slowly. "You sure know how to pick your fights," he commented quietly. "Wouldn't it just be easier to give in to their demands?"

"The green light has not yet been given to our operation," Giora admitted. "Prime Minister Rabin and his cabinet members aren't sold on a mission where our soldiers might hold only one-way tickets. And to be honest, until these landed in our hands," he motioned toward Mutiba's sketches and Elon's photographs, "the only option that appeared viable was the political one. That is if you can consider the barter of innocent lives for those of criminals and terrorists to be politically, or morally, justified.

"Western governments for the most part have downplayed aerial hijackings by Islamic extremists, no doubt because of a dependence on Arab oil," Giora explained. "But Israel does not have the luxury to do so. I have no doubt, however, that the world will eventually come to realize that terrorism constitutes war—aimed directly at democratic freedom and human decency."

Elon solemnly nodded in agreement.

"Not that we haven't capitulated in the past," Giora admitted. "In 1968, Palestinian terrorists were secretly released in exchange for Israeli citizens hijacked on an El Al flight to Algeria. In 1969, we exchanged Syrian airmen and other prisoners for two Israelis who had been held hostage in Damascus. After the Yom Kippur War, we returned over a hundred saboteurs and spies to get back the bodies of a few Israeli soldiers."

"So why not now?" Elon asked.

"In part because the terrorists' demands have escalated to the point of absurdity. They expect us to be responsible for the release of all the detainees—even those not being held in Israel. And they have refused any exchange to take place outside of Uganda. Beyond that, other circumstances mandate that we don't give in.

"For the first time in modern history, a nation and its leader have openly supported international terrorists and blackmailers," Giora explained. "Those terrorists are headquartered in Somalia, which is strategically allied with the Soviet Union. And they are sponsored by Libya, one of the most dangerous countries in the world. If they succeed in Uganda, their efforts will only escalate."

"The same could hold true if they don't succeed," Elon stated the obvious. "So, if you don't mind my asking, what's the plan and how can I help?"

He and Giora turned their attention to a man who repeated in Hebrew the information he was receiving via radio headphones.

"The strike force has left Israel," Giora translated for Elon. "But the cabinet has still not sanctioned the mission," he added worriedly.

Elon gave him a questioning look.

"Four C-130 Hercules transport planes with almost three hundred soldiers and airmen—along with armed jeeps, infantry carriers, and a black Mercedes similar to the one used by Idi Amin—will fly over the Red Sea along commercial air routes," Giora told Elon. "In the eight hours it will take for them to get from Israel to Uganda, they'll have to avoid Russian-made radar, fly between hostile Arab states, and cross Ethiopia into Kenya, flying low over the Rift Valley into Uganda.

"If all goes as planned," Giora added, "they'll succeed in a surprise attack, rescue all the hostages, refuel either at Entebbe or here, and return safely to Israel."

"That shouldn't be a problem," Elon stated sarcastically, shaking his head at the seemingly impossible logistics involved in the daring operation.

"We have Navy ships in position offshore, plus IAF Phantoms with devices that can jam hostile radar and misdirect radar-controlled missiles," Giora elaborated in an effort to make the mission sound more feasible.

"We estimate our causality loss to be perhaps thirty dead, fifty wounded," he stated sadly. "There is an entire medical facility set up in the 707 parked here next to us. The men and women onboard are highly trained in combat, as well as in saving lives. They will remain here while we monitor the mission from the air. What we would like for you to do, Elon, is to stay onboard with us and give us any insights as to the physical terrain, structures, weather conditions—whatever first-hand information you have that might be of help. You're in a unique position to supply us with—"

"'Zanek!'" the man with the headphones excitedly repeated the Hebrew word that he just received.

"'Zanek'—it means 'jump' or 'scramble,'" Giora explained to Elon. "The mission has been given the official word to proceed."

"Count me in," Elon told him

Giora nodded while smiling faintly. "Let me show you around," he offered.

Although Giora didn't introduce him to any of the men manning the command center, Elon was met with friendly nods. He admired the radar screens and other equipment while Giora laid out a set of blueprints. Elon immediately recognized them as plans of Entebbe Airport.

"As you know, we were instrumental in building the military air facilities, as well as the old and new civilian airports at Entebbe," Giora said. "We have made note of any changes according to the information Mutiba and others have provided—as well as from the photos you took. Over there we have a scale model."

Elon studied the model and blueprints. "Can you tell me who's in charge of the ground operation?" he asked.

"Brigadier General Dan Shomron, commander of our Special Air and Commando Service," Giora told him. "Thirty-nine years old, born on a kibbutz, Shomron's been actively involved in every military conflict since the Sinai War of 1956. He has little, or no, tolerance for negotiating with terrorists . . . or for world opinion, for that matter," Giora smiled knowingly.

"Shomron, and Israel as a whole, learned an interesting lesson during the Yom Kippur War," he elaborated. "When that conflict shifted in Israel's favor, the Russians threatened large-scale military intervention and the United States secured an end to the hostilities. We call it a 'stopwatch' tactic—where the hands of the clock move slowly when the Arabs are winning, yet quickly when the tables are turned.

"Shomron's second-in-command is a good friend of mine, Lieutenant Colonel Yehonatan Netanyahu, nicknamed 'Yoni,'" Giora said. "Yoni's commandos are excellent sharpshooters who are highly trained in terrorist reprisals. Yoni was born in America and is currently a graduate student of philosophy at Harvard University. His father is a well-known and respected Jewish historian. Yoni knows where every Biblical event took place in Israel," Giora shook his head with admiration. "His men refer to him by the ancient Hebrew phrase as 'the man of the sword and the Bible.'

"He was wounded in the arm during the Six-Day War, and is considered thirty-percent disabled. But he talked his way back into the commandos. When he was asked why they should let him continue to fight, Yoni answered because he could recite all the poems of one of our greatest poets, Nathan Alterman," Giora laughed softly.

Giora's account of his friend Yoni reminded Elon of his own friendship with Mutiba. "Any chance of getting Mutiba out before the strike force lands?" he asked.

Giora shook his head sadly.

"You still intend to use him, don't you?" Elon asked worriedly.

"He knows to be careful," Giora responded with forced lightness.

Directing his attention to the model of the airport facilities at Entebbe, Elon studied the miniature buildings, helicopters, tanks, Migs, and other armaments. He shook his head at the enormity of the task facing the Israelis. Elon also knew, in spite of Giora's assurance, that there was a strong possibility Mutiba could get caught in the crossfire.

Chapter 11

Not long after the Israeli commandos had begun their perilous journey toward Uganda, President Amin arrived back at Entebbe. Mutiba was on guard duty when Amin addressed the hostages. The smell in the old terminal building was horrendous, as many of the captives were sick with food poisoning, and the toilets were clogged and overflowing.

"The Palestinians have informed me that you have written a letter to your government, as I had suggested," Amin told them. "Your government is gambling with your fate. Let us hope your letter will convince them to be reasonable."

"Excuse me, Field Marshal President Idi Amin—" a young Israeli mother began.

"Do not address me like that!" Amin exploded. "My full title is 'Field Marshal Doctor President Idi Amin Dada!'"

While everyone's attention was focused on the volatile President, Mutiba slipped out of the building. Driving the short distance toward the city of Entebbe, he didn't notice the airman following him. The man had reported what he considered to be suspicious behavior on Mutiba's part to their superiors—and he was assigned to monitor Mutiba's movements. He parked at a distance and watched as Mutiba entered a phone booth.

Although Devin had left Africa, Mutiba had been instructed to continue calling the number in Lamu. He relayed the latest information on the hostage situation to the Mossad agents there.

They in turn relayed it to the Israeli 707-command center that was still parked in the hangar at Nairobi.

"We have just received word that Amin has returned to Entebbe," Giora informed Elon, translating the message relayed by the man with the headphones.

Giora didn't tell Elon that the information had come from Mutiba, but the look on Elon's face showed that he suspected it had.

"It appears the terrorists don't intend to move the hostages, which is fortunate," Giora said. "Our biggest fear is to have the rescue team arrive and find them gone, like the Americans have when attempting to rescue their POWs in Viet Nam."

"What is it you expect Mutiba to do during the operation?" Elon asked worriedly. "And doesn't it bother you that he could get caught up in it?"

"He has been advised to stay away from the hostages and, if possible, to see that the premises are not lit. He has been informed that 'the leopard hunts best in darkness.'"

Giora's forced nonchalance did little to ease Elon's fears.

"It seems that many of the hostages are ill, perhaps from eating spoiled meat. The orthodox Jews, who didn't eat the meat, have not been affected. There are ten terrorists, including the two Germans, guarding the hostages," Giora explained before turning his attention to the moving blips on the radar screen, four of which were the C-130 Hercules transport planes carrying the Israeli commandos and equipment.

"It's not too late for you to bail out," Giora said, turning back to Elon.

"I'm staying. I just hope it's not too late for Mutiba and his family," Elon replied.

Ignoring the warning of the Israeli intelligence agents, Mutiba returned to the hostages. Many of the people were vomiting and had severe attacks of diarrhea. The toilets were still clogged and there was no running water. In spite of the overwhelming stench,

Mutiba was compelled to help in any way he could. He was one of the servicemen who brought the captives clean water to drink.

By now Mutiba was familiar with the faces of all the hostages. He knew there were 104 captives—including 34 women and 11 children. He was concerned when an elderly woman choked on some food during the evening meal and was taken to the hospital in Kampala. Throughout the week, the woman's son had been the one to interpret Amin's speeches to the Hebrew-speaking hostages. Amin had referred to the man as his "translator."

Mutiba felt it was important to relay the information regarding the elderly woman to the Israeli intelligence. But this time, as he drove toward the town of Entebbe, he saw that he was being followed. His heart pounding with fear, Mutiba realized he hadn't been careful when making the call a few hours earlier.

Bypassing the phone booth, Mutiba drove to a nightclub where he ordered a glass of whiskey. The airman soon entered with a friend. They sat at a nearby table, observing Mutiba. With his drink in hand, Mutiba went and greeted them warmly.

"May I buy you a drink?" he offered.

The two men appeared uncomfortable, but they nodded their consent. Mutiba ordered a bottle of whiskey for them to share, and encouraged the men to drink up. Three young women approached, asking them to dance. Mutiba refused, but he insisted that the airman and his friend take the women up on their offer. When they were gone, Mutiba refilled their glasses.

Brushing off the attentions of one of the young women, Mutiba pretended to be preoccupied with getting drunk. Which wasn't easy, considering he wasn't a drinker. When the others weren't looking, Mutiba emptied his glass into the pot of a nearby plant.

After a few hours of feigned revelry, Mutiba was able to slip away from the two men. His head spinning from what little alcohol he had consumed, he forgot about making the phone call and instead drove to the control tower at the new airport.

The leopard hunts best in darkness; Mutiba remembered what the Mossad agent had told him. He knew it meant he should try to see that the airport wasn't lit when the rescue team arrived.

"'The leopard hunts best in darkness,'" Mutiba repeated quietly as he remained in the jeep. Closing his eyes against the nausea from the alcohol, he drifted off to sleep.

Hours later, as lightning pierced the night and a soft sheet of rain began to fall, Mutiba woke with a start—not so much from what he heard, as from what he sensed. He felt as though he was dreaming when he vaguely saw the huge Israeli Hercules C-130 drop down for an assault landing.

Inside the cavernous belly of the Hippo, as the Hercules were nicknamed, thirty-year-old Yoni Netanyahu and his men heard their craft fall out of the air with what sounded like a shriek of twisted metal. With dark curly hair and boyishly-handsome features, Yoni's face and hands were now blackened with make-up, as were those of some of his commandos. They also had on black blouses similar to those worn by Idi Amin's bodyguards.

From where Mutiba remained sitting in the jeep, all he heard was a soft squeal from the Hippo's under-inflated tires as it dropped onto the runway. With the pilot deftly maneuvering the controls instead of loudly reversing the engines, Mutiba watched in awe as the Hercules pathfinder almost soundlessly checked its speed after landing. Glancing at his watch, Mutiba saw that the time was exactly 2400 hours.

Circling five miles above Lake Victoria in the El Al 707, Elon and the others onboard the Israeli command center listened intently to open radio mikes as the rescue mission unfolded. The transmission was being relayed by way of microphones worn by some of the commandos; and was beamed over a secret channel to Tel Aviv, as well as to the airborne command center. The information was being broadcast in Hebrew.

"The airport is fully lit," Giora worriedly translated for Elon. "They could be flying into a trap."

On the ground at Entebbe, Mutiba realized with a jolt that the runway was illuminated. Grabbing his rifle, he ran through the light rain toward the control tower at the new airport.

As the Hercules pathfinder continued to slow down, some Israeli commandos jumped out and positioned emergency beacons next to the runway. Before the craft had come to a complete stop, the rear ramp opened and a black Mercedes carrying Yoni and some of his men rolled off and drove away from the Hippo. It was followed closely by two Land Rovers, also filled with Yoni's men.

With Ugandan flags flying from the Mercedes, the three vehicles headed down the connecting road to the old terminal with their lights on at a steady 40-miles-per-hour, a speed consistent with that of an officer's entourage. As they approached the tarmac apron in front of the building, two Ugandan guards aimed their rifles and shouted for them to halt. Yoni and his men slowed their vehicles as if to stop. When the guards were in range, Yoni ordered his men to shoot. The Israelis opened fire with Berettas fitted with silencers. One of the Ugandan guards died instantly, but the other fell backwards and started shooting before being mowed down by the Israelis.

Inside the flying Israeli 707-command center, Elon and the Israelis heard the shots from the Ugandan guard's rifle. They knew from the radio transmissions that the commandos hadn't yet reached the hostages, and they feared the element of surprise had been compromised.

Yoni and his men drove toward the old terminal at full speed. When they approached, several Ugandan soldiers and one of the Palestinian terrorists were milling around outside. They appeared to be confused by the sounds of the guard's gunshots.

The Mercedes and Land Rovers stopped at the control tower adjacent to the old terminal. When Yoni and his men jumped out of the vehicles and began to attack, the terrorist who had been outside ran into the building yelling, "The Ugandans have gone nuts—they're shooting at us!"

The German terrorist, Wilfried Bose, turned with a look of bewilderment and slowly lifted his rifle. Before he could fire, Israeli bullets from a pistol fitted with a silencer cut him down.

Pacing near the entrance to the building, with a gun in one hand and a grenade in the other, Gabriele Kroche-Tiedemann momentarily seemed at a loss as Bose fell. From a few yards away, an Israeli commando emptied the entire clip from his Uzi into her body. Other commandos stepped over her mangled corpse as they burst into the lounge. Outside, Yoni and his men wiped the black make-up from their hands and faces and tore off their black shirts.

Inside the 707-command center, Elon and the others heard what sounded like all hell breaking loose. Hebrew shouts of "Tiskavu," and "Lie down!" "On the floor!" "Down!" could be heard over the microphones, accompanied by rapid gunfire.

Reaching the control room at the new airport tower, Mutiba surprised the two men manning it. Before they knew what hit them, he knocked them unconscious with the butt of his rifle. At the control panel, Mutiba glanced out at the rain-shrouded runway just as the second Hippo touched down. He switched off the lights, and the airport was plunged into darkness. After binding and gagging the controllers, Mutiba raced from the tower.

Most of the hostages froze where they were when the Israeli commandos burst in through the windows and door. Two Palestinian terrorists inside the lounge area opened fire. Yoni's men sprayed them with a hail of bullets. The hostages piled on top of one another to get away from the bullets and flying glass from the shattered windows. Some of them fled toward the restrooms. Screams of alarm and cries of "Sh'ma Yisrael!" echoed through the building.

A fifty-six-year-old Israeli woman was hit by a terrorist's bullet. Blankets caught on fire and the lounge filled with smoke as pieces of mortar fell from the ceiling. A young girl rose to her knees and was wounded. Caught in a hailstorm of friendly fire from an Israeli Uzi, nineteen-year-old Jean-Jacques Maimoni, referred to by the other hostages as "the barman," died instantly. His surrogate father, Pasko Cohen, the survivor of a Nazi death camp, was fatally wounded as he tried to reach his young friend.

The shooting in the old terminal building lasted less than two minutes. Combing the upper floors, Yoni's men found two armed Palestinian terrorists hiding under a mattress in one of the restrooms. The men quickly surrendered; but as they came toward the Israelis, one of the terrorists was seen to have a grenade in his hand. Both men were immediately fired on before the grenade could be detonated. Their bodies, and that of another terrorist found hiding upstairs, were dragged downstairs and laid next to those of their fallen comrades'. All were photographed and fingerprinted by the Israelis.

Arriving on the scene, Mutiba parked at a safe distance. Leaving his vehicle, he watched undetected as the hostages were rushed from the building and directed into the first Hippo, which had swung around to receive them. The wounded were loaded onto the second Hippo, which contained medical equipment and operating tables. The Israeli doctors and orderlies onboard the second craft quickly got to work.

Israeli half-tracks and jeeps, armed with recoilless weapons, raced toward the outer defense area of the airport. President Amin's residence was less than a mile away. The Israeli commandos expected Ugandan and Palestinian reinforcements to arrive on the scene at any moment with Russian-made tanks and infantry carriers. But they only encountered a squadron of confused Ugandan troops riding in light trucks, which the commandos quickly dispatched.

Turning his attention to the front of the old terminal building as a rain of automatic fire burst out of the adjacent control tower, Mutiba saw one of the Israelis falter.

The cryptic Hebrew heard over the microphones in the 707-command center now mentioned Yoni's name. "Yoni's been hit," Giora explained quietly to Elon, his stoic expression masking his gut-wrenching fear.

Struck in the back by a bullet, Yoni tried to remain standing before he passed out. His second-in-command immediately took over. Some of Yoni's men directed Bazooka shells and Uzis at the tower, quickly silencing the hostile fire.

Mutiba heard an Israeli man yelling something about his mother. Mutiba recognized him as Amin's "translator," whose elderly mother had been taken to the hospital in Kampala. In their haste, the commandos didn't try to understand what the man was saying. *It's just as well,* Mutiba thought, *since there's nothing anyone can do.* He knew the poor woman's fate was sealed—that she would never get out of Uganda alive.

Inside the terminal, the Israelis made one last sweep of the building. The bodies of seven terrorists now lay side-by-side in the lounge area. The Ugandan soldiers and airmen who had been killed in the assault remained where they had fallen.

Mutiba stayed hidden as the Israelis and their vehicles returned to the two Hippos. When the craft carrying the wounded took off, he marveled at how quiet it was. Mutiba watched as the Israeli commander, Brigadier General Dan Shomron, his Uzi aimed in front of him, walked backwards onto the remaining Hippo. As the ramp began to creak shut, Mutiba made his way toward the craft. He stopped and gave Shomron a sharp salute.

Shomron directed his weapon at Mutiba. Seeing that the tall Ugandan was unarmed, Shomron lowered his Uzi and returned Mutiba's salute. Mutiba remained saluting as the hydraulic pistons hissed and the Hippo began to shudder when its turboprops picked up speed after the ramp had closed.

Mutiba stood in the light rain as a shaft of lightning flickered within the clouds, which parted briefly to reveal a pale, crescent-shaped moon. He watched fearfully as the Hippo carrying Shomron, his men, and the uninjured hostages, veered off the runway—getting its portside wheels stuck in the mud. Loaded to full capacity, the craft slid precariously on the slippery ground. The pilot pushed the throttles wide and wrenched the Hippo back onto the tarmac, losing precious distance for take-off. Lake Victoria was straight ahead.

The pilot quickly switched to the emergency procedure for maximum effort take-off: he stood on the brakes and poured on the power. The nose of the plane went down. Applying full throttle, he released the brake. The nose came up and the massive machine lunged forward. At the end of the runway, the Hippo rose toward the sky at an incredible 45-degree-angle. Mutiba slowly exhaled. He'd been holding his breath, fearing that after all they'd been through, the hostages and their rescuers would perish in a watery grave.

With two of the four Hercules safely away, Mutiba turned his attention beyond a small hill to where he could see fires burning at the new airport. As explosions rocked the night, Mutiba realized the Russian-built Migs were going up in flames. From the direction of some of the fires, he could tell that the control tower and radar station at the new airport had also been hit. Hearing continued gunfire, Mutiba knew some Israeli commandos were still at work.

In the El Al 707 circling above Lake Victoria, sounds of the ongoing destruction could be heard over the open microphones.

Giora checked his watch. "The hostages have been rescued in considerably less time than anticipated," he said, shaking his head with disbelief. "But the last two Hercules are still on the ground at the new airport," he added worriedly.

Over the airwaves, the voices of the Hercules pilots could be heard speaking in Hebrew. Elon detected the word "Jumbo"—along with the mention of Yoni's name.

"They have decided to refuel at Nairobi," Giora told Elon with a grave expression. "Excuse me," he said before making his way toward the back of the plane.

Elon knew by the looks on the other Israelis' faces that Giora's friend Yoni was dead. Elon recalled what Giora had told him about the young man of the sword and the Bible . . . the fighter who had the heart of a poet.

Closing his eyes, Elon lowered his head with sadness and exhaustion. As the 707 turned back toward Nairobi, he thought about Rika and Ani, no doubt asleep at the home of Rika's parents in Holland. Elon longed to be with them . . . to feel Rika's soft, warm body against his own . . . to listen to her rhythmic breathing as it lulled him to sleep. But first he knew he had to hold the Israelis to their promise of rescuing Mila, Harun, Rafi, . . . and Mutiba. Elon prayed that Mutiba would make it to Rose Inish safely—and in time.

Soaked from the light rain, and still standing on the runway watching the glow from the fires at the new airport, Mutiba heard vehicles approach. He turned to see a group of Ugandan military personnel rapidly approaching. The airman and his friend, whom Mutiba had entertained hours earlier, were in the lead vehicle.

Mutiba sprinted for his jeep, but he was spotted. As he sped away in the vehicle, the airman tried to block his way. Bullets whizzed past Mutiba's ears. He was concerned one would ignite the fuel he had stockpiled in the back of the jeep. Driving with the headlights off, he didn't see the bodies of the two Ugandan guards the Israelis had killed. Feeling sick when realizing what they were, Mutiba ran over them without slowing down.

Almost reaching the open gate leading out of the airport, Mutiba heard the bullet a fraction of a second before he felt it sear through his left shoulder. He almost lost control of his vehicle. Ahead he saw a squadron of Ugandan soldiers racing toward him. Turning on the jeep's headlights, he stopped to talk to them.

"The Israelis have blown up the old airport!" Mutiba yelled while glancing over his shoulder. The airman's vehicle was coming up fast.

"You need to hurry!" Mutiba told the soldiers as he continued on.

Confused by what Mutiba had told them, and distracted by the explosions and dense jet-fuel smoke that was settling over Entebbe, the soldiers didn't stop Mutiba from driving away. Turning off his headlights, he went a short distance before pulling off the road into a grove of banana trees. The airman and his friend soon sped past.

Mutiba concentrated on slowing his breathing as he felt the wound in his shoulder. The bullet had gone clean through without greatly affecting the mobility of his arm. It didn't seem to be bleeding too badly; and the pain was masked by the adrenaline coursing through his body.

Mutiba stuffed an oil-stained rag between the wound and his shirt before heading toward Rose Inish. He knew he had to hurry—that it would be just a matter of time before he was traced there.

He hadn't gone far on the road leading to Fort Portal when the airman's vehicle passed him, having turned back toward the airport. Recognizing Mutiba, the airman and his friend turned around so quickly that their jeep almost tipped over. Mutiba picked up speed, but the visibility was poor on the fog-shrouded road. Just as his pursuers were about to gain on him, their jeep sputtered and died as it ran out of gas. They cursed into the darkness as Mutiba disappeared from sight.

Elon stood beside a grim-faced Giora, who gazed at his dear friend Yoni's body lying inside the Hercules, which was now on the ground in Nairobi along with the other three Hippos. Studying the face of the brave commando leader, Elon was struck by how young Lieutenant Colonel Yehonatan Netanyahu appeared. And, in death, how peaceful-looking.

Dawn was breaking over the mist-shrouded Ruwenzori Mountains when Mutiba's vehicle sputtered out of gas. Weak and off-balanced, he got out and poured the last of the fuel that he had stockpiled into the tank, spilling much of it onto the ground. Before getting back in the jeep, Mutiba noticed the pool of blood on the seat where he'd been sitting.

Mila waited on the front veranda of Rose Inish with her and her sons' suitcases packed and Rafi standing protectively at her side. The big dog emitted a low growl when the jeep came to a stop in front of the house. Recognizing Mutiba, Rafi happily ran to greet him. Fear gripped Mila's heart at the sight of her eldest son, drenched in blood.

"Where's Harun?" Mutiba asked, ignoring Rafi's friendly greeting. He noticed Mila's stricken expression. "It's nothing," he tried to convince her of his wound.

But Mila knew otherwise as he rushed past her on his way inside the house.

"Bring everything to the barn, we'll wait there," Mutiba told Harun, who was on his way out with more bags.

Harun was also shocked by Mutiba's bloodied appearance. Grabbing some of the bags, Mutiba led the way toward the barn until Rafi started barking excitedly at the sound of an approaching vehicle.

"We need to get to the forest!" Mutiba yelled as he dropped the bags and grabbed his rifle from the jeep. He took hold of Mila and led her through the house.

"Leave those!" Mutiba shouted at Harun when he tried to bring some of the bags. "Come, Rafi!" he ordered.

Thinking it was a game, Rafi followed with his tail wagging as they raced through the house and out the back. Until they reached the edge of the forest, where Rafi refused to go any further.

"Come, Rafi!" Harun yelled.

But Rafi had been taught too well that the forest was off limits.

"Rafi, come!" Harun screamed as Mutiba took him by the arm and dragged him into the forest.

Shots rang out from the direction of the house as the airman and his friend caught sight of Mutiba.

Turning his attention to the intruders, Rafi rushed toward them with a menacing growl. Lunging in attack, he was caught in mid-air by a hail of bullets. His beautiful tawny coat was soon shredded to bloody ribbons.

"Rafi!" Harun wailed from the forest, knowing the gunshots meant the end of the magnificent dog.

Mutiba slapped Harun hard across the face. The boy fell silent as they hurried after Mila. They stopped when they reached a small clearing.

"The leopard," Mila whispered fearfully while trying to catch her breath. Although she hadn't seen the animal, she sensed that it was nearby.

Glancing into the trees, Mutiba caught sight of the tip of the leopard's tail as it twitched below one of the branches.

"Don't look up!" he ordered needlessly, as they all knew that looking into the animal's eyes could provoke an attack. Mutiba held his rifle ready while directing Mila and Harun to continue on.

The leopard snarled angrily as the people disappeared among the trees. Agitated from the sound of the gunshots, she was poised to strike. She watched as two other men entered the clearing. One stooped down and studied the ground. Hearing the leopard hiss, the man made the mistake of looking up into her eyes. Immediately the animal was upon him. The man fell backwards with a terrified scream as the leopard clamped her fangs into his head, puncturing his eye while ripping open his stomach with her hind claws.

A short distance away, Mila and her sons stopped abruptly when they heard the man's screams. They hit the ground when the cries were drowned out by rapid gunshots as the airman directed his weapon at the leopard—finishing off his friend in the process. With his rifle still poised to shoot, the airman looked around fearfully while retreating from the forest.

"They're gone," Harun whispered a few moments after the gunshots had ceased.

Mila crawled toward Mutiba and insisted that he allow her to inspect his wound. Even before looking at it, she knew it was fatal. For a long time Mila had suspected that her eldest son was one of the dark figures in her dream from years ago—one of the three shadowy figures that signified death. Christiaan had been the first. Now Mutiba.

"Harun, go back to the house and get—" she began, fighting the knowledge that Mutiba was beyond help.

"No," Mutiba cut her off in a weak voice. "It's not safe."

He was right, for in the distance they could hear the sound of exploding grenades as the airman angrily set about destroying Rose Inish.

"Come," Mutiba directed as he mustered what strength he had left to lead them deeper into the forest. Eventually he could go no further. Sitting with his back propped against a tree, Mutiba's eyes grew dim as he studied the morning sunlight filtering through the branches.

"Stop that," Mutiba told Harun weakly, seeing the tears streaming down the boy's face. "Rafi died bravely."

"It's not Rafi . . ." Harun choked on his words.

Mutiba slowly reached into his pocket and pulled out the envelope Elon had given him, which was now saturated with blood.

Removing the ring that had belonged to Elon's father, Mutiba placed it in Harun's palm.

"Take care of Mama," he told Harun softly before turning his attention to Mila. Handing her the blood-soaked money from the envelope, he looked into her stricken face.

"Tell Shauna . . ." Mutiba told her quietly as the tears filled his eyes, " . . . I loved her. I love you all . . ." he whispered before losing consciousness.

"Mutiba!" Harun sobbed, his voice echoing through the trees.

Mila gathered Mutiba in one arm, and Harun in the other. She rocked them both gently as the distant beat of helicopter blades traveled throughout the forest.

Harun looked hopefully to the sky, where he could barely see the craft through the canopy of trees. He directed his tear-streaked face toward Mila. She studied him momentarily before slowly shaking her head. Mila knew that the helicopter had come for them—but Mutiba had not yet taken his last breath, and she wasn't about to let him die alone. Nor would she risk losing Harun by letting him return to Rose Inish by himself.

"It's probably Amin's soldiers," Mila lied.

The hopefulness drained from Harun's face as he again surrendered to his grief in his mother's embrace.

Inside the helicopter, approaching Rose Inish from the west, Elon saw that it was burning. The Israelis had been good on their word to try to rescue Mutiba and his family, and they had allowed Elon to come with them. The mission involved the helicopter pilot and three Israeli commandos who had volunteered, as well as Giora and Zev. With the exception of Elon, they all wore camouflage and were armed with Uzi's.

Avoiding Entebbe, they had flown from Kenya to Tanzania, over Lake Victoria and into Rwanda. Flying low across the Zaire side of Lake Edward, they approached Rose Inish from over the Ruwenzori Mountains. Before setting down, they noticed the

Ugandan army vehicles that were leaving Fort Portal and headed in their direction.

Zev and the Israeli commandos hit the ground with their weapons ready. Elon and Giora ran to inspect the burning house and barn, looking for Mila and her sons. Even the cottages, Land Rover, and Mutiba's jeep had been set ablaze. At the back of the house they discovered Rafi's mangled remains.

"Rafi?" Giora asked sadly.

Elon nodded with a hardened expression before directing his attention toward the forest.

Protecting their back with his Uzi, Giora followed Elon into the forest where they discovered the bullet-riddled remains of the man and the leopard. Studying the ground, Elon could discern Mila and her sons' tracks. He followed them a short distance before stopping to inspect a shoulder-high branch with nearly dried blood on the leaves.

"Mila! Mutiba! Harun!" Elon called frantically.

"We don't have much time," Giora told him, remembering the Ugandan troops that were headed their way.

The calm was shattered by the sound of gunshots as the Ugandan soldiers, led by the airman, arrived on the scene and fired on the Israelis. But they were no match for Zev and the highly trained commandos, who within seconds dispatched the Ugandans.

Giora followed Elon deeper into the forest. "Maybe we can see them from the air," he suggested when Elon stopped again to study the ground.

Unable to further detect what direction Mila and her sons had gone, Elon reluctantly agreed. "Mila! Harun! Mutiba!" he called one more time.

When there was still no answer, they turned back. Elon took a moment to kneel at Christiaan's grave. As he absently pulled at the weeds that grew around the little cross, Giora studied him with compassion. Realizing the futility of his action, Elon straightened up. Taking one last look at Rose Inish as it continued to burn, he headed toward the helicopter, followed by Giora.

Elon stared blankly at the bodies of the dead Ugandan airman and soldiers before he and Giora got in the helicopter. Still poised for action, Zev and the commandos backed into the craft. As it lifted off the ground and veered over the smoke from the flames devouring Rose Inish, a larger contingent of soldiers could be seen racing toward them from Fort Portal.

The helicopter pilot made a series of low sweeps over the forest in the direction that Mila and her sons had taken. But it was impossible to see anything other than a thick blanket of trees. When they eventually gave up the search and retraced their route back to Nairobi, Elon suppressed his anguish over Rafi and Rose Inish . . . now that they were lost. But he fervently prayed that somehow Mila and her sons would survive—and that they would soon all be together again.

Deep in the forest, Mutiba died peacefully in his mother's loving embrace. As the helicopter circled out of sight, Mila quietly hummed a lullaby while the tears streamed down her face. When she could no longer deny his passing, Mila got on her knees and began digging his grave with her bare hands.

Harun regarded her with concern. "Mama," he told her softly, his face also streaked with tears. "Don't you remember Mutiba saying that, when he died, he wanted to be left in the bush like a Maasai warrior?"

Mila stopped digging. Closing her eyes, she slowly nodded. Harun was right . . . Mutiba had mentioned more times than once that, when his time came, he didn't want to be placed in a dark hole. He said he wanted to be laid with his face to the sky—to remain a part of Africa in the animals that devoured him.

As a Christian, it was difficult for Mila to honor her son's wish. But, as a loving mother, she knew that she must. She did so not only out of respect but because, although Mutiba's body had grown cold, Mila sensed his spirit hadn't gone far. Harun felt it too as he gently stretched his beloved brother's long, lean frame out on the ground where patches of sunlight played across his face.

Mila kissed her dear son one last time. Putting aside his tears, Harun took hold of Mutiba's rifle with one hand and enclosed his mother's hand in the other. And with that he became a man as he led her toward the mountains, and a harrowing, uncertain future.

Chapter 12

"We've barely been apart a day, but it seems like an eternity," Rika told Elon when he phoned her at her parents' home in Holland.

"I know," he responded from his room at the Nile Star Hotel in Nairobi. "I miss you both terribly," he admitted, his voice quivering. "How are you?"

"We're doing fine. Ani and her grandmamma are getting along fabulously."

"And your father?" Elon asked hesitantly.

"Were you able to get to Rose Inish?" Rika asked, avoiding his question.

"Yes. They weren't there," was all he told her.

There was a pause as they shared feelings of sadness and fear. They avoided any mention of the Israeli rescue of the Air France hostages.

"I love you," Rika stated tearfully.

"And I love you," Elon responded, the pain of missing her tearing at his heart. "I'll be arriving in Amsterdam tomorrow night at nine on Pan Am."

"Ani and I will be there."

"Give her a hug. Tell her I love her. I can't wait to hold you," Elon said as the tears welled in his eyes.

"Sleep well, my love," Rika told him softly before hanging up.

"Was that Elon?" Xandra asked, leading Ani by the hand as they entered the parlor where Rika had been speaking on the phone. They were accompanied by a pair of magnificent Leonbergers, Rafi's parents Hans and Gretchen.

Wiping away her tears, Rika nodded and held out her arms to Ani, who ran to her happily. "Your papa said to tell you he loves you very much. And that he'll be here tomorrow night."

"He is not welcome here!" Owen van Zaun exclaimed as he came into the room. Although not a large man in stature, he had an imposing air about him.

"Owen, please," Xandra begged her husband. "Ani, come, let's take Hans and Gretchen for a walk," she suggested, hoping to spare the child from witnessing her grandfather's wrath.

The dogs barked their approval as Ani again took hold of her grandmother's hand, skipping happily at her side as they left. Rika and Owen remained in the room.

Hearing the front door close, Owen unleashed his anger and condemnation at Rika. "I will not have that adulterer in this house!" he seethed with indignation.

"Then Ani and I will be leaving," Rika responded in a controlled voice.

"How?" he demanded.

"We have money."

"From where? The Nazi friend of that man's sister?" Owen hissed.

"I don't know what you're talking about. And I don't care. But 'that man' happens to be the father of my daughter—your granddaughter. And tomorrow I intend to speak with a solicitor about legally putting an end to the travesty that was my marriage to Lee. God knows it was far from what a marriage should be."

"How dare you mention God's name!" Owen raged. "You seem to have forgotten all that you had been taught about God's will! You have become as undisciplined as your child, who has been brought up in a heathen land! You are nothing more than an animal living by its basest nature!"

"No!" Rika yelled back—for the first time in her life standing up to her overbearing father. "It is *you* who act like an animal! No, not even an animal! Animals can at least feel and give love!" she added, thinking of Rafi. "But you—! You don't know how to love! You have no idea what it means to—! You are nothing but a cruel, self-righteous, pathetic man!"

Owen slapped her hard across the face. Stunned, Rika held her hand to her cheek. As she ran from the room, Owen remained rooted to the floor until the strength drained from his body and he sank wearily onto a chair.

Sleep well, my love, Elon repeated Rika's words in his mind. But he couldn't sleep. Staring at the ceiling in his room at the Nile Star, Elon's mind was flooded with thoughts of Mila, Mutiba, and Harun . . . of Rose Inish burning and Rafi's mangled, bloody remains.

"We'll do everything possible to find them," Giora assured Elon as Zev drove them to the airport the following morning. "It would help if we had a photo."

Elon removed a photograph from his wallet. It showed Mila and her sons with Rika, Ani, and Rafi, celebrating Ani's third birthday. Elon handed it to Giora.

"Shalom," Giora told him solemnly when Elon got out of the car at the airport. "We can never thank you enough."

"Giora. Zev," Elon nodded his goodbyes.

Zev's stoic expression softened slightly as he acknowledged Elon with a nod.

Giora knew how difficult it was for Elon to leave without knowing what had become of his friends. But news of the ninety-minute raid on Entebbe had hit the world with both amazement and controversy; and it wasn't safe for Elon to remain in Africa. Glancing at the photograph Elon had given him, Giora shook his head sadly.

Inside the terminal, Elon bought a newspaper at the gift shop. Seeing a stuffed toy lion, he impulsively bought it for Ani. On the way to the departure gate Elon read the newspaper account of the motion set before the United Nation's Security Council to debate

"Israel's flagrant violation of Uganda's sovereignty"—according to Uganda and its Palestinian and Russian allies, the article noted.

Elon shook his head as he thought about the UN's anti-Israeli bloc and its latest effort to condemn that nation. He remembered what Giora had said about the Soviet Union's "stopwatch" tactic used during the Yom Kippur War.

The paper's pro-Israeli article went on to point out that, in the nine years since the Six-Day War, almost every United Nations resolution condemning the Jewish State had passed. Except in the Security Council, where the United States' veto alone prevented them from doing so. Elon appreciated the comparison the newspaper article made between Israel and the U.S.—and how appropriate it was that the raid at Entebbe took place on the 200th anniversary of America's independence.

Elon read with dismay that one of the hostages, a 75-year-old woman, had been left behind in Uganda. Although the Ugandans claimed she had rejoined the others prior to the raid, her whereabouts were unknown and it was suspected that she'd been murdered. Sickened by the thought of the defenseless woman being left in the hands of an irate Idi Amin and his henchmen, Elon heard the announcement for the departure of his flight. He left the paper behind before boarding.

Clutching the toy lion as the plane gained altitude after take-off, Elon closed his eyes as he leaned his head against the seat. He forced his mind to focus on the happy memories of the past four years—all of which centered on Rika.

Elon recalled the first time he saw Rika smile. Not the robotic smile that masked her pain, but the smile that was reflected in her eyes. It had been on the drive to Rose Inish the day after they'd met. Elon remembered their first kiss, overlooking Murchison Falls. And the first time they made love . . . their bodies coming together in the most natural, overwhelmingly beautiful and spiritual way.

Elon visualized Rika in the tender moments of motherhood, with both Ani and little Christiaan. Against his will, the memory of the lost child cast a gloom over Elon's thoughts and he recalled the sight of Rose Inish being devoured by flames. An image of Rika, standing in the center of the fiery destruction with Christiaan in her arms and Rafi at her side, flashed into Elon's mind. Rika's face was calm and loving as she mouthed the words: *Sleep well, my love.*

Elon's eyes sprang open as he sat up with a jolt. *God, no!* he prayed as he broke out in a sweat.

As the hours dragged on throughout the flight, Elon chided himself for agonizing over the unknown. *You're acting just like Mila,* he told himself. *Just like Mila!* he fearfully realized. *No, God, please! Don't let it be true!* he silently screamed.

Elon's anxiety remained constant. It intensified when he arrived in Amsterdam and saw that Rika and Ani weren't there to meet him.

"Are you Elon O'Shay?" Franz asked, noticing Elon scanning the people who were waiting for the arrival of the Pan Am passengers.

Elon studied the handsome blonde stranger. Seeing the sadness reflected in Franz' eyes, Elon's heart sank even further. He could only manage to nod.

"I'm Franz Kessler, a friend of Shauna's," Franz introduced himself sadly as they shook hands. "Shauna and Xandra are waiting for us outside. Do you have any more items than this?" he asked, attempting to help Elon with his bag.

Elon shook his head as he refused Franz' help. Feeling the need to hold onto something, Elon held fast to his bag while clutching the toy lion. Wordlessly, he followed Franz to a taxi parked in front of the terminal. Shauna and Xandra were waiting inside. Elon could tell from their tearful expressions that something terrible had happened. He wanted desperately to run. But Franz directed him inside the vehicle where he sat in the seat facing the two women. Franz sat next to Shauna as Xandra gave the driver their destination in Dutch. Elon studied Rika's mother, who appeared even more fragile than he had remembered.

As they pulled away from the airport, Shauna looked into Elon's searching eyes. "Rika is dead," she tearfully confirmed his dreadful premonition.

Although her words hit Elon like a bomb, he showed no outward emotion. Turning his head away, he stared out the window.

"How?" he eventually asked in a distant voice. "When?"

Knowing how difficult it would be for the women to answer, Franz quietly responded. "This morning. She was killed instantly by a motorist . . . an American draft-dodger who was high on marijuana. Xandra notified Shauna and me in Austria, and we have just now arrived as well."

Franz didn't tell Elon that Rika had been in Amsterdam to see a lawyer concerning the dissolution of her marriage to Lee Parnell. He didn't want Elon to feel that he might in any way be responsible for Rika's death.

"Ani?" Elon asked hesitantly, still gazing out the window.

"She's fine," Shauna assured him while quietly weeping. "She had stayed with her grandparents . . . She's with her grandfather now."

Elon could barely make out the lights of Amsterdam as they traveled across the flat terrain toward Holyport. He felt both suffocated and strangely comforted by the night. *Sleep well, my love,* Elon remembered Rika's final words to him. *How can I ever sleep peacefully again?!* his mind screamed.

As Shauna regarded her brother with anguish, her tears cut through Franz' heart. When Franz enclosed her in his arms, she buried her face in his loving embrace. Elon and Xandra remained lost in their private grief as the taxi continued on, eventually coming to a stop at the van Zaun home.

From the light of a streetlamp, Elon saw that the house was located next to a church with a small graveyard separating the two. Built of pale stone, the church looked cold and forlorn. The wood-framed, bluish-gray house appeared only slightly warmer, with a single dim light showing through one of the curtained windows.

Franz paid the driver before helping the women out of the taxi. He continued his hold on them as they made their way inside the house. Clutching his bag in one hand and the toy lion in the other, Elon followed in a daze. They all froze when entering the dimly lit parlor where Ani sat rigid in fear, with Hans and Gretchen lying at her feet.

The child was practically swallowed by the chair she was sitting in. She looked like a little porcelain doll in the dress Xandra had put on her prior to leaving for the airport. Ani's eyes were swollen from earlier tears, and her hair had been cut—her beautiful, long golden hair had been savagely cropped around her neck. Her eyes wide with disbelief, she focused on her father.

"Papa?" Ani asked hesitantly, as if fearful of speaking.

Dropping his bag and the toy lion, Elon rushed to her. He swept her in his arms, holding her close while stroking her hair with concern.

"He cut my hair!" Ani whimpered as she glanced toward a corner of the room.

Elon followed her gaze to where he could barely make out Owen van Zaun, sitting in the shadows.

"Why won't Mama wake up?" Ani asked sadly.

Elon's eyes turned to where she was looking.

"Oh, my God!" Shauna exclaimed as she, Franz, and Elon simultaneously noticed Rika's body, clothed in a flowing white gown, lying on a table against the far wall.

Xandra quickly took Ani from Elon's grasp and carried her out of the room, with the dogs following closely.

"You monster!" Shauna yelled at Owen. Picking up the toy lion Elon had dropped, she followed after Xandra.

Franz remained in the room as Elon slowly made his way to where Rika's body lay. The trauma that had killed her hadn't marred her beautiful features. Running his fingers over her pale blonde hair, Elon then gently stroked her cheek.

Franz' eyes misted with tears as Elon gathered Rika's body into his arms and carried it to the chair where Ani had been sitting. Elon held it tight, staring blankly into space. Unable to watch any longer, Franz turned to go. From where he sat in the shadows, Owen regarded Elon's suffering with a glaring look of hatred.

Elon held Rika's body throughout the night. He did not sleep, nor did he cry. He also didn't notice when Owen left. In the morning, it was only at Shauna's gentle prodding that Elon placed Rika's body back on the table and allowed himself to be led from the room to dress for the funeral.

Rika's body was placed in a simple coffin. A young vicar delivered a short yet heart-felt eulogy at the gravesite, located between the church and the home she had grown up in. The news of Rika van Zaun's death had spread quickly throughout the tiny canal-laced community; and practically all the residents came to pay their last respects to the lovely, quiet child who had blossomed into a beautiful woman. The flowers brought by the mourners soon overran the floral arrangements Franz had ordered.

Little Ani, her butchered hair trimmed somewhat neater by Shauna, clung to her father with one arm wrapped around his neck. In the other arm she held the toy lion. Shauna stood at Elon's side with her arm intertwined with Xandra's. Franz stood behind the women with his hands resting on their shoulders. Hans and Gretchen lay quietly at Xandra's feet. Owen van Zaun was not in attendance at the burial of his only child.

Xandra managed to hold back her tears throughout the brief ceremony. But when a clear soprano voice began to softly sing *Amazing Grace,* with the congregation joining in, she could no longer remain strong. Shauna and Franz were already reduced to tears.

Ani regarded the others with concern, not understanding what was happening. She seemed comforted by the fact that her father showed no outward emotion.

Inside the darkened parlor of the van Zaun home, Owen heard the beautiful chorus paying their last respects to his daughter. Against his will, the tears found their way through his hardened heart and down his cheeks. Rika was dead—*lost forever in the depths of hell!* he grieved. But it wasn't too late to save his granddaughter. He had already set in motion the means to do so.

When the singing came to an end and the townspeople quietly disbursed, only the family remained at the gravesite. Xandra softly kissed the tips of her gloved fingers and then transferred the kiss to the coffin. Shauna gently took Ani from Elon's grasp before Franz guided her and Xandra toward the house, with the dogs at their heels.

Elon remained alone at the gravesite, staring absently at the flower-draped coffin. He didn't move until a police vehicle pulled up to the house. Two constables got out and knocked at the front door. Owen let them in.

"What do you mean you're not letting us take her?" Shauna angrily demanded of Owen as Elon entered the house. Shauna handed Ani to Xandra, who quickly carried the child from the room, followed by the dogs.

"You have no right—" Shauna turned back toward Owen.

"I have every right in the world!" Owen bellowed.

Shauna looked at Elon with fire in her eyes. "You're her father! Say something!"

"He was not married to my daughter!" Owen raged. "He has no home to give my granddaughter! And it is because of him that the child's mother is dead!"

Shauna and Franz turned worriedly toward Elon, who seemed unaffected by what was happening. The constables appeared uncomfortable witnessing the domestic dispute.

"Ani and Elon most certainly *do* have a home," Franz stated adamantly when seeing Elon was unable to respond. "With Shauna and me in Austria," he explained, placing his arm around Shauna. "We are to be married soon," he added, anticipating Owen's objection.

Shauna glanced at Franz with surprise.

"Unless you can prove in a court of law," Franz continued addressing Owen, "that it is in the best interest of the child to take her from her father and the secure home we can provide for them, you will not succeed in keeping her. Bear in mind that we will fight you with every financial means we have—which I warn you are almost inexhaustible."

"How dare you threaten me, you Nazi bastard!" Owen shot back. "Do you think I don't know how your family acquired their wealth? By draining the bank accounts of the accursed Jews as they were being slaughtered! Get out of my home! All of you! But the child remains!"

"No!" Xandra boomed as she returned to the room alone.

Everyone turned toward her with shocked expressions.

"You may go," Xandra told the constables. "This is a family matter. Thank you for your time," she added, motioning them toward the door.

"They are not to leave!" Owen attempted to overpower his wife.

"Shut-up!" she turned on him furiously.

Reacting as though he'd been punched in the stomach, Owen sank onto a chair.

"This way," Xandra told the constables firmly.

The two men seemed eager to go as they followed Xandra to the door.

"Leave us," Xandra requested of everyone except Owen when she returned to the parlor. "Get your things together—and Ani's, too," she directed. "I'll meet you outside."

When she and Owen were alone in the room, Xandra knelt at his feet. "I love you very much," she told him softly. "But you are wrong to try and separate that child from her father. We had our chance to be parents, and we raised a beautiful, caring daughter who was very fortunate to find a man who loved her so completely. Elon is a good man . . . and a good father. Rika loved him dearly. We could not have hoped for a better father for our grandchild."

Gazing into his wife's loving eyes, Owen asked himself how he deserved such a compassionate woman. "I had tried to be a good father," he stated sadly.

"You were a good father," she assured him. "Because at heart you are a good man. I know it hasn't been easy for you, with the example set by your own father . . . and his father before him. But it's time to let go of their expectations."

She smiled gently as tears misted Owen's eyes. "I've often felt that you and I grew up knowing two different Gods," she continued softly. "You were taught the God of law, and I was taught the God of forgiveness. For too long now I have allowed your God to dictate our lives—but no longer. No more anger and judgment. We must find peace within ourselves. And we must make peace with our loved ones."

"I want my daughter back," Owen quietly wept.

"I know," she whispered, cradling his head to her breast.

He clung to her desperately as his body shook with sobs. When he had cried himself out, Xandra caressed his weary face, drying his tears with her gentle kisses. She left him with his sorrow as she went to say goodbye to Ani and the others.

Outside, Elon stood beside a taxi, holding Ani's toy lion as she petted the dogs. He stared blankly at Rika's flower-draped coffin, in the nearby cemetery. Shauna and Franz were seated inside the vehicle.

"Hans and Gretchen will miss you very much," Xandra told Ani lovingly as she hugged the child. "And your grandpapa and I will miss you very much, as well. But we hope you and your father, and your aunt and uncle, will come visit us often."

From inside the taxi, Franz looked into Xandra's eyes. She could see how much he'd been hurt by Owen's accusations.

"Please forgive my husband," she quietly asked of him.

Franz nodded vaguely, although he didn't feel the man needed to be forgiven for speaking what was probably the truth about the Kessler wealth—a truth that had haunted Franz ever since he was a boy and had first heard the rumors.

Xandra reached up and gently stroked Elon's cheek. "Please don't let Ani grow up being a stranger to Owen and me," she begged of him.

When Elon responded to the plea with just a blank stare, Shauna answered for him. "Don't worry, Xandra, we'll keep in touch," she assured her.

Xandra nodded gratefully as she kissed Shauna and Franz goodbye before directing Ani into the taxi. Still holding Ani's toy lion, Elon took one last look at Rika's coffin before joining the others inside the vehicle.

With the dogs at her side, Xandra watched sadly as the taxi drove out of sight. She then turned toward two men who had been waiting patiently by the church with shovels in their hands. When she nodded to them, they made their way toward the gravesite. Tears flowed down Xandra's face as the men removed the flowers from her daughter's coffin before gently lowering it into the ground and covering it with dirt.

Inside the taxi, headed for the airport where Franz' private jet waited to fly the group to Vienna, Shauna studied Franz thoughtfully.

"Thank you for what you said back there," she told him quietly. "But you needn't have gone so far as to offer to marry me for Ani's sake."

"It wasn't just for Ani," he admitted. "I've been wanting to ask you to marry me for a long time. But I don't suppose you could consider marrying a 'Nazi bastard,'" he added sadly, repeating Owen's accusation.

"You are no Nazi," she assured him lovingly. "Perhaps the question should be whether *you* could seriously consider marrying a 'cursed' Irish Jew," she smiled softly.

"Does that mean you would consent to be my wife?" Franz asked incredulously.

When Shauna nodded, Franz breathed a sigh of relief. Their lips came together in a soft, gentle kiss. Sitting on her father's lap in the seat facing them, Ani giggled at her aunt's and Franz' display of affection while covering her little eyes with the toy lion.

Gazing out the window, Elon studied the beautiful Dutch farmland dotted with windmills and intersected by canals. *Rika! Why couldn't we have experienced this together?* his heart screamed.

"Can we go home now and see Mama and Mimi and 'Arun and 'Tiba?" Ani asked her father innocently. "And Rafi?" she pleaded.

To stave off the tears, Elon bit his lip with such force that it began to bleed.

Chapter 13

Dressed in formal black slacks and a ruffled pale-peach dress shirt with the cuffs unfastened, Elon stood at a bedroom window in Franz' castle across from the picturesque town of Hallstatt. Glancing out over the lake, Elon imagined that he and Rika were in one of the small gondolas dotting the serene glacial water. As they glided slowly across the mirrored surface of the lake, she gazed at him with smiling eyes.

"Excuse me, sir," Johann addressed Elon from the other side of the door as he knocked lightly.

The vision of Rika vanished from Elon's mind. "Come in," he called while turning away from the window.

Also dressed formally, and looking quite dashing, Johann entered the room. "Herr Kessler asked me to bring these to you," he said as he handed Elon a small velvet box.

When Elon opened the box, his eyes widened at the sight of the sparkling diamond cufflinks.

"They are a gift from Herr Kessler," Johann explained.

"A gift? I can't accept—"

"Please, sir," Johann interrupted. "I have known Herr Kessler since he was born. There is nothing he likes more than to give to others. When Ursula and I were married, he was quite generous."

Elon removed the cufflinks from the box.

"Here, sir, allow me," Johann offered as he took them from Elon and attached them to his shirt.

"Thank you, Johann. Do me another favor?" Elon asked as Johann gave him a questioning look. "Drop the 'sir.' 'Elon' will do."

"Yes, sir—I mean, Elon," Johann smiled. "If you don't mind my saying so, it's a pity your parents could not have lived to see their daughter's wedding day."

"Our mother, perhaps," Elon admitted quietly. *And of course Mila, Mutiba, and Harun . . . and Rika,* he silently wished.

Not having the heart to tell Shauna what had happened at Rose Inish, Elon lied in telling her Mila and her sons were safe. He knew how much Shauna regretted that they wouldn't be there for her wedding. Elon and Shauna had also hoped Devin and Yvette could attend; but they were hesitant to leave Scotland and travel so soon following the incident at Entebbe.

After taking the tailed tuxedo jacket from the armoire and helping Elon into it, Johann stood back and nodded approvingly. "You look quite splendid," he smiled before checking his watch. "If you will excuse me, I must collect Fräulein Wilcox and her brother and his family at the station. Will there be anything else before I go?"

"No thank you, Johann," Elon replied as he straightened the cuffs on his shirt. "Oh, were the women successful in getting Ani into something formal?"

Johann nodded. "Ursula has made her a little tuxedo. But I must say it is sad that the child refuses to wear a dress."

Elon had learned how upset Ani had gotten when Shauna took her shopping for a dress to wear at the wedding. Realizing the child associated dresses with the trauma at her grandparents' home, Shauna hadn't forced the issue.

"I wish you could have seen Ani when her hair was long," Elon stated absently before Johann left.

Turning back to the window, Elon looked down at the activity on the castle grounds where Franz, looking strikingly handsome in his tuxedo and top hat, was seeing to it that everything was perfect. Franz had taken it upon himself, with Shauna's blessing, to plan every detail of their wedding. Everyone was amazed at how quickly, efficiently, and elegantly he'd pulled it all off. Franz had long dreamed of the perfect wedding, although marriage to a woman hadn't necessarily been part of his fantasy. But he loved Shauna dearly—more than he ever thought he could possibly love a woman.

Elon continued to watch from the window as the catering crew put the finishing touches on their preparations while Franz enthusiastically welcomed his guests, who began arriving in everything from gondolas to horse-drawn carriages.

In contrast to Franz' jubilant demeanor, Shauna sat sadly at the antique dressing table in her bedroom. Wearing just her slip, she studied her reflection in the ornate mirror as she slowly brushed her hair.

"What's wrong?" Ursula asked worriedly as she entered the room with Shauna's veil, which she spread gently across the massive antique bed.

"I was just thinking how much I wish Mila and her sons were here," Shauna responded sadly. "I've been so worried about them. But Elon says it's best not to even try and contact them . . . that they're safe at Rose Inish," she repeated the lie he'd told her.

"Auntie Shauna!" Ani exclaimed as she barged into the room accompanied by Tanya, who, like Ursula, wore the stylish pale-peach gown of a bridesmaid.

"My, don't you look pretty!" Shauna smiled as she placed the child on her lap, smothering her with kisses.

Ani feigned annoyance at her auntie's affections.

"Stand back and let me look at you," Shauna told Ani as she set her on her feet.

Twirling around on her tiptoes, Ani showed off her little peach-colored tuxedo. She'd made a concession to having a matching bow put in her hair, which had been trimmed by a professional stylist—yet another traumatic experience for the child.

"Oh, Ursula, you did such a splendid job on Ani's tuxedo!" Shauna raved. "Didn't she, Tanya?"

Tanya smiled and nodded. Now nineteen, she was still rather plump and extremely shy.

"What will people say when you walk down the aisle in *that*?" Ursula asked Shauna, studying her slip disapprovingly. "Come, you must get dressed!" she ordered.

With Tanya's help, Ursula secured Shauna into the wedding gown that had belonged to Franz' mother. A simply cut yet elegant original, it had needed only a few minor alterations to accommodate Shauna's svelte figure.

It was Shauna's idea to wear the dress. When Johann had mentioned how lovely Franz' mother had looked at her wedding—and Franz admitted off-handedly that he still had her dress—they were surprised when, after seeing it, Shauna asked if she could wear it. Franz told Shauna she didn't need to; that he'd understand if she preferred to have something new and of her own. But when Shauna insisted, saying it would be a way of representing his dear departed mother at their wedding, Franz cried with gratitude.

Another reason Shauna wanted to wear the dress was due to the fact that it had aged to a soft-ivory hue. She didn't feel comfortable wearing white. Not that she told anyone, of course.

With the exception of Mila, no one knew of the night Shauna and Mutiba had spent together. Not that Shauna in any way regretted it. Quite the contrary. It was just something that was so dear, so special that she didn't want to diminish it with words.

Besides, what could I say about it? Shauna asked herself before answering her own question: *That there was a boy whom I grew up with as a brother who became my first lover . . . for just one night . . . But it was the most wonderful night of my life!* Shauna forced the bittersweet memory from her mind.

"You look beautiful," Tanya told her softly after Ursula had fitted the pearl-trimmed veil on Shauna's head. "Doesn't your auntie look beautiful?" Tanya asked Ani as she knelt down to her level.

Ani nodded enthusiastically as she put her little arm around Tanya's neck. It was obvious the child felt safe and happy in the young woman's care.

When there was a soft knock at the door, Ursula opened it to Elon and Johann. The breath caught in Elon's throat, and tears misted his eyes when he saw Shauna in her wedding gown. Nodding his approval, he gave her a loving smile. Johann reacted with an appreciative whistle. Ursula smiled and wrapped her arm in her husband's as they left.

Ani ran from Tanya to Elon.

"Look how lovely you are!" he exclaimed while picking her up. The child giggled when he rubbed noses with her.

Tanya smiled at their display of affection. When Elon set Ani down, Tanya took her by the hand and led her from the room.

Elon offered Shauna his arm. "You are simply stunning," he told her as she laced her arm through his. "Ready?" he asked.

Taking a deep breath, Shauna nodded. She was grateful the veil prevented him from seeing the sadness in her eyes as they walked arm-in-arm down the ornately carved staircase, through the foyer, and toward the beautifully landscaped garden.

As the orchestra began playing the bridal theme, Ani threw multi-colored rose petals onto the pathway. Harry and Lisl's three-year-old son, Fredrick, carried the rings on a silk pillow. The three stylishly attired bridesmaids, Tanya, Lisl, and Vivian, followed after the children. Then came Ursula, who was Shauna's maid-of-honor.

Beneath a flower-woven canopy, Franz stood between an elderly Catholic priest and Johann, who was Franz' best man. Harry stood next to Johann, gazing at his former lover with longing. But Franz only had eyes for Shauna, who looked radiant as she walked toward him on her brother's arm.

While everyone focused on the bride, Vivian did a double take when seeing Elon for the first time in person. Just the sight of him practically gave her an orgasm. The plan Vivian had thought of years before, when she saw Elon's likeness in Shauna's photograph, again took shape in her mind. Vivian realized with a sly smile that part of her plan had been realized; for she had thought of getting Franz and Shauna together—if only as a cover for his and Harry's relationship, which Vivian was aware of. But Vivian hadn't bargained on Franz actually going so far as to marry Shauna.

Vivian's interest in Elon was more than simply sexual. Ever since Harry had married Lisl, Vivian's claim on Franz and his financial resources had cooled. She knew his marrying Shauna would further compromise her and Franz' relationship. So, as Vivian now set her sights on Elon—who was not only the most gorgeous man she'd ever seen, but who was about to become the brother-in-law to the most wealthy man she'd ever known—Vivian was determined to become a member of the O'Shay family. She smiled smugly when remembering the woman whom she assumed was Elon's wife had recently died. *But the child could be a problem,* Vivian thought as she glanced resentfully at Ani.

Delivering Shauna to Franz' side, Elon gently kissed her cheek after lifting the veil from her face. He then took his place as one of the groomsmen.

Elon didn't notice the way Vivian looked at him throughout the ceremony, as his attention had wandered to the pair of Lipizzans hitched to a gold-trimmed, white carriage. Both the carriage and the horses' harnesses were laced with flowers. Elon imagined that he saw Rika. Dressed in the flowing white gown she was buried in, she appeared from around the other side of the horses. Stroking the animals on their velvety noses, she gave Elon a loving smile. He smiled back.

When clapping erupted at the end of the brief ceremony, Elon's attention was drawn to Franz' and Shauna's lingering kiss. Looking back toward the horses, he noticed sadly that the image of Rika was no longer there.

"You must be the bride's brother," Vivian stated seductively as she not too subtly laid claim to Elon following the ceremony. "I'm Vivian Wilcox," she purred, offering her hand.

"Elon O'Shay," he introduced himself before softly brushing the back of her gloved hand with a kiss.

"Papa!" Ani ran to Elon, pushing Vivian away. "I'm hungry!" the child whined while tugging on his coattails.

Elon smiled as he picked her up. Vivian's dislike toward Ani flashed in her eyes, but she masked her feelings with a forced smile.

"Vivian, this is my daughter, Anika," Elon introduced them.

"Ani!" the child corrected, ignoring the woman. "I'm hungry!" she repeated, taking her father's face between her little hands and forcing him to look her in the eye.

Elon gave the child a loving laugh. "You'll excuse us?" he asked Vivian politely.

Vivian maintained her smiling facade. "Perhaps I could engage you in a dance later?" she inquired sweetly.

"Now, Papa!" Ani demanded, wanting him away from the woman.

"Perhaps," Elon responded absently to Vivian's offer before carrying Ani toward the tables laden with food.

Vivian's smile quickly vanished. "Boarding school," she muttered. "Nannies and boarding school!" she plotted as a way to deal with the spoiled and demanding child, once her designs on Elon had been realized.

Shauna's wedding day was a storybook event. As she danced with Franz, no one could have guessed that her heart yearned for the feel of another man's hands. Shauna had to remind herself why she had consented to marrying Franz. For one thing, Mutiba hadn't responded to any of the letters she'd written over the past three-and-a-half years since they'd been together. And the last words he had spoken to her, "We can never be," still echoed painfully in Shauna's mind.

Throughout the day, Vivian was relentless in her pursuit of Elon. She monopolized his time on the dance floor, and was standing by his side when Harry raised a toast to the bride and groom.

"Come, it's your sister's wedding!" Vivian encouraged Elon to drink when he barely sipped the champagne from his glass. "Just one won't hurt," she convinced him.

But one drink led to many, and Elon was pretty well plastered by the time Shauna and Franz bid their guests goodbye. In the flower-laced carriage, Johann drove the newlyweds to catch the last train to Vienna, from where they would travel to Trieste and board Franz' yacht for their Mediterranean honeymoon.

Remaining at the castle, Elon fantasized in an alcohol-induced haze that it was Rika whom he danced with, not Vivian. And in his mind it was Rika whom Elon made passionate love to that night, until falling into a drunken slumber.

As Elon lay beside her in her bed, Vivian admired his chiseled profile and well-endowed form. "Mr. and Mrs. Elon O'Shay," she plotted quietly as she ran her fingers over his naked body. She smiled when, in his sleep, Elon again became aroused by her touch.

"Mr. and Mrs. Elon O'Shay," Vivian repeated determinedly as she mounted him for another deliciously satisfying ride.

In his dream, Elon heard the gentle surf lapping on the shore at Lamu as he and Rika came together. He covered her sculpted body with gentle kisses. Clinging to her desperately, Elon fought against waking. But a child's voice roused him from his sleep.

"Tanya!" Ani called happily from outside. "Look, I'm flying!"

Turning his head toward the sound of his daughter's voice, Elon slowly opened his eyes. He quickly shut them against the morning light as the room spun around him.

"Look, Ursula!" Ani called. "We're dancing!"

Vivian groaned in her sleep and turned away from Elon's grasp. He managed to again open his eyes. Already nauseous, he became even more so when he focused on the naked woman sleeping beside him.

As quickly as possible in his hung-over state, Elon put on his slacks. Gathering up the rest of his clothes, he slipped out of the room. He barely made it to the bathroom in his own room before vomiting. Sitting on the cold marble floor while hugging the toilet, Elon felt both physically and emotionally drained. Eventually the sound of Ani's sweet laughter gave him the strength to drag himself up off the floor and go to the window.

Outside, Ani was being held secure in Johann's grasp as they sat astride one of the Lipizzans. On the manicured grounds, where just hours earlier Shauna and Franz' guests had partied, the horse indeed seemed to be dancing. The child squealed with delight as Johann eased the animal into its well-trained routine. Nearby, Ursula and Tanya laughed and clapped at Ani's enjoyment.

Elon turned away from the window to take a shower. As the steaming water flowed over his body, he closed his eyes against the bitter tears. By the time he dressed and joined Ani and the others outside, Elon felt clean—but far from being cleansed.

"Papa!" the child exclaimed happily. "Look, I'm flying!"

Elon smiled vaguely as Johann again put the horse through its paces.

"I should go see to breakfast," Ursula said. "You stay here with Ani," she insisted when Tanya started to follow.

"Are you sure?" the young woman asked with a hint of fear in her voice.

"Ya," Ursula responded before leaving.

Avoiding Elon's gaze, Tanya turned her attention back to Ani and Johann.

"I want to thank you for taking such good care of my daughter," Elon told her.

Glancing into his eyes, the color rose in Tanya's cheeks. She quickly looked away.

"Would you care to ride?" Johann asked Elon, halting the horse in front of him.

"It's been years since I've ridden," Elon admitted.

"You'll do fine," Johann said as he handed Ani down to him.

Elon set Ani on her feet. Tanya opened her arms to her, and the child went to her readily. When Elon eased into the saddle, the well-trained animal responded beautifully to his gentle touch.

"Breakfast is ready!" Ursula eventually called from the house.

"After you've eaten, perhaps you and Ani would care to go riding with me?" Johann suggested when Elon dismounted.

"Can we, Papa?" Ani begged.

"Perhaps," Elon responded as he patted the horse's neck before turning the reigns back over to Johann. Sweeping Ani onto his shoulders, she giggled happily as they headed toward the castle.

Genuinely touched by the loving relationship Elon shared with his daughter, Tanya smiled as she followed them inside.

"You won't be gone long, will you?" Vivian asked Elon with a pout when she joined everyone outside as he and Ani were about to ride off with Johann on the two Lipizzans.

Seeing that Elon had difficulty looking Vivian in the eye, Ursula and Johann exchanged a knowing glance. Tanya studied the ground with a look of discomfort.

"I was hoping we could go into Hallstatt," Vivian explained. "There's a darling little toy store there that I thought Ani might enjoy," she smiled, going over Elon's head.

"Toy store?" the child sounded interested. "Can we, Papa?"

"We'll see," Elon responded vaguely.

"You must be starved!" Ursula told Vivian as she directed the woman inside.

Tanya started to follow.

"Tanya, wait," Johann called to her.

She turned and gave him a questioning look.

"I just remembered something important that I need to tend to," Johann explained. "Why don't you take my place?" he asked, holding the reigns out to her.

"Me? Oh, no, I—" she backed away fearfully.

"Please, Tanya!" Ani begged. "Come with us!"

"Yes," Elon smiled his encouragement.

Gazing into his kind blue eyes, Tanya felt as though her knees would give out. Before she knew it, her uncle had helped her into the saddle. Wearing a lightweight dress, Tanya wasn't prepared to go riding. But Johann knew if they waited for her to change, the moment would be lost.

An accomplished rider, Tanya sat well in the saddle with her skirt tucked around her plump legs. She gave her uncle an accusatory glance, feeling she'd been conspired against.

Johann smiled as he turned Tanya's horse toward the nearby

forest. "No need to hurry back," he told Elon, who held Ani in front of him in the saddle.

"Can we go fast?" Ani begged her father as they followed after Tanya.

"I don't know. I can't ride as good as Tanya and her Uncle Johann," he admitted.

"You ride quite well," Tanya complimented him shyly.

"I see you've definitely inherited your uncle's talent."

"Before he came to work for the Kesslers, Uncle Johann was a trainer at the Spanish Riding School in Vienna," Tanya told him.

"Which do you prefer? Vienna or here?" Elon asked.

"Oh, here! Not because of the castle," Tanya quickly explained, "although it's quite beautiful. But this is what I enjoy best," she added while gesturing to their surroundings.

Elon nodded as he inhaled the crisp, pine-scented mountain air.

"Papa, look!" Ani exclaimed as she spied two deer grazing by the side of the trail.

"I see," Elon told the child softly. "Be real quiet so you don't scare them away."

"Don't worry, they're quite tame," Tanya smiled.

Meeting Elon's gaze, Tanya again quickly looked away—but not before Elon saw the fear in her eyes. He sensed that, sometime during her young life, Tanya had been terribly hurt by a man.

"If you would like, we can let the horses run now," she said, when the trail opened into a meadow.

"Perhaps it would be best if you took Ani," Elon suggested.

When Elon's hand brushed against hers as he transferred Ani onto her horse, Tanya felt as though lightning had passed through her body. Holding Ani tight while letting the horse have its head, the wind beating against Tanya's face did little to cool the fire in her cheeks.

"More!" Ani begged when they halted at the other side of the meadow.

Taking the lead as they galloped back across the meadow, for the first time since Rika's death, Elon felt exhilarated at being alive. The sense of exhilaration quickly vanished, however, when he saw Vivian waiting for them when they returned to the castle.

As Johann helped Ani down from Tanya's horse, Vivian's dislike for the young woman showed in her eyes. But she turned to Elon with a sickening-sweet smile.

"If you and Ani hurry and get cleaned up, we can have a nice lunch in Hallstatt," Vivian told him. She had difficulty hiding her contempt for the horses as she stepped aside when Johann led them toward the barn.

"Can Tanya come?" Ani begged her father.

Tanya appeared embarrassed by the child's request.

"Actually, that might not be a bad idea," Vivian responded, realizing the young woman could help divert some of Ani's attention away from Elon.

"I really don't care much for towns," Elon told Vivian in a flat tone.

"Nonsense," Vivian responded lightly as she hooked her arm in his, leading him inside. "Ani will love it!" she added. "I'll buy you any toy you want!" she turned to the child.

"Any?" Ani asked incredulously.

"Any," Vivian promised.

Against his wishes, Elon soon found himself gliding across the glacial lake with Vivian, Tanya, Ani, and Johann, who manned their small gondola.

"We'll have supper here, as well," Vivian told Johann when they reached the little dock at the other side of the lake. "Be back for us at nine."

Johann watched with a worried expression as Vivian led the others toward the little town of Hallstatt.

"Apparently Rome wasn't yet in existence when this region was already being mined for salt," Vivian informed Elon as they walked up a cobblestone alleyway leading to the town square.

As much as Elon hated to admit it, Vivian was right in thinking he would enjoy the historic little town with its mix of Roman, Gothic, and Baroque architecture; as well as all the flowers that adorned the little shops and pensions.

"Should we eat first? Or visit the toy store?" Vivian asked brightly, anticipating Ani's response.

"Toy store!" the child exclaimed.

"Follow me, then," Vivian told her with a forced smile as she led the way.

Although she gave Vivian a look of distrust, Tanya was appreciative of Ani's enthusiasm. Tanya sadly noticed, however, that Elon seemed lost in melancholy thoughts.

Vivian was good on her offer to buy Ani any toy she liked. The child eventually settled on a teddy bear that was practically as big as she was.

Leaving the toy store, Vivian took them to a little restaurant where they sat outside overlooking the lake. From where they had lunch, they could view Franz' castle on the opposite shore.

Vivian was quite pleased at how well their little excursion was going—although she was disappointed when she couldn't persuade Elon to join her in having a glass of wine with their meal. *But the day's only half-spent,* Vivian reminded herself. Time remained for her to use whatever means necessary to again lure him to her bed.

Following lunch, the group toured a little museum that highlighted the town's five thousand years of rich cultural history. With time to spare, and hoping to impress Elon with her *piety,* Vivian then took them to a small Catholic Church that clung to a rocky hillside. Once there, however, Tanya refused to enter and Ani wanted only to play outside with her teddy bear. Before Elon could balk, Vivian led him inside the ornate Gothic structure.

As they entered the little church, the constant pain of missing Rika became even more intense for Elon. When Vivian made a show of crossing herself and kneeling in prayer with her eyes closed, he slipped outside to the courtyard and made his way toward what he assumed was a wine cellar. Ducking through the entryway, Elon straightened up inside the small, vault-like room. When his eyes adjusted to the dim light, he recoiled in horror at the sight of the human skulls and bones stacked against the walls.

Unknowingly, Elon had entered the church's ossuary. He noticed most of the skulls had names and dates printed on them;

and some were even painted with flowers and other designs. Suddenly seized by the image of his beautiful Rika rotting in the ground, Elon fled from the ossuary and barely made it to the shelter of a nearby tree before throwing up. He remained with his head resting in his hands as his body shivered in the warm, gentle breeze.

"Are you all right?" Tanya asked worriedly in her soft, caring voice.

Playing nearby with her bear, Ani didn't notice her father's distress.

"Elon!" Vivian called from the church.

"I'm fine," Elon responded sharply to Tanya's question. Unable to tolerate the young woman's sympathy, he angrily brushed past her to collect Ani.

Elon's brusque manner and sharp tone left Tanya feeling as though the breath had been knocked out of her. Glancing toward the entrance to the ossuary, she guessed the reason for Elon's behavior. But Tanya was still terribly hurt—not only from the way he treated her, but because she sympathized with the anguish he obviously felt over the loss of Ani's mother.

Tears stung Tanya's eyes as she thought of the deep love Elon had, and probably always would have, for Rika. It was a degree of love that Tanya doubted she'd ever experience personally. Tanya was also terribly saddened from knowing she'd never be able to bear children of her own. And she was consumed with guilt . . . because she was the only one to blame for her misfortune.

Wiping away her tears, Tanya followed after the others. At dinner she looked on sadly when Elon no longer refused Vivian's insistence that he join her in a drink or two. It was difficult for Tanya to watch him drown his sorrows in alcohol.

"Tanya, take Ani back with you," Vivian directed when they'd finished eating. "Elon and I will be spending the night here."

Vivian's tone, and the fact that Ani had fallen asleep in Tanya's lap, kept the young woman from voicing an objection. As did Elon's drunkenness.

"Where are Elon and Vivian?" Johann asked worriedly when Tanya met him at the boat landing with Ani asleep in her arms.

"They're staying here," Tanya told him sadly.

With the help of a waiter, Vivian practically dragged Elon and the giant teddy bear into a room. When the waiter left after settling the drunken man into the bed, Vivian threw the bear on the floor and began undressing Elon. Admiring his nakedness, she smiled while removing her own clothes.

Drawing on her arsenal of tricks, Vivian set about servicing Elon. Covering his body with kisses while stroking him with the tips of her fingernails, she then closed her mouth around him.

Elon soon responded to Vivian's skilled maneuvers. When she mounted him, she continued to massage him while he was locked inside her. As if suddenly springing to life, Elon folded his arms forcefully around her and turned her on her back. To Vivian's total delight, Elon then became the aggressor.

Chapter 14

Shauna and Franz' honeymoon was as outwardly idyllic as their wedding had been. Cruising leisurely down the Adriatic Sea on their private yacht, they made numerous stops within the Grecian Isles.

To the casual observer, the newlyweds appeared very much in love as they toured the sights by day, and danced cheek to cheek in the evenings. But, as they lay in each other's arms at night, their dreams betrayed their union. For in Shauna's heart it was Mutiba who shared her bed. And for Franz, it was Harry.

When the honeymoon eventually came to an end and the couple returned to their home in Vienna, they were met by Elon, Ani, Tanya, . . . and Vivian. Johann and Ursula were still at the castle.

Elon's unkempt appearance and emotional remoteness were quite disturbing to Shauna; and she was far from pleased to see that Vivian had so obviously laid claim to him. Shauna was also shocked when, barely two months after having met, they announced their engagement. That is Vivian announced it. Elon simply stood at her side in an alcohol-induced haze.

"Do you really want to get married so soon after . . ." Shauna asked worriedly when she was able to talk to Elon alone one afternoon while strolling in the courtyard of her and Franz' home in Vienna.

"Vivian's pregnant," Elon admitted with downcast eyes.

Stopping abruptly, Shauna regarded him with alarm. "Are you sure it's yours?"

Elon simply stared at her.

"Assuming it is," Shauna said, "you don't have to marry her, you know."

They walked in silence for a while until Vivian joined them.

"There you are!" she told Elon. Slipping her arm possessively through his, she steered him away from Shauna. "I've made plans for us to have dinner with Harry and Lisl, who can help us plan our engagement party," she informed him cheerfully. "They'll be bringing Fredrick over so Tanya can keep an eye on him and Ani while we're out. You need to hurry and change," she added while checking her watch.

Shauna shook her head sadly as she watched Elon respond meekly to Vivian's commands. It was difficult for Shauna to accept their engagement and subsequent wedding, set for mid-December.

Three days before Elon and Vivian's engagement party, Shauna collapsed from an excruciating pain in the groin. Bleeding profusely, she was rushed to the hospital where it was discovered she'd suffered a ruptured fallopian tube from an ectopic pregnancy. The doctors managed to stop the hemorrhaging but, due to complications, Shauna would never be able to have children.

Franz was as devastated as Shauna. Although his position as a husband was somewhat tenuous, he had always wanted to be a father. Watching Harry interact lovingly with his son Frederick, Franz longed for a child of his own. It was the main reason he had decided to get married.

While everyone was extremely saddened by Shauna and Franz' loss, Tanya was especially sympathetic. On the night before the party, while Shauna was still in the hospital, Tanya quietly confided in her as to why she was also unable to have children.

"About a year before I met you . . ." Tanya began hesitantly, " . . . when I was fourteen . . . I was raped. More than once, by the same man." She took a deep breath before continuing. "I became pregnant. I knew I couldn't tell anyone, so I did what I'd heard could be done to . . . I took a knitting needle and I . . ." her voice became choked with emotion as the tears ran down her cheeks.

Shauna regarded her with shock.

"I nearly bled to death," Tanya continued softly, avoiding Shauna's gaze. "I didn't realize what I had done . . . I didn't mean to . . . but I hurt myself so badly that I can never have children," she quietly sobbed. "My parents disowned me. Uncle Johann and my aunt were kind enough, with Franz' blessing, to take me in."

"Why didn't your parents understand?" Shauna asked with anger and concern. "What happened to the man?"

"I couldn't tell anyone who he was. I knew no one would believe me."

"Why not?"

"Because he was a priest," Tanya admitted for the first time.

Shauna was still in the hospital on the evening of Elon and Vivian's engagement party, which took place at her and Franz' home in Vienna. In Ani's room, the child lay sleeping in Tanya's arms as she rocked her gently while listening to the music and laughter from the guests. When Vivian's shrill laugh was heard above the others', Tanya felt ill as she thought about the woman becoming Ani's stepmother.

On the verge of tears, Tanya suddenly felt a presence in the room. "Is someone there?" she whispered, glancing into the shadows. But she could see that there wasn't.

When Ani stretched in her arms, Tanya carried her from the rocking chair to her bed. Gently tucking her in, Tanya lay down beside her with her arm draped protectively across the child's little body. Grief stricken from having lost Ani and Elon to Vivian, Tanya quietly cried herself to sleep.

Rika's spirit slowly materialized from the shadows and stood over the bed. A loving smile spread across Rika's face and into her eyes. *Thank you,* she silently mouthed to the young woman who so obviously loved her motherless child.

The door opened and Rika's image quickly faded in a shaft of light.

Dressed in formal attire, Elon entered the room. Having had too much to drink, he appeared slightly off-balance as he gazed down on Ani and Tanya while they lay sleeping. Elon's face had a hardened, determined look. He'd finally had enough of the charade with Vivian—of being trussed up like a penguin and paraded around like a trophy. And he'd made a decision as to what to do about it.

More than anything, Elon was tired of living without Rika. Ever since her death he'd toyed with the idea of suicide. It was only his devotion to Ani that had kept him from following through with it. Shauna's misfortune had been the final blow—the straw that broke Elon's desire to go on. Gazing down on Ani as she slept in Tanya's arms, he felt confident his daughter would be well cared for . . . that she would become the child Shauna could never have.

Standing tall with resolve, Elon left, closing the door quietly behind him. When the room was again pitched into darkness, Rika's spirit reappeared. Her face was etched with sorrow from knowing what her beloved Elon was contemplating.

Elon collected his wallet and passport from the room that he and Vivian shared. Taking a thousand dollars of the money the Israelis had given him, he hid the rest in a drawer before leaving, still wearing his tuxedo.

A few blocks from the house, Elon hailed a taxi. "The airport," he told the driver.

At the terminal, as Elon scanned the monitors for the next flight to Ireland, he saw there was one scheduled for Shannon. It was the last flight of the evening, and if Elon had been fifteen minutes later he would have missed it.

The Aer Lingus agent gave him a look of curiosity when Elon paid for his ticket with cash and told her he had no luggage. Soon Elon found himself en route to the country of his father's ancestry, where he planned to accomplish two things: to see Ireland for the first time . . . and to put an end to the months of unbearable sorrow.

Arriving at Shannon Airport after midnight, Elon hired a taxi to take him to Galway. At the cold, deserted ferry station in Galway, Elon finished off the miniature bottles of liquor that he'd bought on the flight from Vienna.

Drifting off to sleep on one of the hard benches, Elon eventually woke with a hangover. The station was buzzing with activity. In the men's room, Elon splashed cold water on his unshaven face.

Boarding the ferry with a group of noisy tourists, Elon remained on deck as the craft headed across the wind-swept bay toward Kilronan, on the Aran Islands. The bitterly cold salt air stung his eyes as he hung onto the rail while the boat lunged over the swells. Staring into the churning water, Elon contemplated jumping. He smiled when realizing he'd no doubt be rescued. With what he had in mind, there'd be no such interference.

When the ferry docked at Kilronan, Elon hired a pony-cart to take him to the ruins of Dun Aengus.

"'Failte go hArainn!' Welcome to Aran! Gerald O'Flaherty and trusty Ginny at your service!" the driver cheerfully introduced himself and his little horse in a thick Irish brogue after greeting Elon in Gaelic.

Elon nodded solemnly as he settled into the cart. He avoided looking Gerald in the eye, not wanting the man's friendly demeanor to possibly compromise his plan. The thought crossed Elon's mind of how different his childhood would have been if his father had shown him as much warmth as this complete stranger was now offering.

"I suppose 'tis the fort you'd be wanting to see?" Gerald asked, trying not to show too much curiosity toward the silent man dressed in a wrinkled tuxedo and sporting a day's growth of whiskers.

Again Elon simply nodded.

"Well, 'tis a bit nippy for a little jaunt. If you're cold, just wrap up in the blanket there. Is it your first time here at Inishmore?" Gerald asked as Ginny set out at a brisk trot.

Elon nodded slightly as he looked out on the wind-swept farmland, dotted by ancient stone fences and whitewashed cottages with thatched or slate roofs. Ginny's hooves made a rhythmic clip-clop on the cobblestone road and the cart swayed gently as Gerald O'Flaherty continued his commentary.

"We have as much history here as you'd care to find anywhere in Ireland. The Fir Bolgs built dun Aonghusa, where we're headed, around five hundred B.C. Their leader was a man by the name of Aengus. And there's been finds of Late Stone Age tombs said to go back two thousand years before that," Gerald marveled.

They passed the ruins of a small stone church surrounded by weathered graves marked with Celtic crosses.

"'Round the fifth century of Our Dear Lord, the Fir Bolgs were converted to Christianity," Gerald informed Elon. "The isle 'tis the resting-place of many a good saint. 'Arainn na Naoimh'—'Aran of the Saints,'" he explained, translating the Gaelic.

Religion was the last thing Elon wanted to be reminded of. He was grateful he hadn't been raised as a Catholic . . . or a Jew—although Elon admired the accounts of courage shown by those Jews who were willing to take their fate into their own hands. From Masada to the Holocaust, suicide was often a noble option for a Jew . . . while a damning one for a Catholic.

"Perhaps you'd care to hear a little music later?" Gerald asked when he noticed Elon studying the bagpipe tucked under the seat.

When Elon didn't respond, Gerald finally gave up trying to draw him into conversation. He turned his attention to Ginny, singing her a rousing Irish tune.

Arriving at the trailhead to the fort, Elon got out of the cart before Gerald brought Ginny to a complete halt.

"I'll wait here," Gerald called after him. "Well, Ginny," he commented while watching Elon make his way up the trail, "I guess some folks just don't have it in them to be friendly."

After a fifteen-minute hike, Elon reached the ruins of the fortress—perched atop a cliff plunging almost three hundred feet to the Atlantic Ocean. Although there were a handful of tourists milling around, no one paid attention to the strangely dressed man standing at the edge of the cold windy cliff, staring at the crashing waves below.

"How dare he do this to me!" Vivian raged at Shauna when she returned home from the hospital on the day after the engagement party. In her anger, Vivian's accent slipped back into its lower-class nuances.

About to enter Shauna and Franz' bedroom with a tray of tea and biscuits, Tanya stopped when overhearing Vivian's tirade from the other side of the closed door.

"Your brother is nothing but a coward!" Vivian yelled at Shauna. "I'm pregnant, you know!" she announced, with complete insensitivity toward Shauna's recent loss.

Vivian's words caused Tanya's limbs to go weak, and she leaned against the door.

"No, I didn't," Shauna lied in response to Vivian's admission. "From Elon?" she asked pointedly.

"Of course! Why do you think we—" Vivian caught herself before going further.

Tanya closed her eyes against the rising tears. She had suspected that was the reason why Elon had consented to marry Vivian.

"Here, let me take that to her," Franz offered kindly as he approached Tanya.

Tanya avoided his gaze while handing Franz the tray. He regarded her with concern as she hurried away. When he entered the bedroom, Vivian's expression immediately changed from anger to feigned hurt.

Glancing in on Ani, Tanya saw that the child was still napping. Wiping away the tears, Tanya went about her chores. Entering Elon and Vivian's room, she started picking up Vivian's clothes that were strewn around the floor. After making the bed and tidying up the room, Tanya went to work in the bathroom. Picking Vivian's robe up off the floor, she hung it on a hook behind the door.

Cleaning around the sink, Tanya started putting away Vivian's toiletries and makeup cluttering the counter. A small, circular container caught Tanya's eye. Absently opening it, she saw that it held birth-control pills. The prescription inside the lid was made out to Vivian, with a refill date from the previous week.

Initially Tanya seemed uncertain as to what she had discovered. But when she realized the significance of the find, she snapped the lid shut and stuffed the container in her pocket just before Vivian entered the room.

"You can finish in here later," Vivian hissed at her.

Tanya quickly left and headed for Shauna and Franz' room. She knocked lightly at the door.

"Who is it?" Franz asked from inside.

"Tanya. There's something important I need to tell Shauna."

Franz opened the door. "Could it wait?" he asked kindly. "She's almost asleep."

"What is it, Tanya?" Shauna asked weakly from the bed.

Franz motioned for Tanya to enter. She did so tentatively.

"I . . . there's something I thought . . ." Tanya stammered to Shauna before glancing worriedly at Franz.

"I'll be in the parlor if you need me," he offered, seeing that Tanya wanted to talk to Shauna in private.

After Franz left, Shauna nodded for Tanya to continue. Pulling the pill container from her pocket, Tanya handed it to her.

Shauna's eyes narrowed with anger when she realized Vivian's deceit. "So, she's not pregnant after all. Where is she?" she asked coolly.

"In her room."

"Tell her I'd like to see her."

Tanya left, soon returning with Vivian.

"What?" Vivian demanded of Shauna.

"I was just wondering if you've seen a doctor about your pregnancy?" Shauna asked, not letting on that she knew about Vivian's deception.

"Why? To tell me what I already know?"

"For your sake as well as the baby's, you really should be under a doctor's care. Why don't we make an appointment with Dr. Schmidt?" Shauna suggested with feigned innocence, giving the name of the prescribing physician listed on the birth-control pills.

Vivian appeared worried.

"Tanya, give his office a call and see how soon Vivian can be seen," Shauna directed. "Be sure to mention she's . . . how far along are you?" she asked Vivian.

Vivian glanced worriedly from Shauna to Tanya and back. Shauna opened her hand, revealing the container of pills. Recognizing them as hers, Vivian reacted as if she'd been slapped in the face.

"You little—" she turned viciously toward Tanya.

"Leave her out of this!" Shauna boomed.

"So I'm not pregnant!" Vivian directed her anger back at Shauna. "But Elon did agree to marry me!"

"Under false pretenses! I want you to leave. Now!" Shauna ordered.

"Leave? This was my home long before you hoodwinked Franz into—"

"It's my home now and you're no longer welcome!" Shauna cut her off.

Tanya regarded the two women with concern.

"You simple-minded ingrate!" Vivian snarled at Shauna.

"Leave before I tell Franz what a lying—"

"'Tell Franz'?" Vivian sneered. "Let me tell you something about your dear sweet Franz," she began in a quiet, malicious tone as Tanya shot her an anxious glance. "Did you know that he and—"

"What's going on?" Franz asked worriedly as he entered the room.

"Vivian is upset about Elon's leaving," Shauna responded quickly, not wanting to involve him in the matter. "She's decided it's too painful to remain here without him."

"I'm sorry," Franz told Vivian kindly. He hadn't heard her threatening to tell Shauna about his relationship with Harry. "But I quite understand. If there's anything you need, don't hesitate to ask," he offered sincerely.

His presence prevented Vivian from continuing her attack on Shauna. After all, Franz wasn't the one she wanted to hurt—*it was his wife and cowardly brother-in-law!*

"You're so kind," Vivian told Franz sweetly, her voice regaining its studied tone. "I appreciate all that you've done for me. And for Harry," she emphasized. She could tell from Franz' reaction that he still had feelings for her brother—just as she'd hoped.

"Shauna's right," Vivian continued with forced tears. "It's too painful for me to remain here after the way her brother has . . ." she paused theatrically.

Shauna and Tanya shared a look of sarcasm aimed at Vivian's performance.

"Don't worry, you'll be all right," Franz tried to comfort Vivian as he put his arm around her. "I'm sure Elon will be back soon. Perhaps—"

"We could never recapture the . . ." Vivian sobbed while fleeing dramatically from the room.

Franz sadly watched her leave. Shauna rolled her eyes at Vivian's theatrics; but Tanya continued to appear worried. Relieved that Elon was no longer bound to a disastrous union with Vivian, Tanya was still quite concerned about his disappearance.

While waiting for his quiet customer to return from the ruins of Dun Aengus, Gerald O'Flaherty reached for his bagpipe. He noticed the wallet and passport partially hidden beneath the blanket in the cart. Opening the passport, Gerald discovered the name of his reticent passenger.

"Oh, Ginny," he commented worriedly to his little horse. "It appears Mr. O'Shay has no intention of coming back."

Tucking the wallet and passport inside his jacket pocket, Gerald grabbed the bagpipe and quickly headed up the trail toward the ruins.

As the cold wind whipped at his face, Elon closed his eyes and stepped nearer to the edge of the cliff. With his heart pounding furiously, he marveled at the courage his grandmother had to enable her to take that final step—until Elon realized it wasn't courage as much as despair.

"Are you sure this is the answer?" the sweet voice whispered in his ear.

Elon's eyes sprang open as he turned his head and looked into Rika's loving gaze. At first he appeared elated, but then his expression hardened. "You're not really here," he accused.

She smiled softly while slowly shaking her head.

"I can't live without you," Elon stated tearfully.

"I haven't left you," she assured him quietly. "Yet, if you do what you're about to—"

"What? God will damn me?" he sneered.

She shook her head. "Whatever hell we live through in both our earthly and eternal lives does not come from God, but from ourselves," she told him knowingly. "If you end your life here, you wouldn't be able to bear the pain of knowing how much it hurt the people you left behind."

"I miss you so much," he choked on his tears. "I love you so . . ."

"I know, my love. I know. The time will come when we will be together again," she assured him.

Closing his eyes, Elon imagined he could feel the soft touch of her gentle caress. Mingling with the wind, he barely made out the strands of *Hey, Jude* played on a bagpipe. Opening his eyes, Elon saw that Rika's spirit was no longer there. He turned toward Gerald O'Flaherty, blowing into the instrument as if someone's life depended on it. *Which it just might,* Elon thought with a sardonic smile.

"I was afraid you were about to have a terrible accident," Gerald shouted above the wind when he finished playing.

"'Accident'?" Elon asked sarcastically.

"Aye, accident. There's been a fair share of accidents from here."

"No suicides?" Elon sneered.

"No, no suicides. Just as there's no divorce here in Ireland, there's no suicide, either. Just terrible accidents."

Elon shook his head at the absurdity.

"Come," Gerald offered kindly, "I'll treat you to a brew at me family's pub."

The invitation sounded quite tempting to Elon, until he remembered Rika's loving presence. "I appreciate the offer, Mr. O'Flaherty, but I no longer drink. I could do with something to eat, though."

"Ah, you're a smart man, Mr. O'Shay," Gerald smiled.

"How do you know my name?"

Gerald pulled the wallet and passport from his pocket and handed them to Elon. Putting a friendly arm around Elon's shoulder, Gerald steered him away from the cliff. Behind them, Rika's spirit reappeared. She smiled softly before fading in the wind.

When he returned to Vienna, Elon was clean-shaven and appeared rested. Having given his tuxedo to Gerald, he was now dressed in a wool sweater and corduroy slacks. Knocking at the door to Franz and Shauna's home, it was opened by a startled Tanya.

"You're back!" she exclaimed happily.

"Papa!" Ani cried excitedly as she threw herself into her father's open arms.

Elon buried his face in her soft hair as he fought tears of joy.

"Where have you been?" Shauna demanded of him as she joined them at the door.

"How are you?" he asked, kissing her on the forehead. "Should you be up?" he inquired with concern.

"I'm doing well. We've been so worried about you!" Shauna admonished him.

Elon placed Ani on her feet. Kneeling at her level, he reached into his pocket.

"I brought you something," he said, handing her a miniature toy lamb made out of wool. "It's from Ireland."

"Ireland?" Shauna demanded.

"Kilronan, actually," Elon elaborated while straightening up.

Shauna gasped as she recalled the story of their grandmother plunging to her death at Kilronan. Tanya gave her and Elon a questioning look.

"Don't worry," Elon assured his sister, "I'm back."

Tears of relief and gratitude flooded Shauna's eyes.

"Tanya, would you entertain Ani while I talk to Shauna?" Elon asked kindly.

Tanya felt as though she would melt from his soft smile and

gentle manner. She held out her hand to Ani, who went with her happily.

"I can't marry Vivian," Elon told Shauna, after following her to the parlor.

"You needn't worry about Vivian."

"I intend to support the child financially, but—"

"She's not pregnant. She only told you that to get you to marry her. And you don't have to worry, she's gone."

Elon breathed a sigh of relief. "I've decided to go back to Africa. Devin and Yvette have given us their camp outside the Mara."

"What about Ani?"

"It would be best if she stayed here."

"As much as we'd love to keep her indefinitely, she needs to be with you. When you get settled at the Mara, or as soon as you can get back to Rose Inish—"

"Rose Inish is gone," Elon finally admitted, with tremendous difficulty. "It was burned to the ground."

Shauna gave him a stricken look as she sank onto a chair.

"There was so much . . . I couldn't tell you before," he apologized as he knelt at her feet.

"Mila? Harun?" Shauna whispered fearfully, unable to mention Mutiba's name.

"I don't know," Elon shook his head sadly.

"Mutiba?" she managed weakly.

"The Israelis flew me to Rose Inish after the hostages had been rescued from Entebbe. Mutiba was supposed to be there with Mila and Harun. But no one was there."

The tears spilled onto Shauna's cheeks.

Elon gently took her hands in his. "The Israelis have offered to help find them. Don't worry, we will," he tried to reassure her, hiding his doubts.

Shauna stared tearfully into space, urgently praying they could.

Chapter 15

Approximately six months after he had left Africa, Elon returned to Kenya. Arriving with little more than what he'd taken with him first to Holland and then Austria, he immediately went to check on the Cessna, which was still parked at Williams Airport. He was relieved to find that the craft and its contents had remained safe in his absence.

Elon then checked in at the Acacia Tree Hotel. Avoiding the Nile Star, he hoped to keep from dwelling on the last night that he and Rika had been together. But memories of Rika constantly invaded Elon's waking thoughts and late-night dreams.

With some of the money he had left over from the original ten thousand dollars the Israelis had given him, Elon purchased a used Land Rover. In town he bought food and supplies for the camp. From the Cessna, he transferred the rifles, ammunition, and other gear that he'd brought from Rose Inish into the Rover before heading for the Maasai Mara Reserve.

Arriving late in the afternoon, Elon found the camp deserted. Contrary to what Devin had been led to believe, it hadn't been maintained. The grounds were overgrown with bush; and the few buildings that remained standing appeared unlivable. Elon set up camp beside the Land Rover. That evening, following a meager meal cooked over an open fire, he settled back and observed the sunset as the sounds of the night came to life.

The bark of jackals and the rhythmic call of hyenas seemed to welcome Elon home. Until they were broken by the low, rumbling roar of a lion—causing the hair to stand up on Elon's neck as he felt the ground slightly vibrate, indicating the beast was nearby. Although he knew the animal was just giving a warning, he still reached for his rifle. Elon realized if the lion were seriously on the prowl, he wouldn't know it until it was too late. To be on the safe side, he decided to spend the night in the Rover.

Elon moved everything back into the vehicle before dousing the fire. He was grateful the night air was cool, as he was hesitant to leave the windows lowered to the point where a lion's paw could strike a fatal blow.

As his eyes grew weary with fatigue after making himself as comfortable as possible inside the Rover, Elon recalled the story of The Man-Eaters of Tsavo—the two lions that were reported to have killed over a hundred people in 1898, halting the construction of the Uganda Railroad, "The Lunatic Express."

Elon thought about another man-eating lion involved in an incident that was also connected to the railroad, and happened around the turn of the century. While hoping to ambush the beast during the night, the Supervisor of Railway Police, Charles H. Ryall, momentarily fell asleep at an open window inside a parked railcar. Just before midnight, the lion strolled into the carriage, broke Ryall's neck with a single swipe of its paw, and then casually jumped through the window with Ryall's corpse dangling from its jaws. Elon shuddered at the mental image before finally drifting off to sleep.

Elon woke in the morning with the sun beating through the windshield, and the sound of cows mooing to the accompaniment of a softly clanging bell. He focused on a young Maasai boy tending a small herd of cattle. Holding a wooden staff and wearing only a strip of brightly colored material across his slim shoulders, the boy had circular wooden plugs in his freshly cut earlobes. He was studying Elon with uncertainty.

Glancing at the ground when leaving the Rover, Elon saw the massive paw prints of a lion. He exhaled with relief for having spent the night in the Rover.

The Maasai boy watched silently as Elon re-lit the fire and prepared his morning meal. Elon offered some to the boy, but it was refused. A teenaged Maasai, dressed in a traditional toga, with his stretched earlobes dangling to his shoulders, eventually joined them. Tall and elegantly proportioned, the teenager chased away the boy and his cattle before approaching Elon with a menacing glare.

Although he was familiar with the Maasai from having accompanied his father on numerous safaris, often at this very site, Elon felt slightly unnerved by the teenager's stare and the sharp-pointed spear he was holding. Elon's relationship with the Maasai had always been cordial, while he respected the fact that they were considered to be one of the fiercest peoples in Africa.

"Sopa," Elon gave the teenager the Maasai greeting. "Elon O'Shay," he introduced himself while extending his hand.

The teenager's expression softened slightly. "My name is James. But we have met before," he stated in perfect Queen's English while shaking Elon's hand.

Elon gave him a questioning look.

"I do not expect you to recognize me. I was not much older than my brother when I last saw you," the teenager explained, referring to the boy who was herding the cattle.

Elon continued to look bewildered.

"Perhaps you remember me by my Maasai name? 'Kijabe'?"

A smile of recognition slowly spread across Elon's face. "Of course, 'The Wind,'" he translated the name from Maa—the Maasai language. "But, if I remember correctly, your English was rather nonexistent back then."

"As the eldest of my father's sons, I was provided with the opportunity of attending missionary school," Kijabe informed him rather derisively.

"Well, I'm glad to see it didn't totally corrupt you," Elon stated sincerely as he studied Kijabe's attire and drooping earlobes. "If you don't mind, I'll call you by your Maasai name. Would you care for some tea?"

While accepting the cup, Kijabe noticed the lion prints on the ground. "I see you had a visitor last night," he commented.

"Have you had much trouble with it?"

Kijabe nodded. "It has killed a few goats, and yesterday a cow. The murrani are hunting it."

"Then I can rest easy," Elon responded, placing his faith in the ability of the young Maasai warriors.

"Will you be staying long?" Kijabe asked.

Elon nodded.

Kijabe glanced around. "You will need some help," he said, trying not to sound too pessimistic.

"Know of anyone? It'd be worth a few cows," Elon offered the currency most valued by the Maasai.

"Yes," Kijabe replied as he rose to leave.

"Ashe maleng," Elon thanked him in Maa.

"A-serian, lo shore," Kijabe smiled in parting, calling him "friend."

Elon appreciated being referred to as a friend. He watched as Kijabe headed toward his village. Turning his attention back to the camp, Elon exhaled slowly as he thought of all the work that lay ahead.

The first thing Elon did was to attack the growth that had overtaken the main building. When it was cleared, he was pleased to find that the structure was relatively sound, although in desperate need of a new roof.

From the top of the building, Elon gazed out across the terrain. The view was breathtaking. Nestled at the base of a network of small round hills, the camp was shaded by numerous acacia trees. It looked out across a fertile, rolling plain with a tree-lined stream leading to a watering hole. A small herd of elephants were headed toward the water; while wildebeest, zebra, gazelle, giraffe, and buffalo dotted the surrounding savannah.

The sound of laughter drew Elon's attention to Kijabe's village, located on the opposite side of the stream. He saw a group of

Maasai women making their way toward the camp. Climbing off the roof, Elon went to welcome them.

"Sopa," he called, much to their delight.

While the younger women giggled at Elon's greeting, as well as his handsomeness, only the elders dared to look him in the eye.

Elon thought perhaps Kijabe hadn't informed the women that he understood their language, as they made numerous sexual comments about him. But he smiled when realizing the women wouldn't have cared if he knew what they were saying, as the Maasai were far from inhibited in sexual matters.

Elon was also neither surprised nor disappointed that Kijabe had recruited women to help him. For thousands of years the Maasai had remained true to their traditions; one of which being that it was women's work to build the homes. The men protected the village, watched over the cattle, and went on raids to acquire more. They refrained from manual work in order to reserve their strength for fighting. Elon appreciated how, more than any other tribe in East Africa, the Maasai had struck fear in the hearts of early European settlers. Even in modern times, lions were known to run at the sight of a proud Maasai murran.

When evening approached, the women left with the promise of returning the next morning. As they walked away, Elon overheard them cautioning one another to be on guard for "ng'atuny"—the lion.

Watching them leave, Elon felt an overwhelming sense of loneliness. As a boy, he hadn't given a second thought to spending a night alone in the bush. But the nights were now long and lonely without Rika. He still craved the numbing effect of alcohol, but he remained strong in his resolve to no longer use it as a crutch.

The sounds of the wild intensified as darkness engulfed the camp. Elon built up the fire, regretting having to spend another night in the Rover. Hearing a noise, he reached for his rifle.

"Sopa," Kijabe greeted him as he approached from beyond the glow of the fire. "I thought you might want some company."

Four of Kijabe's friends also emerged from the shadows, all armed with spears and long knives hanging from their rough cowhide belts. As they wordlessly took positions around the fire, Elon felt a wave of gratitude.

"I remember you and your father quite well," Kijabe told him as he studied Elon's rifle. "And that you were an excellent marksman. Do you still hunt?"

"No," Elon responded.

"Are you still a good marksman?"

"I suppose."

"We are not allowed to have firearms, but I have done some shooting. Perhaps you can teach me how to shoot better?"

"Perhaps. As long as you promise to never take a life needlessly. That you will never kill just for the sake of killing."

"Of course," Kijabe replied, disappointed that Elon felt he had to ask such a thing. But then Kijabe remembered Elon's father and some of the men he had brought to hunt with him in the Mara. "How is your father?" he asked.

"Dead," Elon answered in a flat tone.

"Will your woman be joining you here?"

Elon didn't respond as he poked absently at the fire.

"Should you want the company of a woman," Kijabe mentioned, "there were many here today who said they would be happy to be with you."

"Tell them I appreciate the offer, but no thanks," Elon smiled. "Although I could use their help when my daughter arrives. She's four years old."

Kijabe studied Elon intently, not wanting to ask what had happened to the child's mother. If she were dead, it was the Maasai custom not to speak of it.

"Our women make very good mothers," Kijabe stated suggestively. "What is your daughter's name?"

"Anika. We call her Ani."

"Well, Ani's father, you must get some rest if you are to work as hard tomorrow as you did today. We will watch for ng'atuny."

"Ashe, Kijabe," Elon thanked him.

Retrieving his bedroll from the Rover, Elon spread it beside the fire and was soon lulled to sleep by Kijabe and his friends' quiet singing.

When Elon woke in the morning, Kijabe and his friends were gone. Hearing the laughter from the women as they approached the camp, Elon smiled at the thought of spending another day in their cheerful company.

That afternoon, as he was tearing off the old roof from the main building, Elon noticed a vehicle approach in the distance. When it eventually reached the camp, Elon was surprised to see Giora, the Israeli Mossad agent.

"Shalom," Giora greeted him when Elon came down from the roof. He extended his hand somewhat hesitantly, not knowing if Elon viewed him as friend or foe.

"Shalom, Giora," Elon nodded solemnly as they shook hands. "You still around? Where's your side-kick?"

"Zev and I just recently got back from Israel. We won't be staying long. He's waiting for me in Narok. Devin told us you were here. Great crew you've got working for you," Giora commented appreciatively as he surveyed the women, who regarded him with amused looks. "I was very sorry to learn of your loss," he stated sadly, referring to Rika's death.

Elon looked away. "Would you care for some tea?" he offered distantly.

Giora followed Elon to where a pot of tea was being kept warm on the smoldering fire.

"I regret adding to your sorrows," Giora said, following a long pause as they sipped their tea. "But I have news about your friends."

Elon visibly braced himself for the bad news.

"We learned that somehow, miraculously, Mutiba's mother and brother made it across the Ruwenzori Mountains to a refugee camp in Zaire . . ." Giora began haltingly. "We were told that unfortunately, while they were there, they waded into the area of the lake where the bodies of the people who had died at the camp were thrown."

Fear tightened Elon's throat.

"They were killed by crocodiles," Giora told him quietly, confirming Elon's fears.

A heavy silence settled between them as Elon stared blankly into space. "Mutiba?" he eventually asked.

Giora shook his head sadly. "Apparently he didn't make it out of Uganda."

Elon nodded stoically.

"I'm so sorry," Giora said. "I can be reached through Devin. If there's anything we can do . . ."

Giora studied Elon sadly before turning his attention to the Maasai women, who were leaving for the day. "It's beautiful here," he commented quietly while looking around the camp.

Taking a photo from his wallet, Giora hesitated before handing it to Elon. Knowing there was nothing he could say or do to ease Elon's pain, he rose to leave.

"Giora," Elon called quietly.

Giora turned back.

"Thank you," Elon told him softly. "Shalom."

Giora gave him a bittersweet smile. "Shalom," he responded sadly.

Elon watched absently as Giora returned to his vehicle and drove off. Glancing around the deserted camp, Elon took a deep breath before looking at the photograph. It was the one he had given Giora to help find Mila and her sons. Taken on Ani's third birthday, it was difficult for Elon to comprehend the fact that, in addition to Rafi, four of the five people pictured—Mila, Mutiba, Harun, . . . and Rika—were no longer alive.

Elon remained still as the night approached. He paid no attention when Kijabe and his friends joined him.

"The murrani have killed the lion," Kijabe informed Elon proudly.

Elon gave him a blank stare. Knowing that Elon had had a visitor, Kijabe surmised that the man had brought bad news.

"Come, you must spend the night at our village," he told Elon adamantly, pulling him to his feet.

Elon offered no resistance as Kijabe and his friends led him away.

With the Maasai welcoming him into their homes and their lives, Elon found the strength to carry on. Watching their children play, he longed for Ani. When the camp was completed to the point of accommodating her, Elon sent for her. She arrived in Nairobi clutching her toy lion and accompanied by Shauna and Franz. And Tanya.

The months of being separated from her father made Ani feel a little uncertain of him, and she responded stiffly when, at the airport, he picked her up and showered her with kisses. Shauna and Franz greeted Elon lovingly, but Tanya remained characteristically shy.

"Wait 'til you see what we brought," Shauna told Elon as they headed toward the baggage claim area.

"Don't tell me," Elon feigned disapproval when he spied the animal crate being unloaded with the rest of the luggage.

"Two little Rafis!" Ani excitedly told her father.

"They're a gift from Xandra and Owen," Shauna informed Elon as Tanya opened the crate and the large, three-month-old puppies greeted her with exuberance. "The male is from their pair, but the female isn't related," Shauna explained.

Realizing the male was a full-brother to Rafi, Elon regarded it sadly. "What are their names?" he asked Ani.

"I don't know yet," she responded with concern.

"Which one is 'I Don't' and which one is 'Know Yet'?" he teased.

"No, silly! That's not their names!" Ani admonished him with a giggle.

Tanya smiled at Ani's warming to Elon, until she noticed he was smiling in her direction. With the color rising in her cheeks, Tanya quickly looked away.

On the drive to the Mara, Elon stopped the Land Rover at a turnout overlooking the Great Rift Valley. Gazing down at the primeval terrain, for the first time in Tanya's twenty years she felt vibrantly alive. She could see why Elon had returned to Africa. Franz, on the other hand, seemed totally out of his element. He had offered to come to Africa as a chivalrous gesture, thinking he could help protect the women. But it appeared that *he* was the one more in need of protection.

As they continued toward the camp, Shauna became lost in her thoughts. It was difficult for her to accept the fact that she wasn't headed home to Rose Inish. She wanted desperately to learn if Elon had heard anything about Mila, Harun, and Mutiba. His having said nothing about them made her hesitant to ask. Shauna fantasized they would be at the camp when she arrived. But the only ones to greet them were a group of exuberant Maasai.

Kijabe's entire village turned out to welcome Elon's family—and they were an impressive sight! Wearing lions' manes and black ostrich-feathered headgear, the men brandished spears as their half-naked bodies glistened in the late-afternoon sun. The women appeared even more beautiful than usual; wearing brightly colored sheaths accentuated by copper and beaded jewelry. They emitted a high-pitched trill as their men surrounded Shauna and Tanya while trying to out-jump one another. When the Maasai tightened their circle around the two women, Tanya's eyes grew large with apprehension.

"It's said that the one who jumps the highest is the most proficient in sex," Shauna informed Tanya with a smile.

Tanya felt as though she would faint from fear and embarrassment.

Kijabe made his way over to Ani, who clung desperately to Elon's neck. As Kijabe approached the child, the male puppy jumped out the window of the Rover and headed for the teenager's shins with barred teeth and a fierce little growl. Startled, Kijabe jumped away.

The dancing stopped and the women grew silent as Kijabe fell to the ground, letting the puppy have its way with him. He knew it wasn't capable of doing any real damage. Soon the puppy realized the scary black teenager wasn't a threat after all. Kijabe still pretended he was being eaten alive, when in fact he was closer to being licked to death.

"That's my friend, Kijabe," Elon told Ani with mock concern. "Maybe we'd better save him?"

The child slowly loosened her grip on his neck after he lowered her to the ground. The puppy ran to her happily. When the little female whimpered from the Rover, Franz opened the door so she could join her mate.

As the puppies gathered around Ani, Kijabe studied them from where he sat in the dirt. "So, you are Ani," he smiled. "Keeper of the little lion dogs."

Ani glanced at Kijabe with uncertainty as he untied his leather necklace and held it out to her. Studying it with curiosity, she focused on the curved object in its center.

"It's the dewclaw of a lion," Kijabe told her. "It will protect you."

Ani looked to her father for permission to take the necklace. When Elon nodded his approval, she allowed Kijabe to tie it around her neck.

"What do you tell Kijabe?" Elon prompted.

"Thank you, 'Jabe," Ani responded shyly as she fingered the lion's claw.

Kijabe smiled. "'Jabe' says it's time to eat!" he announced in a loud voice.

The Maasai erupted into shrill cries as they herded everyone to where two goats were roasting over an open flame. Ani and the puppies were soon lured into play by the children; while Shauna and Tanya helped with the meal. Franz appeared uneasy as some of the Maasai women regarded him with suggestive giggles. He had difficulty keeping his eyes off the muscular, sparsely clad young men.

"Your woman is quite lovely," Kijabe commented to Elon as they ate.

"That's my sister," Elon reminded him.

"I'm not talking about your sister."

Elon followed his gaze to Tanya. "She's not my woman," he responded.

Kijabe gave him a look suggesting he didn't believe him.

Elon felt strangely unable to defend his denial. His friend was right; Tanya *was* rather lovely—with her curvaceous body, long brown hair, and soft-hazel eyes. But she wasn't "his woman," Elon told himself as anger swept over him. He glared disapprovingly at Kijabe, who countered with a patronizing smile.

Whether Elon realized it or not, Kijabe could tell he had feelings for the woman who cared for his child. And she for him—for Kijabe saw the glances Tanya stole of Elon when he wasn't looking.

But Elon refused to allow himself to look upon Tanya as anything other than someone he was grateful to for being devoted to Ani. He was angry that Kijabe would suggest anything else. Not that Elon had sworn off sex, for he'd toyed with the idea of taking some of the Maasai women up on their offer to be with him. And, although he hated to admit it, the memory of his sexual trysts with Vivian still excited him. But his involvement with Vivian had been purely sexual, and Elon was too much of a gentleman to consider using Tanya in that way. She deserved much more than he was capable, or willing, to give.

At nightfall, when the party came to an end and the Maasai returned to their village, Elon found himself alone with Tanya as they tucked Ani into bed.

"She hasn't had her toy out of her sight for the whole time you've been apart," Tanya told Elon quietly as they gazed down on the sleeping child, clutching her toy lion.

Feelings of pity and guilt swept over Elon when he realized how difficult the months of separation had been for Ani—as well as for himself.

"I hope you don't mind rooming in here with her," he told Tanya.

"Of course not," she smiled softly.

"I was thinking we could all go on a game drive tomorrow, if you'd like," he suggested hesitantly.

"I'd like that very much," she responded brightly.

"I want to thank you again for taking such good care of Ani, and for being here with her. I thought seriously about having her stay in Austria."

"She needs to be with you."

He nodded appreciatively. "Although Africa can be quite cruel and dangerous," he stated distantly.

"Yet quite beautiful," she commented.

Elon studied her with uncertainty. "You're welcome to stay as long as you like," he offered. "When the time comes that you want to leave, I'll understand."

Tanya nodded in a way that made Elon feel she was disappointed by his statement.

"I can't promise you'll enjoy it here," he elaborated with an edge to his voice.

"I'm not looking for any promises."

Elon seemed to appreciate her response. "'Night," he told her while turning to go.

"Goodnight," she responded softly.

Elon joined Shauna in the front room, where a fire blazed in the stone fireplace. Glancing at the puppies, he saw that they were curled up in a blanket on the floor, fast asleep.

"Where's Franz?" Elon asked as he stoked the fire.

"In bed. I'm afraid he's never experienced anything like today. It may take him a while to adjust. It's not bad here," Shauna offered kindly while looking around the room.

"It's far from what Franz is accustomed to," Elon acknowledged. "And far from how I'd like it to be when I'm finished."

"Franz and I have been talking. If you'd let us, we'd like to help with it."

"The place is as much yours as it is mine. Devin and Yvette intended it to be for all of us to . . ." Elon's voice trailed off sadly.

"When Rika's parents shipped the puppies to Austria, they sent the photo album of Rose Inish. It had been forgotten after . . ." Shauna halted. "I brought it with me."

Elon remembered Mila giving the album to Rika on the day

they left Rose Inish. He'd forgotten that Rika had taken it with her to Holland.

"Have you heard anything about them?" Shauna asked hesitantly regarding Mila, Harun, and Mutiba.

When Elon lowered his head, she knew that he had. "Tell me," she gathered the strength to ask.

"I was told that they made it to a refugee camp in Zaire, where they died," was all that he quietly said.

Tears rose in Shauna's eyes and coursed down her cheeks. Elon folded her in his arms as she surrendered to her grief.

"Mutiba wasn't with them," he told her softly.

Shauna glanced at him with a ray of hope. When he shook his head sadly, she buried her face in his shoulder as she continued to weep.

"Is something wrong?" Franz asked worriedly as he joined them.

"Our friends . . . Mila and her sons . . ." Elon tried to explain.

Franz understood. "I'm so sorry," he stated sympathetically while embracing Shauna, who moved from Elon's arms into his. "Come, my dear," Franz told her lovingly as he led her away.

Elon watched sadly as they left. When one of the puppies whimpered, he saw that they were both at his feet. Stretching out on the sofa, Elon gathered them to him.

"Don't be getting used to this," he warned the puppies sternly as they sprawled all over him before dozing off. Elon remained awake, gazing forlornly at the fire.

In the morning, Shauna and Franz opted out of the tour of the reserve. Elon realized Shauna needed time to come to terms with Mila and Harun's deaths . . . and, no doubt, Mutiba's. Elon felt like backing out of the game drive as well, but he didn't want to disappoint Ani.

As they toured the Maasai Mara Reserve, Elon fought hard against dwelling on the past. But it was a losing battle, as his mind wandered back to the tour of the Toro Reserve, where he first realized he was falling in love with Rika.

When Ani and Tanya admired a pride of lions, Elon recalled Lee Parnell's reference to "the lure of the lion." Elon became angry as he remembered the abusive, obnoxious Texan.

"It's all so beautiful! And exciting!" Tanya enthused. Glancing at Elon, she was saddened to see his hardened expression. "Are you all right?" she asked.

Elon was annoyed by Tanya's sympathetic tone and expression. "I'm fine! There's just a lot that needs to be done," he responded brusquely while starting up the Rover.

"Do we have to go?" Ani whined. "I don't want to go!"

"Don't worry," Tanya quickly assured her before Elon could scold the child. "I'm sure your papa will bring us here again, when there isn't so much to do," she smiled in Elon's direction. But he ignored her.

Elon's hot and cold treatment was extremely upsetting to Tanya. She had to remind herself that she had come to Africa for Ani's sake. She was determined to stay for as long as the child needed her. Tanya held no illusions of ever taking the place of Ani's dead mother . . . or of Elon ever reciprocating the love Tanya secretly harbored for him.

Chapter 16

With Shauna and Franz' physical and financial contributions, the camp soon turned into something much grander than what Elon had envisioned. It was amazing how quickly and professionally things got done when money was of no concern. Hiring construction crews that were artisans at heart, the camp evolved into something far beyond Elon's dreams.

The main building, or lodge, was practically unrecognizable from how it had looked when Elon first arrived at the camp. The plain, rectangular-shaped dwelling now had interesting angles, with floor-to-ceiling windows offering panoramic views. A large dining room extended onto a deck overlooking the watering hole, affording game viewing during the day or night.

A massive stone fireplace took the place of the smaller one in the remodeled front room; and beautifully grained hardwoods replaced the old flooring and trim throughout the building. Three additional bedrooms and baths had been added to the main structure, with eight tent-like guest cottages skirting the property; each with a private bath and sitting room, in addition to the bedroom. The furnishings in both the lodge and guest facilities were remnants of the grand East African colonial era.

Although Elon would have preferred to keep things much simpler, he didn't complain. Without being conscious of it, he and Shauna, with Franz and Tanya's help, had come close to creating another Rose Inish.

"It's beautiful," Shauna stated one evening as they all stood outside admiring the camp when it was completed.

"Yes," Tanya agreed while holding Ani.

"What will you name it?" Shauna asked Elon.

He gave her a blank expression. "I don't want it to have a name," he told her distantly as he recalled Rose Inish being devoured by flames.

Shauna understood Elon's hesitancy in becoming emotionally attached to the place by naming it. "We'll simply call it 'The Camp,'" she suggested.

And so "The Camp" it became.

The first safari clients to visit The Camp were a middle-aged couple from France. While Shauna and Franz stayed behind with Ani, Elon and Tanya drove to Nairobi to meet the couple. Elon arranged to spend the night at the Acacia Tree Hotel. He knew the clients would have preferred the Nile Star, but it still held too many memories of Rika.

"Hemingway said if a person remained long enough here at the Acacia Tree, they'd eventually see everyone they knew," Elon stated when they sat down at the outdoor café that encircled the ancient tree from which the hotel got its name.

As Tanya chatted in fluent French with the couple, Elon's attention drifted to the notes tacked onto the tree, which acted as a bulletin board for travelers. He didn't notice the extremely thin teenaged boy who placed glasses of water around the table. What caught Elon's eye, however, was the ring the boy wore on the outside of his gloved hand. Elon recognized it as his father's ring—the one he'd given to Mutiba.

Instinctively, Elon grabbed hold of the boy's wrist to prevent him from running away. Elon appeared angry with the thief whom he suspected had stolen the ring. But, when Elon looked into the boy's face, he recognized Harun.

"Harun?" Elon whispered in amazement.

The tears spilling onto his cheeks, Harun slowly nodded.

Elon stood up so quickly that his chair toppled over. Picking Harun up off the ground, Elon hugged him tight while they both wept.

The French couple appeared shocked by Elon's behavior; but Tanya's eyes flooded with tears as she realized the significance of the reunion.

"Where's your mother?" Elon fearfully asked Harun when slightly regaining his composure.

Wiping away his tears, Harun motioned for Elon to follow him toward the kitchen. He hadn't told Mila that he'd seen Elon. When Harun spotted him, he had slipped the ring over his gloved finger—hoping Elon would recognize it, if not him.

"Mama," Harun addressed Mila as she labored over a hot stove. "There's someone here to see you," he told her before stepping aside to reveal Elon.

When Mila looked up, the hand holding the ladle she was stirring with froze in mid-air.

"Hello, Mila," Elon smiled through his tears. He hardly recognized her, as she had lost so much weight.

The ladle fell from Mila's grasp as she blinked with disbelief. When Elon came closer, she collapsed into his arms, sobbing.

"What's going on here?" the kitchen supervisor demanded. "Get back to work!" he barked at Mila and Harun.

"You need to find yourself some new help," Elon told the supervisor as he helped Mila out of her apron.

Harun smiled as he removed his gloves. He turned toward a young black girl, barely in her teens, who was staring at him with beautiful, yet frightened, doe-shaped eyes.

"What's this?" the supervisor shouted. "How am I expected to tend to my customers? Who are you?" he demanded of Elon.

"I am this woman's son," Elon responded matter-of-factly as he took out his wallet and removed a wad of money, which he handed to the supervisor. "Send out for whatever you need. I'm taking these people home."

Fearful of being left behind, the young girl began to tremble.

"Come," Harun told her while holding out his hand. "We're going home."

In shock, she grasped Harun's hand as they followed after Elon and Mila.

"Is there anything you need to bring with you?" Elon asked, for the first time noticing the young girl who clung desperately to Harun.

"This is Emi. She's coming with us," Harun informed him.

"Hello, Emi. Welcome," Elon smiled.

Looking totally bewildered, Emi glanced from Harun to Elon and back.

"We have just a few things," Harun answered Elon's question as he continued to hold Emi protectively.

"Get them and I'll meet you outside," Elon suggested, touched by Harun's tenderness toward the girl.

Mila was hesitant to let go of Elon's hand. Smiling reassuringly, he kissed her gently on the forehead.

"Don't worry," he told her quietly. "We'll never be apart again," he promised as the tears again rose in his eyes.

Harun led Mila and Emi away. Watching them go, Elon sensed that, although the boy appeared to have diminished in size, inwardly he had grown into a man.

"I'm sorry, but I need you to stay here while I fly back to The Camp," Elon apologized to Tanya and his clients when he returned to them. "I'll be back in the morning, and we can proceed as arranged."

"We'll be fine," Tanya assured him.

Gazing into her eyes, brimming with tears of joy, Elon's heart went out to her.

"It's a miracle," Tanya told him quietly.

Elon nodded tearfully as he turned away.

Watching him leave, Tanya's joyful expression slowly turned to one of uncertainty. Now that Mila and her son were back in Elon and Ani's lives, Tanya feared she would no longer be needed.

Prior to landing the Cessna at The Camp, Elon buzzed the Maasai village. It was the first time Elon had flown the plane to the Mara, and Kijabe and the others looked to the sky with excitement.

Shauna and Ani were tending to some newly planted rose bushes when Elon brought the aircraft in for a dusty landing on the recently created airstrip. Relaxing on the front veranda of the lodge, Franz looked up from the book he was reading as the now nearly full-grown puppies woke from their nap at his feet.

Shauna watched as the plane rolled to a stop. Her breath caught in her throat and her eyes widened with disbelief as she slowly recognized the passengers Elon was helping out of the Cessna. Dropping the spade she was holding, Shauna forced herself to move. Soon she was running—breaking into tears as she and Mila embraced.

Concerned by Shauna's behavior, the young dogs ran barking from the veranda to "protect" Ani. Emboldened by their presence, Ani cautiously made her way over to where her aunt was crying in the arms of someone who seemed only vaguely familiar to the child.

Emi looked fearfully to Harun, uncertain of all these overly emotional people she had encountered in the past few hours.

Franz stood on the veranda, smiling and shaking his head with amazement. Like Tanya, Franz knew he was witnessing a miracle.

"Ani, it's Mimi," Shauna told the child when seeing Ani wasn't certain who the woman was.

Too choked up to speak, Mila knelt down and gave the child a tearful smile. Still not sure who Mila was, Ani allowed herself to be gently hugged by the woman.

With Mila's attention drawn to Ani, Shauna turned to Harun. He tried not to cry when she embraced him, but he couldn't help it.

Emi watched with total incomprehension as Harun and the strange white woman made a complete spectacle of themselves.

"Shauna, this is Emi," Harun introduced them through his tears.

Emi's eyes widened with uncertainty when suddenly finding herself in Shauna's loving embrace.

When Franz joined them, Shauna directed him toward Mila. "Mila, this is my husband, Franz," she introduced them.

"It is such a pleasure to meet you," Franz smiled while hugging Mila.

Mila hadn't lost her powers of perception. In Franz' embrace, she immediately guessed his secret. But she also sensed that he was a good person at heart, and that Shauna was fortunate to have found him. Especially now that Mutiba . . .

"Hello, little one," Harun smiled down at Ani.

"'Arun?" she asked hesitantly as she slowly remembered him.

He smiled and nodded tearfully.

"Where have you been?" Ani asked sternly, as if he'd been naughty in staying away so long. When he cried and smiled at the same time, Ani looked concerned. "Don't cry," she pleaded, reaching up to him.

Gathering her in his arms, Harun bit back the tears as he breathed a deep sigh of relief. "Where's your mama?" he asked innocently when he had composed himself.

"With the angels," the child responded sweetly, repeating what she'd been told.

Harun appeared shocked. He looked to Elon and Shauna to discount Ani's words, but it was obvious they couldn't.

Mila simply looked away. For a long time she had suspected that Rika was the third shadowy figure in her dream from many years ago.

"I hardly recognize you, you've gotten so thin!" Shauna told Mila worriedly. "Come, you must be exhausted," she said, directing Mila toward the lodge.

Harun carried Ani in one arm and held onto Emi with the other as they followed with the young dogs at their side. Harun regarded the animals sadly. "Rafi . . ." he uttered, looking to Elon with tears again rising in his eyes.

"I know," Elon responded sadly as he carried Mila and Harun's few belongings. "I know," he repeated in a reassuring tone, indicating there was nothing more to be said.

Entering the lodge, Mila shook her head with admiration.

"We've only recently finished it," Shauna told her. "There are six bedrooms and baths in here, plus eight tent-like cottages outside. You can have your pick of—"

"Emi and I will share one of the cottages," Harun spoke up.

Shauna and Elon exchanged a look of surprise; which intensified when Mila nodded her approval of Harun's suggestion.

"Come along, then," Elon told Harun, who continued to hold Ani in one arm while encompassing Emi with the other. Before they left, Mila took her small bundle of belongings from Elon.

Elon led Harun and Emi to the tree-shaded complex of tent-like cottages. As they entered the one closest to the main lodge, Emi's eyes widened with amazement.

"Welcome home," Elon said as he placed Harun and Emi's bundle of clothes on the sofa in the sitting room. "Both of you," he smiled at Emi before taking Ani from Harun and leaving them alone in the room.

Unable to move, Emi simply stood back and blinked. Never in her thirteen years had she imagined making herself at home in such a beautifully decorated, modern facility!

Harun smiled as Emi cautiously, and then excitedly, inspected every inch of her new home. When she had taken it all in, she turned to him with tears of joy. Harun knew how much she wanted to express in words all that she was feeling. But Emi's tongue had been maliciously severed, and she was unable to speak.

"Are you sure you don't need my help with supper?" Mila asked when Shauna and Franz led her to the room that would be hers, inside the lodge.

"Absolutely," Shauna stated with conviction. "Believe it or not, I've learned to cook. Although I'm sure there's still much that you can teach me."

"She's quite a good cook," Franz proudly attested to his wife's accomplishment.

"You just get some rest," Shauna encouraged Mila as she hugged the dear woman. "When you feel up to it, you can tell us all that's happened since . . ." her voice trailed off sadly.

Mila knew Shauna was both anxious and hesitant to ask about Mutiba—and she hadn't forgotten the message he'd asked her to give to Shauna. Uttered in his dying breath, Mutiba's words were best not shared with Franz. Now that Shauna was married, Mila wasn't sure when, or if, she should convey them.

When Shauna and Franz left her alone in the room, Mila appeared dazed. It had been almost a year since she and Harun had fled Rose Inish—a harrowing year of terror, hunger, . . . and death. It was difficult for Mila to comprehend that she was finally "home."

Sinking to her knees while clutching her bundle of belongings to her breast, Mila began to tearfully pray. She prayed and wept not for all that had been lost, but in gratitude for all that had been found.

"I came back for you," Elon told Mila that evening, as he stood staring into the gently blazing fire in the parlor's fireplace. He, Mila, and Shauna were the only ones in the room. Guilt-ridden for failing to rescue Mila and her sons, Elon avoided her gaze.

"Yes, I know," Mila admitted.

Elon and Shauna regarded her with surprise.

"Mutiba arrived from Entebbe early that morning," Mila began in a quiet voice. "But he had been followed. And he'd been shot. We escaped into the forest, where we heard the helicopter—and shooting. We knew Rose Inish wasn't safe . . . that we could not return . . . Mutiba died that afternoon," she softly wept.

Shauna closed her eyes as the tears found their way down her cheeks.

"Harun and I made our way over the Ruwenzoris," Mila continued, painfully recalling the freezing nights and lack of food—not knowing where they were going, or what they would find. What they found was hell.

"We met Emi at a refugee camp near Kasindi," she told them, avoiding any description of the terrible conditions they encountered there.

"I was told you had died there," Elon informed her quietly.

Mila gave him a questioning look.

"The Israelis were looking for you. I'd given them a photograph to help find you. They learned you made it to Zaire," Elon explained.

Mila realized she needed to explain why the Israelis believed that she and Harun were dead. "Emi's parents had been killed in Uganda," she began with the girl's story. "She and her older brother escaped to Zaire. She was just twelve years old. Her brother disguised her as a boy, but that didn't stop some of the soldiers who guarded the camp from wanting her. They killed her brother and took Emi into the forest to rape her. Harun and I were nearby, looking for firewood. When we heard her screams, we ran to help. By the time we reached her, they had cut out her tongue to keep her quiet."

Covering her mouth with her hands, Shauna gasped with horror. Anger flashed in Elon's eyes.

"Harun managed to get hold of one of the soldier's rifles . . . He used it on them." Remembering the horrible, bloody scene, Mila swallowed the nausea rising in her throat.

"When they heard the shots, other soldiers came running toward us," she continued with much difficulty. "We made it to the river and knew we could go no further. We could see the crocodiles. Harun tore off Emi's bloody clothes, wrapped them around a rock, and threw them in the water."

Shauna and Elon remained stunned as Mila collected herself before continuing.

"We waded in the shallows along the shore, then ran back into the forest. The soldiers saw the crocodiles snapping at the clothes and they must have thought we had perished, because they didn't try to look for us. It took us months until we arrived in Nairobi," she sighed deeply, remembering the exhausting journey. "We'd been working at the Acacia Tree for just a few days."

In the silence that engulfed the room, only the crackling of the fire was heard as Mila ended her account.

Flying back to Nairobi the following morning, Elon rejoined Tanya and his clients at the Acacia Tree Hotel. Tanya appeared as physically and emotionally drained as Elon was, having spent the long night contemplating her future. By morning she'd made a difficult decision. Tanya waited until she and Elon and his clients arrived at The Camp before informing Elon of it.

"I'll be going back to Austria with Shauna and Franz when they leave," Tanya told him, avoiding his gaze.

Her words took Elon by surprise. When he didn't respond, she fled to her room.

"You're not going to let her go, are you?" Shauna demanded of Elon when she learned of Tanya's decision.

"If she wants to go, there's nothing I can do!" he responded defensively.

"Do you want her to leave?"

"No," he finally admitted.

"Then tell her!"

"Why? What good would it do? She's young and has her whole life ahead of her! Who the hell am I to keep her from finding what she wants—what she deserves?!"

"What she wants is you and Ani!"

Elon stared at Shauna with a combination of surprise and relief; followed by renewed anger.

"Rika is gone," Shauna continued, her voice softening. "I know how much you miss her. I miss Mutiba. I'll miss him for as long as I live. I love Franz, but . . ." she stopped before saying something she might regret. "Tanya cares deeply about you and Ani. If you'd only—"

"She deserves a loving husband! And children of her own!" Elon cut her off sharply. "Neither of which I'm willing to give her!"

"Like me, Tanya can never have children," Shauna told him quietly.

Her words startled him.

"I won't betray her trust by telling you why," Shauna continued. "But I will tell you this, in case you don't already know—her eyes light up when she's with you and Ani! She's the best substitute mother your daughter could ever have. And she'd be an excellent companion for you. Don't let her go."

Elon studied her thoughtfully before turning away. As much as he tried to deny it, he knew Shauna was right.

Elon waited until almost the last minute to ask Tanya to stay. She was in her room, packing, when he knocked lightly at her door.

"I wish you wouldn't go. Ani needs you," he told her, having difficulty admitting the whole truth.

Tanya regarded him with skepticism.

"Not just for Ani's sake," he finally mumbled. "But for mine as well."

She seemed apprehensive.

"I doubt I'll ever love another woman the way I loved Rika," Elon confided. "But I also doubt that Ani and I will ever find someone we care about as much as we do you."

Tanya's look of apprehension turned to one of confusion.

"I realize it isn't fair of me to ask, considering our age difference and the fact that I never intend to marry—or to have any more children," Elon said without letting on that he knew about Tanya's secret. "But, if you're willing to take a chance on a man who can offer you devotion, if not love, then I'm asking . . . I'm begging you . . . please stay."

Tanya sank onto the bed with a look of total bewilderment. Too shocked to speak, she remained silent as Elon looked around uncomfortably.

"I just wanted you to know," he told her quietly before leaving.

After he left, as Tanya came to her senses, tears rose in her eyes and a smile spread slowly across her face.

Two nights after Shauna and Franz left for Austria, Tanya garnered the strength to go to Elon's room. When she quietly slipped in bed beside him, he gently curled his body around hers. She trembled in his arms as he held her tight, asking nothing of her. As he had with Rika, Elon waited until she was ready. When that time came, he treated Tanya with such tenderness that all her defenses melted away . . . and together they found a safe refuge in each other's touch.

Chapter 17

In the fall of his senior year of high school, seventeen-year-old Cole Lightfoot went hunting with his father and Lee's friend, Ray. They hunted deer in the wild animal park that Lee and some of his colleagues had created on the vast ranch in Texas where Cole had grown up, which was still managed by the Bennetts. The park had an impressive array of exotic and domestic game, which Lee and his friends hunted within its fenced parameters.

On this autumn day, Lee and Ray were trying their hand at high-tech bow and arrow hunting. Cole preferred to stick with his rifle, although his heart wasn't into hunting. In addition to his natural aversion to the practice, the Bennetts had impressed upon Cole that the taking of another creature's life should never be done lightly.

With Simon and Juanita's encouragement, Cole had grown up learning how to target shoot.

"You never know when you might need to put an animal out of its misery," Simon had told him. "You'd want to do it as quickly and painlessly as possible. So learn to shoot straight. And never leave a wounded animal to die—always follow it to the end."

Cole was an excellent shot, which seemed to be one of only two things that pleased Lee Parnell about his illegitimate son—and accounted for why Lee became so irate when, during this particular hunting trip, Cole seemed to purposely miss a young buck that had been perfectly positioned within his sights.

"Damn it, boy!" Lee yelled. "I swear, if you've grown up to be some bleedin' heart animal lover, I'll—"

"Ah, lay off the kid, Lee," Ray intervened with a smile. "He's probably just having a bad day. Huh, Cole?"

Cole shrugged his shoulders as he returned Ray's smile with a half-hearted one of his own.

"Come on!" Lee barked. "That bugger can't have gone far!"

As he traipsed after the men through the leaf-carpeted woods, breathing in the cool crisp air, Cole realized how much he loved autumn. He loved the whole outdoors . . . especially the animals!

Ever since he was thirteen, when he assisted Simon in helping Star's daughter Noelle give birth to her first foal, Cole was determined to become a veterinarian. The colt had been rather large for Noelle to deliver on her own and, if Simon and Cole hadn't been there, both mother and foal might have died.

When Cole decided to become a vet, his attitude toward formal education changed drastically. Although he hadn't applied himself to his full potential throughout grade school, Cole's academic standing was now within the top-five-percentile of his high school class. Which was the other thing that pleased Lee about his son, as he had designs on the boy following in his professional footsteps. Cole hadn't found the courage to tell his overbearing father that he had no desire to do so.

"There it is," Ray whispered when they came upon the young buck that Cole had previously missed.

They were at the boundary of the park, where the frightened animal had come to a stop in a corner of the twelve-foot, chain-link fence.

"Let me have a go at him," Lee said quietly as he raised his powerful bow, placing the animal within its sights.

The arrow whizzed through the air, penetrating the buck's flank. The wounded animal let out a terrified scream as it threw itself against the fence. Ray also shot at it, and soon the poor creature had almost half-a-dozen arrows puncturing non-fatal areas of its body. Cole raised his rifle and put it out of its misery with a single shot to the brain.

"See, Ray. Told you the kid could shoot," Lee boasted.

"Yeah, yeah," Ray smiled.

"Let's get it gutted," Lee said as he and Ray made their way toward the kill.

Cole stayed put, glaring at the men. He was incensed that they showed absolutely no remorse for the horror they had inflicted upon the innocent creature.

"Get your butt over here!" Lee barked at him.

Reluctantly, Cole did as he was told.

"The boy's good with a knife, too," Lee bragged to Ray as he held the skinning knife out to Cole.

Cole gazed into the buck's eye, turning dull in death. He hated skinning and gutting his father's trophies; although he did so willingly with the cattle, sheep, and chickens on the ranch. But, like the Bennetts, Cole felt he had no right to take the life of a wild animal.

"Domestic animals owe their lives to mankind," Juanita had explained her and Simon's philosophy to Cole one day. "It's our responsibility to see that they are well cared for, and that their deaths are as painless as possible. But a wild animal owes nothing to us, and we have no right to take its life unless it's needed for our survival."

Cole, of course, had no way of knowing this philosophy, which became his own, matched that of the man whom he most despised. The man who had taken Rika away from him, and whose name Cole would never forget—Elon O'Shay!

"We don't have all day!" Lee snarled at Cole, bringing him back to the present.

Cole took the knife from Lee and knelt beside the carcass of the buck. Closing his eyes, Cole silently prayed in the way that his birth mother had explained to him when he was just a child. It was the way of her Comanche ancestors, whose lives had been dependent on the bounty of nature. Only Cole's prayer over the dead animal wasn't one of gratitude for giving its life so others might live; but rather it was one of forgiveness for the useless and cruel manner in which it had been killed.

When he had finished his prayer, Cole angrily pulled the arrows from the animal's hide and deftly went to work.

"Your pa's right," Ray told Cole appreciatively as he and Lee lit cigars. "You're good with that knife."

"What'd I tell you?" Lee smiled while puffing away. "Gonna make a great heart surgeon, just like his ole man!"

The hell I am! Cole felt like screaming at his father. Up to his elbows in blood, Cole ripped the intestines from the carcass. He wanted to yell that he was going to be a veterinarian—*a 'bleedin' heart animal doctor'! And to hell with your plans for my future! To hell with you!*

The blood on Cole's hands smeared his forehead as he swept the hair from his eyes. It was his job to carry the gutted animal back to camp. Draping it across his broad shoulders, he did so with little effort. Growing up on the ranch, Cole was quite strong and healthy. He was also extremely good-looking, with his dark-brown hair and soft, brown eyes. Although he didn't flaunt his looks, Cole knew from the way girls treated him that he was attractive to them. Not that he'd admit to noticing, let alone liking the attention.

"Ever have a lion in your sights, Ray?" Lee asked as they sat in the woods around a roaring campfire that night.

The two men were again puffing on cigars while they guzzled whiskey. Gorged from their evening meal, they often burped and rubbed their extended bellies.

Cole was left with the dishes, but he could overhear the conversation.

"You know with my schedule I can't be running off to Africa. I'm waiting on you to bring some here," Ray responded hopefully to Lee's question.

"I'm working on a deal. Shouldn't be too long now. You know, it's the lion more than anything that draws people to Africa," Lee stated knowingly.

"Do tell, Hemingway," Ray teased.

"It's 'the lure of the lion,'" Lee smiled. Recalling the day he'd first made the comment, Lee's smile waned as he became consumed with anger when thinking about Elon O'Shay . . . and Rika. Lee wasn't aware that Rika had been dead for five years. Of the few letters she'd sent, Lee had returned the first one, addressed to Cole, back to Africa unopened. The others Lee had simply discarded, again without opening them. As he hadn't been pushed regarding a divorce, Lee took pleasure in knowing that Rika hadn't married *that son-of-a-bitch Elon O'Shay!*

"Bring us another bottle!" Lee angrily demanded of Cole.

Finishing the dishes, Cole did as he was ordered, taking his place beside the fire.

"Tell you what, boy," Lee smiled through an alcohol-induced haze, "how about you and I take a trip to Africa? We could get us a couple of lions . . . maybe even a two-legged creature while we're at it," he sneered under his breath.

Cole guessed the identity of the "two-legged creature" Lee was referring to. Although he dreamed of someday going to Africa, and had often fantasized about putting an end to the man who'd stolen Rika away from him, Cole had no desire to go there with his abusive father. But he held his tongue and watched silently as Lee and his buddy Ray drank themselves into a stupor.

Tending to the campfire, Cole noticed how its glow flickered on the bloodied coat of the young buck, hanging upside down from the limb of a nearby tree. Focusing on the animal's dull eyes, which had been so bright in life, Cole's own eyes clouded with rage.

On the day of Cole's high school graduation, he finally got up the nerve to inform his father of his decision to become a veterinarian. Cole wished he'd been able to do so prior to Lee's having secured a position for him in pre-med studies at Louisiana State University, in Baton Rouge. With Simon and Juanita's help, Cole had changed his course of study to pre-veterinary medicine. He knew, however, that without his father's financial support, it was questionable if he could accomplish his dream.

On hand to help Cole celebrate his graduation were Simon and Juanita; as well as Lee's chauffer Isaac, Isaac's wife Vera, who was noticeably pregnant with their third child, and their ten-year-old son and seven-year-old daughter. Lee and his latest sex-interest, Marjorie Lynn, were also there.

Looking quite impressive in his cap and gown, Cole smiled as everyone congratulated him following the ceremony, which took place on the high school's football field.

"We're just so proud of you, sweetie!" Marjorie Lynn cooed to Cole. Her voice had a quality of Southern honey to it; and her bright-red lips matched the bottled color of her big, fluffy hair.

"This is for you," she told Cole, handing him an envelope. "It's a gift certificate for two at Chris' Steak House in Baton Rouge, so you and your daddy can have a good meal when he helps you get settled in at LSU!" Knowing the best ways to a man's heart were through his stomach and his kids, her graduation present was a combination of the two—and was intended for Lee's enjoyment as much as Cole's.

"Thanks, Marjorie Lynn," Cole smiled.

"And this is from me," Lee told him proudly, taking an envelope from his pocket.

Opening the envelope, Cole pulled out an airline ticket.

"It's to Johannesburg," Lee told him. "We're set to go in six weeks, after you've gotten your shots and all."

"Great," Cole responded with mixed feelings.

"Your daddy's so proud that you're gonna be a heart surgeon just like him!" Marjorie Lynn gushed.

"No, ma'am," Cole responded after taking a deep breath. "I'm going to be a veterinarian."

Simon and Juanita exchanged looks of concern with Isaac and Vera. Although they were grateful that Cole had finally found the courage to tell his father of his dream, it was perhaps not the right time or place for him to do so.

"Kid's got a great sense of humor, hey Marjorie Lynn?" Lee smiled, not taking Cole seriously.

"It's true," Cole stood his ground. "I've already registered for the classes."

It took Lee a few seconds to realize Cole wasn't joking. When he did, he exploded. "You ungrateful bastard! I'll be damned if you think I'm gonna send you to school to become some goddamned bleedin' heart animal doctor!"

Simon and Juanita rallied around Cole, while Marjorie Lynn appeared shocked. Isaac and his family wisely stayed out of the ruckus.

"I suppose you put him up to this!" Lee accused Simon.

"The boy's got his own mind," Simon responded calmly.

"You little son-of-a-bitch bastard!" Lee turned back to Cole. "You can bet I'm not paying for your goddamned education—or a trip to Africa!" he raged while grabbing the ticket away from Cole.

"Come on!" Lee bellowed at Marjorie Lynn, taking her by the arm as he left in a huff. As he led her away, she almost tripped in her skimpy, high-heeled shoes.

Realizing he had sabotaged his own future, Cole stared sadly at his feet. He hadn't expected his father to react so viciously. Without Lee's money, Cole's prospects of becoming a vet looked bleak.

"Isaac! Vera!" Lee yelled back for them to join him.

"We're very proud of you," Vera told Cole as she gently kissed his cheek before herding her children toward Lee and Marjorie Lynn.

"Yes, sir, right proud!" Isaac beamed as he pumped Cole's hand. "Mister Simon and Miss Juanita have a little something for you from Vera and me," he told Cole, exchanging a knowing smile with the Bennetts before joining Vera and the kids.

Cole watched sadly as Isaac and his family followed Lee and Marjorie Lynn to Lee's limousine.

"We were going to wait until later to give this to you," Simon told Cole as he removed an envelope from his coat pocket and handed it to him.

When he opened the graduation card, Cole wasn't expecting to find the check made out in his name. "What's *this*?" he gasped, his eyes wide with disbelief.

"An answer to your dreams," Juanita smiled.

"*Seventy-five-thousand-dollars?!*" Cole asked incredulously.

"Whether it matters or not, your father paid for your education after all," Simon told him.

Cole gave him a questioning look.

"It's the money your father had his lawyer, Walter Hansen, send to us over the years for your care," Simon explained. "Plus some extra that Isaac and his family, as well as 'Nita and I, threw in."

"But that money was meant for you!" Cole objected.

"Nonsense," Juanita countered kindly. "What your father doesn't know is that Simon and I would have gladly paid *him* for the pleasure of your company."

"But I can't accept—"

"Yes you can," Simon stated firmly. "No more arguing! Let's go eat! Then you've got a graduation party to go to with your friends," he reminded Cole.

"I think I'd rather spend the evening with you two," Cole replied, shaking his head while studying the check.

"Don't be silly," Juanita told him gently as she hooked her arm in his and steered him away. "We're not about to let you stay home with us old fogies!"

"Who are you calling an 'old fogy'?" Simon took offense.

"I love the two of you," Cole admitted quietly as the tears rose in his eyes. Although the Bennetts had often told Cole how much they loved him, he had never before verbalized his love for them. He'd been fearful of loving anyone since losing Rika.

"Not just for this," Cole told them as he held up the check, "but for always being there for me. Thank you," he added tearfully.

Juanita placed his face lovingly between her hands. "It's *we* who thank *you*," she smiled.

"Are we going to stay here all day lollygagging? Or can we go get something to eat?" Simon playfully lamented.

"I swear," Juanita told him while lacing one arm through his and the other through Cole's, "there's nothing like a hungry man!"

"Ain't that the truth?" Simon responded suggestively.

"Stop that!" she gently elbowed him in the stomach.

"Ouch!" he feigned hurt.

Wiping away his tears, Cole smiled at their antics. "How 'bout we all go for a ride tomorrow?" he asked.

"Sure. That is if you have the energy for it after staying out all night with the girls," Simon winked suggestively at Cole.

"Don't be giving him any ideas!" Juanita scolded her husband with another, this time not so gentle, elbowing to the stomach.

"Don't worry, you're the only gal for me," Cole assured her with a hug—although it wasn't entirely true, as Rika would always have a hold on Cole's heart.

Over the next five years, Cole realized his dream of becoming a veterinarian. He also met and became engaged to a young woman who viewed Cole as the answer to *her* dreams.

Eugenie Beauchamp spied Cole on the campus of LSU, where she was majoring in an MRS degree. The progeny of a well-to-do New Orleans family whose roots in Louisiana dated back to the time of Napoleon, Eugenie's comment to her girlfriend when she first laid eyes on Cole was: "I'm gonna marry that boy!"

The fact that the handsome young Texan was working on becoming an animal doctor—and that Eugenie had no use for any four-legged, feathered, or especially scaly creatures—didn't deter her from her goal. *He's just too gorgeous to let get away!* she'd sighed. *Besides, professions can always be changed!* she reasoned. As her mother had helped her father in determining what was best for him, Eugenie felt confident she could do likewise with the man of her dreams.

That Cole was the son of an extremely wealthy doctor didn't escape Eugenie and her family. The fact that his parents had never married was rather non-important to them, as all families had a skeleton or two in their closets. And, although Cole tried to impress upon Eugenie that his father had disinherited him, she was confident that could be remedied as well. After all, her daddy was a lawyer—*a very good lawyer!*

So, without his knowing exactly how or why, in his final year of vet school Cole found himself engaged to a petite brunette Louisiana peach who seemed to think the sun rose and set in his eyes.

"Isn't it beautiful?" Eugenie had exclaimed over a ring one day when they wandered into a jewelry store.

"Would you like to try it on?" the saleswoman offered kindly.

"Oh, pleeease!" Eugenie purred.

"Perhaps you should slip it on her," the saleswoman told Cole while handing him the ring. She stood back with an expectant look on her face.

Not really thinking about what he was doing, Cole did as she suggested when Eugenie thrust her left hand in his face.

"Have you set a date yet?" the saleswoman asked.

"Date?" Cole asked absently.

"For your wedding."

Cole made the mistake of looking into Eugenie's big brown eyes, staring into his with longing and adoration. He didn't have the heart to deny the saleswoman's assumption, or Eugenie's expectation. After all, they had talked about getting married. Or, rather, Eugenie had talked about it.

"I presume you're engaged?" the saleswoman asked sweetly.

"Yes," Cole muttered, still locked into Eugenie's pleading gaze.

Eugenie's eyes widened with joy and relief as she threw her arms around his neck, squealing with delight while smothering his face with kisses. "Wait 'til I tell Mommy and Daddy!" she exclaimed, admiring the ring.

The saleswoman gave them a congratulatory grin.

Forcing a smile, Cole swallowed his fear and uncertainty as he paid for the ring.

Before Cole had time to fully comprehend the reality of his engagement to Eugenie, he found himself arriving at the formal party her parents were hosting for them at a country club in New Orleans.

"Daaaamn!" Eugenie drawled as she tried to avoid a muddy puddle when stepping out of the limousine. "I wish the whole world was cemented!" she whined as Cole helped her navigate the landscaped walkway leading to the country club.

Her outburst was rather disturbing to Cole. More than anything she'd said to date, it impressed upon him their differences. Whereas she wished for a world covered in concrete, he longed for open spaces and the scent of pine trees in the cool morning air.

My God! What have I done? Cole asked himself as he smiled gamely when being greeted by Eugenie's family and friends at the party. But he was too much of a gentleman to bow out.

One of the things Cole hated about his father was the way Lee used and abused women—and Cole didn't want to emulate it. Ironically, in a roundabout way, it was Lee who provided Cole with the opportunity to end his engagement. Or at least postpone it.

Early one morning, barely two weeks before the wedding, the phone rang in Cole's modest apartment in Baton Rouge.

"Cole, this is Walt Hansen, your father's lawyer. I'm sorry to have to tell you, but your father just passed away," Cole was told when he answered the phone.

Rubbing the sleep from his eyes, Cole tried to comprehend what Walt was saying.

"Are you there?" Walt asked.

"Yes. How . . ."

"He had a massive coronary. Again, I'm sorry."

There was a long pause as Cole absorbed the information. He wasn't surprised that he didn't feel anything. Except perhaps curiosity as to what was expected of him. Before he could ask, Walt continued.

"He had left instructions as to funeral arrangements, which Marjorie Lynn is helping me with. I'll phone back with the details. After the service, we'll need to talk."

"Fine," Cole agreed before slowly hanging up. He stared vacantly at the ceiling.

"Who was that?" Eugenie asked in a sleepy voice as she stirred beside him.

"My father's dead," he told her in a flat tone.

"Oh?" she responded, her voice conveying more relief than shock. "I'm so sorry," she told him, feigning sympathy as she reached out for him.

Cole gave Eugenie what she wanted, and took from her what he needed.

"You are your father's primary heir," Walt informed Cole when they met alone at Walt's office in Houston the day after Lee's funeral. They sat opposite each other at Walt's desk.

"You, of all people, should know that he disowned me," Cole responded while studying the photo of five smiling kids of various ages, displayed on the desk.

"We lawyers tend to be rather busy. And, with raising my kids on my own after my wife died, . . . I just never got around to filing the papers," Walt explained lamely.

Cole regarded Walt with more amusement than surprise. For a long time Cole had known that Walter Hansen wasn't an ordinary lawyer—*he had a heart!* The money that had been sent to the Bennetts for Cole's keep throughout the years had come through Walt's office. It could have easily been misdirected.

"Nice kids," Cole commented, regarding the photo of Walt's smiling brood.

"They're my life," Walt admitted with a melancholy smile. "Technically, your daddy was still married to Rika," he returned to the business at hand.

Cole looked surprised. But then he remembered overhearing the telephone conversation Lee had with Walt many years ago. Cole could still hear the anger in his father's voice, directing Walt to make life miserable for Rika and "that son-of-a-bitch Elon O'Shay!" *That son-of-a-bitch Elon O'Shay!* Cole repeated bitterly in his mind.

"Lee was quite wealthy. He left considerable holdings, in addition to his practice," Walt continued.

"I don't want any of it," Cole stated absently.

"Well, you should!" Walt responded angrily. "If any two people deserve some compensation for the shit Lee Parnell dished out, it's you and Rika!"

Cole blinked with surprise. *Not only does Walter Hansen have a heart, he has a temper as well!* Cole realized.

"I've taken the liberty of trying to find Rika," Walt said as he composed himself. "I couldn't locate her in Uganda. Her parents live in Holland, but they're apparently doing missionary work in South Africa, and I haven't been able to get hold of them."

Seeing Cole's hardened expression, Walt studied him with concern.

A wave of resentment had swept over Cole as he remembered how he'd felt when he was seven years old, waiting at the airport with a bouquet of wilted roses. Roses Cole had picked himself to give to Rika. But she never showed up—because a man by the name of Elon O'Shay had taken her away from him!

"She loved you very much," Walt told him, sensing Cole was thinking of Rika.

Cole regarded him with a blank stare.

"I know how hard it was for you to lose her," Walt said. "But, to be honest, I hope she was able to find in Elon O'Shay what she couldn't find in your father."

Cole refused to acknowledge that Rika might have remained in Africa of her own volition. It was easier for him to blame Elon O'Shay, even after all these years. Cole narrowed his eyes with anger as he glared out the window at the Houston skyline, seen from Walt's high-rise office.

Walt wasn't sure if Cole knew who Elon O'Shay was. Seeing Cole's expression, Walt realized that he did. He was concerned by the hatred registering on Cole's face.

"There is one thing," Cole said as he turned his attention back to Walt. "The animal park. I'd like to buy out the partners and turn it into a sanctuary."

Walt nodded with relief, feeling Cole's love of animals could be his saving grace.

"What about these?" Walt asked as he removed half-a-dozen

automobile keys from a drawer, placing them on his desk. The keys had tags identifying the vehicles they belonged to.

Cole was well aware of his father's expensive car collection. Studying the keys, the one to the late-model Chevy truck interested him. "For the Bennetts," he explained, handing the key to Walt, whom Cole knew would get the vehicle to them.

A thought seemed to cross Cole's mind as he pocketed the keys to the Porsche.

"Give Marjorie Lynn whichever one she wants," he directed, regarding the remaining vehicles. "As well as the house and some financial support."

"That's very considerate of you," Walt nodded, admiring his generosity.

"She deserves whatever she can get," Cole explained. "It amazes me that she put up with the womanizing son-of-a-bitch for as long as she did. Let your kids look over the rest," he offered, motioning to the keys. "Some of them look old enough to drive," he added, glancing again at the photo. "Oh, and I'd like to do more for the Bennetts. And something for Isaac and his family . . . And any charities that you think might—"

"Whoa!" Walt laughed as he held up his hands. "Don't go giving it all away. There's still Rika to consider. And when you and Eugenie are married—"

The phone rang.

"Yes?" Walt answered. "Right," he eventually responded. "Let me know if you find out anything else. Thanks."

After hanging up, Walt appeared conflicted. Cole's obvious hatred toward Elon O'Shay made Walt hesitant to pass on the information he'd just received.

"We've located Elon O'Shay," he decided to inform Cole. "He's operating a safari camp near the Maasai Mara Game Reserve, in Kenya."

Cole nodded solemnly. "Eugenie and I were originally going to Kenya for our honeymoon. I even got all the shots and visas. But then she decided on Paris."

"Paris would be better," Walt said, concerned how Cole's

animosity toward Elon O'Shay could manifest itself if they were to ever meet.

"Maybe," Cole responded vaguely as he rose to leave.

"I'll see you at the wedding," Walt smiled as they shook hands in parting. "We'll talk more after you've gotten back from your honeymoon. Oh, the Porsche is parked in the garage at Lee's office. I'll call the attendant and tell him you'll be picking it up. I'll send whatever you need to register it. And the same for the Bennetts, with the truck."

"Thank you, Mr. Hansen, for everything," Cole told him.

"Please, call me Walt."

"Walt," Cole nodded.

Walt sadly watched Cole leave. He'd always had a soft spot in his heart for the young man, looking on him as almost one of his own. Walt was grateful that Cole had found what seemed to be a fine young woman, and would be settling down soon.

But, as Cole drove Lee's fire-engine-red Porsche out of Houston, he was glad Eugenie wasn't with him, as she and her family had flown back to Louisiana after Lee's funeral. Eugenie's lament that the whole world should be cemented came back to haunt Cole. By the time he arrived at the little apartment they shared in Baton Rouge, he'd made the decision to go to Africa after all—without Eugenie.

As he'd mentioned to Walt, Cole had already gotten the required inoculations and visas, and it took him only two days to prepare for the trip to Kenya. He didn't tell Eugenie that he was leaving. As he looked down on her while she slept in the pre-dawn hour on the morning of his departure, Cole felt a pang of guilt. Their wedding was scheduled for the following week.

Cole placed a note for Eugenie on the nightstand, in which he'd written that his father's death left him with some unfinished business—business that would prevent him from getting married at this time. He apologized to Eugenie for any hurt he caused her.

Laying the keys to Lee's Porsche and the tickets to Paris next to the note, along with a thousand dollars in cash, Cole then picked up his few bags and went outside to wait for the taxi.

On the ride to the airport, Cole had mixed feelings as to what lay ahead. He both prayed for and dreaded a reunion with Rika. *And meeting that son-of-a-bitch Elon O'Shay!* Cole thought with renewed anger.

Chapter 18

Three teenaged Maasai murrani loped confidently across the savannah. They were proud in the knowledge that they hadn't brought dishonor upon their families during their initiation as warriors—for they hadn't flinched or cried out when being circumcised.

Wearing short togas made from new cloth symbolizing their exalted status, their bodies were adorned with brightly colored bead ornaments made for them by their girlfriends. Their stretched earlobes hung low with beaded hoops, and red ochre mixed with animal fat coated their plaited hair. Red ochre had also been applied to their long trim legs, with zebra-like patterns drawn in a way that exposed the rich dark skin beneath.

With them they carried the tools of their position: short double-sided swords called "pangas," secured in cowhide sheaths attached to beaded belts; bows slung across their shoulders, with poison-tipped arrows stored in leather quivers; buffalo-hide shields painted with designs signifying bravery; wooden clubs called "o-rinkas," that had smooth rounded heads; and long spears with formidable steel blades that now reflected the morning sun.

Reaching the crest of a small hill, the three young warriors momentarily halted. Below them the vast savannah was blackened with perhaps a million wildebeest, as it was the time of the great migration. Suddenly the morning air was shattered by the sound of rapid gunfire, startling the animals into a stampede. The murrani broke into a run and headed in the direction of the shots.

In a wooded area next to the river, they stopped and stared at a scene of unfathomable carnage. Their hearts caught in their throats at the sight of a small herd of elephants being brutally and systematically slaughtered.

The poachers had known to dispose of the herd's matriarch first. The remaining adult elephants made valiant, though confused and terrified attempts to shelter the younger ones. But none were spared. When the sounds of their anguished cries were silenced and the guns were stilled, the butchers sprang upon the magnificent beasts and hacked away the ivory even as some weren't yet dead. They were unaware of being watched.

With fury burning in their eyes, two of the young murrani raised their spears and were about to attack the poachers when the other murran stopped them. Recognizing the power and cold determination of the killers, he knew it would be suicidal to try and avenge the slaughter on their own. He offered to go for help while the other two remained behind to see what direction the poachers headed once their work was done.

Before leaving, the young murran took note of how many men had taken part in the massacre, as well as the weapons they carried. Of added concern was the uniform some of them wore and the emblem displayed on their vehicles; for it was the symbol of the organization designed to protect the animals whose blood now soaked the ground.

As the cries of the slaughtered elephants still rang in his ears, the young warrior ran to report the carnage to his older brother Kijabe, who worked as a ranger in the Maasai Mara Reserve.

With Tanya at his side, Elon waited on the veranda of The Camp's lodge as a caravan of olive-green Land Rovers arrived at the well-manicured grounds. Still exceedingly handsome, with his dark hair graying around the temples, Elon's face reflected a rugged maturity from years of exposure to the African environment. Seemingly content, only his sky-blue eyes betrayed any occasional glimpse of earlier sorrows.

The years had been quite kind to Tanya, who had matured into a very lovely woman who appeared happy, although not inwardly secure, in being Elon's companion. As she now stood beside him on the veranda, she gave him a gentle smile.

Half-a-dozen Leonbergers, descendants of the pair Rika's parents had given to Ani eleven years earlier, greeted the arriving vehicles with raucous barking.

At the wheel of the first vehicle, Harun got out and gave Elon a forced smile. Though not as tall as his brother Mutiba had been, Harun had grown into a fine-looking young man with an easy-going nature that seemed to be unaffected by the horrors he had once experienced.

Harun had much to be thankful for. He and Emi were married and now had three young children: two boys, eight-year-old Beni and six-year-old Juba; and an infant daughter, Tessa. Beni and Juba ran with the dogs as they greeted Harun and the safari guests.

Remaining on the veranda, Elon returned Harun's smile with a forced one of his own. He knew Harun felt as he did, that their clients would have to be tolerated even if they weren't really welcomed. For Elon had long dreaded this day—when Hollywood invaded The Camp.

When he was growing up, Elon had accompanied his father on safaris that involved the making of a movie. The fact that these guests were shooting a documentary did little to ease Elon's resentment, as they were still from Hollywood—*That place with a state of mind giving men license to be rude, demanding, and smug in the belief that theirs is the greatest endeavor on earth!* Elon lamented.

"Aren't you going to welcome them?" Tanya asked him.

"Why don't you greet them while I go for a drive?" Elon suggested through clenched teeth, with the smile plastered on his lips.

But he complied when she took him by the arm and directed him down the steps.

"Welcome to The Camp," Tanya greeted their clients after quieting the dogs.

"Mr. and Mrs. O'Shay, I presume? Sam Bloomstein, director," the group's leader introduced himself as his cameraman took shots of The Camp.

Tanya was grateful Elon didn't contradict Sam's assumption that she and Elon were married. "Call me Tanya," she smiled as she shook Sam's hand. "And this is Elon."

She narrowed her eyes at Elon, indicating he should be polite. He broadened his plastic smile as he and Sam shook hands.

"How was the journey from Nairobi?" Tanya asked their guests.

"Full of potholes and dust," one of the men quipped.

"Don't suppose you have hot-running water and flushing toilets?" another asked.

"Of course," Tanya responded kindly. "Every tent has—"

"Tents? Sam, I thought you said this place was top end!" another whined.

"I'm sure you'll find them quite comfortable," Tanya said, her patience beginning to fray. "Elon, why don't you and Harun get them settled in while I help Mila and Emi with lunch?" she suggested before leaving.

Elon regarded the cameraman with displeasure as he filmed Sam, who was narrating into a microphone. To Elon's dismay, with the camera still rolling, Sam came and put his arm around his shoulder as if they were long-lost friends.

"This is Elon O'Shay, whose father Quinn was one of the last Great White Hunters. Elon and his charming wife Tanya have operated this camp for how long now?" Sam inquired before shoving the microphone in Elon's face.

Elon appeared to squirm in the spotlight. "Eleven years," he mumbled.

"Eleven years in one of the most untamed corners of the world—Kenya's Maasai Mara Reserve," Sam addressed the camera.

He drew his finger across his throat, indicating the cameraman to "cut."

Elon went to help Harun with the luggage. "It's just for a week," Elon whispered, trying to sound upbeat.

Harun rolled his eyes, suggesting a week could seem like an eternity.

"Not bad!" Sam reacted appreciatively as he followed Elon inside one of the tent-like cottages. "This should suit us quite nicely. I'm afraid some of my crew aren't as adventurous as I'd like," he told Elon.

Elon surmised that Sam Bloomstein wasn't all that adventurous himself. "So, you're filming a documentary," Elon commented. "On the migration?"

"Actually," Sam lowered his voice and looked around to make sure he wasn't being overheard, "we're doing kind of a counter-culture piece. You know all the current sentimental crap against poaching and how it could throw certain species into extinction? Well, my film addresses the idea that Kenya's wildlife would be better served if hunting were again legalized. The theory being that, in the long run, it actually amounts to better conservation. Like with deer and duck hunting in the States."

Sam studied Elon's expression for signs of approval, but it told him nothing.

"In my research," Sam continued, "I discovered that your father was not only known for his hunting skills, but he hobnobbed with the best of 'em. Not to mention his association with other interesting characters . . . Hemingway, for one."

"Hemingway was a lousy shot and drank too much," Elon offered coolly.

"Regardless, he epitomized the *chutzpah*, the *machismo* of that rare and virile breed known as 'Great White Hunter.'"

"He killed himself," Elon reminded Sam of Hemingway's not-so-elegant demise.

"Whatever. When I learned that Quinn O'Shay's son ran a safari camp, I thought perhaps the apple might not have fallen far from the tree. I hope I—"

"Lunch is ready," Harun called from outside, while ringing a cowbell.

"Good!" Sam enthused. "I could eat an elephant!"

"I'm afraid elephant isn't on today's menu," Elon responded with forced friendliness. "But we do have three of the finest chefs in Kenya," he said before turning to go.

"I'll just clean up a bit and be right there," Sam called after him.

"One week!" Elon shook his head as he, Harun, Beni, and Juba made their way toward the lodge where Mila, Tanya, and Emi were putting the finishing touches on the luncheon buffet. Elon hadn't exaggerated—the food looked like works of art!

In the years since her and Harun's harrowing escape from Uganda, Mila had regained much of the weight that she'd lost. Her hair was now almost completely gray, and her physical strength had diminished. But mentally Mila was as perceptive as ever.

Emi, of course, had changed the most over the years. Now the mother of three children, she had blossomed into a full-bodied, strikingly beautiful young woman. Her love and devotion to Harun and their children were heartwarming, as was theirs for her. For although Emi was unable to speak, her family had no difficulty in deciphering her every need, wish, and emotion.

Entering the dining room, Harun greeted Emi and little Tessa with gentle kisses. The infant, who was strapped to her mother's back, gave her papa a gurgling smile.

Harun playfully slapped his sons' hands as they reached for the food. "Beni, Juba, wash up first," he directed, herding them toward the bathroom.

Elon furrowed his brow as he checked his watch. "I told Ani to be back by now."

"Don't worry, she'll be here," Tanya stated in Ani's defense.

"She'd better be," Elon responded sternly as Sam and his crew joined them.

"Look at this spread!" the cameraman exclaimed while photographing the buffet.

"Hey, Sam, why can't craft services look like this?" one of the crew asked.

"What have we here?" the cameraman commented salaciously as he directed the camera beyond the back deck, where fifteen-year-old Ani had brought her jeep to a grinding stop. From a distance, the vehicle's exterior appeared to have a variegated, olive-green camouflaged-look; but it was actually a beautifully designed collage of African animals that Ani had painted herself.

Dressed in shorts and a T-shirt, Ani stretched her long, shapely legs from out of the vehicle.

Harun and his young sons returned to the dining room just as it echoed with a collective gasp out of the men from Hollywood as they focused on Ani.

Running her tanned fingers through her long, blonde hair after shaking it in place, Ani wasn't aware of the drooling looks she was eliciting. She playfully acknowledged the dogs when they happily ran to greet her. A family of warthogs squealed in delight, begging for their share of her attention. A young vervet monkey leaped onto Ani's shoulder and hung on tight as she sprinted with the grace of a gazelle toward the back entrance to her room inside the lodge.

Tanya, Mila, and Emi came from the kitchen with the last of the food. They were surprised to see their guests frozen in awe as they stared toward where Ani had disappeared.

Taking his place at the table with his sons, Harun looked amused when realizing what had happened.

"Who was *that*?" the cameraman asked breathlessly as he lowered the camera.

"My daughter," Elon replied in a threatening tone.

"She's gorgeous, even by Hollywood standards," Sam stated appreciatively. "How old is she?"

"Fifteen," Mila responded, surpassing Elon's threatening tone.

With the exception of Sam, the men took the hint to back off as they settled into their chairs.

"Will she be joining us?" Sam asked. "What's her name?"

"Anika," Tanya told him, trying to remain friendly although she too was concerned by the men's reaction. "We call her Ani."

"She could easily be a model, perhaps even an actress," Sam said. "In fact, if—"

"She'll be going to school in Switzerland the end of—" Elon cut him off until he himself was interrupted by the sound of chairs scraping the floor as the men hurriedly stood when Ani entered the room.

Beni and Juba appeared clueless as to why the men were suddenly standing. Harun seemed even more amused.

Her face and hair slightly damp from the water she'd quickly splashed on it, Ani seemed surprised, and then amused by the attention her entrance had created. Until she saw the disapproving look on her father's face. As she took her place at the table, Sam and the cameraman practically tripped over one another to pull the chair out for her.

"Thank you," Ani told the men with a soft smile and melodious voice reminiscent of her mother's.

"You're quite welcome," Sam replied as he returned to his seat. "Ani, is it?"

She nodded. Her green eyes, a shade between Rika's pale-green and her Aunt Shauna's emerald ones, had a mischievous glint to them.

"I'm Sam Bloomstein, film director. And this is my crew," Sam introduced himself and the others with a sweeping gesture.

"We were just discussing the possibility of your becoming a model . . . or actress," the cameraman ventured.

"But your parents tell us you're about to be shipped off to Switzerland," Sam stated with disappointment.

Ani shot a resentful glance in Tanya's direction. "Tanya is not my mother," she responded coolly. "She and my father aren't married."

Tanya's eyes sank with her heart. It wasn't the first time Ani had been so insensitive. Tanya knew it was mostly Ani's age talking—along with the teenager's erroneous assumption that Tanya was behind the decision to send her away to school. Plus it was apparent that, as Ani had grown older, she'd become rather possessive of her father . . . and resentful of his relationship with Tanya. Hoping it was just a stage Ani would eventually grow out of, Tanya tried not to take it too personally. But it was difficult to do so when Ani's feelings toward her were made so public.

Tanya noticed the sternness reflected in Elon's eyes as he regarded his daughter. *But what can he do?* she thought sadly. *Ani had only spoken the truth.*

"Perhaps you would tell us about the movie you're making," Mila suggested to Sam, hoping to diffuse the tension that she saw was mounting between Elon and his daughter.

"It's a documentary. It addresses the changing environmental and political climate of East Africa since the end of colonialism. Specifically in regards to the wildlife and Kenya's current prohibition against hunting," Sam stated in a broad half-truth while glancing in Elon's direction.

"We're naturally most interested in the 'Big Five': elephant, rhino, buffalo, leopard, and of course, lion," the cameraman elaborated.

"There are very few rhino left in the area, due to poaching," Harun stated sadly.

"I happened to see one this morning," Ani offered brightly.

"Perhaps you could show us where?" Sam asked hopefully.

Ani looked to her father for permission.

"No," Elon told her sternly.

"Is it true that rhinos have god-awful eyesight?" one of the crewmembers asked.

"And that your grandfather played matador with one?" Sam asked Ani.

Ani wasn't aware of the documented event. She gave her father a questioning look, but he didn't respond.

"I never knew my grandfather," Ani told Sam. "But I've heard of Maasai children sneaking up on a sleeping rhino and placing pebbles on its back."

"I'd love to see that!" Sam laughed.

"Speaking of Maasai," the cameraman stated respectfully as he stared toward the entrance to the room, where Kijabe stood dressed in his ranger uniform with his hat in his hand, flanked by two traditionally-attired Maasai elders.

No longer the lanky teenager who had befriended Elon when he first arrived at The Camp, Kijabe was now considerably taller and more muscular. He still had an imposing air about him.

"Hello, Kijabe," Mila greeted him, acknowledging the elders with a nod. "We were just having lunch. Would the three of you care to join us?"

"Thank you, but no," Kijabe responded with a smile that evaporated when he looked toward Elon. "Can I have a word with you?" he asked.

"Of course," Elon replied, realizing something was wrong. He followed Kijabe and the elders outside to where Kijabe's brother, the young murran who'd witnessed the massacre of the elephants, sat rigid in Kijabe's official jeep.

"Sopa, Gilisho," Elon greeted the young warrior. "What's up?" Elon asked as he turned back to Kijabe.

"Poachers. Wiped out a herd of elephants," Kijabe responded with anger flashing in his eyes.

Elon looked alarmed—and angry. "Where? When?" he asked.

"This morning, east of the Loita. Eight of them, armed with AK-47s. Three are wearing uniforms, and their vehicles are identified as belonging to the Global Animal Protection Agency," Kijabe told Elon with quiet rage. "If you come along, there will be five of us."

Studying the two Maasai elders, Elon knew they weren't included among the five. He, Kijabe, and Kijabe's brother Gilisho made three.

"Who are the other two?" Elon asked.

"Gil's friends," Kijabe replied.

Elon knew exactly what was being asked of him—and why. Poaching was an insidious cancer that permeated Kenyan society, even at the highest level of government. If Kijabe were to ask his colleagues for help, more than likely he wouldn't come back alive. Elon knew the same applied to them all. *Two men and three teenagers against a pack of killers armed with AK-47s!* Elon shook his head. *And I'm the only one who can shoot worth a damn!*

"Count me in," he responded, hiding his reluctance.

"Bring your rifle," Kijabe suggested needlessly. "I'll be back soon," he told Elon as he and the elders got in Kijabe's jeep and headed for their village.

As he watched them drive away, Elon thought of the animal rights activists and their fund-raising efforts to support GAPA—the world's foremost wildlife protection organization. Little did they know that much of those funds simply lined the pockets of corrupt officials; or provided the organization's own people with the means to destroy what they were supposed to be protecting.

"Is everything all right?" Tanya asked worriedly as Elon removed one of his rifles and some ammunition from the gun cabinet in the lodge's office.

"I'd appreciate it if you and Mila would pack some food and water, enough for five people for maybe as long as four days," he told her quietly as he loaded the rifle before stuffing his pockets with ammunition and relocking the gun cabinet.

Tanya's concern intensified.

"Don't worry, I'll be fine," he tried to reassure her with a gentle kiss on the cheek.

Before returning to the dining room, Elon propped the rifle against the wall in the entryway. "I need to take care of some business for a few days," he explained to Sam and his crew as Tanya, Mila, and Emi quickly disappeared into the kitchen. "Harun and Tanya can show you around while I'm gone."

"And me?" Ani asked hopefully.

"No. I want you to stay here and help Mila," Elon told her sternly.

Ani slumped in her chair with a sullen expression as she watched him leave, followed by Harun. Remaining at the table, Beni and Juba studied Ani with curiosity—still wondering what she had done to elicit so much attention from the strangers.

Sam took advantage of the fact that Ani was left without any chaperones. "Interesting necklace you're wearing," he commented.

"It's the dewclaw of a lion, which is what it uses to disembowel its prey," Ani told him. "When I was very young, it was given to me by the ranger who was just here."

"I can see you making a lot of money in Hollywood," Sam told her, changing the subject. "I know your father thinks you're a bit young, but when the time comes, look me up," he offered, handing her one of his business cards.

Ani's mood visibly brightened as she took the card from him.

Outside on the veranda, Harun waited with Elon for Kijabe to return. "Are you sure you don't need me to come along?" Harun asked as he studied Elon's rifle with concern.

"It's important that you stay here," Elon told him.

Tanya and Mila brought the food and water Elon had requested. Kijabe and his brother Gilisho soon arrived without the elders, whom they'd left at the village.

Remaining on the veranda with Mila, Tanya watched fearfully as Harun helped Elon carry the supplies to Kijabe's jeep. Loading them next to Gilisho on the back seat of the vehicle, Elon glanced at the teenager's feet and saw the firearms Kijabe had brought. *They're not AK-47s, but they'll have to do,* Elon thought as he added his rifle to the small arsenal before sitting next to Kijabe in the front passenger's seat.

Elon and Harun exchanged a look of mutual understanding as the jeep pulled away. Mila put her arm around Tanya in an attempt to comfort her. Without having to be told, Harun and the women knew why Kijabe needed Elon's help—and they greatly feared for the men's safety.

Elon, Kijabe, and Gilisho drove in silence toward the site of the massacre. Vultures circling overhead helped mark the spot from the air. Hiding the jeep in a small ravine, they took their weapons and walked the remaining distance in case the poachers were still around. But only the two young murrani were there, watching silently as hyenas and jackals tore at the carcasses of the slaughtered elephants.

Seeing the devastation, Elon was consumed with rage. Noticing a movement different from that of the scavengers, his fury intensified when he saw an infant elephant swaying next to the body of its dead mother, trying to rouse her with its little trunk.

For a fleeting moment Elon imagined the baby being nurtured by the women and children at The Camp. And, from the looks on Kijabe and the three murrani's faces, it was obvious they also agonized over the tiny elephant. But they all knew that taking the time to save it would mean giving the men who orphaned it the freedom to create more orphans. And to put a merciful end to it with a swift bullet to the brain could alert the poachers that they were being followed.

Realizing there was nothing they could do for the doomed infant, Kijabe and the murrani sadly turned away. Elon followed at a distance.

Returning to the jeep, Gilisho's mates pointed out the direction the poachers had gone. At nightfall they caught up with them. Leaving their vehicle parked at a distance from the killers' camp, they crept up on them by intermittent moonlight shining through gathering storm clouds.

The fact that the poachers had built a fire indicated they had no idea they were being hunted. By the fire's glow, six poachers could be detected. Then a seventh, as the man staggered out of the bushes while zipping up his pants.

The murrani had counted eight men who'd taken part in the massacre. Kijabe motioned toward a bedroll spread between a lorry and a jeep, both vehicles bearing the GAPA emblem. It appeared that the eighth man was bundled within the blankets.

Kijabe indicated to Gilisho that he and his two friends should circle the camp and cover it from the opposite direction. They took off soundlessly into the night.

Elon lay prone on the ground next to Kijabe, glaring at the poachers with his rifle gripped in his hands and one of Kijabe's pistols tucked in his belt. With his heart pounding rapidly in his ears, Elon waited with Kijabe for what seemed like hours—but was actually only twenty-minutes.

They watched as the poachers got progressively drunk on beer. Eventually one went into the bushes to relieve himself. When he didn't return after several minutes, his drunken friends called to him. When he still didn't respond, one of them went looking for him while the others remained by the fire, making crude suggestions as to what might be detaining their friend.

Kijabe and Elon crept closer as the men's laughter echoed through the camp. Pausing within thirty-feet of the poachers, they watched as one of them stood and faced the direction where the other two had disappeared. The man took one step forward before falling backwards with a startled expression as an arrow pierced his throat. Unable to scream, he thrashed about as the arrow's poison quickly spread throughout his body. A blood-curdling Maasai cry shattered the night as two more arrows and a spear found their targets.

The poachers screamed in fear and agony as the murrani fell upon them, attacking them with their pangas. With his o-rinka, Gilisho crushed the skull of one of the men before thrusting his spear through his body with such force that it was skewered to the ground.

Elon and Kijabe rushed to where the last poacher remained hidden in the bedroll. When Kijabe pulled back the blanket, Elon recognized the man as one of Kijabe's colleagues. Even more shocking was the sight of the young Maasai woman who had been sleeping next to the ranger.

Elon watched as the man rose to his knees, begging Kijabe for mercy. With obvious difficulty, Kijabe shot him through the heart at close range.

As the ranger convulsed violently before dying, the woman emitted the high-pitched warbling cry of the Maasai. Kijabe and the murrani remained motionless. Elon knew they would do nothing—as their culture strictly forbade them from killing a woman. Elon also knew that, as a witness to their revenge, the woman could not be spared.

Recalling the scene of the brutally slaughtered elephants, and the infant trying to rouse its dead mother, Elon aimed the pistol at the young woman's forehead and silenced her forever. It wasn't until she fell dead on her back that Elon realized with a jolt that she was pregnant.

The stillness that followed was almost deafening. A streak of lightning and a clap of thunder eventually roused Elon and the others from their collective state of shock.

On weakened legs, Elon staggered to the edge of the poachers' camp and vomited. He had to force himself to return to where Kijabe and the murrani had gathered the poachers' bodies into a pile. As they brought the bodies of the two men who had disappeared into the bush and added them to the pile, Elon saw that their throats had been cleanly slit.

Elon tried to suppress the realization of what he, Kijabe, and the murrani had done. But, as the young woman's cry reverberated in his mind, Elon knew that her death—and the death of her unborn child—would haunt him for the rest of his life.

Going to the poachers' vehicles, Elon pulled back the tarp covering the bed of their lorry, exposing the bloodied ivory and one lone rhino horn.

Finding a can of petrol in the poachers' jeep, Kijabe doused the bodies with the fluid and then ignited them. As the flames leapt into the air, Elon ripped off pieces of the blanket the ranger and the woman had been wrapped in. He stuffed the pieces like fuses into the gas tanks of the poachers' two vehicles.

Picking up a stick, Elon lit it from the burning bodies. He motioned for Kijabe and the murrani to leave. Gilisho and his friends made a hasty retreat toward their jeep, but Kijabe hung back, watching as Elon lit the makeshift fuses.

When Elon remained motionless by the vehicles, Kijabe rushed toward him. Grabbing hold of Elon, Kijabe had to practically drag him away. They hadn't gone far before the vehicles exploded behind them, knocking them to the ground.

Suddenly the sky crackled with thunder and lightning as rain poured down in slanted sheets. Kijabe and Elon remained where they had fallen as the earth turned to mud around them, mingling with the blood of the slain poachers. Regaining their senses, Kijabe pulled Elon to his feet and together they joined the murrani at the jeep.

As they drove away, Elon and the others sat in stunned silence while shivering in the open vehicle. They trembled not only from the cold night rain, but also from the realization that the evidence of their killing spree wouldn't be destroyed after all.

Lying awake in their bed at The Camp, Tanya listened silently as Elon returned in the pre-dawn darkness.

Standing in the shower, fully dressed, Elon watched the mud and blood swirl down the drain until the hot water ran out. Removing his clothes, he scrubbed his body with cold water and soap. After drying off, he quietly slipped into bed.

As Elon lay down beside her, naked and shivering from the cold shower and emotional trauma of the night's events, Tanya gently wrapped her arm around him. He was grateful that she didn't speak. Warming to her touch, he eventually fell into an exhausted, haunted sleep.

Chapter 19

Elon sat up in bed with a jolt. Gasping for air, his naked body drenched with sweat, he recalled the nightmare that woke him. He swallowed back the rising nausea when realizing it wasn't just a bad dream.

Looking toward Tanya's side of the bed, Elon was relieved to see she wasn't there. Glancing at the bedside clock, he saw it was almost noon.

After showering and shaving, Elon went to the kitchen where Mila and Emi were preparing lunch. "Where is everybody?" he asked Mila.

As usual, little Tessa was strapped to Emi's back. The baby smiled and reached out for Elon, but he uncharacteristically ignored her.

"At the manyatta," Mila told Elon, referring to the Maasai village. "They took the dogs with them, so you could sleep," she added, regarding him with concern.

"Ani?" Elon asked worriedly, avoiding Mila's gaze.

"She's out by the pool. Shauna radioed yesterday evening. She'll be arriving in Nairobi this afternoon at three."

"Today? She wasn't supposed to be here until next week!"

"You should take Tanya with you when you pick her up," Mila suggested. "And have supper in town. Perhaps stay the night."

"What about our clients? And I'm not about to leave Ani here with those—"

"Harun, Emi, and I will take care of the guests and keep an

eye on Ani," Mila assured him. "I feel it's important that you and Tanya spend some time with Shauna by yourselves," she stressed. When Mila had spoken with Shauna over the radio the previous evening, she could tell something was wrong. She wondered if Shauna had finally found out about Franz' secret.

Mila was grateful that Elon left without countering her suggestion. She knew it would be good for him to get away for a while; and that he needed time to recover from what Mila sensed had been an extremely harrowing night for him.

Mila was also concerned by a dream she'd had during the night—of a dust storm rising from the west, and a large shadowy figure that she knew signified death. Forcing the image from her mind, Mila returned to the task of preparing the mid-day meal.

Joining Ani at the pool, Elon looked disapprovingly at the skimpy bikini she was wearing. She was attempting to read a book, but her pet monkey wanted her to play with him, and he was making it hard for Ani to concentrate.

"Tanya and I will be flying to Nairobi to pick up your Aunt Shauna, and we won't be back until tomorrow," Elon told her. "I want you to get dressed and go help Mila. You're to mind what she says, and not leave The Camp while we're gone."

"But—" Ani started to object.

"I'm not going to argue with you!" he warned. "I want you to get dressed now! And watch what you wear while I'm away!"

Ani rose with a pout and resentfully did as she was told, with the monkey hitching a ride on her shoulder.

Elon had often seen his daughter in a bikini, as had previous safari guests. But it hadn't bothered him before now—with the men from Hollywood so blatantly admiring her. Elon mentally counted the days until Ani would be safely tucked away at the all-girls' school in Switzerland.

"I'd rather just go directly to The Camp," Shauna told Elon and Tanya when they met her at the international airport in Nairobi later that afternoon.

Shauna hardly seemed to have aged a day over the past decade. But Mila was right—Shauna did appear stressed. And it did concern Franz. Only not to the extent that Mila had imagined. Franz had grown rather distant from her, and Shauna couldn't understand why. She largely blamed herself . . . for not being able to give him children.

Seeing how Franz looked at Harry and Lisl's son Fredrick, who had grown into a very handsome teenager, Shauna felt that Franz regretted not being a father. Over the years they had talked a few times about adopting; but with the demands of his businesses, her musical engagements, their travels, and the responsibility of maintaining their properties, they never got around to doing it.

Tanya had been looking forward to spending time with Elon and Shauna in Nairobi, and she was disappointed that they wouldn't be staying the night. But she kept her disappointment to herself; as well as the hurt she felt when seeing how relieved Elon was that they weren't staying.

On the way back to The Camp, when glancing down at the passing landscape while at the controls of the Cessna, Elon noticed a solitary rhino resting in a dry riverbed. Remembering the rhino horn that had been part of the poachers' bloody loot, Elon made a mental note of the animal's location. He gave only a cursory glance to the olive-green Land Rover headed toward the riverbed, followed at a distance by a tan-colored Rover.

When they landed at The Camp, Shauna was given a jubilant welcome.

"Beni! Juba!" she exclaimed after exchanging hugs and kisses with their parents and grandmother. The boys smiled when finding themselves in Shauna's loving embrace.

"And this must be little Tessa!" Shauna gushed over the baby strapped to Emi's back. "You're so gorgeous! Just like your mama!"

Although Emi seemed somewhat embarrassed by the compliment, it was obvious that she and Harun appreciated Shauna's love of their children.

"Where's Ani?" Shauna asked. "And all the dogs?"

"Ani is in her room, and the dogs are over at the manyatta," Mila responded as she led Shauna toward the lodge, followed by Tanya and Emi.

"And our clients?" Elon asked Harun as they collected Shauna's bags from the plane.

"Resting before supper," Harun told him. "Except for Mr. Bloomstein and his cameraman, who wanted to go back to the manyatta by themselves. I didn't see any harm in—" he was interrupted by Kijabe arriving in his jeep.

"I was at the manyatta and saw you fly in," Kijabe told Elon. "I heard you went to meet Shauna. Did she arrive safely?"

Like Elon, Kijabe appeared to be suffering from a lack of sleep. Although the previous night's ordeal was painfully fresh, and indelibly etched in their minds, there was an unspoken understanding between them that it would never be mentioned.

Elon nodded in response to Kijabe's question about Shauna. "I hope our clients aren't causing too much trouble over there," he said as Kijabe helped carry Shauna's bags toward the lodge.

"Where's that?" Kijabe asked.

"At the manyatta," Harun said.

"None of your clients are at the manyatta," Kijabe replied.

Elon stopped in his tracks and stared at Kijabe. He wondered why Sam had lied about where he was going. And then he remembered seeing the olive-colored Land Rover that was headed toward the dry riverbed where he'd spotted the rhino. Looking for Ani's jeep, Elon saw that it was parked nearby.

"Kijabe!" Shauna exclaimed as she ran from the lodge to greet him.

Dropping the bags, Kijabe smiled as he whisked the hat from his head. He seemed almost beside himself when she threw her arms around his neck and kissed him on the cheeks.

"How's your family?" Shauna asked while lacing her arm through his as they walked toward the lodge, followed by Elon and Harun, who collected the bags that Kijabe had dropped.

"Doing well," Kijabe mumbled. He was obviously quite smitten with Elon's sister.

"Come help me find Ani," Shauna told him, her arm still locked in his as they entered the lodge. "She's not in her room. Maybe she's out by the pool," she speculated as Mila approached.

"She's not at the pool," Mila said, giving Elon a worried look.

"Where can she be?" Shauna wondered.

Dropping the bags, Elon sprinted to the gun cabinet in the office, where he removed the still-loaded rifle that he'd taken with him when he and Kijabe went after the poachers.

"Come on, Kijabe, we need to take your jeep!" Elon directed, stuffing his pockets with ammunition while racing toward the vehicle with the rifle in hand.

Shauna gave Mila a look of bewilderment as Kijabe took off after Elon.

Mila and Harun shook their heads with anger and concern over Ani's apparent disobedience of Elon's directive to remain at The Camp.

Against her father's orders to stay put, Ani had offered to take Sam and his cameraman to where she'd last seen the rhino. Sneaking out of her room, she felt confident that she could sneak back in without being missed—especially since her father wasn't due back from Nairobi until the following day.

While at the wheel of one of Sam's rented vehicles, Ani hadn't given any thought to the tan-colored Rover they passed that was headed toward The Camp. Nor did she notice when it turned around and followed them.

Slowly coming to a stop at the crest of an escarpment overlooking the dry riverbed, Ani was pleased to see the rhino off in the distance, sleeping in the warm sand. Quietly getting out of the vehicle, she started picking up some pebbles while Sam helped the cameraman mount the camera on a tripod. When they were ready, Sam nodded for Ani to proceed. Making her way down the steep trail of the escarpment, she didn't see or hear the tan-colored Rover as it turned into a grove of nearby trees.

From inside the Rover that he'd rented on his arrival in Kenya, Cole watched as Ani reached the sandy base of the riverbed. He'd been on his way to The Camp, as he'd learned it was called, when he saw Ani at the wheel of the olive-colored Rover. Her resemblance to Rika made Cole do a double take. Out of curiosity, he turned his vehicle around and followed her at a distance.

Cole guessed that the teenager was Rika's daughter, as there were many similarities between them—especially in the graceful way the girl moved. Even from a distance, Cole could tell she was quite beautiful. As he watched her walking in the dry riverbed, he wondered what she was up to. And why the two men were filming it. Spotting the sleeping rhino, Cole was shocked when realizing the girl was purposely headed toward it.

"Shit!" Cole exclaimed as he sat straight up. He debated what to do. If he honked his horn, he feared it would waken and aggravate the rhino. He hoped the animal would remain sleeping. If not . . . "Damn! I wish I had a rifle!" he swore.

A jeep came to a grinding stop next to the girl's Rover. Cole watched as two men got out: a black man wearing a ranger's uniform, and a tall white man with dark hair.

Cole turned his attention back to the girl, who appeared frozen while staring at the two men who'd just arrived. Beyond her, Cole saw that the rhino had gotten to its feet. The tank-like beast shook the sand from its hide, and then glared at the girl. With its head and tail held high, it snorted while trotting forward a few paces. Then, lowering its head, it charged. The girl had turned back toward it, but she seemed unable—or unwilling—to move.

Cole glanced at the ranger and the other man, who now each had a rifle aimed at the charging animal. Almost simultaneously, both men fired.

The rhino let out a shrill scream as it fell on its chin, coming to a sliding stop a few feet from where the girl remained immobilized.

Seeing the animal fall, Cole slowly exhaled, not realizing he'd been holding his breath. He watched as the white man said something to the ranger before making his way down the steep trail to the riverbed, still clutching his rifle.

Cole was surprised to see the ranger point his rifle at the two men with the camera, who practically tripped over one another while hurriedly gathering up their equipment and putting it back in their Rover. The ranger accompanied the men as they got in the vehicle and drove away.

Directing his attention back to the girl, who still seemed rooted to the ground as she stared at the rhino convulsing at her feet, Cole again wished he had a rifle—to put a merciful end to the animal. But the man who helped shoot it was now standing over it. Aiming his rifle behind the rhino's ear, he fired. It jerked once before lying still.

Cole watched as the man lowered his rifle and let it fall to the ground. The man studied the dead beast before turning toward the girl. What he did next wasn't surprising to Cole, as it was what *he'd* do if a daughter of his ever pulled a stunt like the girl had. For Cole felt certain that the man was the girl's father . . . and that he was the person whom Cole had grown up despising more than anyone else in the world—Elon O'Shay.

Elon approached Ani while removing his belt. She offered no resistance as he wheeled her around and whipped her soundly. When he was finished, Elon pointed her toward Kijabe's jeep. Replacing his belt before picking the rifle up off the ground, Elon gave the dead rhino one last glance before following after Ani.

Cole's vehicle had been idling throughout the entire incident. He slowly backed it out of the trees and headed toward The Camp without anyone knowing he'd been there.

"I want you dressed and at supper on time!" Elon ordered Ani in a furious tone when they arrived back at The Camp in Kijabe's jeep.

Ani nodded tearfully before running to her room.

Removing his hands from the steering wheel, which he'd been gripping with such force that his knuckles had turned white, Elon noticed they were shaking.

Elon was furious at Ani for what she'd made him do. Not only for his having to kill an extremely endangered animal—but for making him take his belt to her! More than anything, it's what sickened and angered Elon . . . for it made him feel that he had become just like his father—which was the second greatest fear of Elon's life. His worst fear was of losing Ani . . . like he had lost her mother.

Harun joined Elon, who remained sitting in the jeep. "I'll drive our clients to Nairobi," he offered, studying Elon worriedly.

Elon stared at Harun as if he didn't know who he was. He turned his attention to where Kijabe had his rifle pointed at the men from Hollywood while overseeing their hurried evacuation from The Camp. Elon didn't notice Cole's vehicle, parked in front of the lodge.

"Take Emi and the children with you," Elon told Harun when regaining his senses. "You could all use a holiday," he explained as he got out of the jeep. "On me," he offered, taking a considerable amount of cash from his wallet and handing it to Harun.

Grabbing his rifle, Elon headed for the office inside the lodge.

Harun went to tell Emi that they were going on a little vacation.

At the front desk, Tanya was having Cole sign the guest registry. She gave Elon a worried look, and Cole shot him a furtive glance, as Elon walked by without acknowledging them.

A few moments later, Elon came out of the office, where he'd left the rifle, and joined Harun on the front veranda.

"Give this to the bastards," Elon directed angrily, handing Harun a check. "It's a full refund," he explained.

Taking the check, Harun went to join his family and Sam and his crew.

From the veranda, Elon watched as Mila helped Emi get the kids settled into one of the vehicles while kissing them goodbye. Elon narrowed his eyes in anger as the caravan of Land Rovers drove off with the men from Hollywood. Turning his attention to Kijabe, who was still holding his rifle, Elon and he exchanged a knowing glance. They nodded slightly before Kijabe got in his jeep and drove away.

"Elon," Tanya called from behind him.

When he turned around, Elon came face-to-face with Cole.

"This is Simon Hansen. Simon, I'd like you to meet Elon O'Shay," Tanya introduced them.

Cole had registered under an alias, combining Simon's first name with Walter's last. As he stared into Elon's sky-blue eyes, still registering anger, Cole didn't know whether to offer his hand or to punch the man in the jaw.

"Pleased to meet you," Elon extended his hand as the anger drained from his face.

Cole's hand had been balled into a fist. He slowly opened it to shake Elon's.

"I was telling Simon how fortunate it is that we can accommodate him," Tanya told Elon, giving him a look suggesting she hadn't explained *why* they could accommodate him.

Elon smiled vaguely. Studying Cole's soft brown eyes, Elon felt there was something both familiar and slightly disturbing about them.

"Simon, this is Mila Kitande," Tanya made the introductions when Mila joined them. "Mila and her son Harun and his family are co-owners of The Camp," she explained.

"How do you do?" Cole smiled at Mila.

Like Elon, Mila felt there was something very familiar about the young man.

"Simon is from . . . Where is it again?" Tanya asked Cole.

"Louisiana," Cole responded, catching himself before saying he was actually from Texas.

"If you'll excuse me, I'll go tend to your accommodations," Tanya told him before leaving.

"I'll see you at supper," Elon informed Cole, as he also left.

Cole felt somewhat uncomfortable being left alone with Mila. He had the feeling that when she looked into his eyes, she had guessed his deceit.

"Come," Mila told him gently, directing him inside.

"It's very nice here," Cole stated appreciatively as he looked around the lodge while following her to the parlor.

When Mila busied herself straightening up the room, Cole admired the photographs lining one of the walls. He froze at the sight of an enlargement of the photo Elon had given to Giora to help locate Mila and her sons after they had fled from Uganda. Taken at Ani's third birthday, it also pictured Rafi . . . and Rika. The child was shown being embraced by her smiling mother.

Mila noticed how motionless Cole had become while fixating on Rika's likeness. And then it dawned on Mila that Rika's stepson had finally come to Africa.

"That's a picture of Elon's daughter, Anika, when she turned three," Mila told Cole quietly as she stood at his side. She kept her knowledge of his identity to herself.

"These are my sons," Mila pointed to their likenesses in the photo. "And Ani's mother, Rika, who died tragically just seven months after this photograph was taken."

Sensing Cole's shock, Mila realized he hadn't been aware of Rika's death.

"I thought all the guests had left," Shauna said when seeing Cole as she entered the parlor.

"Shauna, I'd like you to meet . . ." Mila turned to Cole with a questioning look.

"Oh . . . Simon . . . Simon Hansen," Cole responded, turning his attention away from Rika's image to the beautiful redheaded woman with emerald-green eyes.

"Shauna is Elon's sister," Mila informed Cole. "Perhaps you could entertain Mr. Hansen while I see to supper?" she asked of Shauna.

"Of course!" Shauna replied enthusiastically as she laced her arm through Cole's. "Come, we're just in time to see the sunset. Oh, Mila," she called after her, "is Ani back yet?"

"Yes," Mila responded with more than a hint of anger as she headed toward the kitchen.

"Have you met my niece?" Shauna asked Cole while leading him to the back balcony, overlooking the watering hole.

"No," Cole answered truthfully.

Gazing out at the beautiful African landscape, bathed in hues of purple and orange from the setting sun, Cole bit back tears of anguish as the impact of Rika's death swept over him.

"There's my elusive niece!" Shauna exclaimed when Ani entered the dining room later that evening.

They hugged and kissed before Shauna held Ani at arm's length. "My, you look gorgeous!" Shauna raved.

Cole rose from his chair when Ani joined him and Elon at the table. *Yes,* Cole silently agreed with Shauna's observation of Ani—*she's absolutely gorgeous!*

Ani was wearing a brightly colored wraparound sheath, the type of simple everyday garment worn by African women. Only on Ani it looked like a Paris creation. It was the first time since her mother's funeral that Ani had worn a dress, which she'd borrowed from Emi's wardrobe. Ani had nothing of her own that was comfortable enough to wear after the whipping her father had given her.

The lion's claw necklace stood out against Ani's bare neckline as her long hair, still damp from the shower, was pulled up into a twist. She wore no make-up, and didn't need any. Ani hadn't put any effort into looking beautiful, as it just came naturally.

"Simon, I'd like you to meet my niece, Ani. Ani, this is Simon Hansen," Shauna introduced them. "Simon's from America," she informed Ani.

Seeing her up close, Cole was even more stunned by the teenager's resemblance to Rika. He could only manage a weak smile.

Ani practically ignored him, until noticing that her father appeared concerned by the way Cole was looking at her. Seizing the opportunity to in some way get back at her father, Ani gave Cole an alluring smile. The whipping Elon had given her hadn't completely cured his daughter's rebellious streak.

"Ani, you look lovely," Tanya complimented her when she and Mila brought the food from the kitchen to the table.

Ani shot Tanya a look of resentment, until seeing her father's stern expression. "Thank you," she responded to Tanya with forced sweetness as she gingerly took her seat when Cole held the chair out for her.

The perfect gentleman, Cole remained standing until all the women were seated.

"Where are Emi and the kids?" Ani asked.

"They went with Harun for a little holiday in Nairobi," Shauna told her. "Ani, it may interest you to know that you and Simon have much in common," she informed her niece as they passed around the food.

Mila looked up with a startled expression, thinking perhaps Cole had confided his real identity to Shauna.

"Simon is a veterinarian," Shauna explained to Ani. "I told him you've often mentioned that's what you'd like to be someday."

Mila slowly exhaled a sigh of relief. She felt the time wasn't right for Cole to divulge his secret—especially to Elon, who was studying the young man with a look of fatherly protectiveness of Ani.

"Is there any particular animal that interests you the most?" Tanya asked Cole.

"I'm rather partial to rhino," Cole replied, gratified when Elon and Ani glanced at him with concern. "And, of course, lion," he added, so as not to appear too obvious.

"*Everyone* comes for the lion," Shauna stated knowingly.

Cole was reminded of his father's reference to "the lure of the lion." The phrase came to Elon's mind as well; but he still didn't make the connection between the person who'd coined it and the young man who now sat at his table.

"Elon, I think Ani should show Simon around the Mara tomorrow," Shauna suggested.

"Yes," Tanya quickly concurred.

"I agree," Mila spoke up before Elon could object.

Feeling over-ruled, Elon angrily narrowed his eyes at the women. He'd planned to keep Ani grounded at The Camp until she and Shauna departed for Ani's school at the end of the month.

"All right," he reluctantly consented.

Ani smirked slightly at having been paroled. Glancing at Cole, she felt a certain queasiness as he gave her a soft smile. With the color rising in her cheeks, Ani quickly looked away.

Chapter 20

With piercing yellow eyes, a black-maned lion studied the small herd of Maasai cattle and the two boys who watched over it. Its massive 500-pound body low to the ground, the beast inched forward with its gaze set on a half-grown calf. As it exploded out of the bushes, the lion caught the young animal by its flank when it leapt into the air as the rest of the herd scattered around them. Pinning it under its huge paws, the beast tore at the calf's tender belly as it screamed in terror and agony.

The two Maasai brothers remained perfectly still with their staffs clutched in their hands, fearfully watching the lion as it devoured its victim. The older boy silently, carefully, motioned for his brother to go for help. The youngster cautiously backed away before turning and fleeing.

With the calf's blood dripping from its jaws, the lion snarled angrily at the brother who remained behind. The boy stood motionless with his gaze directed away from the beast's eyes. In spite of the boy's non-threatening posture, the lion charged.

While Cole waited in front of the lodge for Ani to join him for their tour of the Mara Reserve, he admired her jeep with its African-animal-motif.

"Nice paint job," he commented when Ani joined him with a picnic-basket in hand. "Did you do it yourself?"

"Yes," she responded as he held the door open for her. She looked surprised when seeing the pillow he'd placed on the seat. But her surprise quickly turned to anger as she thought of his knowing about the whipping she'd gotten the day before.

Throwing the pillow in the back, Ani got behind the wheel. When her foot hit the accelerator, however, she wished she had left the pillow where it was.

Cole smiled at Ani's willfulness as they raced off. He knew that every bump they hit, every hole they went over, was painful for her.

Ani wondered how he could have known about the whipping. And then she remembered the vehicle she had passed on the way to the riverbed. *It was his, and he must have turned around!* she realized. Seething with anger, she thought of how to get back at him. Heading away from the entrance to the Mara, Ani eventually pulled to a stop at the base of a rocky incline.

"Stay here, I need to pee," she told Cole before quickly sprinting from the jeep with the keys to the ignition.

Cole watched as she disappeared behind a large boulder. Looking away, he saw something move in the bushes just ahead of the vehicle.

From her hiding place behind the boulder, Ani smiled as three young, yet fully-grown cheetahs emerged out of the bushes into the sunlight. They stretched and yawned before ambling toward the jeep, where Cole sat frozen with fear.

"Oooh, shiiiit," Cole whispered.

He remained still as the animals sniffed around the vehicle. One pounced on the hood, baring its fangs in a yawning growl. Cole's eyes looked as though they were about to bulge out of their sockets.

Ani had difficulty suppressing her laughter, until she detected a wild, pungent odor. Slowly turning around, she gazed into the angry yellow eyes of the black-maned lion. Panting laboriously, the beast's mouth and paws were smeared with the blood of its morning's prey.

Ani had had close encounters with lions before. But she sensed there was something different about this one—something extremely threatening. Lowering her eyes, she remained perfectly still.

Baring its bloodstained teeth, the lion emitted a menacing growl at the same time Cole frantically honked the jeep's horn.

When Ani cautiously looked up, she saw that the lion had turned and was walking away. Exhaling slowly, she clutched the lion's claw necklace that she constantly wore. Leaving her hiding place, she went to "rescue" Cole.

As Ani approached the jeep, the smallest of the three cheetahs was sniffing at Cole. Cole sat rigid with his eyes squeezed shut and his face contorted in fear.

Ani clapped to get the animals' attention.

Slowly opening one eye, Cole watched as the trio raced toward Ani, knocking her to the ground. Cole sprang from the jeep to save her. But, by the time he reached her, Ani's screams of terror had turned to laughter.

Cole's knees gave out and he sank to the ground. "Damn you," he told her sternly. "I was never in any real danger, was I?" he demanded.

"Of course not," Ani replied in a tone suggesting he was stupid.

The smallest of the three cheetahs went to Cole, rubbing against his shoulders with a purring growl. Cole cautiously stroked its luxurious coat. The animal collapsed at his feet, stretching like a contented house cat.

"That's Leia," Ani told him. "And this is Luke and Hans," she added while playfully romping with the two males.

"Then we must be on the planet Tatooine," Cole responded, being well versed in the *Star Wars* movies. "So what's their story?" he asked as Luke and Hans also vied for his attention.

"They were orphaned when they were about two months old. We think their mother was killed by a lion," Ani explained, as she glanced worriedly to where the black-maned one had disappeared beyond the hill.

"And?" Cole asked.

Ani turned back to him. "A friend of mine, Kijabe, found them. I helped raise them. We've just recently released them back into the wild," she told him while rubbing her cheek across Leia's forehead.

Her gesture was quite sensuous to Cole. "How old are you?" he asked quietly.

"I'll be sixteen the end of December. And you?"

"Twenty-four. Has Kenya always been your home?"

Ani shook her head. "I was born in Uganda. We moved here when I was four."

"Are your parents from Uganda?"

"My father was. My mother was from Holland. I don't remember too much about her. She died when I was three."

I can tell you about her! Cole wanted to scream. *She was the most loving, beautiful person I've ever known! And I hate your father for taking her away from me!*

"How long has your father been married to Tanya?" Cole asked, hiding his anger.

"They're not!" Ani shot back with resentment.

"Oh? I assumed—"

"Did you know that cheetahs are more closely related to dogs than cats?" Ani asked, changing the subject. "See how their claws don't retract?" she demonstrated on Leia's paw. "And their dispositions are more like a dog's. You can never fully trust a cat," she added knowingly.

"Don't move, I'll be right back," Cole told her while easing away from Luke and Hans, who went begging for Ani's attention.

Cole soon returned with his camera. He shot half-a-roll of film capturing Ani with the Star Wars gang—or "babies," as she called them.

When they eventually left the three young cheetahs behind, Ani appeared worried. Wanting to tell Kijabe about the lion, she drove straight to the ranger station.

"Is Kijabe here?" she asked one of the rangers.

"He's at the manyatta," he informed her.

The ranger watched with disdain as Ani and Cole headed toward the village. He was the cousin of the poacher Kijabe had killed, and was concerned because his cousin hadn't been seen or heard from in two days. The ranger suspected Kijabe and the girl's father had something to do with his cousin's disappearance.

Arriving at the Maasai village, Ani and Cole were bombarded by women, children, and dogs—including the ones from The Camp, which had been left there since the previous morning when Elon slept late following the encounter with the poachers.

"What type of dogs are these?" Cole asked with admiration as he returned their friendly greeting. He recalled seeing Rafi in the photo taken at Ani's third birthday.

"Leonbergers," Ani told him.

"They're beautiful."

"I didn't expect to see you out and about so soon," Kijabe told Ani with a stern expression as he walked toward them.

Cole recognized Kijabe as the ranger who had been with Elon during the incident with the rhino.

"Kijabe, this is Simon Hansen, from America," Ani introduced them, ignoring Kijabe's remark.

Cole shook Kijabe's outstretched hand. "Would they mind if I took their picture?" Cole asked as he motioned toward the women and children.

"Go ahead," Kijabe told him.

"Maybe you'd prefer that the women were bare-breasted?" Ani asked Cole with feigned innocence as he aimed his camera at the smiling Maasai. "Most men undoubtedly come here hoping to see bare-breasted natives."

"That's all right," Cole responded as he snapped away. "In your case, I doubt there's much there," he teased.

Kijabe smiled at Cole's remark. When Ani spoke to the women in Maa, they and Kijabe broke out in laughter.

"What did she say?" Cole asked Kijabe.

"She said you are a very poor man and you have no cattle with which to buy a wife. But that it's just as well, as you wouldn't know how to service one anyway," Kijabe told him.

Lowering his camera, Cole glared at Ani as he addressed Kijabe. "Perhaps you'd be so kind as to inform Miss O'Shay and her friends that, contrary to what she has said about me, I have no trouble with women. And I happen to own approximately five-thousand head of cattle," he admitted, referring to Lee's herd, which Cole had inherited.

Ani blinked with astonishment.

"That's too bad," Kijabe responded to Cole's statement with mock seriousness. "For that makes us enemies."

Cole gave him a questioning look.

"God, or Engai as we know Him or Her, had three children," Kijabe explained by relating the Maasai story. "Engai gave an arrow to the first child, so he could live by hunting. The second was given a hoe, so he could dig into the earth and grow crops. The third received a stick to use for herding cattle. This third child was Natero Kop, the father of the Maasai. Engai gave all the cattle in the world to Natero Kop and his children after him. And it is the duty of the Maasai to reclaim them from others."

"Well, you'll have to come to . . . the States to do so," Cole had almost slipped and said Texas.

"We just might someday," Kijabe responded, still pretending to be serious.

Cole smiled at the prospect of the Maasai descending on the state of Texas to reclaim *their* cattle. His thoughts were interrupted by a young boy running toward the manyatta while screaming something in Maa.

"Ol-ng'atuny—a lion has attacked the boy's cattle," Ani translated for Cole as the Maasai sprang into action around them. "It could have been the black-maned one I saw a while ago, near the babies," she told Kijabe worriedly.

He and Cole regarded her with alarm.

"Perhaps I can be of help?" Cole offered.

"He's a veterinarian," Ani told Kijabe.

"Come along, then," Kijabe said as he and the boy, along with half-a-dozen spear-totting Maasai, headed toward Kijabe's jeep.

"What do you have in the way of medical supplies?" Cole called out to Kijabe as he and Ani got back in her jeep, with as many armed Maasai as it could hold.

"They're at the station," Kijabe responded as he sped off in that direction.

They stopped briefly at the ranger station to pick up the medical supplies before following the boy's directions to where he'd left the herd . . . and his older brother.

Remaining at the station, the poacher's cousin glared with hatred while watching Kijabe's and Ani's jeeps speed away.

At the scene of the attack, the boy jumped out of Kijabe's vehicle before it came to a complete stop, with Ani's jeep close behind.

As the boy called frantically for his brother, Kijabe and the others stared with disbelief at the devastation spread across the savannah. Not being content in killing just the calf, which remained only partially eaten, the lion had gone on to kill at least two more cattle and wounded a handful of others. Hyena and other scavengers were already at work.

The only sound responding to the boy's calls to his brother were the plaintive cries of the injured animals. Kijabe and the boy conversed hurriedly in Maa.

"Kijabe asked if there'd been more than one lion," Ani translated for Cole. "But the boy saw only the black-maned one."

"One lion did all *this*?" Cole asked incredulously. "I didn't think lions killed just for the hell of it!"

"They usually don't. Apparently it's also taken the boy's brother," Ani told Cole fearfully.

Kijabe removed two rifles from his jeep. "Know how to use one of these?" he asked Cole.

When Cole nodded, Kijabe handed him one of the rifles. Cole expertly checked to see if it was loaded, which it was. Ani seemed impressed.

Studying the ground, the Maasai determined where the lion had attacked the boy and the direction it had taken him.

"The lion is probably a young adult," Kijabe speculated as he, Cole, and Ani followed the Maasai. "Even with the cattle being such easy prey, an older animal would not have had the stamina to do what this one did. It is no ordinary lion," he added, supporting Cole and Ani's impression of the beast.

"It's more like a killing machine," Cole commented quietly.

And a man-eater, their suspicions were confirmed when they came across what remained of the boy, lying in the center of a swarm of buzzing flies. The bloody mess was difficult to distinguish as having once been human. The boy's feet were missing, and there was almost no skin left on the head and torso. The raw face held only one eyeball, which stared toward the sky in frozen horror.

The younger boy trembled in shock as he gazed at his brother's remains. Ani stood back with a stunned expression; while Cole watched with a mixture of curiosity and revulsion as Kijabe and the Maasai carefully laid the boy's body on its left side with the legs drawn up, head toward the north, and face turned to the east. They then bent the left arm under the head as a pillow, and folded the right arm over the chest, with the hand resting on the heart. In positioning the boy's body in this manner, the Maasai were affording it a great recognition—as it was how they honored a fallen warrior.

The Maasai turned to go. They left in a single file while singing a sad song. Kijabe picked up the young boy and took him with him. Ani continued to stare with shock at the older boy's remains, until Cole gently pulled her away.

Returning to Kijabe's jeep, Cole exchanged the rifle for the medical supplies. After the Maasai chased away the scavengers, it was determined that one of the injured cattle was beyond hope. The Maasai put it out of its misery by suffocating it. They then went looking for what was left of the scattered herd.

The young boy stayed close as Kijabe and Ani helped Cole tend to the injured animals. They watched with growing admiration as Cole deftly got to work.

When he finished suturing the last animal, Cole wiped the sweat from his brow with the back of his bloodstained hands. "I could use a large supply of antibiotics," he told Kijabe.

"We can get some in Narok," Kijabe told him.

Ani didn't object when Cole got behind the wheel of her jeep. They followed Kijabe back to the manyatta, where they left the young boy and some of the Maasai. The rest of the Maasai had stayed behind with the cattle.

After Cole, Kijabe, and Ani quickly rinsed the blood off their hands, they headed for Narok in Kijabe's jeep.

At a medical facility in Narok, Ani and Kijabe watched as Cole asked for an impressive array of items. It included bandages of all shapes and sizes, syringes with various calibers of needles, suturing material, plastic tubing, and a good-sized quantity of antiseptic and antibiotics.

"Let me," Cole offered to pay for all of it when Kijabe pulled out his wallet.

"No," Kijabe objected.

"Please," Cole insisted.

Realizing how much it meant to the young American vet to pay for the supplies, Kijabe reluctantly consented. On their way to the jeep, Ani and Kijabe exchanged a look of amazement over Cole's generosity.

"Cole?" Walt Hansen called out to him from across the street.

Turning around, Cole regarded Walt with a look of shock.

"Dad!" Cole responded, thinking fast as he went to Walt. "Play along, and don't call me Cole," he whispered as they hugged. "Come, I want you to meet some people."

Walt worriedly studied Cole's filthy, bloodied appearance as he was being led across the street.

"This is Ani O'Shay and Kijabe. My father, Walt Hansen," Cole introduced them.

As they shook hands, Walt noticed that Ani and Kijabe were also covered with dried blood and dirt. He regarded Ani sadly while managing a weak smile.

"How did you get here?" Cole asked, also wanting to know *why* Walt had come to Africa.

"I took what I thought was a small bus from Nairobi," Walt responded, shaking his head with concern.

Ani and Kijabe exchanged a knowing smile.

"It's called a 'matatu,'" Ani told Walt.

"You are lucky you got out of it alive," Kijabe added in regards to the death-defying, privately owned means of public transportation.

"This was as far as it went. I was looking for a way to meet up with you . . . at 'The Camp,' I believe it's called?" Walt told Cole before glancing at Ani.

"If you don't mind, I need to speak with my dad," Cole told Ani and Kijabe as he took Walt by the arm and led him out of hearing range.

"'Dad'?" Walt smiled.

"I told them my name was Simon Hansen. What are you doing here?!"

"I wanted to tell you what I'd found out about Rika," Walt explained sadly.

"I already know," Cole responded quietly. "But you needn't have delivered the news in person!"

"I hoped to catch up with you before you went looking for Elon O'Shay. But I see I'm too late," Walt said while glancing over at Ani. "She looks so much like her mother," he observed sadly.

"She's got a lot of her father in her, as well," Cole stated rather resentfully.

Walt regarded him with concern.

"How'd you get here so fast?" Cole asked.

"When I heard from Rika's parents in South Africa, and then found out from Eugenie that you'd left, I booked a flight. Fortunately I'd already gotten the required shots and all from my recent trip to the Orient. And a friend of mine, who knows someone in the State Department, helped put a rush on the visa."

"Now that you're here, you might as well come with us."

"To The Camp?"

Cole nodded. "But first there's some injured cattle I need to get back to."

"Ah! That explains the look!" Walt stated with relief while studying Cole's appearance.

As if noticing it for the first time, Cole glanced at the dirt and dried blood on his clothes. "Remember, I'm your son, Simon," he reminded Walt.

"No problem. I've always thought of you as one of my kids,"

Walt smiled, putting his arm around Cole's shoulder as they headed toward Kijabe's jeep.

"It looks like a battlefield," Walt commented when they returned to the dead and injured cattle. He gave the spear-totting Maasai a look of apprehension.

"More of a massacre," Cole said before he started inoculating the injured animals, with Ani's help.

The looks of admiration that Ani gave Cole weren't lost on Walt and Kijabe.

"That's all I can do," Cole stated, when he finished with the cattle.

"Ashe. Thank you," Kijabe told him in first Maa and then English as the Maasai herded the injured cattle and survivors toward the manyatta.

"I was wondering if you would take a look at a young girl who is not doing well?" Kijabe asked Cole when they arrived back at the village.

"What's wrong with her?" Cole asked.

"Ani, you should drive Mr. Hansen to The Camp," Kijabe instructed in a tone that left no room for argument.

Ani wanted Kijabe to come with her to look in on the babies, but she knew it wasn't the right time to ask. *Besides, the lion is probably exhausted from the morning's massacre,* she thought, feeling nauseous when remembering what had remained of the young boy.

Calling for her dogs to follow, Ani and Walt got in her jeep and took off for The Camp at a pace the dogs could easily keep up with.

"This way," Kijabe told Cole as he brought the medical supplies with him. He led Cole inside one of the mud- and dung-covered huts.

It took a while for Cole to adjust his eyes to the dimly lit interior. The only light came from shafts of sunshine streaming in through two baseball-sized holes in the roof, which blended with whiffs of smoke spiraling up from a smoldering fire.

Tending to the fire was a wizened little old woman.

"My grandmother," Kijabe informed Cole reverently.

Kijabe and his grandmother spoke softly in Maa.

Cole noticed a young girl, about twelve years old, curled up on a raised cubicle lined with goatskins. The girl regarded Cole with glazed eyes. There was a baby goat sleeping in the nook of her arm.

Kijabe's grandmother left the men alone with the girl.

"My niece," Kijabe quietly told Cole while gesturing toward the girl.

"What's wrong with her?" Cole again asked.

"She has not been able to recover from being circumcised."

"'Circumcised'? What do you mean 'circumcised'?" Cole demanded as he felt the girl's forehead. She was burning with fever.

"It is our custom," Kijabe responded simply.

Cole gave him an incredulous look. "I need to look at the wound," he said.

Neither Kijabe nor the girl objected as Cole gently straightened her legs and pulled up her skirt without disturbing the baby goat nestled in her arms.

"My god!" Cole turned toward Kijabe with anger after seeing the jagged wound. "How was this done?" he demanded.

"With a piece of sharp metal."

"Any anesthesia?"

Kijabe shook his head. "Girls are expected to cry out—it disgraces their families if they presume to have the courage of a boy," he explained. "But if a boy 'kicks the knife,' as we say, his parents are spat on and their cattle are beaten. And no one eats the food, or drinks the honey beer, that took months for the family to prepare in honor of the circumcision."

Kijabe didn't tell Cole that most girls fainted from the excruciatingly painful procedure . . . and some even died.

"What was done to this girl is not circumcision!" Cole seethed with indignation. "It's genital mutilation! If a comparable procedure had been done on a boy, it would be considered complete castration! Tell me, do you *men* take pleasure in doing this to them?" he demanded to know.

"It is not the men who do it," Kijabe calmly informed him.

Cole appeared even more incensed at the thought of the women subjecting the girls to such primitive brutality. He turned his attention back to his patient.

"She's suffering from infection and shock," he told Kijabe.

Kijabe's grandmother returned with a dried gourd containing a foaming, pink-tinted liquid. She lifted the girl's head to drink, but most of it ran down her chin.

"What is she giving her?" Cole asked Kijabe.

"Cow's blood mixed with milk."

Cole's anger kept him from admitting to Kijabe that the concoction was the next best thing to a transfusion, which the girl also probably needed. Taking the medical supplies from Kijabe, Cole filled a syringe with antibiotic and injected it into the girl's thigh. He also gave her a shot of anesthetic before gently covering her with her skirt.

"I don't know what else I can do," Cole stated sadly. "I'm an animal doctor, not a people doctor."

"You are a very good doctor," Kijabe told him with admiration.

Cole studied the man whom he wanted to consider as a friend. *How can someone as obviously educated and caring as Kijabe stand by and let such a barbaric practice take place?!* Cole fumed. *And his sweet-looking little old grandmother, who no doubt had been subjected to the same abuse, how can she and the other women perpetuate it?!*

Kijabe's grandmother again spoke softly in Maa.

"She's offering us a cup of chai," Kijabe told Cole.

Cole watched as the ancient-looking little woman blew gently on the smoldering embers, coaxing them to ignite. She then rubbed some ash around the inside of a pot and rinsed it with a little water contained in a dried calabash. Placing the pot on a grate over the fire, she poured some fresh milk and heaping spoonfuls of sugar into it.

Waiting for the milk to heat, she cleaned out two mugs in the same way she had cleaned the pot—with first ash and then water. Pouring some hot tea from a kettle into the mugs, she then added the warm, sweetened milk. She handed both mugs to Kijabe, who passed one on to Cole.

Sipping the chai tentatively, Cole was surprised at how good it tasted. "It's been a while since I've had fresh, whole milk," he admitted, his anger subsiding.

"Milk is the main item in our diet," Kijabe told him.

"Not cow's blood?" Cole asked with a hint of derision.

"We drink cow's blood only during the dry season, or for special ceremonies . . . or when the warriors need strength, or after a woman has given birth," Kijabe explained, not taking offense at Cole's tone. "We rarely slaughter our cattle. When we do, we never drink the milk and eat the flesh in the same day. It shows disrespect toward the animal to feed on it while it is both dead and alive."

Cole thought about Kijabe's words as he sipped his chai. "I read somewhere that the Maasai are possibly descended from a lost legion of Roman soldiers," he mentioned.

"Perhaps that's true," Kijabe admitted. "All we know for certain is that Engai created the Maasai and gave us all the cattle in the world . . . and the grass to feed them. Without grass there are no cattle, and without cattle there are no Maasai. If we want to make peace with an enemy, we hold out a handful of grass."

Something about grass being used as a peace offering stuck in Cole's mind. He was also reminded of Eugenie's wish that the whole world was paved with cement.

"If our enemy does not stop fighting when we hold out grass to him," Kijabe continued, "then he is a 'Ndorobo'—a man who does not know cattle. A man whom the Maasai hate."

Finishing his chai, Cole handed the cup back to Kijabe's grandmother. When she smiled, Cole noticed her two lower incisors were missing. In his medical training, Cole had learned that the teeth were often removed so sufferers of tetanus could be fed.

"How do you say 'thank you'?" he asked Kijabe.

"In Maa? 'Ashe.'"

"Ashe," Cole told the old woman, whose smile broadened.

Cole again felt the girl's forehead. "You need to keep her cool. I don't know how long her fever will last, or if she'll pull through this," he told Kijabe worriedly.

"It is in Engai's hands now," Kijabe said. "Ashe for helping her."

Wishing he'd been able to do more for the girl, Cole followed Kijabe out of the hut and into the waning sunlight.

Glancing around, Cole felt as though he had stepped back in time as he viewed a people whose customs and attire hadn't changed for thousands of years. He watched as the Maasai prepared for nightfall. Teenaged boys brought the cattle into the center of the kraal, while some of the younger girls and boys herded goats, sheep, and a handful of donkeys in with them. The dogs, many of them obviously crossbred from the Leonbergers, helped with the task. Some of the men were shoring up the thorn-bush barricade for protection against the nights' predators.

Children played their last games of the day while being tended to by the elders. Women sang as they carried loads of firewood on their heads, or milked the cattle for the evening meal. Teenaged girls giggled suggestively in Cole's direction, as their brothers and boyfriends gently chastised them.

One image in particular went right to Cole's heart. It was a father playing with his infant child with a look of such intense joy and love that Cole had to look away—as it impressed upon him the lack of love he had received from his own father. And it reminded him of Rika's unconditional love. Feeling a combination of resentment and loss, Cole followed Kijabe to the jeep.

They hadn't driven far from the village when they stopped for a herd of zebra that thundered across the dirt road. The whites of the animals' coats reflected the pastel shades of the setting sun. The scene took Cole's breath away.

"It's all so beautiful," he stated softly. "Yet so horrific," he shook his head sadly.

"Africa?" Kijabe asked.

Cole nodded.

"To survive in Africa, you must become like the giraffe," Kijabe said.

Cole gave him a questioning look.

"One of the giraffe's favorite foods is the tender leaves of the acacia tree," Kijabe explained. "But it must learn how to take what is good while avoiding the thorns."

Cole slowly nodded at Kijabe's observation as they continued toward The Camp.

Chapter 21

"Did I mention I was adopted?" Cole asked at breakfast the next morning at The Camp when Walt proudly showed a photograph of his five kids to Shauna, Mila, and Tanya.

Only Mila seemed to pay attention to Cole's comment; while Shauna and Tanya admired the photo, which was a smaller version of the one Cole had seen on Walt's desk in Houston. Not one of Walt's smiling brood remotely resembled Cole.

"Simon was away at school when that picture was taken," Walt fabricated, explaining Cole's absence in the photo.

"Walt, they're absolutely beautiful!" Shauna exclaimed, handing back the photograph.

As their eyes met, there was an instant of shared attraction. Seeing the exchange, Mila had a premonition that all would be well with Shauna.

"Here I've been monopolizing everyone's attention," Walt apologized as he directed his gaze away from Shauna. *She's a married woman,* he reminded himself. "What about you three? Any photos to brag about?" he asked.

Tanya glanced down sadly as Shauna answered for them both.

"I'm afraid neither Tanya nor I were fortunate enough to have children. But Mila had two handsome sons," Shauna offered with a melancholy smile when reminded of Mutiba. "And she has three beautiful grandbabies!" she brightened. "They're on a little holiday with their parents," she added, explaining their absence.

"Speaking of children," Cole piped in, "where's Ani?"

"In case you haven't noticed, my dear Simon," Shauna admonished him gently, "Ani is hardly a child. Although her father refuses to acknowledge it as well."

"He and Ani left at dawn to check on her babies," Tanya said. "Elon wouldn't let her go on her own, not with that rogue lion on the prowl."

"'Babies'?" Walt asked.

"A trio of orphaned cheetahs," Cole explained. "Named for characters in the *Star Wars* movies."

"You should feel privileged to have met them," Tanya told him. "Ani doesn't introduce them to just anyone, you know."

Cole smiled sardonically at the "privilege" of meeting Ani's babies.

"Hopefully they'll get back soon," Shauna lamented while checking her watch. "I've promised Ani a little shopping spree. Knowing Ani, I doubt she has anything appropriate to wear on our trip. Elon's agreed to fly us to Nairobi."

"So you'll be packing her off to Switzerland? To an all girls' school?" Walt pondered. "Not a bad idea. I'll have to think about that for my own daughters."

Everyone at the table, especially Shauna, knew he was joking—that the last thing Walt wanted was to be separated from any of his kids for any length of time.

"Here's Elon now!" Tanya smiled as he entered the dining room. "How are Ani's babies?" she asked him.

"You can see for yourself," he said, shaking his head with feigned disgruntlement.

Mila helped Elon get his breakfast as the others left to go outside, where they saw the dogs playfully greeting Ani and the babies. Recognizing Cole, Leia ambled over and rubbed against his legs. Walt smiled at the rapport Cole had with the animal.

"Ani, I know I promised you a girls-only shopping trip, but what would you say if we invited our guests?" Shauna asked quietly.

"Of course," Ani brightened at the suggestion while glancing at Cole.

"Listen up, everyone," Shauna announced. "Ani and I have decided to make a party of our little outing, and we'd appreciate it if you gentlemen would join us."

"It would be a pleasure," Walt responded sincerely.

"Why not?" Cole tried to sound enthusiastic, although he would have preferred to go on a game drive instead of a shopping spree.

"I need to see if Kijabe can keep an eye on the babies while we're gone," Ani said.

"Mind if my dad and I tag along?" Cole asked.

"Of course not," Ani smiled shyly as Cole and Walt followed her to her jeep.

At the ranger station, they were told that Kijabe had left at dawn to hunt the black-maned lion with one of the other rangers.

When the poacher's cousin had impressed upon Kijabe that they should go after the lion, Kijabe didn't realize until it was too late that he was being led into a trap. At a secluded spot near the Mara River, he and the ranger pulled to a stop where two men waited in a small lorry.

As soon as they got out of their jeep, the ranger aimed his rifle at Kijabe. When the two men stepped out of their vehicle, Kijabe saw that they were Maasai. Seeing the AK-47s the men were holding, Kijabe immediately made the connection between them and the poachers—and, more specifically, the young Maasai woman Elon had killed.

Having made the connection, Kijabe didn't seem surprised when the Maasai pulled back a tarp covering the bed of their truck, exposing the charred remains of the ranger's cousin and his woman—their bodies frozen in grotesque poses.

There wasn't a word spoken by either the men or Kijabe, although Kijabe knew he was going to die. All he could do was to face death like the brave murran he had once been.

It wasn't an easy death, as the three men took studied pleasure in their revenge. When Kijabe finally drew his last breath, it appeared as though he'd become another victim of the man-eating lion. Hardly an inch of skin remained intact on his once handsome body, as lions were known to lick the salty skin from their human prey, often causing them to slowly bleed to death before the real feasting began.

When Ani, Cole, and Walt arrived back at The Camp from the ranger station, it was decided that the group would postpone their excursion to Nairobi. But at mid-morning, when Harun and his family returned from their holiday and offered to stay with Mila and watch over the babies, the shopping spree was back on.

Before leaving for Nairobi, Shauna watched with a melancholy expression as Walt playfully interacted with Beni and Juba—and especially little Tessa.

Although Shauna, Tanya, and Ani obviously enjoyed their time in town, it was apparent that Elon and Cole simply endured it. Walt, however, seemed grateful to be included in the girls' outing, and to spend time in Shauna's company. But he was too respectful of her marital status to let Shauna know how he felt about her.

That evening, following supper at the Hillside Hotel, the group found their way to the hotel's ballroom. Shauna took Cole by the arm and led him onto the dance floor. Walt offered his hand to Ani, while Elon and Tanya followed.

It had been a long time since Tanya was in Elon's arms on a dance floor, and her heart leapt at the opportunity. Until the music slowed and the singer broke into a perfect imitation of Roberta Flack's *The First Time Ever I Saw Your Face*. Elon momentarily froze before leading Tanya back to their table, where he sat lost in his thoughts.

Knowing Elon was thinking about his beloved Rika, tears stung Tanya's eyes. Glancing at the dance floor, she saw that Walt and Cole had changed partners. Shauna was gazing unabashedly into Walt's eyes; while Ani had hers closed, resting her head against Cole's shoulder.

Ani trembled in Cole's grasp; not knowing their first dance together was to the accompaniment of the same song as her parents' first dance:

> "And the first time ever I lay with you,
> I felt your heart so close to mine.
> And I knew our joy would fill the earth.
> And last 'til the end of time, my love.
> And it would last 'til the end of time, my love . . ."

When the group arrived back at The Camp later that night, the dogs and cheetahs greeted them excitedly. Harun was waiting on the veranda with an anguished look on his face.

"Kijabe has been killed," he informed Elon and the others quietly, realizing there was no easy way to break the news.

His announcement was met with stunned silence.

"He was attacked by a lion," he explained to everyone's horror.

"Oh, my god!" Shauna exclaimed, clasping her hand over her mouth.

She and Tanya rushed tearfully into the lodge; while Elon and Ani remained frozen in shock. Cole and Walt regarded them with compassion. Cole wanted desperately to comfort Ani, as he knew her pain at losing their friend was far greater than his own.

"Apparently it was the same lion that killed the Maasai boy," Harun said.

"We need to get the monster," Cole stated with quiet determination.

"'We'?" Elon asked distantly.

"He's an excellent shot," Walt offered, remembering what Lee had told him about Cole's marksmanship.

Ani's legs went limp. Sitting on the steps of the veranda, she ignored the dogs and babies while staring at the star-filled sky. Cole sat beside her as the others went inside.

Cole and Ani remained on the veranda without a word spoken between them. Eventually she leaned her head against his shoulder.

He held her tight as she succumbed to her grief, sobbing uncontrollably.

"We want to help track the lion that killed Kijabe," Elon told the poacher's cousin when he and Cole showed up at the ranger station the next morning, armed with Elon's rifles.

The ranger regarded them with a look of irony, having Elon O'Shay play right into his hands! But he appeared skeptical about the American coming along.

"I appreciate the offer," the ranger responded. "I'll radio some of my friends to come with us," he said before disappearing inside the station.

"They'll meet us at the Sand River," the ranger stated when he returned. "They said the lion was spotted there," he added truthfully while leading Elon and Cole toward Kijabe's jeep, leaving Elon's Rover parked at the station.

The ranger drove to where they met up with the two Maasai who'd helped murder Kijabe. So as not to appear conspicuous, the men were now armed with rifles instead of AK-47s.

"We'll take their vehicle from here," the ranger told Elon and Cole.

"We should bring these," Cole said of the medical supplies he'd bought in Narok, which were still in Kijabe's jeep. He brought the supplies with him.

The Maasai had arrived in a Land Rover that had two side seats facing each other in the back. After placing all their weapons on the floor between the two seats, one of the Maasai got in the back while Elon and Cole sat in the middle seat. The ranger sat in the front seat next to the other Maasai, who drove toward where they'd seen the lion.

Although Elon's instincts told him to beware, his wits were compromised from a lack of sleep—starting from the night he and Kijabe had gone after the poachers. And he of course agonized over Kijabe's death. As he was a considerably better marksman than

Kijabe, Elon wondered why his friend hadn't asked for his help in going after the lion. Elon wasn't aware that the ranger sitting in the vehicle he was riding in was the cousin of the poacher Kijabe had killed. Or that the two Maasai were the brothers of the woman Elon had shot.

Elon was lost in his thoughts as he and Cole scanned the landscape for any sign of the lion. They didn't notice when the Maasai sitting behind them secretly exchanged the bullets in Elon's rifle with blanks.

"That could be it," Elon pointed out the solitary black-maned lion he saw in the distance, stretched out in the sandy riverbed. It was asleep in the morning sun, not far from what remained of the rhino Elon and Kijabe had shot.

They came to a stop at the crest of the escarpment before the Maasai had time to sabotage Cole's rifle in the same way that he had Elon's.

After making their way down the steep trail to the base of the dry riverbed, the ranger motioned for Cole and the two Maasai to fan out in one direction while he and Elon went in the other. As the men encircled the lion, it suddenly sensed trouble. It sat up in a regal, Sphinx-like pose while sniffing the air.

The men froze. From his position directly in front of the beast, Elon slowly raised his rifle. Watching from a short distance away, Cole saw the ranger step back, leaving Elon alone to face the lion. There was something about the ranger's action, and the look on his face, that alarmed Cole.

With the lion in his sights, Elon fired. He knew he'd hit it between the eyes, but the bullet seemed to have no impact as the animal rose with a tremendous burst of speed. It charged at Elon with its body close to the ground, clawing the earth with its massive paws. With its ears laid flat and tail raised straight in the air, its jaws snapped repeatedly in anticipation of the kill.

Elon fired once more, but again the bullet had no effect. Cole had his rifle aimed at the lion but, before he could pull the trigger, a bullet struck the ground at his feet. Glancing at the ranger, Cole saw that he had his rifle aimed at *him*—not the lion! Seeing the ranger was about to fire again, Cole shot him in the head, killing him instantly.

Elon heard the two shots ring out, but they didn't stop the lion. Sinking to one knee, he positioned his left arm at an angle in front of his face while propping the useless rifle in the sand, pointed toward the beast. It was the pose taken by the Maasai when faced with a charging lion—only instead of an ineffective rifle they had a sharp-pointed spear on which they hoped the animal would impale itself.

The lion was instantly upon him. Grabbing Elon by his left forearm, its jaws snapped the bone like a twig as its claws raked into Elon's chest.

Seeing him being whipped about like a rag-doll in the lion's grasp, for a fleeting instant Cole felt his animosity toward Elon O'Shay be vindicated. But then he thought of Rika . . . and her daughter.

In the lion's grip, Elon relaxed as he resigned himself to dying. When another shot rang out, the beast crumpled on top of him. Buried under the pressing weight of the animal, Elon heard the trilled war cry of the Maasai, followed by four more shots. Darkness and quiet enveloped Elon as he lost consciousness.

Realizing that he and Elon had been set up, Cole had turned his attention to the Maasai after killing the lion and quickly reloading his rifle. Fortunately, like the ranger, the two men were lousy shots, as they fired at and missed Cole before he killed them.

Cole ran to help Elon. With considerable difficulty, he moved the 500-pounds of dead weight off of him. Tearing off his shirt, Cole used it as a tourniquet to bind the gaping wounds on Elon's torso. When Cole swung him across his shoulder, Elon's left arm dangled at a grotesque angle. Cole tried to bring their rifles, but he could only manage to carry Elon. He left the weapons lying in the sand.

By the time Cole made the difficult climb out of the riverbed to the Rover, he was drenched with sweat and coated with Elon's blood.

"Damn!" Cole swore when seeing the keys weren't in the vehicle's ignition. Losing precious time, he managed to hot-wire it. Before speeding off, Cole glanced at Elon. Stretched out in the middle seat and covered in blood, Elon was barely breathing.

Mila stood on the back balcony, gazing in the direction from which her intuition told her Elon and Cole would be coming. She stiffened when she saw the cloud of dust rising in the distance. It was a vehicle, approaching from the west. Mila recalled the dream she'd had—of the dust storm rising from the west and the large shadowy figure of death.

"What is it?" Tanya asked when seeing Mila's worried expression as she joined her at the balcony. She followed Mila's gaze to the approaching vehicle.

Together they watched as Cole brought the Rover to a skidding stop. Again swinging Elon across his shoulder, he hurried toward the lodge. Tanya gasped when seeing that Cole and Elon were covered with blood. She ran to meet them.

Mila quickly went to the manicured lawn at the front of the lodge where everyone, including the dogs and babies, was playing a makeshift game of rugby. Ani's pet monkey chattered excitedly at the group from his perch on the veranda railing.

"Ani, you and Emi take the boys to their rooms. Now!" Mila ordered. "The rest of you come with me!"

Emi rounded up her sons and headed for their cottage, followed by a hesitant Ani.

"What's wrong?" Shauna asked Mila as she, Harun, and Walt followed her inside.

"*Elon!*" Shauna screamed when she saw Cole carry him toward them.

Harun and Walt quickly took Elon from off of Cole's shoulder.

"Bring him in here," Mila said, leading them to the parlor.

"Lay him on the floor," Cole directed while trying to catch his breath. He noticed Mila worriedly scanning his bloodied appearance. "I'm all right," he assured her before helping Harun remove Elon's shredded, blood-soaked clothes.

"What blood type is he?" Cole asked.

"O positive," Mila replied.

"The same as me," Shauna offered weakly, slightly recovering from her shock.

"Good," Cole responded. "Harun, there are some medical supplies in the vehicle we came in," he remembered.

There was no mention of flying Elon to Nairobi for treatment, as it was obvious to everyone that he wouldn't make it. Harun took off at a run for the supplies.

"Come," Mila said as she grabbed hold of Tanya, who was in a state of shock. "We need to get water, soap, and—"

"Before you go, I need some alcohol—whiskey, anything!" Cole told Mila.

She brought him two bottles of Scotch they had on hand for their safari guests.

When Harun ran back with the supplies, Cole had him pour some of the whiskey over his hands while Cole rubbed them together to sterilize them. He then filled a syringe with antibiotic and injected it into Elon.

"Lie down, face up," Cole instructed Shauna as he motioned to the nearby coffee table.

Before Shauna did so, Harun swept the magazines and books off the table. Shauna nodded in gratitude when Walt placed a small pillow from the couch under her head.

Finding the wad of tubing and the needles that he'd purchased with the other supplies, Cole disinfected Shauna and Elon's forearms before inserting the needles into their veins and connecting the tubing. Soon the blood was flowing from Shauna's arm down into Elon's.

When Mila and Tanya returned, they carefully washed the blood and debris from Elon's body. Cole motioned for Harun to pour the remainder of the Scotch over Elon's gaping wounds, and again over his hands before Cole began the delicate job of suturing. There was neither time nor the need for anesthesia.

It took Cole almost two hours to close the gashes in Elon's torso. He then directed his attention to Elon's shattered and mangled left forearm, which had become horribly swollen. With Harun's help, Cole positioned it back in place as best he could before mending and securing it.

When he was finished, Cole slowly exhaled while rubbing his eyes with his bloodied palms. He was obviously spent—and worried, for he doubted that Elon would make it through the night.

"He'll need surgery on his arm," Cole said while disconnecting the tubing from Shauna and Elon's forearms. "When he's stabilized, we should get him to a hospital where he can be monitored by a real doctor," he added, trying to sound optimistic.

"He could never receive any better care than he has from your hands," Mila told him sincerely.

Seeing the love reflected in Mila's eyes, Cole was reminded of Rika. The strength drained from his body as he sank onto the couch. Resting his head in his hands, tears of exhaustion and loss escaped from under his closed eyelids.

"Harun, Walt, please carry Elon to his bed," Mila requested. "Tanya, you watch over him while I see to lunch. Shauna, come and get some rest," Mila suggested, helping Shauna to her feet and then to her room while the others did as Mila directed, leaving Cole alone in the parlor.

When Mila returned, she wasn't surprised to find Cole sound asleep on the couch. She gently removed his boots and spread a blanket over him.

"You did good, my dear Cole," Mila whispered as she eased the hair away from his eyelids. "Rika would have been very proud of you," she added tearfully.

"Is he all right?" Harun asked worriedly when he came into the room.

"Yes. He just needs to rest," Mila told him, wiping away her tears.

"I'll clean up in here," Harun offered.

Mila nodded her thanks. "I'll see to lunch," she told him before leaving.

After Harun finished washing away the blood and had disposed of the used medical items, he sat in a chair opposite the couch where Cole slept.

In his troubled sleep, Cole's mind replayed what happened when he and Elon met up with the lion. Everything was in slow motion: the look on the ranger's face when he moved away, letting Elon face the animal alone; the ranger shooting at Cole rather than the charging beast; the Maasai trying to kill Cole before he shot them. And, in the way dreams have of righting mistakes, Cole imagined he was able to bring the rifles with him when he carried Elon to the Rover—that he hadn't been forced to leave them behind as evidence of their involvement in the deaths of the three men.

"The rifles!" Cole exclaimed as he woke with a jolt.

"What about the rifles?" Harun asked.

"I had to leave them behind," Cole responded distantly, not focusing on Harun.

"I'll go get them," Harun offered as he rose from the chair.

"Yes," Cole agreed. "I had to shoot the ranger that was with us," he slowly recalled as his face and voice maintained a distant quality, as if Cole were talking to himself rather than Harun. "And the two other men, who looked like Maasai, but they weren't wearing traditional clothes . . . I had to kill them also," he said, explaining his concern over leaving the rifles as evidence.

Harun appeared shocked by Cole's admission.

"They were trying to kill Elon and me . . . it was like they set us up," Cole stated in a quizzical tone, wondering why the men wanted them dead.

"Where did it happen?" Harun asked. "And where's our Land Rover?"

Cole blinked as if unable to comprehend Harun's question.

"The Rover that belongs here at The Camp," Harun explained. "Where is it?"

Cole looked at Harun as if seeing him for the first time. "At the ranger station," he responded slowly, as his gaze locked into Harun's. They both realized that, even if they retrieved the rifles, the Rover being left at the station would connect Elon and Cole to the men's deaths.

"I'll go with you," Cole offered. But when he tried to stand, he was too weak to do so.

"Just tell me where the rifles are," Harun told him.

"The ranger referred to it as Sand River . . . near where the rhino had been shot," Cole managed weakly before again stretching out on the couch and falling asleep.

Harun went to the kitchen where Mila was preparing lunch.

"What's wrong?" she asked with alarm when seeing his stricken expression.

"Simon just told me what happened," he responded as he proceeded to tell Mila all that Cole had told him; including the fact that The Camp's Rover had been left at the ranger station.

Mila quickly determined what needed to be done. "Have Walt go with you to get our Rover. Use the vehicle Cole . . . I mean Simon . . . rented," she corrected herself without Harun seeming to notice. "Bring our Rover back here, and then have Walt follow you in Simon's vehicle when you take the one that Simon and Elon arrived in back to where . . ." she suggested, unable to finish. "I'll radio Dr. Abrams while you're gone."

Before leaving, Harun shared a look with Mila that suggested their contacting Dr. Abrams would involve more than his being informed of Elon's condition. There was also a shared understanding between them that, no matter what they did to try and cover it up, there would be major repercussions resulting from the incident at Sand River.

During the night, in a fitful state of unconsciousness, Elon hallucinated that he was standing at the edge of the cliff on the Isle of Aran. The wind was whipping at his face as he heard *Hey, Jude* being played on a bagpipe. Elon needed to take only one step forward to join Rika . . . who stood suspended above the ocean, churning almost three hundred feet below them. But Rika shook her head slowly while mouthing the words, "Sleep well, my love." And then she was gone.

"Rika!" Elon cried out in his sleep as Tanya was placing a cool cloth on his burning forehead.

His cry shattered Tanya's heart as the tears flooded her eyes.

"I'll watch him for a while," Cole offered quietly when he entered the bedroom. He had showered and shaved, and looked relatively rested.

Tanya quickly wiped away her tears before leaving. Cole sadly watched her go, although he hadn't heard Elon cry out for Rika. Sitting in a chair beside the bed, Cole took Elon's pulse.

In his dream, Elon was again on the cliff at Aran. He heard Rika's sweet voice calling his name. Turning around, he gazed into her loving eyes. She smiled and stepped aside . . . revealing an image of Tanya, bathed in bright sunlight.

"Tanya?" Elon whispered as he slowly opened his eyes. It took a while for him to focus on Cole. Elon gave him a questioning look. Making an attempt to sit up, Elon gasped from the excruciating pain of his injuries.

"The lion," Cole reminded him. "It's what brings most people to Africa," he elaborated. "As I once heard my old man say, it's 'the lure of the lion.'"

The realization of Cole's true identity slowly dawned on Elon. "You bastard," he stated weakly, angered by both Cole's deceit and the memory of Lee Parnell.

Elon's accusation struck Cole like a dagger. "Technically, yes," Cole admitted. "But then the same can be said of your daughter, can't it?" he countered.

Elon's anger visibly intensified. He hadn't told Ani that he and her mother were never married. His reluctance to do so was tied in with his fear of hurting, and possibly losing her.

"Get the hell out of here!" Elon painfully hissed at Cole as Mila entered the room.

"He's all yours," Cole told Mila angrily, brushing past her on his way out.

"Wait, Cole . . . there's something I want to show you," Mila told him softly.

Cole stopped abruptly. When he turned to face her, he seemed only vaguely surprised that Mila knew who he was.

Mila took him by the arm and led him to the parlor, where she had him sit on the couch while she got out the photo album of Rose Inish, which was stored in a cabinet. She sat next to Cole and opened the album.

"This was my son, Mutiba," Mila pointed out her favorite photo of her eldest son. "He died a long time ago," she stated simply as she turned the pages of the album. "And this was Rika's son, Christiaan," she informed Cole.

The photograph was one that Devin had taken in Lamu. It showed Rika with Elon, who held little Christiaan lovingly in his arms.

Cole's eyes widened with surprise, for he could tell that the child and he shared the same father. He gave Mila a questioning look.

"He lived only one year," she told him quietly.

Cole studied the photograph. *Rika looks so happy. They all look so happy!* he realized with a mixture of resentment and relief as he focused on her and Elon's smiling images.

"Elon loved Christiaan as if he were his own," Mila informed him.

Cole kept his eyes glued to the photo as Mila took an envelope from the album.

"This is for you . . . from Rika," she said, holding it out to him.

Cole's hands shook as he tentatively took it from her. He blinked back the tears while slowly opening the letter that had remained sealed for so many years.

Mila left him alone as he read Rika's loving words.

Chapter 22

"How is he?" Ani asked worriedly about her father when she joined the others at breakfast the next morning.

"He's going to be fine," Mila assured her.

Ani breathed a sigh of relief. "Where's Simon?" she asked, noticing he and Harun were the only ones besides her father who weren't at the table.

Mila and Walt exchanged a knowing glance before Mila nodded for him to explain who Simon really was.

"His name isn't Simon. And he's not my son," Walt admitted. "His real name is Cole."

"'Cole'?" Shauna played the name over in her mind. "Wasn't that the name of Rika's—" she glanced worriedly at Tanya before finishing.

Tanya looked drained, having spent a restless night caring for and worrying about Elon. She was also still terribly hurt by his calling Rika's name in his sleep. It reinforced what Tanya had long feared—that Elon still, and always would, love only Rika. The revelation of Cole's identity was yet another reminder of Rika.

"Yes," Walt responded to Shauna's unfinished question. "Cole is Lee Parnell's son."

"He left this morning before dawn," Mila said.

"Left?" Ani practically cried as she sank onto a chair. "Where'd he go? And who's Lee Parnell?"

"Emi, it would be best if you took Beni and Juba out," Mila suggested.

Although they appeared disappointed not to be included in the adults' conversation, the boys went with their mother without complaining.

Walt cleared his throat and took a deep breath before addressing Ani. "Lee Parnell was your mother's husband," he began. "He was a great doctor, but an extremely abusive man. Cole was his son from a woman he'd had an affair with. She committed suicide a year before Lee met your mother. When Lee and your mother married, she and Cole became very close."

Walt gave Ani time to absorb the information before he continued. "When your mother and father got together, Lee was so angry that he refused to grant her a divorce. Therefore, when your mother died, she was still legally married to him."

Ani stared at Walt with incomprehension. "Then that means I'm a—"

"It means you have inherited a considerable fortune," Walt interjected. "Lee died a very wealthy man. Cole and Rika were his only heirs, so your mother's share is now yours. I'll need some time when I get back to Texas to work out all the details, but Cole and I talked about it briefly before he left this morning. He'd like you to have your mother's share of Lee's estate in cash . . . if that's all right with you."

Not knowing what to say, Ani simply blinked.

"Unless your mother had other legal representation," Walt glanced at Mila, who shook her head, indicating Rika didn't have another lawyer. "Then, as attorney for both your mother and Lee, and taking into consideration what your mother probably would have liked," Walt told Ani, "I'll establish a trust fund which will provide you with a substantial monthly stipend until you're twenty-one, at which time the funds will be yours to manage."

Looking at Mila, Walt speculated she might be wondering why Lee Parnell hadn't taken measures to insure that Rika wouldn't inherit any of his wealth. As with his not getting around to Lee's directive to disown Cole, Walt had purposely done the same with Lee's wishes concerning Rika.

But Mila simply nodded gratefully at what she perceived to be Walt's safeguarding of Rika's interests—and, by extension, Ani's.

Everyone at the table remained silent while Ani tried to come to terms with all that Walt had told her.

Shauna regarded Walt with a look of sadness, mixed with accusation for having deceived them. But, as she thought about what an honest and caring person Walt obviously was, Shauna's feelings turned to gratitude, admiration, . . . and love.

With her head bowed, tears flowed down Tanya's cheeks. Like Ani, Tanya had always assumed that Elon and Rika were married. She was hurt that Elon hadn't told her the truth. It made her feel as though their relationship was based on a lie; and that their years together had been a waste of her time, devotion, . . . and love.

Harun entered the room and took his place at the table. "He's sleeping," he stated regarding Elon. He'd been watching over Elon while the others were having breakfast.

"I'll go stay with him," Shauna said.

Walt sadly watched Shauna leave. He worried that she thought less of him because of his involvement in Cole's deception.

"After I eat, I'll be flying to Nairobi to pick up Dr. Abrams," Harun told Mila as she served him his breakfast.

Ani studied Harun with interest.

"Ani, you should eat something," Mila told her gently.

"I want to see the babies first," Ani replied distractedly as she rose to leave.

Although Mila suspected what Ani was planning, she didn't try to stop her.

When Harun flew the Cessna to Nairobi to pick up Dr. Abrams, he didn't realize he had a stowaway onboard. Landing at Williams Airport, Harun took a taxi to the doctor's office.

Seeing him drive off, Ani came out from her hiding place inside the aircraft. Carrying a small suitcase that she'd brought with her, she also hailed a taxi. Starting at the Hillside, she made her way to practically every hotel in Nairobi, hoping to find Cole. After two hours, Ani ended up at the Nile Star.

"Is a 'Simon Hansen' or a 'Cole Parnell' staying here?" she asked the desk clerk.

"No," the clerk responded after checking the guest registry.

Sadly, Ani turned to leave.

"Wait," the clerk told her while checking the book more closely. "We do have a 'Cole Lightfoot' registered."

Ani's face brightened. "Where does it say he's from?" she asked.

"America . . . Texas," the clerk told her. "He's in room 326, by the pool."

"Thank you," Ani said, feeling as though she could kiss the man.

The clerk smiled at Ani's obvious delight as she hurried away.

Knocking first gently, and then vigorously on the door to Cole's room, Ani looked disappointed when he didn't answer. Curling up on a small divan in the hallway, she soon fell asleep.

"Ani?" Cole shook her awake a little while later.

Rubbing the sleep from her eyes, she sat up. "Cole!" she smiled, until seeing the anger reflected in his eyes.

"What are you doing here?" he demanded, before a worried look clouded his face. "Your father? He isn't—"

"He's going to be all right," she assured him. "I just wanted to—"

"Do they know you're here?" he asked sternly.

She slowly shook her head.

"Just great! Come on," he told her while angrily pulling her up off the divan. Grabbing her suitcase, he practically dragged her inside the room. "There's the phone! Now call and tell them where you are!"

"I can't!" she shot back, on the verge of tears. She couldn't understand why he was so angry with her.

"Why not?" he demanded.

"Because there's no phone at The Camp! Only a radio!"

"Right," Cole remembered, following a pause. "They probably have one at the front desk," he said, calming slightly. "We'll radio from there, and then get some lunch."

"I'm not hungry," she pouted.

"You're going to eat!" he glared at her, sounding disturbingly like her father.

Ani glared back at him. But, as her gaze locked into his, something happened between them. Without knowing exactly how, Ani had her arms around Cole's neck and was kissing him. And he was kissing her back! Passionately! Until his eyes sprang open. Pushing her away, Cole held her at arm's length.

"No! It's not going to happen!" he forced himself to say, although his body screamed otherwise.

"Why not?" she asked as sadness and anger melded with her physical desire.

Cole studied her as if uncertain of the answer. "Ever heard of the term 'jailbait'?" was all he could come up with.

"This is Africa!" she countered. "But it's not that as much as it's my father, isn't it?" she accused. "You hate him, don't you? I can understand why you—"

"Yes I hate him!" Cole shot back with fire in his eyes. "Or at least I thought I did! I grew up blaming him for taking Rika away from me! But I realize now how much they really loved each other! And how much your father loved my little brother . . ." he choked on the rising tears.

Ani reached out to comfort him.

"No!" he told her while backing away. "Just stay here while I radio The Camp!" he ordered before leaving, slamming the door behind him.

Ani stood staring at the door. Throwing herself on the bed, she began to sob.

Leaning against the other side of the door, Cole heard her crying. It was all he could do to keep from going to her.

"Ani's here at the Nile Star with me," he told Mila when she answered his radio call to The Camp, which he made from the hotel's office.

"Yes," Mila responded knowingly. "Harun will meet you there later this afternoon. You need to come back here with her."

"Why?" Cole demanded.

"It's important," was all she told him before signing off.

Heading toward the hotel's café, Cole realized Mila was right; that he needed to return to The Camp, as he and Elon had some unfinished business to take care of.

When he returned to the room with a tray of food for Ani, Cole heard the shower running. Ani's clothes left a trail leading to the bathroom. Cole focused on her bikini panties, lying on the floor. When the water stopped running, he set the tray on the bedside table before leaving.

Ani came from the bath with a towel wrapped around her, while drying her hair with another. Seeing the tray of food, she glanced sadly at the closed door.

"Beer!" Cole ordered as he sat on one of the stools at the hotel's bar. Glancing around, he noticed two strikingly beautiful blondes sitting at a nearby table, eyeing him seductively. He turned away when the bartender brought him his drink.

"Excuse me, but would you care to join us?" one of the blondes asked Cole in a melodious Scandinavian accent as she approached him at the bar.

Cole studied the gorgeous woman before glancing at her friend, who smiled invitingly. "Why not?" he replied while paying for his beer. He took it with him as he followed the woman to her table.

"I am Brita," she introduced herself to Cole. "And this is Ingrid."

"Stewardesses?" Cole guessed correctly as he and Brita sat down.

"Ya," Ingrid smiled. "For SAS."

"Cole," he introduced himself while shaking their perfectly manicured hands.

"American?" Brita asked hopefully.

Cole nodded. "From Texas," he elaborated.

"Ah, Texas!" the women cooed simultaneously. "We have been to Dallas!"

"Where are you two from?" Cole asked.

"Copenhagen," Ingrid responded.

"Are you here alone?" Brita asked Cole.

"No, my little sister is here with me," he replied with a sly smile. "What are you ladies drinking?" he asked.

"Nothing strong," Brita told him. "We have to fly later this afternoon. But our pick-up isn't until a few hours," she added suggestively.

"I've got some time to kill as well," Cole said, not picking up on Brita's implication. "What would you two like to do? See a museum or something?"

"Why don't we do 'something'?" Ingrid purred before giving Cole a long, juicy kiss.

Following the kiss, it took Cole a moment to catch his breath.

"What the hell," he said while letting himself be led to their room, where they quickly stripped and had their way with him.

Entangled in a mass of shapely naked bodies, Cole woke with a start after dozing off. Glancing at the bedside clock, he saw that it was 2 p.m.

"Damn!" he whispered as he slipped out from under Brita and Ingrid's arms and legs. He nearly fell over as he hurriedly pulled on his pants.

When one of the women moaned and moved in the bed, Cole quickly gathered up his shirt and shoes, and left.

"Cole?" Harun asked when Cole walked by him in the hotel's lobby, still carrying his shoes and shirt.

"Harun!" Cole greeted him, trying to act as if there was nothing unusual about his being half-dressed. "Stay here, I'll get Ani," he said.

"I'll be in the café," Harun called after Cole, who was walking away with a false show of dignity. Harun didn't know whether to feel alarmed or amused by Cole's appearance.

Letting himself into his room, Cole saw that Ani was sleeping. She was still wearing only the towel, which barely covered her shapely little butt.

Noticing the red marks her father's belt had left on Ani's upper legs, Cole wanted desperately to lie down beside her . . . to gently caress her wounded bottom . . . to take her in his arms and feel himself inside her. Angrily forcing the thought from his mind, he went to take a cold shower.

After quickly shaving and showering, and with just a towel wrapped around him, Cole left the bathroom to get his clean clothes.

"Ani?" he called when seeing the only thing on the bed was the towel she'd had on. He also noticed that her suitcase was gone.

"Ani?" he called again. "Damn it!" he swore angrily, rushing out of the room still clad in nothing but the towel.

In the hallway, Cole startled a family with two small children. Shielding her youngsters' eyes from the partially naked man, the mother hurriedly led them away while the father glared disapprovingly at Cole.

Cole seemed clearly embarrassed. "Sorry," he apologized to the man while backing into the room. When Cole shut the door and turned around he saw Ani, with her suitcase in hand. She'd been out on the room's balcony.

Cole appeared relieved, then angry. "Get dressed!" he ordered without really looking at her.

"I am dressed!" she shot back. "You're the one who isn't!"

Cole angrily tightened the towel around his waist. Grabbing some clean clothes, he headed for the bathroom. "Don't move from there!" he barked at Ani before slamming the door shut.

When he soon emerged from the bathroom, fully dressed, Cole grabbed Ani's suitcase in one hand and took hold of her arm with the other. He marched her to the hotel's outdoor café, where Harun was having something to eat.

Seeing Harun, Ani slumped angrily onto a chair at the table where he was sitting.

"Would either of you care for anything?" Harun asked. He was relieved to see from Ani's attitude that her little escapade hadn't panned out in the way she had hoped.

"Coffee. Strong," Cole told the waiter, who brought menus for him and Ani.

The waiter looked to Ani, who ignored him. She sat with her arms folded and legs crossed, her foot swinging impatiently as she glared toward the street. Cole regarded her sternly. Harun tried to suppress a smile as he glanced from Ani to Cole and back.

"Just coffee," Harun repeated Cole's order to the waiter, who seemed anxious to get away from the fuming customers.

The waiter soon returned with Cole's coffee, and then quickly left.

"Cole!" Brita called excitedly as she and Ingrid were leaving the hotel with their fellow crewmembers. Making their way over to Cole, the women gave Harun warm smiles before directing their attention to Ani.

"Is this your baby sister?" Ingrid asked Cole.

"She's adorable!" Brita gushed.

Ani glared angrily at the tall Scandinavian beauties, dressed in stylish airline uniforms. "Baby sister" was the last thing Ani wanted Cole to think of her as! Her resentment toward him was visibly growing by the minute.

"It was nice spending time with you!" Brita cooed to Cole before planting a kiss on his cheek.

"Ya!" Ingrid agreed enthusiastically, adding her lipstick print next to Brita's.

"If you ever get to Copenhagen—!" Brita smiled suggestively as they left. She didn't need to finish the invitation, as everyone in hearing range got the drift.

Harun's smile broadened as he watched the women join the flight crew in a taxi and drive away.

Cole wiped the lipstick from his cheek, while Ani seethed with anger.

"We should go," Harun said, leaving the money for his meal and Cole's coffee on the table, along with a tip.

Eager to leave, Ani practically leapt out of her chair. Taking her suitcase, she headed for one of the available taxis parked in front of the hotel.

"Women!" Cole stated with displeasure as he followed after Ani.

Harun smiled at Cole's outburst.

"Williams Airport," Harun directed the taxi driver as he sat in the vehicle's middle seat, which faced the back seat where Ani and Cole sat as far away from each other as possible, glaring out their respective windows with Ani's suitcase acting as a barrier between them.

"So, what are your plans for when you return to America?" Harun asked Cole, attempting conversation.

Cole gave the question some thought before answering. "I might take a few courses at LSU for exotic animal care," he replied. "Then set up practice in Texas. Who knows, maybe I'll marry the little Louisiana peach I left behind . . . and together we can pave the world!" he added with forced enthusiasm.

Glancing at Ani, who remained staring out her window, Harun saw that she appeared hurt from Cole's mentioning he might get married.

When they arrived at Williams Airport, Cole and Ani simultaneously reached for her suitcase. A slight struggle ensued over it until Cole raised his arm as if to backhand her. Everyone in the vehicle, including Cole, appeared surprised by his action. On the verge of tears, Ani shoved the suitcase at Cole's chest before fleeing from the taxi.

Harun pulled out his wallet to pay the driver, but Cole beat him to it. The driver shook his head as he watched Cole take the suitcase and follow Ani to the Cessna.

"Lovers," Harun told the driver, who smiled and nodded knowingly.

As they flew toward The Camp, Cole sadly studied the passing landscape. *God, I don't want to leave this!* he silently screamed.

At the controls of the aircraft, Harun looked worried when he noticed a police vehicle and two army trucks carrying armed soldiers that appeared to be headed toward The Camp. He was grateful that Dr. Abrams was there, tending to Elon.

When they landed, Ani ran from the plane while ignoring the dogs and babies, as well as her pet monkey. She also raced past Mila, who was standing on the veranda.

Carrying Ani's suitcase, Cole slowly approached Mila. Harun remained at the Cessna, removing something from its storage compartment.

"How's . . ." Cole asked Mila hesitantly.

"Elon is improving," she told him. "Dr. Abrams is with him. Come, you two should meet," she suggested, leading him inside the lodge.

When Cole placed Ani's suitcase by the front desk, he glanced curiously at all the others that were there. "Where is everybody?" he asked as he followed after Mila.

"Shauna, Walt, Beni, and Juba are on a game drive . . . but they'll be back soon. Tanya and Emi are preparing supper," Mila told him.

"Dr. Abrams, I'd like you to meet Cole," Mila introduced them quietly when she and Cole entered Elon's room, where he was sleeping. "Cole took care of Elon after he was attacked," Mila explained to the short, balding physician who wore thick-rimmed glasses.

"Ah! So pleased to meet you!" Dr. Abrams whispered appreciatively. "You did a splendid job! It is too bad you will not be staying in Africa, as there is much work you could do here!"

There was something about the doctor's accent and statement that were a bit unsettling to Cole. When they shook hands, Cole noticed a series of numbers tattooed on Dr. Abrams' forearm. As the physician looked to be in his early-fifties, Cole correctly surmised that he'd been a young survivor of a Nazi concentration camp.

Tanya rushed into the room. "There are soldiers and police outside," she explained worriedly. "They want to see Elon."

"Yes, we expected as much," Dr. Abrams replied calmly for both himself and Mila as he removed a semiautomatic pistol from his medical bag.

Tanya and Cole appeared shocked by the doctor's action, but Mila was unfazed—for she knew that, in addition to being an excellent physician, Dr. Abrams was an Israeli intelligence agent.

Elon hadn't been aware that, throughout the years, the Israelis continued to watch over him and Mila and their families. Giora had kept in touch with Mila and Harun rather than Elon, as he felt Elon's pride might prevent him from ever asking for help. Dr. Abrams was the Mossad contact Giora had given them.

"Do you know how to work this?" Dr. Abrams asked Cole, regarding the pistol.

Cole hesitated slightly before taking the weapon.

"Good," Dr. Abrams smiled at Cole's expertise in handling the pistol as he checked to see if it was loaded, which it was. "Now, let us go see what the Gestapo wants," Dr. Abrams stated calmly before leaving with Cole and Mila.

Remaining with Elon, Tanya gazed worriedly out the window to where the soldiers had their rifles aimed at the snarling dogs. The babies were huddled off to one side, seemingly fearful as to why the dogs were so upset. As with all Kenyan police, they were unarmed.

When they saw the little physician come to the veranda with Cole, armed with the pistol, the soldiers directed their weapons at the two men.

The final scene in the movie *Butch Cassidy and the Sundance Kid* came to Cole's mind as he viewed the standoff. Glancing over at the Cessna, he noticed Harun had a rifle trained on the soldiers' commanding officer. *At least it won't be a total bust!* Cole thought sarcastically. He and Harun waited for the soldiers to fire the first shot. But, before that happened, Ani's jeep pulled into The Camp, followed by three Land Rovers.

With steady ease, a stream of about a dozen men, including Zev, emerged from the Rovers. Wearing outlandish shirts and hats, with their eyes obscured by expensive sunglasses, they appeared to be horribly dressed tourists. But they were actually Mossad agents, armed with Uzis. They pointed their weapons at the Kenyan soldiers, who seemed at a loss as to what to do.

"What the hell is going on?" Shauna demanded, glaring at the soldiers and Mossad agents as she, Walt, Beni, and Juba got out of Ani's jeep.

Giora stepped out from behind the wheel of the vehicle. Dressed as ridiculously as his cohorts, he took Shauna by the arm and led her toward the lodge.

"Let go of me!" Shauna told Giora while trying to wrest her arm away from his grasp. "Who are you?" she demanded as he delivered her to Mila who, along with Emi, now stood beside Dr. Abrams and Cole on the veranda.

"Mila, Emi," Giora greeted the women solemnly while removing his hat and sunglasses. Although his blonde hair was now streaked with gray, he had hardly aged in the decade since he'd last been at The Camp.

"Giora," Mila nodded.

"Do you know this man?!" Shauna asked Mila incredulously, as Walt and the boys joined them.

"Yes," Mila admitted with a faint smile.

"We were touring the reserve when these men cut us off and forced us to come back," Walt explained worriedly. Seeing the pistol in Cole's hand, Walt looked as though he was about to be sick.

"Papa!" Beni called from the veranda when he spotted Harun at the Cessna. Harun quickly lowered his rifle.

"No!" Mila told the boys as Giora stopped them from going to their father.

"Emi, take Beni and Juba inside," Mila told her.

Emi took the boys by the hand and did as Mila said.

"Shauna, Walt, you need to pack all of your things," Mila directed.

"Why? What's going on?" Shauna asked worriedly.

"Please, just do as I ask," Mila requested. "Quickly."

Still looking dumbfounded, Shauna and Walt headed for their respective rooms.

"Where is he?" Giora asked Mila.

"This way," she told him with a glance that included Cole.

Cole and Dr. Abrams followed Mila and Giora to Elon's room, where Tanya stood at the window with a stricken expression.

"Tanya, please go help Emi finish packing," Mila requested quietly.

Mila knew Tanya was already packed. She also knew, without having been told, that Tanya had made the difficult decision to leave Elon and return to Austria.

When Tanya left, Giora sat in the chair next to the bed. He studied Elon worriedly.

Dr. Abrams went to the window; while Mila and Cole, who still held the pistol, stood behind Giora.

"They're leaving," Dr. Abrams informed the others as he watched the soldiers and police return to their vehicles and drive off, under the watchful eyes of the Mossad agents.

Dr. Abrams went to take Elon's pulse.

Elon slowly opened his eyes. "Giora?" he asked weakly, thinking he was dreaming when seeing his friend.

Giora smiled and nodded. "Shalom," he greeted Elon.

"Nice shirt," Elon told him sarcastically before closing his eyes.

When Giora and Dr. Abrams conversed in Hebrew, Elon again opened his eyes. "So you're one of them," he accused the little doctor. Then he noticed Cole. "What are you doing here?" Elon demanded angrily, with what little strength he could muster. He appeared alarmed when noticing the weapon Cole was holding.

Cole turned to go, but Mila held him back.

"I want you to listen closely," Giora told Elon in an authoritative voice. "We know what happened when you went after the lion . . . and the poachers."

The color drained from Cole's face. Elon blinked as if trying to remember what Giora was talking about.

Giora glanced briefly at Cole before again addressing Elon. "No doubt that's why the soldiers and police were here. You know as well as I do that they don't intend to just ask you a few questions . . . and that they'll be back."

Elon breathed deeply before slowly nodding.

"After Mila radioed Dr. Abrams yesterday, he contacted me in Israel. Zev and I have been traveling all night to get here—so don't argue with me when I tell you what's going to happen!" Giora told Elon in no uncertain terms.

"Harun will fly you, Ani, Shauna, and Tanya to Nairobi," Giora explained to Elon. "Dr. Abrams and I will go with you; while Zev and the rest of our men will escort Mila, Emi, and the children—and your guests—in our vehicles. There's a private jet waiting in

Nairobi to fly all of you to England. Once there, whoever wants to will be taken to Devin's estate in Scotland. We know that Devin and Yvette left the estate to you before they died. We've arranged for you to get medical care in London. You can join the others in Scotland as soon as you're well enough to do so."

Neither expecting nor wanting a response from Elon, Giora turned to Mila.

"We're all packed," she told him before he could ask.

Mila had already accepted the fact that they would all be leaving Africa for good. From her dream, of the dust storm rising from the west and a large shadowy figure, Mila had come to realize that the storm was Cole . . . and the figure of death was Africa.

"We need to be going," Giora said as he rose from the chair and went to open the window. "Zev!" he called.

With his sunglasses pushed up on his head and his Uzi swung across his shoulder, Zev soon joined them. The years had added even more harshness to Zev's dark, brooding features. He and Giora carefully lifted Elon from the bed and carried him out of the room.

Cole handed the pistol back to Dr. Abrams, who returned it to his medical bag before he and Cole followed after the Israelis.

Mila went to help Emi with the children, while Cole remained on the veranda, watching the evacuation of The Camp. He realized Harun must have explained to Shauna and Walt what was going on, as together they were hurriedly packing Shauna's belongings into one of the Mossad agents' Rovers.

"If you and your husband ever get to Texas," Walt told Shauna with a bittersweet smile as he handed her one of his cards, "my kids and I would love to have you visit us."

Tears misted Shauna's eyes. "You're a kind man," she told him after kissing him gently on the cheek. Shauna was devastated, thinking they'd more than likely never see each other again.

Clutching her toy lion, now limp and bedraggled with age, Ani loaded the last of her bags into one of the agents' vehicles.

"What about the dogs and babies?" she asked worriedly, petting as many of them as she could while the monkey ran from the veranda and jumped onto her shoulder.

"Shoot them," Elon told Zev when he overheard Ani's question as he was being carried to the Cessna.

Responding to Elon's directive, Zev solemnly nodded as he and Giora settled Elon onto a makeshift bed on the floor of the plane.

"No!" Ani screamed. "You can't kill them!"

The monkey jumped from her shoulder and ran off screeching when Giora wheeled Ani around, forcing her to look him in the eye.

"Do you have any idea what the soldiers will do to them when they find that all of you have gone?" he demanded.

"Please don't shoot them!" Ani pleaded with tears streaming down her face.

"I'll take care of it in a humane way," Cole offered, coming up behind them.

Ani didn't know whether to hate Cole more, or be grateful to him. She didn't have time to decide before Zev grabbed her by the arm and marched her to the plane.

Walt and Zev stood next to Cole as the aircraft taxied for take-off, with Harun at the controls and Elon, Ani, Shauna, Tanya, Dr. Abrams, and Giora as passengers. Mila and Emi, along with Beni, Juba, and little Tessa, were loaded into one of the agents' Rovers and quickly driven away, followed by a second Rover carrying most of the agents.

Only Cole, Walt, Zev, and two of the agents were left at The Camp—along with three vehicles: the agents' remaining Rover, Ani's jeep, and the Rover that belonged to The Camp.

As Cole sadly studied the distraught dogs and babies, the monkey came and wrapped his little arm around Cole's calf while screeching pathetically.

Zev turned to Cole with an icy stare. They silently shared an understanding of what needed to be done.

Chapter 23

An ambulance with two attendants, along with two private vehicles carrying half-a-dozen Mossad agents, were waiting when Harun brought the plane in for a gentle landing at Williams Airport in Nairobi. Under Dr. Abrams' guidance and the agents' protection, the medics transferred Elon into the ambulance. Before they shut the rear door, Elon gazed at the Cessna for what he knew would be the last time. Of all the memories the aircraft evoked, the one that stood out the most in Elon's mind was of the trip to Murchison Falls with Rika.

Forcing the bittersweet memory from his mind, Elon concentrated on the wave of pain that swept over his body. Seeing Elon wince, Dr. Abrams administered another round of morphine while the ambulance headed for the same hangar near the international airport that the Israelis had used during the rescue of the Air France hostages, twelve years earlier.

The private vehicles followed the ambulance with Giora and the other agents split between them. Harun and Tanya rode in one of them, with Shauna and Ani in the other. On the way to the hangar, Shauna sadly studied the card Walt had given her. She was surprised by how much she missed him. Wondering why, Shauna realized it was because no other man had looked at her with so much longing and understanding . . . since Mutiba. She bit back the tears as she dwelled on the still painful loss.

Clutching her toy lion, Ani stared out the window, her face streaked with tears. The thought of her beloved pets being destroyed was tearing at her heart. And it was inconceivable to her that she might never be able to return to Africa . . . or see Cole again. Ani was terribly conflicted by the feelings she had for him—feelings of physical attraction, empathy, . . . and hatred!

When they arrived at the hangar, everyone was quickly escorted onto the private jet. Tanya helped tend to Elon, who was now heavily sedated. Although she knew her love for Elon would last until the day she died, Tanya felt strongly that her decision to leave him was the right thing to do . . . for his sake. She felt her continued presence in Elon's life would only interfere with his memories, and undying love, of Rika.

Harun and the others were extremely relieved when Mila, Emi, and the children joined them a few hours later. As the jet taxied for take-off, Shauna and Ani looked anxiously out the windows, hoping to see Walt and Cole. But only Dr. Abrams and most of the Mossad agents watched from the ground as the jet lifted into the air.

Giora and a few of the agents, along with the two medics, accompanied Elon and Mila and their families to London. During the long flight, Giora convinced Shauna that it would be best if she and Ani flew immediately to Austria from England. Everyone but Mila looked surprised when Tanya stated that she would also be leaving for Austria.

As soon as they landed in London, Elon was rushed to a hospital. Harun, Emi, and the children were driven directly to Devin's estate in Scotland, which now belonged to Elon, although Yvette's daughter and her family still resided there. Living into their mid eighties, Devin and Yvette had passed away a few years previously.

Mila insisted on staying in London with Elon. Giora secured a small flat for her to stay in that was near the hospital. When he was assured that Elon would recover from his injuries, Giora returned to Israel without giving Elon a chance to say goodbye. The Mossad agents stayed behind to ensure Elon and Mila's safety; and to take them to Scotland when Elon was well enough to travel.

Although his arm was still in a cast, it was two months before Elon's other injuries were healed to the extent that he and Mila could join Harun and his family. They were driven there by two of the Mossad agents. Located in the beautiful Scottish countryside outside of Sterling, the damp and dreary weather made it difficult for Elon and Mila to fully appreciate their new home. Accustomed to the warmer African climate, they shivered as the chill Scottish air penetrated to their bones.

When they turned off the main road onto the narrow dirt one leading to the estate, Elon studied the few sheep and woolly-coated Highland cattle contained behind a network of crumbling stonewall fencing. It was soon apparent to Elon and Mila that the animals, and the entire estate, hadn't been as well maintained as they undoubtedly were when Devin and Yvette were alive. Yvette's daughter Gwendolyn, along with Gwendolyn's husband Dirk and their teenaged children Eric and Valerie, resided in the large stone mansion located on the premises. It was their responsibility to care for the estate, which they had obviously neglected to do.

Coming to a stop in front of a small thatch-roofed cottage located behind the mansion, Elon and Mila were greeted excitedly by Harun and his family. The Mossad agents smiled at the joyous reunion. Refusing Mila and Harun's offer for them to stay and have tea, the agents soon left.

"Come," Harun directed Elon and Mila into the cottage, where a fire blazed at the stone hearth.

The cottage's dimly lit front room served as parlor, kitchen, and dining area; as well as sleeping quarters for Harun and Emi. One of the two bedrooms had been designated for the children and Mila, while the other was reserved for Elon. The toilet was situated in a small cubicle outside. It was all a far cry from the opulence of first Rose Inish, and then The Camp.

Harun helped Elon settle into a chair in front of the fire. Emi tucked a blanket around him before handing him a steaming cup of tea. Beni and Juba sat at Elon's feet, staring at him as if he had returned from the dead. Little Tessa, who had grown considerably since her grandmother and Elon had last seen her, regarded them shyly.

"We've done what we could with the place since we've been here," Harun told Elon and Mila before he was interrupted by a knock at the door.

Emi opened the door to Gwendolyn and her family.

"This is Yvette's daughter Gwendolyn, her husband Dirk, son Eric, and daughter Valerie. Gwendolyn, this is Elon O'Shay, and my mother, Mila," Harun made the introductions.

"We met many years ago, if you remember," Gwendolyn told Elon with an edge to her voice.

Elon nodded that he did remember. Dirk, a mousy-looking man, muttered a tentative greeting, while Eric and Valerie stood back and glared at Elon with open disdain. The teenagers were dressed in punk attire, with numerous facial piercings and spiked, orange- and red-tinted hairdos.

Gwendolyn had none of the dainty finesse of her mother. It was easy to see that she and her family were far from happy about the African invasion into what they considered to be *their* territory.

"I'll get right to the point," she addressed Elon. "I know my stepfather made arrangements for you to stay here, but my husband and I have engaged a solicitor to contest Devin's having given the estate to you. This has been our children's home for as long as they can remember, and we won't be leaving without a fight!"

"No one is asking you to leave," Elon managed weakly.

"Well," Gwendolyn huffed. She appeared slightly off kilter, having been geared for a fight that hadn't occurred. "And we shouldn't have to accommodate any of you in the large house, as we—"

"We will be more than comfortable here!" Mila cut her off sternly. "Now, if you and your family will leave, Mr. O'Shay needs to get some rest!"

Harun held the door open as Dirk made a hasty retreat, followed by his wife. Eric and Valerie ambled out with sneers directed at Beni and Juba. Harun slammed the door shut behind them.

Mila turned her attention to Elon, who sat slumped in the chair grasping the now lukewarm tea. She was visibly angry over Yvette's daughter not having the decency to wait a few days before confronting Elon. Mila felt certain that Gwendolyn knew of Elon's weakened condition—*she could see his arm is still in a cast! But it obviously has no bearing on her self-centeredness!* Mila fumed.

Of even more concern to Mila than Elon's physical state, which was still mending, was his emotional well being. Mila feared he might never recover from the losses and emotional trauma he'd experienced. And, although Ani was better off at school in Switzerland, Mila knew Elon missed his daughter terribly—as they all did. Then there was Tanya. But Mila couldn't fault her for leaving Elon. After all, Mila doubted Elon had ever told Tanya that he loved her.

"Here, I'll reheat that," Mila offered, taking the cup of tea from Elon.

Elon sat in silence, staring at the fire as his thoughts wandered back to Kenya. Recalling the sounds of the African savannah, he was sitting by the open fire on his first night at what would later come to be called The Camp. Remembering the roar of the lion rumbling through the ground, Elon shuddered as his mind returned to the dank Scottish evening.

During Ani's Christmas holiday, Shauna met with her in Innsbruck for a skiing jaunt that included some of Ani's classmates. Although she enjoyed spending time with her niece, it wasn't long until Shauna began to feel like a fifth wheel among Ani's peers.

"I think I'll go back to Vienna a few days early," she told Ani as they waited to be served lunch at a glass-walled mountaintop café, overlooking the ski runs.

Shauna and Ani looked quite stylish in the new ski outfits they'd purchased for the outing. At a nearby table, Ani's classmates giggled among themselves. The boys that were with them were obviously smitten with Ani, as they had trouble keeping their eyes off her.

"I'll go with you," Ani offered in response to Shauna's statement.

"No, you stay with your friends. We'll be together again soon—for Christmas," Shauna reminded her.

Ani appeared far from enthused over the prospect of spending any more time with her relatively immature and flauntingly rich "friends." The boys were especially annoying to her. Being around them only intensified Ani's longing for Cole. But she was still very confused by her feelings toward him. While there were times when she craved the feel of his hands caressing her body, she often felt like she hated him for rebuking her advances—and for his willingness to destroy her pets!

"It's not too late to accept your grandparents' offer to spend Christmas with them in Holland. Or to go to Scotland," Shauna said, interrupting Ani's thoughts of Cole.

"No! I don't want to go to Scotland!" Ani responded angrily.

Shauna studied her with concern. "I know you're hurting. We all are—especially your father. He's lost so much . . . Rose Inish . . . The Camp . . . your mother."

"Why didn't he tell me they were never married?" Ani demanded quietly.

"You need to try and understand how difficult things were in Uganda under Idi Amin," Shauna answered in a soft tone. "On the day she died, your mother was in Amsterdam to meet with a lawyer about putting an end to her marriage to Lee Parnell."

Ani looked surprised.

"Your parents loved each other in a way that most people only dream about," Shauna told her wistfully. "It hasn't been easy for your father to live with the fact that they weren't legally married. And the older he's gotten, the more proud he's become. He now refuses to accept any financial help from Franz and me. And how do you think your mother's inheritance makes him feel? Don't get me wrong, he's grateful you'll never have the financial worries that he and I grew up with—and which he still has. But for him to know he wasn't the one to give you that security . . . that it came from a man whom your father despised . . ."

Ani regarded her with a look of confusion.

"Your father loves you dearly. He's done the best he could for you," Shauna continued. "I know how difficult it must be for him to be away from you. And I know how much both of you miss Africa—and especially your animals. I also know how you felt . . . perhaps still feel . . . about Cole."

"I don't want to talk about it," Ani looked away sadly.

"First loves are always the most exquisite . . . yet the most painful," Shauna stated knowingly.

"Was Franz your first love?" Ani asked quietly.

As she met Ani's gaze, Shauna seemed to debate whether or not to answer truthfully. When she shook her head, Ani gave her a questioning look. "Mutiba," Shauna responded simply.

"Mutiba? Mila's son?" Ani appeared surprised.

Shauna nodded. "I *do* love Franz," she added guiltily. "We just don't share the passion that . . ." her voice trailed off sadly.

"Maybe someday you'll again find someone like Mutiba," Ani told her.

"Perhaps. Perhaps I already have," Shauna responded quietly, thinking of Walt. "But I could never leave Franz. He's been so kind . . . so supportive. Speaking of whom, I think I will leave for Vienna tomorrow," she convinced herself as the waiter brought them their meals.

Shauna didn't inform Franz that she would be returning home early. He was alone at their place in Vienna. Tanya, Johann, and Ursula were already at the castle in Hallstatt, where Shauna, Franz, and Ani would join them when Ani arrived from Innsbruck later in the week.

While riding in a taxi from the airport, Shauna thought of the options Ani had for spending Christmas. Xandra and Owen van Zaun had recently returned from their mission in South Africa, and had invited Ani, Shauna, and Franz to come to Holland for the holiday. But Shauna had already made plans to spend Christmas in Hallstatt. She had asked the van Zaun's to join them there, but they didn't feel up to traveling so soon after returning from Africa.

Throughout the years, due to Xandra and Shauna's efforts, Ani had visited and grown close to her grandparents. Although Owen van Zaun had developed a loving relationship with his granddaughter, Shauna suspected that warmth didn't necessarily extend to Franz—or Elon. Owen hadn't seen either man since the day of Rika's funeral.

In hopes of reconciling Ani with her father, Shauna had also invited Elon, Mila, Harun, and his family to join them for Christmas. But Elon used his responsibilities at the estate as an excuse to decline the offer; and Mila and her family opted to stay there with him. It was just as well that they weren't coming, Shauna now realized, as she remembered Ani's reaction to her suggestion that she go to Scotland for the holiday. Shauna knew the rift that had developed between Ani and her father needed more time to mend.

When the taxi delivered her to her destination, Shauna entered a darkened home. "Franz?" she called.

Assuming he was out for a late supper, she went to the bedroom and switched on the light. What Shauna saw was almost incomprehensible to her. Harry lay on the bed, naked, while Franz, also naked, was pumping him from behind. Seeing Shauna, both men froze. Harry gazed sadly into her startled eyes, while Franz collapsed on top of him.

In a daze, Shauna turned off the light and slowly backed out of the room. Quietly closing the door, she rested her head against it before making her way to the parlor. Sitting in the dimly lit room, she eventually heard the front door open and shut. Shauna knew that Harry had left, perhaps Franz as well. But he silently joined her in the parlor. His nakedness covered by a robe, Franz knelt at her feet. Resting his head on her lap, he broke down and cried.

Shauna gazed down at Franz with a distant look. But then she seemed to melt.

"It's all right," she told him lovingly, gently stroking his hair. "It's all right," she repeated with growing conviction as she realized that, indeed, everything would finally be all right . . . for both of them.

Elon, Mila, Harun, and his family spent a quiet, cold Christmas in the cramped little cottage in Scotland. Gwendolyn and her family had resigned themselves to the African invasion—mostly because of Elon, who, when he regained his physical strength and his arm was no longer in a cast, had directed his energies to turning the estate back into the "gentleman's farm" that Devin originally created.

Although Harun worked diligently at Elon's side, it was difficult to get much help out of Beni and Juba—who seemed to be taking their cue from Eric and Valerie. His sons' belligerent behavior forced Harun into the roll of a strict disciplinarian. But, like Elon had with Ani, Harun hated becoming even remotely like Elon's abusive father.

Mila and Emi kept busy maintaining the cottage, fixing the meals, and tending to the vegetable garden. And watching over Tessa, who was fast becoming a handful.

Although the toddler was engagingly adorable, Elon fought against becoming attached to her. He fought against getting close to anyone or anything. The only thing preventing Elon from becoming completely detached were the few animals on the estate. Although he tried hard to look on them as mere livestock, it was difficult for him to do so. One animal in particular captured Elon's heart: an old woolly-coated Highland steer with the disposition of a gentle dog.

One bright spring morning, when the trees and flowers were in full bloom and the birds had returned in chattering flocks, the old steer wandered out of its paddock when Beni failed to secure the gate. The boy had been coaxed into taking a few hits of marijuana that Eric and Valerie had secreted. They weren't aware that the steer had gotten loose until they heard the screech of tires and the animal's braying screams amid the honking of auto horns. Beni, Eric, and Valerie rushed toward the highway to see what had happened, followed by both sets of parents, Juba, Mila, and Elon.

"I knew this would happen someday!" Gwendolyn screeched above the din of noise as the steer thrashed in agony from the impact of the vehicle that had hit it. "I told you we should have gotten rid of all the animals years ago!" she turned on her husband, who shrank from her wrath.

One of the motorists pulled a shotgun from his lorry. When he fumbled while trying to load it, Elon took it from him and calmly did so before pointing it at the steer's head.

The animal gave Elon a frightened, pleading look. Gazing into its eyes, Elon's mind traveled back to Africa. He recalled the desperate attempts of the infant elephant trying to rouse its dead mother. He saw the frightened look in the Maasai woman's eyes before he silenced her forever. Again he stood over the rhino as it convulsed in the sandy riverbed before he pumped a bullet into its brain. And then he saw the lion—its eyes blazing and jaws snapping as it lunged through the air at him.

When Elon pulled the trigger of the shotgun, something seemed to snap within him. Only the echo of the shot could be heard in the silence that followed. Still clutching the weapon, he turned and walked away from the dead steer. Mila started to follow, but Gwendolyn held her back.

"Where do you think you're going?" Gwendolyn demanded of Mila. "It's you people who'll have to pay for whatever damage that animal caused!"

Her words started a general buzz of complaints and accusations on the part of the motorists whose morning commute had been interrupted by the incident with the steer. Eric and Valerie regarded Beni and Juba with newfound respect for their association with Elon O'Shay. Other than in the movies and on the tele, they had never seen anyone actually shoot and kill another living being. And to do so with the calm and precision that Mr. O'Shay had shown! The teenagers seemed totally impressed.

Elon was beyond feeling anything as he made his way to the back of the cottage. Placing a chair against the side of the building, he sat with the shotgun propped under his chin. Kicking off his boot, he pulled off his sock and started to curl his big toe around the trigger as a peaceful look crept over his face.

Suddenly the phone rang from inside the cottage. Elon blinked as if he forgot what it was—or what he should do about it. The noise woke Tessa from her nap, and soon her crying blended with the ringing of the phone.

Angry at the interruption, Elon stormed into the house with the shotgun in hand. "What?" he barked into the phone.

"Elon?" Shauna asked from the other end.

"What?" he repeated loudly, above Tessa's wails.

"It's Shauna. I'm calling from Texas."

"Texas?!"

"Yes, Texas! I'm calling to tell you I'm marrying Walter Hansen!"

"Who? Where?" Elon asked in a confused and angry tone.

"Are you all right? Is Mila there?"

Elon looked toward the door as Mila and the others entered the cottage. Emi went to pick up Tessa, who soon quieted. Glancing at Elon's bare foot and the shotgun he was holding, Mila immediately guessed what he had tried to do. The accusatory look on her face brought Elon back to his senses.

"It's Shauna," he told her, holding the phone out to her.

But first Mila took the shotgun from him. She gave it to Harun, who went to return it to its rightful owner. Elon left to retrieve his sock and boot.

"Hello, Shauna?" Mila spoke into the phone. "Texas? Walter Hansen?" she smiled knowingly as Shauna confirmed the premonition Mila had in Africa—that Shauna had found a soul mate in Walt.

Within three weeks, Shauna had arranged for Elon, Mila, Harun, and his family to fly from Scotland to San Antonio, Texas. She coordinated their arrival with Ani's from Switzerland. Lee's former chauffeur, Isaac, met them at the airport with a bright smile spread across his still handsome, black face.

Although Ani lovingly greeted Mila and her family, her reunion with her father was more reserved. It was difficult for the others to see that Ani still harbored a considerable amount of resentment toward him. Elon simply seemed to take it in stride.

As everyone else chatted throughout the drive from the airport to what was now Cole's ranch, Elon directed his attention to the Texas landscape. He was struck by how closely it resembled Kenya's Maasai Mara Reserve.

When Isaac eventually headed the limousine down the long driveway leading to the ranch, Elon—and especially Ani—were shocked by what greeted them.

"I don't believe it!" Ani exclaimed, running from the vehicle before it came to a complete stop. Sinking to her knees, she was bombarded by all the dogs from The Camp—who were as ecstatic over the reunion as she was! Some of them ran to Beni and Juba who, like Ani, were crying with joy and astonishment.

Shauna came from the house with Simon, Juanita, . . . and Tanya. After exchanging hugs and kisses with the adults, Shauna introduced them to the Bennetts.

"This is the *real* Simon and his wife, Juanita," she introduced the still youthful-looking seventy year olds. "My brother, Elon. And our dear friends Mila, Harun, Emi, . . . and Beni and Juba!" she exclaimed as the boys got up from the dirt and ran to her open arms where, much to their delight, she smothered them with kisses.

"And little Tessa!" Shauna kissed the toddler's cheek. "Look how you've grown!" she gushed as Tessa smiled while shyly tucking her head under her father's chin.

Everyone exchanged warm greetings, except Tanya and Elon, who kept their distance. It was achingly apparent how difficult it was for them to be so near . . . yet so emotionally apart.

"And that's my niece, Ani," Shauna told the Bennetts as she shook her head with feigned dismay over Ani rolling on the ground with the Leonbergers.

With the tears streaming down her face, Ani gave her aunt a questioning, accusatory look. "Why didn't you tell me they were here?"

"And have you leave school and catch the first plane out of Switzerland?"

"But how did they get here?!"

"Come on inside, everybody!" Shauna announced, ignoring Ani's question.

"Isaac, come join us for supper," Juanita called as he headed back to the limo.

"Thank you, Miss Juanita," he smiled. "But I need to get back to the family. I'll be making another run in a few days," he reminded her.

"Ursula and Johann . . . and Xandra and Owen . . . will be here," Shauna told Elon as they walked toward the house.

Although Elon didn't visibly react to Shauna's mention of Rika's parents, Tanya appeared hurt.

Mila watched with a melancholy expression as Isaac drove away—for he had reminded her dearly of Mutiba. Before following the others inside, Mila admired the newly remodeled homestead. From the flowers to the surrounding cottages, she had the impression that Rose Inish and The Camp had come together . . . and that Cole was behind it. She nodded knowingly when remembering she'd shown him the photo album of Rose Inish.

Simon hung back, watching Ani as she continued petting the dogs. "I'd heard you had quite a way with animals," he told her appreciatively.

Gazing into Simon's kind eyes, Ani guessed her Aunt Shauna had told him that . . . although she wished it had been Cole.

"Maybe you and your father might want to take a tour of the ranch with me tomorrow," Simon mentioned as he helped Ani get up off the ground.

"That would be great!" Ani enthused.

"Do you like to ride horses?" he asked, as they headed toward the house with the dogs frolicking at their heels.

"Very much!"

"Good," Simon smiled.

"This is Star, her daughter, Noelle, and Noelle's daughter, Nicole," Simon introduced Ani and Elon to the three generations of Arabian mares when they met at the barn the next morning. "If you don't mind, I'll take Star," he suggested. "Elon, you can have Noelle. Ani, I'm confident you can handle Nicole."

With the dogs following, they rode away from the homestead on what soon became a nostalgic tour for both Elon and Ani—as the landscape was painfully reminiscent of East Africa.

After an hour's ride, they came to a redwood lodge fronting a twelve-foot, chain link fence. Following Simon's lead, Elon and Ani dismounted and tied their horses to a hitching post in front of the building.

"Stay!" Simon told the dogs, who readily obeyed.

Elon and Ani followed Simon inside, where they immediately froze while staring with disbelief at the three-by-four-foot photograph of Ani and her cheetah babies. It was an enlargement of one of the photos Cole had taken on the day he'd met Ani's pets.

In a daze, Ani turned toward a group of chattering monkeys contained in a large, nicely-landscaped, fenced enclosure. Her eyes brimmed with tears when she recognized her pet, screaming hysterically for her attention. Through the fence's lacing, Ani and the monkey shared a gentle kiss. And then Ani heard the sound that often invaded her dreams—dreams that invariably turned to nightmares. It was the call of a cheetah.

"Leia?" Ani asked doubtfully, turning toward the pacing animal.

Recognizing Ani's voice, Leia let out a mournful cry. Two male cheetahs ran inside from the outdoor area of their separate enclosure to see what was wrong.

"Hans? Luke?" Ani sobbed as she rushed toward them. Unlatching their gate, she knelt on the ground between them, burying her face in their luxurious coats as they greeted her with happy, rumbling purrs.

Glancing at Elon, Simon saw that he had tears running down his face.

"Lee Parnell was one of the meanest men the Dear Lord ever had the misfortune of creating," Simon told Elon softly as he directed his attention back to Ani and her babies. "But the same can not be said about his son."

Studying Simon through his tears, Elon shook his head, amazed at how Cole—with Walt, Zev, and the other Mossad agents' help—managed to save *all* of Ani's pets.

Throughout the following week, everyone pitched in to help with Shauna and Walt's wedding, which was to take place at the ranch.

When Ursula, Johann, and Rika's parents arrived, Shauna watched anxiously as Owen approached Elon. When the two men shook hands without hesitating, Shauna breathed a sigh of relief.

Cole was conspicuously missing as Shauna's wedding day approached. Even as she and Walt stood under the flower-laced canopy on the day of their nuptials, he still hadn't shown up.

Although she was happy for her Aunt Shauna, Ani was heartbroken that Cole wasn't there. Whatever feelings of uncertainty or hesitation she had in seeing him were now eclipsed by the fear that she wouldn't.

When the ceremony evolved into a party, all the couples: Simon and Juanita; Johann and Ursula; Owen and Xandra; Isaac and Vera; and Harun and Emi, took turns dancing with each other's spouses to the accompaniment of a mariachi band. It was heartwarmingly apparent that Harun's family had bonded easily with Isaac's; especially the children, who took to one another like long-lost cousins.

As she danced with her new stepchildren, it was also obvious that Shauna had taken Walt's five kids into her heart . . . and that they had taken her into theirs.

Mila swelled with gratitude at the sight of everyone getting along so beautifully; with the exception of Elon and Tanya, who remained aloof from one another. And Mila would have been concerned by Ani's obvious sadness over Cole's absence, if she hadn't felt confidant that he would eventually show up.

As usual, Mila was right. Just as the sun was about to set, a jeep pulled up to the ranch. When everyone directed their attention to Cole as he stepped out of the vehicle, looking strikingly handsome in his tuxedo, even the band stopped playing. Ani gasped—not just from seeing Cole, but because the jeep he arrived in was hers! From The Camp!

Carrying a bouquet of yellow roses, Cole headed toward Elon. He stopped to pull a handful of grass from the manicured lawn, which he held out to Elon. It was what Kijabe had told Cole the Maasai do when they want to make peace with their enemy. The group from Africa immediately understood the gesture, especially Ani. But they appeared uncertain, and somewhat fearful, as to how Elon would respond.

Elon studied Cole with a blank expression. And then he bent down and also pulled up a tuft of grass, which he held out to Cole.

The two men broke into laughter as they threw the grass over their shoulders. They embraced warmly while everyone clapped. Elon stepped aside and nodded toward Ani, as if giving Cole permission to go to her. Tears streamed down her face as he approached.

After he gave her the roses, Cole handed Ani the keys to her jeep. In the gesture, Ani felt utterly and totally complete—realizing the most important things she thought she'd left behind in Africa hadn't been lost to her after all. Because of Cole!

With the keys in one hand and the flowers in the other, Ani folded her arms around Cole's neck. He picked her up off the ground as their lips came together in a passionate kiss.

Elon went to the bandleader and requested a song. He then turned toward Tanya. Elon knew exactly where she was, for his eyes had never left her; except when he saw her glancing in his direction, at which point they had both quickly looked away.

As he made his way toward her, the band began to play and the singer started singing the Righteous Brothers' *Unchained Melody.*

"I love you," Elon told Tanya adamantly as he reached out to her.

She gazed tearfully into his eyes before melting in his embrace. He held her tight as they swayed gently to the music.

Mila's smile was radiant as she gazed on the jubilant crowd. Walt and Shauna came to her, showering her with hugs and kisses. Walt whisked Mila onto the dance floor, where Cole cut in, and then Elon. Laughing at all the attention, Mila felt as though her heart would burst with happiness as her eyes filled with tears of joy.

The End

BVG